P9-ARL-488

AUG 0 0 2022

Praise for
For the Love of the Bard

"A delightful ode to complicated family relationships, growing up in the theater, and opening your heart to a second chance with your first love. . . . I wish I could move to Bard's Rest immediately!"

—Jen DeLuca, author of *Well Played*

"A sizzling second-chance romance full of witty banter, quirky characters, and a sensational Shakespeare-infused setting. . . . For anyone who never got over their high school crush or who adores Shakespeare, this is an absolute must-read!" —Jenn McKinlay, *New York Times* bestselling author of *Paris Is Always a Good Idea*

"Jessica Martin's rollicking and bighearted debut is a love letter to all things Shakespeare, filled with whip-smart banter that would make the Bard himself jealous, a supporting cast I'd love to share an ale with, and best of all, a second-chance romance that's the stuff of sonnets."

—Victoria Schade, *USA Today* bestselling author of *Dog Friendly*

"Sweet and Shakespearean, *For the Love of the Bard* sweeps small-town charm and second-chance swoon up into a delightful rom-com fit for the stage." —Emily Wibberley and Austin Siegemund-Broka, authors of *The Roughest Draft*

"Brimming with Shakespeare references to delight the brain and a slow-burn, banter-filled romance to melt the heart, this rom-com captivates. . . . A fabulous, laugh-out-loud experience!"

—India Holton, author of *The League of Gentlewomen Witches*

"This charming romance with its cast of quirky, lovable characters will enchant you. . . . If the question is to read or not to read, the answer is: definitely read." —Amanda Elliot, author of *Sadie on a Plate*

For the
LOVE
of the
BARD

JESSICA MARTIN

JOVE
NEW YORK

A JOVE BOOK
Published by Berkley
An imprint of Penguin Random House LLC
penguinrandomhouse.com

Copyright © 2022 by Jessica Gorbet
Readers Guide copyright © 2022 by Jessica Gorbet
Penguin Random House supports copyright. Copyright fuels creativity,
encourages diverse voices, promotes free speech, and creates a vibrant
culture. Thank you for buying an authorized edition of this book
and for complying with copyright laws by not reproducing,
scanning, or distributing any part of it in any form without
permission. You are supporting writers and allowing
Penguin Random House to continue to
publish books for every reader.

A JOVE BOOK, BERKLEY, and the BERKLEY & B colophon
are registered trademarks of Penguin Random House LLC.

Library of Congress Cataloging-in-Publication Data

Names: Martin, Jessica, 1981- author.
Title: For the love of the Bard / Jessica Martin.
Description: First edition. | New York: Jove, 2022.
Identifiers: LCCN 2021054945 (print) | LCCN 2021054946 (ebook) |
ISBN 9780593437438 (trade paperback) | ISBN 9780593437445 (ebook)
Subjects: LCGFT: Romance fiction.
Classification: LCC PS3613.A77964 F67 2022 (print) |
LCC PS3613.A77964 (ebook) | DDC 813/.6—dc23/eng/20220217
LC record available at https://lccn.loc.gov/2021054945
LC ebook record available at https://lccn.loc.gov/2021054946

First Edition: June 2022

Printed in the United States of America
1   3   5   7   9   10   8   6   4   2

BOOK DESIGN BY KATY RIEGEL

This is a work of fiction. Names, characters, places, and incidents either
are the product of the author's imagination or are used fictitiously, and
any resemblance to actual persons, living or dead, business
establishments, events, or locales is entirely coincidental.

For Em

Though you may only be little for a short while longer, may you always be fierce.

··········

For the Love
of the Bard Cast

Miranda Barnes ....our flame-haired heroine

Adam Winters... veterinarian, former high school jerk

Ian Grant..lumberjack hipster

Isabella Barnes ....college professor, bookstore proprietor and matriarch of
    Clan Barnes

Peter Barnes .... college professor, bookstore proprietor and patriarch of
    Clan Barnes

Portia Barnes ....eldest sister of Clan Barnes, scary lawyer

Cordelia Barnes.................................youngest sister of Clan Barnes, baking goddess

Candace Thornton...event planner, gorgon

Tillie Perkins... shoe store proprietor, matchmaker

Opal Perkins ....Tillie's niece, student, director

Dan Townsend... proprietor of kitchen wares, director

Jazz Jones ....student, Titania

Cat Jackson .... adult shop proprietor, Viola

Byron Greene...lawyer, Orsino

Puck.. intern, imprudent eater of inadvisable things

Hathaway Smith .... fictitious bestselling author, total pain in the ass

For the Love
of the Bard

ACT ONE

·········

June

Scene One

. . . .

The Offices of Valhalla Literary

I stared morosely at the screen, where "ELF SHOT THROUGH THE HEART AND HATHAWAY SMITH'S TO BLAME, SHE GIVES YA A BAD NAME" glared back at me in a rather shouty font. Instead of being a productive human and packing up everything I needed to work from my childhood home this summer, I'd gone down the rabbit hole on SpillThatTea.com, yet another teen social media platform where readers went to blast my latest book.

From the floor, the intern let loose a particularly fragrant dog fart.

"Who gave you duck?" I demanded, but Puck just rolled over and yawned.

I rubbed my temples, tucking a stray wave of crimson hair behind my ears, and wished for the billionth time that I'd never invented Hathaway Smith or the Elf Shot series.

Through the glass panels of my office, I spied Ian, my business partner, and Mathilde Mathison, our accountant, squaring off, their gazes set to stun mode. Like the other handful of employees of Valhalla Lit, I politely pretended not to notice the tender shoots of hipster lust blossoming before our eyes. That, and I didn't want to be collateral damage of that doomed relationship.

Catching Ian's eye, I pointed to the novelty book clock over my desk that he'd given me on my birthday. He nodded and said something to Mathilde that was no doubt both pithy and flirty and strode purposefully toward my office.

After he closed the door, I asked, "Do I have to remind you it's not a great idea to badger or bed the person who keeps our books?"

Ian sighed dreamily. "She is a force of nature."

"What is it with you and French women? Is it the way they tie scarves? Because I'll grant you that's pretty impressive."

"That obvious?" Ian didn't even feign sheepishness. It would have looked all wrong on him anyway. A good-looking man with chestnut hair and eyes the color of shamrocks, Ian had that capable-woodsman-meets-urban-hipster vibe. And it was working for him. At least for ninety-nine percent of the female population. Ian and I were strictly in the "friends who do not take each other's clothes off" zone. "She used to be a yoga instructor before she got her CPA," Ian said wistfully. "Can you imagine how smart and bendy she must be—"

"You know how I always say you need to find some guy friends? This is one of those instances where a dude wouldn't feel obligated to punch you on account of the girl code."

He snorted.

"How are we looking? I haven't had a chance to go through this quarter's numbers yet." Flicking one warning finger toward him, I added, "Don't you dare make some sort of weird accounting and yoga double entendre about flexible balance sheets."

"Why must you stifle my creativity?" Ian pouted, then continued, "The books are fine. I think we can make those upgrades to our firewalls this quarter. Maybe even upgrade the hardware."

"The duct tape on your laptop is getting rather ratty," I agreed.

"Speaking of books, can we talk about yours?"

"Why are you so bad at conversational transitions?"

"Because I've spent two decades getting by on my looks and uncanny ability to quote movies from the eighties?" he offered, not the least bit chagrined.

"I'll remember that the next time I need a *Lost Boys* reference."

"You're stalling."

He had me there. "Fine. The beginning's not terrible, but I can't figure out how to move forward. Forget about an ending. After the last one . . ." I trailed off.

"Barnes, how many times do I have to remind you that you can't please everyone? You did the right thing. Readers are a fickle bunch. The critics loved you."

"Critics don't buy books."

Ian smirked. "You know you can do this. You'll find a way, like you always do. Because you're a good writer, and that's what good writers do. They shut out the noise and find the truth in their words."

"Easy for you to say," I mumbled. "I'm still under contract for two more books."

It must have been something he heard in my voice, because Ian's expression sobered. "We can hit pause on this. You can take some time. All the time you need. Or, hell, you can walk away from this. We'll figure it out."

We couldn't walk away, of course. Not if we wanted to keep the agency afloat. But I loved him anyway for offering.

"Hathaway Smith keeps the lights on."

"We can find other ways," Ian insisted.

I shook my head. "You're right. I need to shut out the noise. Get somewhere quiet and reconnect with the characters. I've been buried in reviews and comments and I feel like my fans are breathing down my neck. I don't understand how real writers do this."

"Umm, Barnes? You are a real writer. See, we do this thing where you write books and we sell them for a tidy profit." He flicked his fingers upward. "Lights on, remember?"

"I meant, how do writers ever write under their own names? Who can take that kind of heat? Do you have any idea how pissed my readers are about me killing off Thad? I mean, the guy was a traitor who sold his friends out. And I'm the one they want to strangle? What if a fan figures out I'm Hathaway Smith? What if they start showing up at our door?"

"We'll move out in the night and not tell anyone our forwarding address?"

I growled at Ian. At the sound of it, Puck rose and padded over to him, pressing his head against Ian's thigh in solidarity. Furry traitor.

I glared at them. "You gave him duck, didn't you?"

"What better way to spend ninety minutes in a car than with a mutt who's consumed his weight in waterfowl jerky?" Ian rubbed Puck behind the ears until my dog's tongue lolled out and his eyes rolled up in his head. "Say the word, Barnes. I'll call New York and we'll figure something out."

"I appreciate that," I assured him, "but I'll finish it while I'm home. I write my best stuff in the attic."

"Said every maladjusted writer ever," he said with a practiced eye roll. "When can you get me a draft?"

"You don't get to push me around," I said, jabbing a finger in his direction. "You're basically a glorified beta reader at this point."

Ian clutched his chest. "You wound me. Besides, I don't care what you say. Susannah's great and all, but I'm still your favorite editor. Official or not."

"Susannah's better with grammar than you are."

"Blasphemy," Ian cried. "I taught you what a gerund was, plebe."

"This is exactly why you can't red-pen my stuff anymore," I pointed out, trying to hold in my laugh. "We're supposed to be partners. Equals."

"We will never be grammatical equals," Ian sniffed.

I shrugged. He wasn't wrong. Several years ago, Ian, then a junior agent at a top literary agency in New York, had plucked my manuscript out of the slush pile. He'd offered me representation and we'd spent the next six months trading revisions on my book. The man had an eye for grammar and sentence structure, and though I'd never admit it, he'd helped make me into the semicolon- and run-on-sentence-abhorring writer I was today.

After Ian sold my book to the largest YA publisher and *Elf Shot* rocketed to the top of the *Times* bestseller list, I'd taken the train from Boston to New York to meet him in person, and it was instant like at first sight. Ian was not only the fiercest champion of my book, he was everything I never knew I wanted in a best friend: confident, honest, warm and ever the gallant, always offering to show up with a shovel and a bag of lime at any time of night, no questions asked. I'd never wished for a brother, but somehow fate saw fit to send me Ian anyway.

Somewhere between the runaway success of my first book and scrambling to crank out the sequel, *One Foot in Sea* (a nod to a famous Bard line), to capitalize on the momentum of the first, I'd spent New Year's Eve at Ian's microscopic but trendy studio apartment in Manhattan. After a raucous party that had included body paint artists, contortionists, scores of influencers and all of Ian's clients, we'd taken it upon ourselves as a personal challenge to finish every bottle of champagne left open after the other guests had departed in a haze of glitter and Ubers. It was there in the early hours of the new year that we decided to start our own literary agency.

Six months later, we'd opened the doors to Valhalla with the royalties from my book and Ian's commissions. He taught me everything he knew about being an agent and I fell in love with scouring the slush pile in search of that next voice. And while my introverted ass didn't always love the outward-facing aspects of my job, I'd gotten comfortable enough with it over the years, cultivating relationships with publishers.

After we opened Valhalla, Ian and I had agreed that for the sake of our friendship and business partnership, Ian shouldn't read my drafts professionally anymore. That's where Susannah, my gerund-obliterating editor out of New York, came in. As a bonus, she used less anatomically specific threats about my use of the passive voice than Ian did. So really, I'd traded up.

When Ian and I had decided to embark on this whole "Miranda is a co-owner, but also a client" thing, we hired my sister's law firm to set up some ground rules to clear away any conflicts of interest. I paid for my own overhead as a client: publicity, expenses, etc.

Unorthodox? A little. Ethically gray? I'd like to think not so much. It was just easier to continue on with Ian as my agent. I trusted him completely, and it was one less person who knew Hathaway's true identity.

That had been Ian's idea too, after I'd had an epic meltdown shortly after signing my book deal. Far too late, I'd come to the realization that I'd written a slightly racy, though still teen-appropriate, elf hookup scene and that the whole world—including such notables as my third-grade teacher, my dentist and my handful of ex-boyfriends—would be able to not only read my books but comment on them. I'd wanted to pull the plug on the whole thing, until Ian calmly explained that the announcement hadn't gone out yet and I could adopt a pen name, if only I would stop hyperventilating for thirty seconds. And so Hathaway Smith was born to bear the brunt of bad Amazon reviews and fan rants.

The bad Amazon reviews had been so few and far between that I'd almost felt silly about Hathaway Smith. Then my last book dropped. While I'd always appreciated the love and devotion to the series that my readers bestowed on Elf Shot, with that came the ever-rising tide of expectation to make the third book that much *more* than the last—something I thought I'd achieved with *Inconstant Moons*, another cheeky nod to the Bard and a veiled reference to the traitorous Thad. My readers thought otherwise and made their displeasure known. And, very much like the Dane's dagger, it cut me to the quick.

But much as I might want to curl into the fetal position, never to take a risk while writing again, Elf Shot was the reason we had an agency. We now had four agents, including Ian and myself, and a client base in the fifties and rising. Valhalla was a neat, cozy operation that kept all of us well-read and relatively well-fed without having to sell organs on the black market to make rent. But maybe someday, it wouldn't need Elf Shot or Hathaway Smith anymore.

"Fine, you can read it as soon as it's finished, before I send it to Susannah. If nothing else, it will give me an excuse to limit my involvement in helping Dad build sets."

Ian's eyes widened. "Pardon, I must be drunk. I thought you said you were going to build sets."

"I did."

"I see." He waited a beat and said, "Do you remember when you stapled your hand to the bulletin board trying to put up those respectful workplace training materials?"

"I don't recall that."

"Do you recall the time your skirt got stuck in the shredder?"

"That could have happened to anyone. What's your point?"

"That was office equipment. Stage sets imply the use of tools far beyond even your uncanny ability to avoid lasting damage to your person."

"Cut me some slack. Most tools are made with right-handed people in mind."

"I know plenty of left-handed people and none of them have a track record like yours."

I scowled. "Fine, I'm just going to design the sets. Dad will do most of the actual building."

Ian tried and failed to hide his relief.

"Oh, shut up." I jabbed a finger at him. "Or I will tell Little Miss Sun Salutation out there about the time you got your chest waxed."

He threw up his hands in the universal sign of surrender. "I'm sorry, I'm sorry. I just think it would be easier to write your book with all ten digits." He waggled his fingers for emphasis. "Since you're leaving sooner than initially announced, does that mean I can come to town early for the festival?"

"Centennial," I corrected him. "Hundred-year anniversary of the Shakespearean Summer Festival."

"The implication being that this would be bigger and better than the normal festival. Which would imply there would be even more stuff to entertain me. I'll go pack my bag."

"Great plan. Except you're supposed to be running things around here while I'm gone," I teased. "Besides, there won't be any throngs of Bardolators yet for you to gawk at. That's more of an August thing."

"I do adore that term," he said, in reference to the locals' affectionate nickname for the tourists who descended upon our town every summer in search of all things Shakespeare.

"Fly your freak flag proud or not at all."

"You know, Barnes, if you're serious about breaking this bout of writer's block, you could find yourself a comely Bardolator, take him back to your . . ." He faltered.

"Take him back to my parents' place and have my lascivious way with him in my childhood bedroom?" I scoffed. "Also, who says 'comely'?"

"Says the woman who just dropped 'lascivious.'"

I waved him off with a vague hand gesture as I powered down my laptop. "I don't need some sweaty entanglement with a Shakespeare-obsessed tourist to finish my book."

"I'm just saying. It's a surefire way to cure what ails you."

"Please tell me that's not the advice you give our clients."

"Of course it is. A little no-strings sex to get the creative writing juices going never hurt anyone."

"Don't say 'sex' and 'writing juices' in the same sentence. You're sullying the craft."

"Purist," Ian scoffed, studying me for a long moment. "So why are you leaving a week early, anyway?"

"Because Cordy sent me one of her maddeningly cryptic texts over the weekend telling me I needed to get home as soon as possible."

Ian's eyes gleamed with a gluttonous light. "Do you think she's decided to move down here and open up a restaurant? Or, even better, she's reconsidered the offer to be my personal chef and culinary muse?"

"You couldn't afford her."

"I know," Ian sighed. "But a foodie can dream." Sobering, he added, "Everything okay at home?"

I shrugged. "Your guess is as good as mine. Cordy's definition of an emergency runs the gamut from 'there's a fluctuation in responsibly sourced cacao prices' to 'I burned down the café for the insurance money.'"

"The next time I complain about being an only child, please regale me with tales of growing up with Cordy and Portia."

I checked my watch. "I've gotta jet to catch Cordy before the lunch rush. You need anything else?"

"Nah, go write your book."

"You still okay to look in on my place?"

"Of course. I'll kill all the plants before you return. Text me if you need anything. Now go get your Bard on," Ian said, flashing me a cheesy double thumbs-up.

"Don't sink the agency while I'm gone."

"Don't staple your fingers to the stage," he countered. "No one likes a bleeder."

"It's just a flesh wound," I called over my shoulder.

Fishing my car keys out of my pocket and tucking my laptop under my arm, I nodded my head at Puck. "Gird your loins. We're going back to our roots."

Bard's Books

As we cruised into my hometown with twenty minutes to spare before the lunch rush, Puck pressed his face against the glass and commenced slobbering. Before rolling down the window, I gave him my best "don't even think of vaulting from the car again, even if you smell hot dogs" stink eye. He thumped his tail happily and thrust his head out. His tongue lolled in the breeze as we drove down What's in a Main Street, past the Shakespearean-themed storefronts of The Merry Wines of Windsor, Measure for Measure Hardware, All the World's a Pancake, Two Gentlemen of Daytona and Tempest Tossed Pizza.

Nestled in a corner of New Hampshire so close to Maine you could spit over the border, Bard's Rest had resisted the encroachment of the Walmarts and Targets over the years. Even Wi-Fi had trouble getting a foothold, as the city stood flanked on three sides by a forest and nature preserve for local exotics like white-tailed deer and moose.

But just as Walmart and Target had passed over the town, so had the staunch and puritanical influences of early settlers. Founded in 1698 by a dozen or so families deemed too radical (aka liberal) for the times, Bard's Rest became a haven for actors, artists and academics who worshipped at the altar of a different deity: Shakespeare.

As the town grew, so did the shops and eateries, all paying tribute to the man whose words had left an indelible mark upon the page and stage. Word got around about this literary love letter of a town, and tourism slowly increased with each passing year. Eventually, the town's founders instituted an annual two-week summer festival to honor the Bard, causing tourism to skyrocket during the front half of August. From the summer solstice to Labor Day, we were like a Cape Cod beach town. Only with iambic pentameter and doublets.

I eased my car into the parking lot and opened the door. Never one to wait, Puck clambered out across my lap and broke for the bushes. Rolling my eyes, I strode toward the two-story shop built in the classic Tudor style of contrasting browns and whites. Absently, I ran my hand over the familiar quill carved into the wooden sign, which read "Bard's Books."

The shop was their fifteenth wedding anniversary gift to each other. My father spent months transforming the abandoned summer home into a bookstore, and he hand-carved this much-loved and oft-photographed sign while my mother turned the bedraggled garden around it into a riot of wildflowers and burbling fountains.

As I pushed open the door, I whistled for Puck, who was busy rolling in some early June phlox. That heavenly smell of books and coffee hit me, my jaw relaxing as I crossed the threshold. Weaving my way through the lofty main room, strategically sectioned off by tidy bookshelves and overstuffed leather armchairs, I navigated the familiar grooves in the floorboards. I smiled, noting the new additions—a pair of wingback chairs sat by the window, additional soft lighting glowed by the stone fireplace, and rounded display tables were piled high with books.

Of course, the books were not all Shakespeare. I smiled at the couple sharing a laugh over an early Bill Bryson, their faces half hidden in the sun-dappled light. Turning right, I carefully avoided the feet of a teen who had foregone the comfy chairs and plopped down in the middle of the fantasy aisle with a Jim Butcher paperback. She looked vaguely familiar. Maybe I'd known her back when she'd been in pigtails, reading Harry Potter novels upstairs in Will's Loft, the children's section, where beanbag chairs and oversized chessboards waited to tempt young readers.

I turned to Puck. The bookstore may not have been dog friendly per se, but being the grand-doggy of the proprietors had its perks. "Go find Grandpa." Puck shook himself and trotted off in the direction of the decidedly less charming, yet infinitely more practical, back room, where you could order, at a generous 20 percent discount, textbooks for nearby Keene State College, where both of my parents taught classes.

I turned from the contented sighs of readers and the whisper of turned pages toward the Much Ado About Pastry Café, which my parents built a few years ago after Cordy graduated from culinary school. If the bookstore was a stalwart sentinel keeping watch over the antiquities of the written word, the café was its sparkly, modern sister, with its gleaming silver appliances and the promise of sweets calling like a sugary siren song.

Upon spotting me, Cordy came barreling across the café in a flour-speckled "I Like Big Bundts and I Cannot Lie" tee, her hair spilling out of an artful topknot and her cheeks red from the oven. She would have knocked me to the floor if I hadn't braced myself against the glass case full of mille-feuille, religieuse and mendiants. Cordy had trained in Paris and worshipped at the altar of ganache.

"Missed you too," I managed breathlessly and peeled my little sister off me. A few of the patrons looked up from their pastries, but most of them were used to Cordy's antics.

Whatever genetic prankster had gifted me unruly red hair and sea glass green eyes had been in a more generous mood when outfitting my sister with raven curls, morning glory blue eyes and curves for days. Best of all, Cordy had one of those mouths that always curl up slightly, as if she constantly had a secret or a filthy joke to share. Which she most often did.

She rubbed her hands together gleefully and slid a violet-hued opera cake adorned with a sprig of lavender onto a dainty plate. "Sit," she commanded.

Obeying, I sank into the chair and marveled with the reverence one of Cordy's creations deserved. Finally, I marred the glass-like perfection of the cake, slicing a sliver off with my fork and sliding it into my mouth. "I think my blood just turned to sucrose," I moaned. "Totally worth it though."

Cordy beamed. "You like?"

"Of course I like. You made it." I wiped at my mouth, the lingering taste of lavender and chocolate and . . . a bribe made just for me still on my tongue. I gazed up at Cordy's guileless face, but her fingers—those talented culinary creators—twisted her apron strings, giving her away. "Spill it."

Cordy shook her head and another curl escaped her knot. "Not when you're hangry."

"I'm not hangry."

She rolled her eyes. "You're always hangry between the hours of eleven and one. Once you finish that, come find me out back. I'll get Jazz to cover the floor."

At the sound of her name, a young woman with cerulean-dipped braids and luminous umber skin sauntered out of the kitchen. "I got you, Cord," she called as she swept past us with a pad in hand.

"Jazz?"

"Janelle Jones. But everyone calls her Jazz. Theater major, working at the dinner theater this summer and picking up extra hours here when she's not at rehearsal."

"Gotcha," I said, before wolfing down the rest of the cake. Belly full and sated, I followed Cordy into the kitchen. It was pristine save for a wooden table covered with dough lumps and brown sugar. From the looks of it, I'd interrupted Cordy in the middle of some sort of streusel explosion.

She slumped against the table, all of the smile and bubble slipping out of her. "It's Mom," Cordy said without any preamble. "She has a lump."

"Shit." I sagged beside her, the air in my lungs whooshing out of me. "When?"

"Two weeks ago." She winced. "She made me promise not to tell you. Said she'd talk to you about it when you got here."

"What changed?"

"I overheard a message on the machine from her doctor reminding her to schedule her biopsy because apparently the mammogram is inconclusive. When I scanned through the old messages, I found four others. They sound . . . urgent."

"Did you ask her about them?"

"Of course. Her exact response was, 'The blasted thing can wait until the centennial is over.'"

I scrubbed my hands over my face, trying to push down the unwanted memories of Grandma Bea. A lifelong devotee of Christmas cacti and Herman Hesse novels, Grandma Bea had breast cancer that had already metastasized to her lungs when they found it the summer I finished fourth grade. She was dead by December. Even years later, the memory of her empty rocking chair on that first Christmas morning without her still made my throat tighten. But they had better detection methods now than they did in Grandma Bea's day. Even if my mother was determined to ignore them. "So her grand plan is to use the centennial as an excuse not to get it checked out?"

"You know she lobbied to be chairperson for years. She's not going to give it up."

"It's a biopsy," I fumed. "It can't take that long."

"A biopsy that could lead to an operation, and maybe some chemo or radiation. There's no way she's going to do anything about it until after the centennial, and by then, it could be much worse."

"Well, that is just the cherry on top of the bull pizzle sundae. How's Dad taking it?"

"He's a wreck. He can't get her to budge either. Which is why I texted you. You always make her see reason."

I rubbed my temples. "Please tell me you have something in mind?"

Cordy wrung a dish towel in her hands so hard I swear I could hear the fibers squeak. "Maybe if we had something to entice her, she'd schedule the biopsy sooner."

"Like what?" I asked suspiciously.

"How about first dibs on reading your latest book? You've finished, right?"

"Keep your voice down," I hissed and glanced furtively around.

Cordelia swept comically wide eyes over the empty kitchen. "Right, because the petits fours might hear us."

"Sorry, you know how I am."

"Yes, you privacy freak. But you've finished it, right? Mom would do anything to be the first to read it."

"Yeah, that would be super convenient if I'd written it yet."

"You haven't finished it? But I thought—" Cordy paused and then reconsidered her next words. "Well," she said brightly, "now you'll be extra motivated to get it done so you can get Mom to do the biopsy."

"Since when am I humanity's last hope?"

"She's a word junkie, not a sugar one." My sister frowned. "Plus— and I don't mean to sound selfish—I'm swamped with all the desserts for the centennial, plus all three nights of dinner theater. This could be my big break if I get noticed by the right food people."

I nodded. As much as Cordy loved being the pastry chef at the café, it was the career equivalent of living in our parents' basement. At least she didn't actually live in their basement. Cordy had a tiny but adorable condo on What's in a Main Street.

"Fine, I'll figure something out. Lock myself in the attic or whatever. But while I'm here, you will be my second in any familial feuds that result from my efforts, got it?"

"Sure," she said, shrugging, "but if it were me, I'd want Portia as my second. She's like a honey badger. I'm more cute and lovable and prone to throwing things. Like a pangolin."

"If this blows up in my face, I'm coming to stay at your place," I warned her.

"Make sure you call first so I can clear off the couch."

"Why? Is it currently occupied?" I asked, waggling my eyebrows suggestively.

"Yeah. By my laundry."

Snickering, I swiped a package of macarons and a dozen dark chocolate turtles. "I'm going to say hi to Dad on my way out. Put these on my tab."

"They're on the house if you can get her to schedule the biopsy," Cordy called after me.

With a sigh, I wandered out of the kitchen, the weight of the news settling in my stomach alongside the opera cake. They were not happy seatmates. After everything that had happened with Grandma Bea, how could Mom ignore this?

I wound my way back to the inventory room, where I found one contented dog laid out across my father's feet. I pointed to the giant antler lodged in Puck's jaws. "When you ask me why you can't have two-legged grandkids, this is why."

"Hello, lambkin." Dad grinned, setting down his clipboard.

"I'm on the dark side of my twenties, hurtling toward thirty. You're going to have to give that one up sooner or later."

"Portia's thirty and she still lets me call her that."

"To her face?"

"I say it softly enough that I'm not sure she can hear me. But yes, to her face." His grin—so much like Cordy's—broadened. "How was your drive?"

"Redolent of classic rock and dog farts."

"My daughter the poet. How I've missed you." He smiled up at me, the lines at the corners of his eyes crinkling, the same shade of cornflower blue as Cordy's. Personally, I always thought he looked like the academic version of Paul Newman, with those baby blues and his silvery hair.

"Cordy told me what's going on," I said carefully. "How're you doing?"

"I love that woman more than I love life itself, but I just don't understand her sometimes," he said with a dejected sigh.

Of course he didn't. The man liked process and rules as much as my mother liked the cerebral and hypothetical. My dad was a full tenured professor at Keene State, and his class offering included Syntax of Shakespeare and the Science of Set Design, while my mother, also enjoying her fully tenured professorial status, taught seminars on the role of apparitions in the Bard's works and advanced directing courses.

If the situation had been reversed and his test results had come back wonky, he'd have been in the next day for the follow-up. It was one of life's great mysteries that he'd gone and married my mother, an unpredictable tempest.

Still, the two of them had ruined me for life in the relationship department. Sure, their spars were epic and involved insults no one had used since the days of codpieces, but most of their arguments ended over shared tea in the garden. They were life partners, aligned in their eccentric interests and their shared passion for Shakespeare, teaching, their kids and the bookstore. I'd be damned if I'd let cancer split them up.

"I've tried everything, including unmanly tears," Dad continued. "I even threatened to withhold doing household repair and cooking Sunday breakfast, but apparently my bacon doesn't have the same power over her that it used to."

I blanched, sincerely hoping he was talking about actual bacon. "I'll talk to her," I offered. "I might have a plan."

Dad blew out a breath. "What's your angle?"

"Dangle first crack at my book?"

"You finished it? Did Meg brush up on her crossbow proficiencies like I suggested?" he asked, alluding to my main character. "I mean, with this whole elf war thing you've been foreshadowing, you need archers."

"Have you been listening to *The Two Towers* in the shop again?"

"There's nothing quite like Tolkien's prose when you're using a belt sander."

"I'll take your word for it." I offered him one of the macarons I had swiped from Cordy. "So, is the attic still available for a wayward writer months behind deadline?"

He patted my hand. "The attic is always yours, sweetheart. As is our tea stash. Just make sure you set some boundaries with your mother in terms of your time. Otherwise, you'll be co-opted into service like the rest of us. I didn't, and now I'm building sets for all of the plays."

"Dad, you always build the sets."

"There are *three* plays this year *and* the dinner theater."

"Fair point. I forgot about the extra play. Wait, there are sets for the dinner theater?"

"Apparently, they have a budget this year."

"Good to know," I said, sliding him another macaron. "Go ahead. You need it more than I do. Besides, you gave me a great idea. I could trade a little bit of sweat equity *and* my book to Mom in exchange for her getting this lump checked out. She won't be able to resist me."

"Well, you let me know if you need support. I've tried everything." He sighed. "Short of knocking her out with a tranq dart and driving her hog-tied to the appointment, I'm out of ideas."

"I'll let you know if we need a tranq gun," I assured him, "but I'm hoping to avoid large-game sedatives if possible." I crouched down and rubbed Puck's belly. "C'mon, we gotta get you home before you gas out the patrons."

Puck whined and rolled to his feet. He gave me a baleful look and pressed himself into Dad's legs.

"Who's my good boy? You're a good boy, Puck," Dad cooed.

My dog looked triumphantly back at me. "See, I'm a good boy," he seemed to say.

I shook my head. "C'mon, let's put those puppy dog eyes of yours to use."

The Barnes' Manse

The woman is incorrigible. It's a freaking biopsy."

Puck nodded, his eyes wide and understanding as we drove the short distance out of town and barreled down a dirt road that had seen horses and carriages and the invention of cars but nary a single infrastructure improvement.

"The damn procedure will take less than an hour. I spend longer than that on the yoga mat. And I don't even like yoga." I blew out an exasperated breath.

Puck sighed and swiped his paw across his nose.

"I know, right?"

I didn't bother with a blinker as I turned onto Verona Lane, muscle memory taking over. I cruised down the canopied embrace of golden weeping willows. Opening the windows, I inhaled the familiar scent of honeysuckle and lavender. *Deep breaths, Barnes. You got this.*

One more turn and the Barnes' Manse, such as it was, came into view. A cacophony of curved towers topped with turrets, bay windows and patterned shingles united by a soothing New England blue gray greeted me.

No one was out front. No one was ever out front. All the good stuff—the pond, the dock, the gardens and the gazebo—was in the back. The front was nothing but a parlor for the temperamental trees and ornamental shrubs that only a green thumb like my mother's could coax into thriving.

I squared my shoulders as I slowly rolled onto the gravel driveway. "I'm here to eat opera cake and kick ass. And I'm all out of opera cake," I told Puck. He rolled his doggy eyes skyward.

As suspected, I found Isabella Barnes in the back gardens. She was bent over a pistachio hydrangea bloom, the afternoon sun behind her silhouetting her in a corona of light. Her hair, red like mine with a touch more gold, was pulled back off her face in one of those effortless twists she'd no doubt mastered during her childhood in the Loire Valley, and as usual, it somehow managed to looked polished and glossy, while mine always looked like something out of a Euripidean tragedy.

She must have sensed me, because she turned my way and wiped her garden glove across her forehead. Of course, there was no dirt. My mother was too glamorous for mere earth to light upon her brow. *Light upon her brow.* I groaned softly. I'd been here a grand total of an hour and I was already talking hard-core Bard.

"Hi, Mom." I skirted my way around the delicate boughs to wrap my arms around her. She squeezed me tight, her scent a familiar mixture of gardenia and rosemary.

"You look lovely, Miranda," she said in that oh-so-subtle and melodic-until-provoked French accent. "Have you done something new with your hair?"

I could have just survived the zombie apocalypse in a gore-splattered tank top and been wielding a chain-covered baseball bat, and my mother would still have found something nice to say about my appearance. Bard, I loved this woman. But I had not ruled out the possibility of wringing her swan-like neck over her reckless and wanton disregard of medical advice.

"How's the book going? What have you got in store for my beloved fae queens?"

I crossed my arms over my chest, ready for battle. She was scary, sure. But I had the element of surprise. "Just fine. How are you?"

"I'm up to my ears in asps and Antonys, and I'm in serious de-Nile over it," she quipped.

"I bet," I said, refusing to smile at our long-standing *Antony and Cleopatra* joke. That alone should have tipped her off. "How are you feeling?"

"Like I'm treading water in a maelstrom."

"Taking your lumps as they come, I suppose." I narrowed my eyes.

Her expression faltered. Subtle, I was not.

For the briefest of seconds, storm clouds swept over the green moors of her eyes. Maelstrom indeed. "I'm under a deadline," Isabella said, her tone maddingly even. "Something you should understand better than anyone. Speaking of deadlines, have you hit yours?"

I shook my head firmly. "Don't change the subject."

My mother waved her gloved hand in the air like she was swatting away a honeybee. "You know how excitable Cordelia can be. It's a very small lump."

"So the doctor told you it was benign on the mammogram and didn't need to be biopsied?" I arched an eyebrow and looked down at her. I didn't have much going for me in a stare down with the formidable Isabella Barnes, but at least I had Dad's height. She stood a scant two inches over five feet. I had at least six on her.

"Honey, it's a very busy time for me. You know how important this is to the town. We have just over two months to pull off the centennial of all centennials. I don't have time for this right now."

I bit my lip and prayed for patience. Of course Isabella Barnes didn't have time for something so trivial as her health. Isabella Barnes, one week past her due date, had attended a production of *The Tempest* and was so engrossed that she ignored her water breaking and delivered me during intermission. At the freaking festival. I was born on Will's Island, the uninhabited but admittedly picturesque island where the mainstages were held, in what I surmise had to be pretty rustic conditions, because Isabella Barnes would never let something as silly as labor ruin a good Shakespearean event.

"Mom, you can't mess around with this." Grandma Bea's name was on my lips, but I managed instead: "Given our family history."

"You're just like your sister. Whatever it is can keep until September."

"Says who? What if it's full of malignant cells? It could spread to your lymph; it might already be in your lymph."

My mother arched a wry brow. "By that logic, there's nothing to be done and you should let me live out my dying wish to oversee the centennial."

I clenched and unclenched my fists, resisting the urge to growl. Why did my mother have to be such a devil-may-care badass? Why couldn't I have a normal mother who fussed and clucked and demanded to know when she'd be getting grandkids?

There was nothing left, it seemed, but to play dirty. "If you don't get this checked, I'm not letting you see my book before I send it off to the publisher. You'll have to wait for it like everybody else. I mean it. No advance reading copies, nothing. You will get it when the public gets it."

Her eyes widened. "But, Miranda—who will fix your tenses?"

"I dunno, Mom. I guess that's a chance I'll have to take."

She crossed her arms over her chest. "I don't believe you. You wouldn't shut out your own flesh and blood like that."

"Wanna bet?" I mirrored her posture, folding my arms over my chest. "You know how I overuse the passive voice. Do you really want to leave that kind of responsibility in Ian and Susannah's hands?"

Isabella Barnes, tenured English professor and bastion of books, wavered. I could see it in the downward tilt of her chin. Hell, I'd read those angles like tea leaves during my teen years.

"But if you were willing to get this lump checked out now rather than, say, waiting until September, I'd be happy to let you have the first read of it."

She narrowed her eyes. "Before Ian?"

"Before Ian." I nodded. My mother adored my best friend but took it as a personal slight that I always sent my final draft to Ian first, because Bard forbid the first person I have look at it be someone who read manuscripts for a living.

"Lovely, email it to me and I'll call the doctor as soon as I'm finished here. If nothing else, it will get the lot of you off my back."

"It's not quite finished yet," I hedged.

Her lips quirked. "I see."

"I'll have it finished by mainstages," I said, doing some quick math in my head. It was ambitious, but under the right conditions, I could get a novel done in under three months. "You'll be so busy with the centennial between now and then, the time will fly right by," I assured her.

I could tell from the way her lips went from quirk to full-on grin that I'd opened a door for her to walk right through.

"You're right, the centennial planning is quite the undertaking. Maybe you could give me a hand with it."

Since I'd already resigned myself to being pressed into service, I nodded gamely. "Sure, I could be your gopher behind the scenes. As long as you call the doctor today and you agree to do any required follow-up pending the results."

She lifted an imperious brow. "Look at you grandstanding. Portia would be so proud."

I thought of my scary attorney sister, who would never have stopped here, even when she was up against someone as crafty as our mother. "The first available appointment," I clarified. "Not some far-off date in the fall. The first available."

Mom sighed. "Very well. You have yourself a deal, daughter of mine."

I extended my hand to mock shake on it, but it was at that moment that a black blur of Labrador-husky mix streaked by us. I grabbed for Puck's collar in an effort to prevent the trampling of some beloved snapdragon, but I whiffed in a big way. In fact, all I caught was a glimpse of Puck's muzzle. In his teeth he had the bags of sweets from Cordy. "Craptarts," I gasped and broke into a run after my dumbass dog.

Never one to back down from a challenge, Puck kicked into high gear. "Drop it," I yelled as he widened the distance between us. "Drop it, furball!"

Puck stopped and rounded on me, a doggy grin on his face. He tore open the bag and wolfed down the macarons as I dove for him.

"Oh, come on!" I yelled as I tried—and failed—to wrestle away the turtles. My sister only used cacao that was 348 percent dark and likely a controlled substance in some states.

Behind me I heard the familiar tread of boat shoes.

"Mom," I managed through clenched teeth, "do you have Dr. Winters' number?"

....

The Winters' Tail

Y ou are a furry jerk face," I informed Puck as we drove back down the tire-eating road. He was lucky that Dr. Walter Winters, the kindly local vet who had tended all of my pets over the years, would know what to do with a dog who clearly had a gastronomical death wish.

Puck had bounded into my life via a former roommate who worked at an animal shelter. Sam often brought home some of what she charitably called "the special cases" until she could place them with people who she knew wouldn't return them. One such specimen was an impish pup who invaded our apartment one Christmas Eve and consumed all of our toilet paper and stockings before Sam could even get her jacket off. Full of Charmin and yarn, the little jerk promptly curled up in my lap and commenced snoring. I only half listened as Sam poured us each a mug of mulled wine and went off about the shallow state of humanity and the adopters who routinely passed over the shelter's black animals. She needn't have bothered. From that first Wookiee snore, Puck was mine and I was his. I'd be damned if I'd let his gluttonous ways take him from me now.

Pulling into the driveway of The Winters' Tail, we clambered out of the car, up the steps, and past the meticulously painted porch swing. The waiting room, which was more homey front parlor than seating area, was empty. Glancing at my watch, I realized it was after two, which explained why no one picked up the office line. Dr. Winters always closed up early on summer afternoons to golf at Guildenstern's Greens. The receptionist must have forgotten to lock up. I reached for my phone to call Mom to see if she had Dr. Winters' personal number so I could text him. Unlike most people who had helped Moses carry down the tablets from the mountaintop, Old Man Winters was quite tech savvy.

"May I help you?" A voice that decidedly did not belong to Dr. Winters sounded from the back room. Out stepped someone in a white lab coat. A promising start. The man was tall, but not overly so, with a swimmer's build and blond hair peeking out at odd angles from beneath a Sox hat.

"I'm looking for Dr. Winters. Do you have his number? I need to get in touch with him. My dog ate chocolate. And some maca-rons," I added for posterity. "But it's the chocolate I'm worried about."

The man stepped around the counter and knelt by Puck. From this angle, I could see that under his coat he was sporting a blue-and-green-checked flannel shirt that Ian would have coveted. The YA writer in me mentally revised the prior description of blond hair to caramel with golden wheat undertones. Shame the hat was block-ing his face.

Puck collapsed into his belly rub position and panted happily.

"How much chocolate did he ingest?"

"A half dozen chocolate turtles. I'm sorry to be rude," I said to the man still rubbing my dog, "but I really need to speak to Dr. Winters."

"I *am* Dr. Winters," he replied amiably, his back still turned to me.

"Yeah, so last time I checked, Dr. Winters was a cuddly teddy bear of a man with a pack-a-day Werther's Original habit. You are not him." Taking several steps back, I glanced nervously around the waiting room. Maybe this guy was an intruder who'd murdered the real Dr. Winters and stashed him out back? Could I reach that crystal canister full of dog treats on the counter and brain him with it before he realized I was onto him? I glanced quickly at Puck, who was completely oblivious to the potential danger. Honestly, my dog had no sense of self-preservation.

The imposter rose, turning to look at me square on, a thoroughly amused expression on his now upturned face. Only then did I glimpse the hazel eyes under the cap.

"Good to see you, Miranda." Adam Winters, the son of the aforementioned cuddly vet, extended his hand.

I stared down at it as if he'd offered me one of Puck's backyard deposits and took another step back. The murderous burglar scenario would have been preferable to this.

"Where's your father?" I demanded, dropping all pretense of politeness.

"In St. Petersburg recovering from a double bypass. Sending him out of state was the only way to ensure he wouldn't come to work," Adam said dryly.

"I'm so sorry," I stammered, my anger momentarily subsiding. "Is he okay?"

"He tried to talk my mother into letting him golf eighteen today. I think he's going to make it. Despite his general disregard of all medical advice other than his own."

"That's good," I said, more than a little relieved. I really liked Dr. Winters. Well, Dr. Winters the elder. "We'll get out of your hair."

"Miranda." In those three syllables I heard the ask to be forgiven for a decade-old hurt.

I held up a hand without looking at him. "I'm good," I replied in my Miranda the Frost Giant voice as I fumbled for Puck's leash.

"The nearest animal hospital is twenty miles away. Please let me give him some hydrogen peroxide and an activated charcoal chaser. Given his size, I don't think that amount of chocolate is going to do any lasting damage, but we should treat him right now and not take any chances. Okay?"

I looked at Puck, who gazed up at me with his gas-flame-blue eyes, the sole mark of his husky lineage. Shoulders slumping in defeat, I sighed. Who was I kidding? I'd have gladly sold a non-regenerating organ to ensure his well-being. I was not going to let something as silly as a devasting "girl done wrong on prom night" scenario get in the way of Puck's health. I was a dog parent, damn it. "Okay," I said and dialed back my chilly tone. "As long as I can stay with him while you give him the peroxide and the charcoal. He's not good at vomiting."

Adam lifted a golden brow. "Does Puck vomit often?"

"When he eats dead things," I replied archly.

"Ah, an imprudent eater, then. Bring him to the exam room. I'll be right back."

When he'd gone, I glared at my dog with the heat of a thousand suns. "Really?" I hissed. "You had to go and eat chocolate on *his* watch? I thought we were friends." With some serious side-eye, I ushered my giant albatross of a dog into the exam room.

When Adam returned with a bottle and one of those oral syringes, he looked between Puck and me. "Is he going to bite if I try and put this in his mouth?"

One could only hope.

I offered a noncommittal shrug. Puck was the world's biggest sweetheart. He'd never bite anyone. But Jackass, MD didn't need to know that.

For his part, Puck took the peroxide without complaint and glanced between the two of us like we were particularly entertaining squirrels.

Adam went over to the stainless steel sink and washed his hands. "Now we wait." He gestured for me to sit in one of the plastic chairs. I ignored him and leaned against the wall. "You in town for the centennial?"

I gave him a single nod. He'd taken his hat off, but somehow his mussed hair looked good. I knew, without needing to step any closer, that it was still long enough to cover the tiny crescent scar at his left temple where a line drive had grazed him in middle school.

"Isabella is the committee chair, right?"

Again, the nod.

"Well, your mother beat mine out for the honor. I'd still be hearing about it if she hadn't gone to Florida with Pops."

Could I opt for the nod a third time? I found I could, even as my lips quirked. Bunny Winters had big hair and an even bigger mouth. Little happened in Bard's Rest that Bunny hadn't already heard and formed an opinion about. She'd driven Adam crazy as a teenager, and I hoped the same was true for his adult life. Despite his unfair genetic advantage and veterinary medical degree, at least I could take solace in the fact that Adam had the town gossip for a mother.

"I'm serving as the Winters' representative," he said, a note of resignation in his voice. When I still didn't say anything, he added, "Are we really going to sit here in silence while we wait for the drugs to take their course?"

Poor Adam. He'd asked the wrong Barnes sister. Portia and Cordelia couldn't have remained silent if the survival of the human race depended on it, but as Miranda the middle, Miranda the peacekeeper, Miranda the introvert, I was as likely to seek satisfaction in silence as I was in a pithy remark. And since I had nothing to say to Adam, silence suited me fine.

It wasn't that I didn't like Adam. I *loathed* Adam. I loathed him in the way that one loathes their most vivid memory of being embarrassed, heartbroken and humiliated. The kind of memory that follows you into adulthood and echoes through the corridors of your entire existence.

"I heard you moved to Cambridge," Adam said into the silence that lingered between us like a stale Puck fart.

"Somerville," I said automatically, without meaning to speak. But damn it, I did not want to be lumped in with the stuffy denizens of Cambridge.

"What's the difference?" Adam asked and then smiled at my horrified expression. "I'm kidding. I went to Tufts. Just wanted to see if I could get some sort of reaction out of you." I nodded stiffly. But Adam was not to be deterred. "I'm home for the summer to cover here while Dad recuperates," he volunteered. "I live in Seattle."

Surprised, I blurted out, "I love Seattle."

He raised an eyebrow, which seemed to tug half of his smile up with it. Bard, that lopsided smile and chin dimple had done things to me in high school. "Yeah?"

"My favorite conference is there," I explained. "Over by the Space Needle. Every year my partner and I find a rental in a different part of the city. Last year we did Belltown. I had to talk him out of getting a Biscuit Bitch tattoo." I half smiled, half cringed at the memory.

Adam groaned. "I could so go for a hot mess bitch right now." He froze, the nostrils of his long, thin nose flaring. "That came out wrong. Obviously, you know because you've been there—that's a menu option and not indicative of how I think or treat women or—"

"At ease, Winters," I said, allowing him the smallest scrape of a smile. At the sight of it, he looked genuinely relieved, like somehow my good opinion might actually matter to him. Or maybe he didn't want anyone thinking he called women bitches. Really, either of those options was fine by me.

"I live on the top of Queen Anne Hill. You ever stay there?"

I had. Our second year at the conference, Ian had found a condo over by Kerry Park where we'd caught watercolor sunsets over sweeping views of the Seattle skyline and Puget Sound. Of all the places we'd stayed, the Queen Anne neighborhood, with its lineup of unabashedly hipster restaurants and treasure trove shops full of vinyl records and magic tricks, had been my absolute favorite.

Allowing myself a sidelong glance at Adam, I tried to reconcile the high school baseball star version of him with the white-coated professional who worked in urbane Seattle and came up empty. The Adam who'd crushed me versus the Adam calmly keeping watch over my dog. "Yeah, we stayed in Queen Anne once," I said, non-committally.

"I used to rent downtown, but Lucille needed outdoor space. She's—"

I was saved from having to hear about Adam's perfect girlfriend/fiancée/wife, who was probably an underwear model and a humanitarian with a deft hand in the kitchen, as his words were drowned out by a rumble straight out of Mordor. Puck's eyes widened as he shook himself and began to retch. I scrambled to his side, my hands stroking his back and my voice soothing. What followed was an unholy exit of chocolate and intestinal juices, the likes of which should never be smelled by the noses of mere mortals. Somewhere in the midst of his lurching, Puck managed to get some on Adam's shoes. I tried to feel bad about it.

When Puck had finished throwing up everything he'd eaten from the time he was a puppy, Adam wordlessly went off in search of something strong enough to clean up industrial-grade waste. I knelt by Puck and cradled him. My poor pup rested his head on my knees, completely spent. Massaging that spot he loved behind his ears, I softly praised him for the sorority-girl-worthy mess he'd made of Adam's shoes. Puck thumped his tail weakly, but happily. After a few minutes of copious ear scratching, his body relaxed as he began to snore.

"That was . . . something," Adam noted as he reappeared. He expertly slid a dog bed and blanket under Puck's bulk, without even waking him. Rubbing Puck's head fondly, Adam whispered, "It's okay, buddy. I always pass out after I hurl too."

I gave Adam a speculative look.

He shrugged. "When you deliver a baby camel, you can judge me. Until then, let's just say I've seen things." Adam held up a pair of violently yellow rubber gloves. "It smells like the ass end of a petting zoo in here. Why don't you head home? I'll be up late doing some paperwork and will keep an eye on him overnight. I'll give you a ring in the morning to let you know how he's doing."

I stared down at Puck. "I don't want him to wake up and think I left him alone."

"He won't be alone," Adam assured me. "If he wakes up, he can watch a movie with me. He looks like the kind of dog that would enjoy the Marvel universe."

"What happened to your paperwork?" I asked, raising an eyebrow.

"I've yet to meet a batch that can't be done with *Captain Marvel* on in the background." He grinned. "Or you're welcome to stay here with me. We could order a pizza—" He stopped when he saw my expression of slack-jawed horror. "Okay, maybe neither one of us will want to eat anything ever again after what we just witnessed."

I glanced at Puck, who had incorporated a whistling element into his snoring. Oh yeah, he was out. I loved my dog, but would he really know if I went home and came back in the morning? Even if he did, I'm pretty sure he'd forgive me for not wanting to spend any more time than necessary with Adam, who would no doubt spend the next couple of hours regaling me with tales of his perfect life in Seattle, which I suspected would read like some sort of mash-up of Patagonia and Pottery Barn catalogs. Model-gorgeous Lucille would be woven throughout, looking stunning in some sort of puffy jacket and wool cap, and Adam would be there beside her, looking equally photogenic in an outdoorsy vest. With a kayak. And a golden retriever named Buddy. Yeah, he was definitely the kind of guy to have a dog named Buddy.

"Okay," I relented, "but call me if something changes." We exchanged numbers, me saving his under "Jackass, MD" when he wasn't looking. I took one last lingering look at my snoring dog, then walked out on Adam Winters and his ruined shoes without a second glance.

STRIPPED OF MY furry sidekick, I wasn't sure what to do with myself. After Puck's gastrointestinal performance, the idea of eating was unappealing. I also wasn't keen to go home yet, in case Mom decided to take a second bite at the apple and negotiate for naming rights of a new character or something. Not that I'd told her I was introducing a new character. Mainly because I didn't yet know myself whether I'd write in someone new. At this point, nothing really felt certain about this book.

I'd ended my third book with the death of Thad. Never had I felt so sure that a character deserved what he got. And never had I experienced such an adverse fan reaction to the point that even now, months later, every time I sat down to write, I couldn't separate my imagined fan response from the story. I found myself wondering if they'd approve of this latest plot twist or reveal. Or whether I could get away with this thread or that character. In short, I was getting nowhere with the specter of my fans looking over my shoulder.

Without really realizing what I was doing, I veered off the main road toward Oberon's Woods. Pulling into the parking lot, I rummaged around for the battered Moleskine journal I kept in the glove box.

Shrugging into my Valhalla zip-up—the one that I convinced Ian did not need a busty Valkyrie emblazoned on it, thank you very much—I picked my way down from the trailhead. Breathing in the scents of juniper and sap, I passed by Cobweb's Corner, the picturesque mile loop around the pond, and headed for Mustardseed's Meadows.

Tourists and locals flocked to the woods for Bottom's Boulders, an impressive grouping of rocks that, if you managed to climb to the top of them, provided views of the whole pond and a bit of the town. But the real draw for me had always been the Meadows.

Unassuming, green and sparse, as most meadows are, Mustardseed's Meadows were often overlooked in favor of the other charms of the woods. There were no stone statues of fairies, as there were down by the pond. No bronzed sculpture of the half man, half ass keeping watch over his rocks, his long donkey ears drooping. But for me, there had always been something about this place, ringed by trees and shielded from the main trails.

I made my way to the middle of the Meadows and sank down,

tracing my hands over the grass that had long ago grown over a decade-old fairy ring. Not a real one, mind you. Otherwise, it would have been made of mushrooms or flowers, as befitted the handiwork of fairies. No, this one had been made of plain old stones by a heartbroken teenager who'd found her way here when she'd needed nothing more than to be alone. A teenager who had built a fairy ring and then wished with her cleaved heart she could disappear into another world. A world that didn't have Adam Winters or Portia Barnes in it.

Of course, I hadn't disappeared into the fairy ring. Well, not the way I'd intended anyway. But I had started to envision another girl, a girl with a face full of freckles and adventure in her blood. A girl who, along with her motley crew of friends, stumbled into a fairy ring on a school trip and vanished from the mortal realm. *Meg.*

I picked up a small stone, no bigger than my thumbnail, and rubbed its smooth, dry surface between my fingers. I placed it in the grass beside me. Then I reached for another. And another. Before I knew it, I had built a smaller version of my first fairy ring, ragged and uneven, but an unbroken circle all the same.

I blew out a breath. Then another. And another. Until my breathing stretched long and steady. *Alone.* I was entirely alone, sitting there as the sun abandoned me and the finches disappeared into the trees. I waited. And waited. Until I could see Meg, her hair swinging behind her as she stepped into the ring, looking over her shoulder at me with daring eyes.

I reached for my notebook and pen.

Scene Five

....

The Kitchen

I awoke to the sound of metal grating against ice. Blearily, I peered at my watch and decided that that couldn't actually be the time. Another glance confirmed that someone was indeed blending ice before seven in the morning, and there was only one person I knew capable of such a monstrous act. Portia.

Yawning, I rolled out of bed, casting one longing glance at my laptop. After my impromptu outing to the Meadows, I'd written through most of the night like the house was burning down. Only it wasn't the house that was on fire. I'd gutted the structure I'd planned and started over. While it had been a scary prospect to toss my outline and opening chapters, soon it was like that first day back to work after a bad cold: I felt like myself again.

After running a brush through my impressive bed head and shrugging on my navy blue Colby sweatshirt, I made my way down the stairs to the kitchen, where I found my big sister poised over the blender. I marveled at how perfect the back of her hair was. When I bothered to straighten my crimson waves, I always half-assed the back, assuming that if I couldn't see it, what did it matter? But Portia—Portia had tamed every strand of ice blond hair into silken submission. And even though it was well before any decent hour, she wore nylons. In June.

Apparently sensing my unspoken horror, Portia turned from the blender, a fistful of kale in one hand. "Good morning, Miranda."

"Hey, Porsche."

She smiled thinly, and that little vein over her eyebrow throbbed. She hated when I called her that. Well, if my fancy big sister didn't like it, then maybe she should give up tooling around in such an obvious status symbol of automotive snobbery.

"Smoothie?" She held out a frosty glass of grainy, green liquid.

Like a vampire when flashed the cross, I shrank away and retreated to the safety of the cupboards. When there was any whiff that I might be coming home, Mom stocked the shelves with Pop-Tarts, bags of little chocolate Hostess donuts and the variety pack of cereal boxes chock full of sugar bombs that turn the milk an unseemly color.

"Honestly, Miranda. Have you ever read the label on those? There's not a single ingredient in there that could even remotely be classified as a nutrient."

"That's what makes them taste so good," I chirped as I deftly maneuvered the chocolate fudge pastries into the toaster, not bothering to tell Portia that I'd switched to steel-cut oats and fruit in the morning back home. Let her think I ate like this all the time. "They're not bound by the normal limits of mere sustenance."

I surreptitiously checked my phone. Adam hadn't called yet. Of course, like the rest of the diurnal population, he might still be sleeping.

As the aroma of frosting-filled goodness permeated the kitchen, I eyed Portia's sheath dress, tastefully cut and—like a Sphinx of garments—giving nothing away. Only my sister could have driven the five hours from New York in that dress and not have a single crease. "What time did you get in?"

"This morning. I wanted to speak with Cordelia before she left for work."

Since Cordy generally left before five to head over to the café, I gave my big sister an appraising look. "All-nighter?"

"You know me"—and a flicker of warmth dipped its toe into the surface of her smile—"I don't need more than a few hours to function."

"Big deal keeping you up?"

"My biggest one of the quarter," she agreed and knocked back the smoothie. "But when Cordelia texted me, I knew I needed to be here." She gestured to an imposing leather bag that Puck could have easily fit in and still have room to turn around three times. "I brought everything I need to work remotely. In case anyone needs some help convincing our mother to do what's best," she said, tipping the glass to her lips and swallowing.

I nodded, trying to tear my gaze away from the bits of green floating around the bottom of it. It looked like someone had blown up a head of lettuce. There were no survivors. "She's already agreed to have the biopsy if I let her read my final draft before any of you."

Portia's fjord blue eyes widened. "You've finished it?"

"Bard no." I extracted the fragrantly fudgy tarts from the toaster. "I'm taking a page from your playbook, using that as leverage against her and a motivator for me. I actually knocked out a few chapters last night when I got home."

"You went out last night?"

I opened my mouth, and there it was. The thing we didn't talk about. No, the person we didn't talk about. "Yeah, just around town," I said evasively, leaving out Puck's brush with the dark side of cacao, my less than cordial reunion with Adam and—since sleep had clearly been out of the question—my three-hour writing bender where I'd finally found the golden thread that had been eluding me in the opening chapters.

"Did a flourishing night scene arise in my absence?" Portia probed.

I nodded and crammed a Pop-Tart into my mouth. "The Bard After Dark," I said and waggled my eyebrows.

Portia blanched. "That's a thing now?"

No it wasn't, but I was enjoying her situational ignorance just a tiny bit. Besides, she had offered me kale, so really, she deserved it.

I lingered over the Pop-Tart, licking crumbs off my fingers. "So how long are you here for?"

"I can work remotely for most of this deal." Her eyes flicked to the window that showcased Mom's garden in a golden morning glow. "It's my favorite time of year to be home," she said a little wistfully. "But the sell side attorneys are being difficult, so we'll see how much of the centennial I actually get to see."

"That's a nice way of saying you'll stick around until you're satisfied we've handled things with Mom," I said lightly, our eyes locking in an age-old battle: her need to control versus my need to be judged competent enough to manage shit on my own.

"Think of me as your backup." Her smile was radiant and cold.

A funny choice of phrase, considering my unfortunate high school nickname, Backup Barnes. A nickname that Portia had no small part in bringing about.

I returned her smile, just as bright and insincere as her own. If I'd learned anything the hard way, it was never to turn your back on Portia. You might just find a knife sticking out of it.

My big sister hadn't become the youngest partner at a top ten New York law firm by playing nice in the sandbox. She'd climbed to the top just like she had in high school, one stiletto pick at a time, stepping on the neck of anyone foolish enough to get in her way. Without consciously meaning to, I rubbed the back of my neck.

Pushing unwelcome thoughts of our past away, I shoved the last of the Pop-Tart into my mouth. Now I'd not only have to contend with my mother's pigheaded medical aversions but Portia would be looking over my shoulder, drawing up a detailed timeline and providing other "helpful" suggestions that would probably take the form of Outlook calendar invites. Great—I'd just add that to the list after retrieving my dog from the jerk who'd broken my heart in high school. Along with writing a long-overdue book before my fans figured out who I was and showed up at my office with torches and tweets. No sweat. I eyed the green-streaked residue dripping down the sides of the blender. Maybe I should eat some kale.

No. I shuddered. No need to do anything drastic.

"Well, I'm off to run some errands in town. Can I get you anything while I'm out? A multivitamin? A green vegetable? We can start slow, nothing too exotic. How about a cucumber?" Portia smiled sweetly.

I was about to tell her exactly what she could do with that cucumber when the pocket of my sweatshirt vibrated. I somehow had a missed call from Adam. But no text. Maybe something had happened to Puck and the news was too bad to send a message? My sugar-laden breakfast sloshed uneasily in my stomach. I waved the phone at Portia and stepped through the door, a chill riffling through the hairs on my arm. *Please let Puck be okay,* I prayed as I hit the number.

The phone rang, and I heard it. Not over the line, but right in front of me. Frowning, I looked up to find Adam standing in my driveway with a grin on his face and my dog sitting contentedly on his feet. If he'd been up all night, it certainly didn't show. If anything, he looked even better in the morning light, the sun glinting off his cheekbones and lending a healthy overall glow to his skin. I thought being a doctor—whatever the specialty—was supposed to age you, not make you look like some sort of earthbound embodiment of Apollo.

"Curbside service is no extra charge." Adam winked. "I'd actually like to think I brought him back to you in better condition than I got him in. I bathed him and tended to his oral hygiene."

"Puck let you brush his teeth?" I asked, slightly awed. At the sound of my voice, Puck broke for me, scrambling up the porch and plowing into my shins. His tail thumped the floorboards in an audible *rub me, rub me, rub me* Morse code. I sank to my knees, throwing my arms around him and surrendering to doggy kisses.

"'Let' is a relative term. There was a lot of cajoling and groveling on my part." The morning sun had shifted, now highlighting the caramel in Adam's hair. For one brief instant, I imagined what it would be like to run my hands through it. I shook the thought away and pressed my face in Puck's admittedly pleasant-smelling fur. *Get it together, Barnes,* I scolded myself. Just because he saved your dog's life and brought him home smelling nice does not erase the craptastic backstory. Reluctantly releasing Puck, I said, "I would have come over to pick him up, you know. You could have run my credit card right there and then."

"No charge." He smiled easily. "Old friends discount."

"We're not old friends."

"New friends discount?" he asked hopefully.

I shook my head. "Send me a bill." Just to make sure he got my point, I added, "I insist."

Hurt flashed across his face, but he covered it with a cautious smile. "Fine, I have an ulterior motive. I was hoping I could drive you into town."

"Why would you want to do that?" I asked, eyeing him suspiciously.

"Because your mother emailed the centennial committee last night and said you'd be joining us as its newest member. I thought you might appreciate the lowdown on the goings-on from someone under the age of fifty."

All I managed was, "She did what?" I was supposed to be Mom's assistant behind the scenes. This sounded front and center—as in, an introvert's seventh circle of hell.

"Besides, I thought maybe if I rolled into Bard's with you in tow, your sister might heat up a croissant for me instead of always serving it cold," he added sheepishly.

I tried not to smirk. I really did. While Cordy had ostensibly never picked sides since that fateful prom night, she'd apparently been making her displeasure known in the form of unheated breakfast fare. Bard, I loved my little sister and her passive-aggressive pastry tactics.

Despite the urge to turn on my heel with my beloved mutt and retreat inside, I paused to consider Adam's offer. Riding with him would afford me the opportunity to grill him on internal politics and committee drama. On the other hand, I would actually have to talk to Adam.

Luckily, I was saved from deciding when the screen door whined behind me and the familiar click of stilettos sliced through the morning air. "Adam?" Portia asked in a clipped tone. "What are you doing here?"

Adam already had eyes big enough to border on Disney prince territory, but they seemed to widen even farther. "Portia," he said, straightening and staring up at the corporate version of the fairy-tale princess.

Now painfully aware of my leggings and rumpled sweatshirt, I backed toward the door. I might as well have been frizzy-haired teen Miranda in her prom dress, standing in the path of her perfect older sister, a few hot seconds from being mowed down and left dateless.

"C'mon, Puck. Let's get you some breakfast." Without looking at Adam, I said, "Thanks, but I'll find my own way." And with that, I left Bard's Rest High's 2010 prom queen and king on the porch to stare at each other.

Scene Six

....

The Centennial Meeting

I'm going to kill you," I whispered to my mother as I plopped down beside her on an overstuffed chair.

"Don't kid yourself, darling," she murmured. "You'd never spill blood on the books like that." She nudged a steaming mug into my hands. "Extra Earl Grey."

"What happened to me being your assistant behind the scenes?" I protested as I reached for a coaster and set the mug down well away from a pile of Austen paperbacks. She was right, of course—I'd never risk the books like that. Particularly not my beloved Jane. But that wouldn't keep me from treating my mother to some serious side-eye.

"We could use an extra pair of hands this year, particularly artistic ones like yours. I didn't think you'd mind."

I bit down on my lip, stemming back a torrent of responses, which included "Of course I mind, I have a long-overdue book to write" and "People skills are not my skills" and "I'm your flesh and blood, how could you?" Instead, I sucked in a deep breath, inhaling the fragrant bergamot of my tea, and reminded myself that I was playing a long game and needed to suck it up if I wanted Mom to prioritize her biopsy. "Did you call the doctor?"

"Called her this morning. I'm scheduled for next week. You can give me a lift since I'm not allowed to drive after it. I'd ask your father, but he's been hovering about like I'm made of glass."

"Oh, I'd say you're entirely comprised of sass and stubbornness."

"Don't be so dramatic," she said cheerfully, rising from the couch. "Want anything from the café?"

"My forgiveness cannot be bought with breakfast pastries."

"So, a chocolate croissant, then?" she said airily.

"Two. I want two of them. One for now and one for when I realize the magnitude of what sitting on this committee actually entails."

Smiling, she shook her head at me and floated off toward the café. I watched her go, slipping off my shoes and tucking my feet up beneath me on the chair, I basked in the stillness of Bard's. The café opened at 7:00 a.m. sharp, and the clink of plates and the hiss-pop of the espresso machine drifted in alongside the smells of warm butter and melted chocolate, but the blue velvet rope between Cordy's domain and the bookstore remained in place until 9:00 a.m. Of course, accommodations had been made for the centennial planning committee, who were now trickling in, and—unaccustomed to the early hour—the floorboards of Bard's creaked in sleepy protest.

Tillie Perkins, a vision in a lavender pantsuit and her signature salt-and-pepper topknot, stopped short when she saw me. "I haven't seen you in ages. Come over here and give me some sugar." I rose and dutifully submitted to lipstick kisses from the proprietor of The Taming of the Shoe, who'd patiently helped me select heels for dances and running sneakers that always had an unnaturally long trail life. She also moonlighted as the wardrobe master for all of Bard's major productions and was a general badass of the highest order.

Sensing the proximity of pastry, Puck emerged from beneath my chair with a hopeful expression.

"Better watch that scone," I warned Tillie. "Puck loves lemon."

Puck huffed and shot me a decidedly unfriendly doggy glare.

I glared right back at him. "I cannot afford to take you back to the vet." I wasn't talking about money. My dignity did not come cheap.

Tillie chuckled and, shifting the scone to her other hand, offered Puck a consolation ear rub. "So, your mother has called in reinforcements, huh?"

"If by that you mean she's emotionally blackmailed her own flesh and blood into working as her personal lackey, then yes." I winked. "Are you costuming all three productions this year?"

"And the dinner theater." Tillie grimaced.

"Since when does the dinner theater warrant town-funded costumes?" I asked. The dinner theater was staged at Titania's Bower, a darling of the New England foodie circuit. It had always been a strictly amateur, easygoing affair, an opportunity for the less adventurous residents of the town to try their hand at acting without the pressures of the mainstages.

"A lot has changed since you last visited, pumpkin." Tillie rolled her eyes. "At least Iz managed to talk them out of doing *Titus Andronicus*."

"Why, were they planning on serving Goth meat pies?"

Tillie shuddered. "That's exactly what your mother said." She broke off a piece of scone and chewed it thoughtfully. "So did you bring home someone special?"

I widened my eyes. "I knew I forgot something."

Happily married to Alice Randall, the town librarian and adjunct professor at Keene State, Tillie still had that starry-eyed, lovestruck glow, as if she were on a third date and not snugly nestled in thirty years of domestic bliss. Tillie wanted every heart to be paired up with its true match, just like hers was. I couldn't blame her, really.

"I'm between soul mates right now," I deadpanned, pointing to Puck. "He'll have to do."

Again with the indignant dog glare. Maybe Puck really was my soul mate.

Now, normally, this is where the town matchmaker would make some cheeky comment like "Don't wait too long, sugar, or all the good ones will be gone" or "Ticktock, there goes your clock." Instead, Tillie leaned in and dropped her voice to a conspiratorial whisper. "Well, there's a new place in town—opened up last winter. Comedy of Eros. You should check it out."

"Oh?" I raised an eyebrow. "Did we get a comedy club full of lonely-heart singles like myself?"

"It's an adult store, dear." Tillie winked. "For those long, lonely nights. I worry about you single gals."

My jaw dropped as Tillie cackled and waggled her fingers at Stan Hobbs, another committee member and the third-generation owner of Measure for Measure Hardware. Close on his heels, toting steaming eco-friendly mugs and matching yoga mats, were Aaron and Dan Townsend. Their charming culinary shop, Two Gentlemen of Daytona, occupied the storefront across from Stan's. Bringing up the rear and sipping that bewilderingly strong iced coffee that Cordy brewed was Kitty McMahon, who catered to all of the town's floriculture needs—from wedding bouquets to funeral wreaths—down at Sweet Williams. I was surrounded by about a dozen of Bard's Rest's most successful merchants. My mother hadn't just amassed herself a team of volunteers—she'd assembled a centennial SEAL team.

"Backup Barnes. Long time no see."

"Here we go," I muttered. For as long as I lived, that nickname would haunt my days. I smiled, which I'm sure came off as perfectly natural and not at all forced. "Byron," I managed. "Great to see you." And it actually was—Byron Greene had been a good-looking kid who'd grown into an even better-looking man, with wavy jet-black hair and dark eyes.

"Great to see you too," he said warmly, leaning in for a hug.

Surprised, I awkwardly accepted it. In high school, we hadn't been on hugging terms. We hadn't even been on eye contact terms. Like every other halfway decent teenage crush I'd harbored, Byron had run in Portia and Adam's golden circle of athletes and class presidents.

"What are you up to these days?" I asked as Puck wedged himself between Byron and me, gazing up expectantly for a pet that never came.

"I have a legal practice here in town. Real estate matters, trusts, wills and estates. You need anything, you come see me." With a deft hand, he reached into his pocket and extracted a linen-colored rectangle. "My card." He lowered his voice. "You know how it is. Sitting on these committees is great for business." He smiled, and it did interesting things to the dimple in his chin. "Oh, and my deep appreciation and respect for the Bard, of course."

"Of course."

"I have to say, Barnes," Byron murmured appreciatively, his smooth espresso eyes lingering on my face, "I'd heard you'd run off to the city. It certainly agrees with you."

Before I could reply with something that I'm sure would have been just idiotic enough to call attention to my general social awkwardness, my furry sentinel shot forward, his tail cutting dangerously close to that pile of Austen paperbacks.

"Puck—" I called after him, but stopped when I saw who he had barreled into.

Adam braced himself, clutching a decidedly unheated croissant wrapped in a piece of wax paper. "Hello, my imprudent eater," he said fondly, setting down his baked good and giving my traitorous dog his full attention. Puck stopped, dropped and rolled onto his back for maximum belly rubbing. The good doctor, who I'm sure was a real crowd-pleaser with both the fairer sex and the canine set, didn't disappoint. The two of them looked like they belonged in one of those calendars. *Small-Town Medical Practitioners and Their Ridiculously Photogenic Dogs* or something.

Adam finally looked up from Puck to offer me a cautious smile. "Sorry, he's just so rubbable—" His smile faltered when he saw Byron beside me. For his part, our former classmate seemed oblivious, giving Adam the bro nod before settling into the chair nearest me. Lips thinned into surgeon's stitches, Adam chose a lumpy couch across from us. Poor Puck; he looked from Adam to me and back to Adam. He heaved a great big doggy sigh and trotted back over to me.

"Good boy," I whispered. "All signs point to bacon in your future."

Puck's ears perked up at the word *bacon* as he settled into a sitting position on my feet.

With her uncanny sense of timing, my mother reappeared, deftly deposited a plate with a pair of chocolate croissants in front of me and reclaimed her spot on the couch. Rolling her shoulders back and slipping on her most disarming smile, she delicately cleared her throat. "All right, now that everyone's here, let's get started. We've got just a little over eight weeks to pull together the finest celebration this town has ever seen, and you all know what the Bard would say: defer no time, delays have dangerous ends," my mother said in her perfectly modulated professorial tone. "First, a housekeeping matter. For those of you who don't know my daughter Miranda"— she gestured to me with a flourish that would have looked ridiculous on anyone lacking French heritage—"she'll be joining our committee. Miranda brings a wealth of knowledge of the theater with her."

There were polite smiles and friendly nods from those who remembered me as the weird theater kid. Byron winked at me, while Adam gnawed on his bottom lip and stared holes through the other man. Had Byron stiffed Adam on a vet bill or something? No, that didn't seem likely. Byron didn't seem like a pet kind of guy. More of an artisanal hair pomade kind of guy.

Oblivious to my efforts to sink into the folds of the chair alongside the lost change and fossilized crumbs, my mother turned her attention to reviewing the previous meeting's minutes and action items. It was all terribly efficient and, quite frankly, terrifying. I had never realized the festivals I'd enjoyed as a kid required so much planning. I'd just thought my favorite plays and fried delicacies magicked themselves into my town each summer, bringing joy (and, in the case of the fried dough stand, powdered sugar) before tidying themselves up and disappearing once again. At some point, I'd definitely suspected fairy involvement.

"Miranda will be joining the mainstage subcommittee with Tillie, Dan, Kitty, Adam and Peter."

"What now?" I asked, sitting up. The mainstage subcommittee? How was I going to fit that in? Particularly when I'd just hit restart on my book? I looked over at Adam to gauge his reaction, but he was unfazed and picking unenthusiastically at his cold croissant. I stared down at my own plate of croissants, wondering if Mom would notice if I shoved the entire thing into my mouth. Probably. I settled for half. This meeting was getting worse by the minute.

"Two comedies and a tragedy," my mother continued. "Selections due Friday, with auditions and casting to follow. Rehearsals should start shortly thereafter. Please make sure you coordinate with the dinner theater to avoid any duplication." She said "duplication," but I heard the undercurrent there. It would have been beneath Isabella Barnes to use the words *turf war*. But I heard her loud and clear.

Once she'd covered all of the other open tasks—that miraculously didn't require my participation—she thanked all of us, ending on a gentle reminder to send her all subcommittee meeting notes within twenty-four hours of the meeting occurring. Having received our marching orders, we all stood up, brushing crumbs from our laps. Puck leapt to life and zoomed around like a canine vacuum while I made a beeline for my mother. "I never agreed to the join the mainstages, and if you think I'm directing—"

"Darling," my mother said, pitching her voice low, "a deal is a deal."

"This wasn't the deal," I hissed.

"You agreed to help out." She chucked me under the chin. "Besides, it's not like your book is ready for me yet. This way, I get a little something, you get a little something . . ."

"You're worse than Portia," I grumbled.

"Who do you think taught Portia how to negotiate?"

I threw my hands up. "Fine, I'll do it. But no second-guessing my choice of plays for the mainstages."

"As long as it's not *Titus Andronicus*, I'm sure I'll love it."

I shuddered at the thought of Shakespeare's bloody meditation on violence and vengeance. "Yeah, I tend to avoid the ones where people end up baked in pies."

"Great, it's settled, then," she said, her eyes already on her next centennial target. With a flutter of her fingers in my general direction, she headed over to intercept Stan Hobbs from making his getaway.

I looked down at Puck. "C'mon, dog wonder. Let's—" I spun directly around to find a wall of lean muscle barring the way to the safety of Cordy's kitchen.

"I'm handy with sets," Adam offered by way of explanation. "Pete asked me if I'd help out since there's an extra play this year. In case you're wondering why I'm on the mainstage subcommittee."

I wasn't wondering, actually. Also, had he just called my dad Pete? I could count the number of people who called my dad that on one hand. "Great, looking forward to working with you." But I could tell from Adam's expression that I hadn't quite sold that platitude, so I added, "Thanks again for taking care of Puck like you did. He's my world."

The resulting mega-wattage from Adam's ensuing smile made me want to take a step back. "He's such a good dog. Top-notch movie buddy." The sincerity—that all-in quality—in his voice did something to me. I reminded myself he was probably like that with all his patients—caring and invested and—wait, was I staring? I was staring. "I have to see Cordy . . . about something," I said finally, gesturing behind me as if he didn't know where the café was.

"Sure, I'll text you."

I raised an eyebrow.

"About the sets."

"Right, great." Then we did that awkward thing where we both tried to get out of the other's way and only managed to knock into each other. Classic.

When I'd crossed the threshold to the café and was sure Adam was out of earshot, I called out, "My kingdom for a croissant."

"What happened to the plate I sent Mom out with?" Cordy

asked, wiping her hands on her "Drop It Like It's Hot" cookie dough–patterned apron. Seeing my face, she added, "That bad, huh?"

"You have no idea. Do you think you could heat up a croissant for me and put it on an actual plate, or is there an upcharge for that?"

She gave me a sly smile. "Ah, you noticed."

"Of course I noticed. Adam did too. That is why you're my favorite sister." I sank down into a bistro chair. "Do you know he came to our house this morning to drop off Puck?"

Cordy clucked sympathetically. "That's why I don't live at home. Too many people know where we live. Is Puck okay? Mom texted me this morning. I feel awful."

"Entirely my fault. I shouldn't have left chocolates where a furry jerk face could reach them. Puck is fine. Adam's shoes, on the other hand, are on life support." I filled her in on the gory details.

"That's fantastic." Cordy snorted.

"I know. I love that dog." I toyed with the napkin dispenser. "But it was so awkward sitting there with Adam making small talk. Why can't he just acknowledge that there's always going to be this weirdness between us?"

"Because you're both adults and maybe he thought you could move beyond high school?"

"Says the woman who won't heat up the man's croissant."

"Sisterly devotion runs deep." She slid me a plate with a warmed chocolate croissant. "Besides, I never claimed to be the mature one. But maybe it's time to let bygones be bygones and crap."

"I don't think that's the expression," I said dryly. "But I may try it anyway. We're on the mainstage subcommittee together. So I can't afford to be openly hostile to him in front of Mom or Dad."

"Oh wow, she conscripted you for the mainstages? Are you going to direct?"

"Bard knows," I said, between mouthfuls of croissant. I couldn't even begin to fathom the amount of hours I would be putting in on the mainstage. Oh wait, yes I could. Because I'd been doing mainstages since I could talk. A mainstage was like an eight-week workout boot camp where instead of body-punishing weights and sprints at dawn, it was death by rehearsal and prolonged talking in Early Modern English. "Speaking of conscription, I heard you're doing the dinner theater dessert menus. What are they up to this year?"

"*Romeo and Juliet* reimagined."

"As what?"

"Star-crossed lovers at a robotics summer camp."

I snorted. "You're not serious."

"Wait until you see the menu," Cordy singsonged. "Was that Byron I saw you talking to?"

"What, is Portia not up to her duties today as head inquisitor? Are you filling in?"

"Sweetie, you can't sit up in the attic the entire summer. That never worked out for any of V. C. Andrews' characters. Besides, Byron is easy on the eyes. I bet he'd be easy on the—"

"I don't need to get laid, Cordy. I need to finish my book." Byron was a smooth-talking, good-looking man, but I just wasn't ready for another round of crippling inadequacy in the face of easy man charm. I had a book to write. That was more than enough crippling inadequacy and self-doubt to sustain me. I polished off the last of the croissant and raked a napkin across my mouth. "Holing up in the attic and writing at night is exactly what I plan to do, since I now have a de facto day job on the committee," I said.

"A little nocturnal extracurricular activity might do you some good," Cordy insisted.

The clearing of a throat had Cordy straightening up and me choking on the remains of the croissant. "Why do I get the sense my daughters are talking about something that would scandalize their dear old father? I just wanted a scone."

"I'll get you two if you promise never to bring up what you just heard ever again," Cordy said, wincing.

"Deal," my father said, his eyes twinkling.

"What's this I hear about being replaced as your set assistant by Adam Winters?" I demanded.

Dad looked down at his hands. "I've been meaning to talk to you about that. Your mother and I think it's wonderful you've agreed to help out on the mainstage subcommittee. But I do think your unique talents would be best put to use somewhere other than sets."

"He's afraid you're going to set the shop on fire again," Cordy crowed.

"That was one time!" I shot back. "Okay, twice." I turned on my father, who was doing a piss-poor job of hiding a laugh. "Traitors, all of you."

"We're just worried about your personal safety, lambkin."

"And the safety of everyone else," Cordy stage-whispered.

"Fine," I grumbled. "But he's not going to be as good company as me."

"Of course not," my father said solemnly. "But you did say you need time for your writing. Meg's crossbow skills aren't going to write themselves." His face brightened when Cordy returned with two lemon and blueberry iced scones and a frosty glass of milk.

"Wait, Meg is going with the crossbow?" Cordy demanded. "My girl needs a sword!"

I groaned softly. I guess this was slightly better than the great Thanksgiving debate as to whether Meg's fairy mount should talk or not. And if he did talk, should he be a smart-ass or a straight shooter? The debate had threatened to spill over into dessert, until I'd finally put my foot down and declared that for the love of Bard, Meg didn't need a talking horse.

"There you all are!" My mother breezed into the kitchen. "I think that went well."

I nodded, grateful for any diversion that took us off weapons selection. "I could never control a room like that."

"Of course you could," Mom said staunchly, "but two decades of teaching a hundred freshmen Shakespeare 101 doesn't hurt." She leaned across me, a gust of gardenia and rosemary, and brushed a kiss across my father's cheek. "You can stop being cross with me. I'm in next week for the biopsy. Miranda will drive me. You can all relax."

"That's wonderful, Iz," Dad said, kissing her back, relief evident in his tone. Then he flashed me a covert thumbs-up.

"I don't know why you're all fussing over me," Mom tsked. "I'm sure it's nothing."

"Of course," Cordy said, her cheerfulness bright but brittle as spun sugar. "But that's why we get these things checked out."

"Did I tell you that Miranda has graciously volunteered to direct one of the mainstages?" my mother asked cheerfully, deftly changing the subject.

"'Volunteer' is a strong word," I said.

Isabella waved an indifferent hand and gripped my elbow. "You and I have much to discuss. Dan is going to try and jockey to direct the tragedy, but I think you should take it. You have beautiful taste . . ." And with that she led me into the store, chattering my ear off about strategies for mainstage selections and completely forgetting her earlier promise not to second-guess my selection.

....

The Hood of Miranda's Car

All in all, it had been a busy morning. In addition to acquiring a much-larger-than-anticipated committee assignment, I found that I'd picked up a hood ornament as well.

I squinted at the pert blond in enormous sunglasses lounging against the hood of my car. Clearly, she'd never lived in a big city, where touching another person's vehicle was strictly verboten. Although, given her sky-high peep toes, maybe she was just using my car for balance.

As I drew near, the skin on my arms prickling despite the summer heat, the blond looked up from her phone, brushing at her rosé-hued skirt that showcased her mile-high tan legs. Well, at least she wasn't wearing nylons. This made her at least one-eighth less scary than Portia.

Puck pressed against my leg, alert and wary—not quite at a place where he felt the need to bark at the stranger, but within spitting distance of it.

"May I help you?" I asked politely.

"Are you Miranda Barnes?"

"The one and only."

"Candace Thornton." She extended her hand, finally lifting her barre-class-sculpted ass off my car. "I'm the head event coordinator at Titania's Bower."

Of course she was. Titania's hadn't just gotten themselves an event coordinator, but a head one, implying she had minions. I shook her artfully manicured hand without any enthusiasm. I'd had many an interaction with event coordinators over the years for launches and other press events. In my experience, they were all kind of the same: like shots to the arm, some stung more than others, but they all pinched.

Candace smiled sweetly at me. "I heard you joined the centennial committee. I wanted to come over and introduce myself."

"That was fast." Considering I'd just left my first meeting, it was unsettling that she knew that. I mentally adjusted her scary quotient to put her back on par with Portia.

"I have my ways." She pushed her sunglasses up, sending her honey-golden hair cascading over her shoulders in perfect, Pantene-commercial-worthy waves. Definitely as scary as Portia, if not scarier.

Like Byron, she offered me a tasteful linen business card. Honestly, I didn't understand why professionals still bothered handing out business cards anymore when you could find anyone on social media. The little paper suckers should have gone the way of take-out menus and phone books, and yet there I was with my second one of the morning.

"I'm in charge of this year's production of *Romeo and Juliet*," she continued, her eyes the electric blue of those poison dart frogs you see in zoos.

"So I heard." When those unnaturally bright eyes narrowed, I hastily added, "My sister Cordelia is doing the catering."

"She's not doing the catering," Candace snapped. "She's doing the dessert trays. Jerome insisted we bring her in after our head pastry chef declared she was taking her full maternity leave."

I huffed out an annoyed breath. I didn't know the head pastry chef over at Titania's, but I was pretty sure that commenting on another woman's audacity for daring to take her full maternity leave was a clear violation of lady law. And regular law. Candace's dismissive tone felt like some sort of slight to Cordy as well, so I threw some sisterly shade in the event planner's direction for good measure.

At my indignant exhale, Puck subtly maneuvered himself between Candace and me. I wasn't certain whether it was for her protection or mine.

"Well, it was a real pleasure, Candace." I gestured to my car. "Now, if you don't mind—"

Candace advanced, the too-sharp bouquet of her jasmine perfume grabbing hold of me with cloying hands. "I was hoping you could do me a favor and tell me what plays the committee has settled on." She pursed her peony-glossed lips. "I would just hate for there to be any overlap or clash with the dinner theater's selection."

"Selections are due Friday. But I doubt there's any, uh—appetite for *Romeo and Juliet*." I thought this would assuage the petite and vaguely menacing dynamo standing between me and the safety of my car. But she kept advancing, and was it me, or did her gel mani look rather sharp?

"Miranda," she tutted, like I was the petulant child in this standoff. "I informed your mother of our selection weeks ago. I know you wouldn't have the bad taste to stage a dueling version of the Bard's most tragic love story. I just want to make sure we don't have too much overlap, so I was hoping we could coordinate so that the committee doesn't pick anything with a tragedy or romantic theme too close to ours. So I'm thinking no *Pericles, Cymbeline, Much Ado About Nothing*, or *The Tempest*," she said, ticking off each play on her fingers. "No *Twelfth Night, A Midsummer Night's Dream, As You Like It, All's Well That Ends Well, Love's Labour's Lost*, or *Measure for Measure*." She paused, frowning because she was out of fingers. "Probably best to stay away from *Othello, The Winter's Tale, Antony and Cleopatra, Troilus and Cressida, Hamlet*, and *The Taming of the Shrew* because of the tragic romance themes."

"*The Taming of the Shrew* is not a tragic romance," I protested. "It's just dated." *Nice going, Barnes. That'll show her.* Beside me, Puck planted his feet and let loose a fortifying grunt.

"If your dog isn't friendly," Candace said pointedly, "then he needs to be on a leash. Maybe with a muzzle."

That did it. This gorgon had just insulted my dog. My hands curled into fists at my side as I leaned forward and employed my best "don't even think of trying to screw over my clients" tone, which I occasionally had to use with publishers. "You do realize you've put sixteen of the thirty-eight plays off-limits? You've basically left me with the royals and *Timon of Athens*."

"Right, so there's more than half left for you and the committee to choose—"

"I can do math, Candace," I bit out. As much as I wanted to let loose my inner Ariel and bring the storm winds and gales down on this land-grabbing, furry-soul-mate-insulting usurper, I quelled the spirit of air within. I would not shame the Barnes clan by engaging in a cat fight outside our bookshop. Instead, I called upon the wisdom of Portia—the Bard's creation, not the Barneses'—and the quick thinking of Viola and rounded my rising anger into a polite, detached mask. "I just don't think the centennial committee can accommodate your request, Candace. The mainstage plays are the biggest revenue generators of the festival." I smiled acidly. "I'm sure you can understand why we can't allow them to be creatively restricted." Good thing I'd been paying attention during the committee reports so I actually sort of sounded like I knew what I was talking about.

Candace's glossed lips curved into an exaggerated pout. "Well, I guess I'll just have to call my good friends over at the chamber of commerce and get this straightened out."

"You do that," I replied blithely, knowing there was no teeth to that threat. There was one monarch supreme of the centennial, and I happened to share DNA with her. "Pleasure meeting you." Stepping around her, I swung open my car door, ushered Puck in and closed the door with a little more force than was absolutely necessary. Candace just stood there, glaring at me.

I turned to Puck. "That is one crazy—" I stopped myself. Just in case Candace could read lips or something. Instead, I slipped my phone into its car mount and hit Ian's number, sighing in relief as Candace stalked off, never once wavering in her heels.

He picked up on the third ring, but before I could launch into my woeful tale of small-town turf wars and Puck's near brush with death, the sound of chattering people and the clink of dishes stopped me. Was that the whistle of an espresso machine?

"Are you at Diesel without me?" I demanded.

"When you're out of town," he said archly, "only the charms of nitro-infused caffeine will do."

"Ugh, I miss the good stuff."

"Why are you calling so early?"

"It's after ten."

Ian cleared his throat.

"You dog! Give me all the details."

"Mathilde and I went out for dinner at Spoke. Spent the whole night talking over candlelight and a wine list that would make you swoon. One thing led to another and I woke up with the perfect woman in my arms."

"Wow, how will you ever follow that up for a second date?"

"I know," Ian said miserably. "I know, I know. It was magical. She is everything I would wish for in a partner, right down to her exquisite taste in Lambrusco." He sighed wistfully. "Now, are you calling to tell me you've had a breakthrough on your book, or did you cut off a third of your digits in a tragic tabletop saw incident?"

"The former, you jerk. Must be the air up here or something, but I did have an epiphany of sorts. It required me to rewrite quite a bit, but I feel much better about where to go with it."

"Excellent. Trust your gut. You've got great instincts."

"Thanks for the ego boost as always, but I really called to tell you about why Cordy wanted me home early."

"Barnes, you okay?"

I cleared my throat. "Not really." As calmly as I could, I relayed what I'd learned about Mom's health over the past few days.

"Wow," Ian said, all trace of levity gone from his voice. "I can be there in two hours."

I rubbed my eyes. I would not cry. I would not cry. "Nah," I managed. "Just needed to tell someone."

"Anything you need, you call me, okay? Even if it's just heavy sedatives—for you or her. I'm here for you. Always."

I knew he meant it, which brought the tears back to my eyes. Desperate for any conversational lane change that didn't end in me ugly crying, I asked, "Do you remember how I told you my nickname in high school was Backup Barnes?"

"Have we finished the serious part of our conversation?"

I managed a watery laugh. "Let me have this one. For my dignity, such as it is."

"All right," he said gamely. "Tell me all about it. How could anyone forget the Backup Barnes saga? You win the award for the most traumatic prom story I've ever heard, and trust me, I have heard some shit. This buddy of mine got his date's press-on nail glue on his hands, and he—"

"Can we focus for a moment?"

"I'm just saying, I've never heard someone shriek like that." He clucked sympathetically. "Did you run into a former classmate?"

"No. I mean, yes. But that's beside the point. The guy. The guy who stood me up at prom is here."

"Please tell me he's a balding, potbellied townie living in his mother's basement with Aquaman figurines still in the box."

"Sadly, no. He's a successful veterinarian out of Seattle who happens to be home for the summer covering for his ailing father, because in a past life I must have been the monster who invented those flute recorders kids use in school to deserve this kind of karmic sucker punch." Fuming, I filled Ian in on Puck's toxic snatch-and-grab and my reunion with Adam. But I left out the part about Adam being as good-looking—if not better-looking—than I remembered, because it wasn't central to the story, just an added annoyance. "Then there's this evil event coordinator who put the entire first folio on the no-fly list because she thinks it will somehow clash with her robotics camp retelling of *Romeo and Juliet*—"

"Can you please take a breath before you pass out?" Ian chided gently. "Can we back up to the part where the canker blossom from your past saved Puck? That must have been a little"—he fumbled for the right words—"emotionally confusing."

"Right? Also, he showed up this morning at my house with Puck in tow and he had bathed him, brushed his teeth and trimmed his nails."

"So, is he no longer the scum of the earth because he saved our beloved intern, or do we still hate him on principle?"

"We hate him on principle."

"Okay, but it sort of sounds like maybe this guy is trying to mend fences. Do you remember the time Puck snatched his Scooby-Doo toothbrush out of your hand and swallowed it whole? The pup's got teeth issues. Adam's lucky he has all his digits." Ian hesitated. "He does still have all of his digits, right?"

"It gets better. I then got to watch his reunion with Portia. You should have seen his face when she came out on the porch. I felt like the leftover Cherry Wheat beer in the mix pack."

"Barnes, you're better than that."

"Fine. I'm the Cranberry Lambic. But you get the point."

"Did Portia rub her hands together like a praying mantis and prepare to rip off his head and eat it in front of you?" Ian asked gleefully. "What did you do?"

"Collected my dog like a mature adult."

"And then?"

"I turned tail and ran."

"Thatta girl." Ian paused, presumably to take a sip of his coffee. "I know you don't want to hear this, but high school assholes can occasionally mature into well-adjusted, even likable adults. I mean, this guy did help Puck. You could at least try to not treat him like social herpes."

"That's exactly what Cordy said. Without the upsetting STD reference."

Ian snorted while I beat back the memory of crying my eyes out on the front porch after Adam drove off with my sister. Well, Ian was right about the "high school asshole" part. The jury was still out on "well-adjusted adult."

"So," Ian said. "Did the vet call you Backup Barnes? Because that seems in poor taste."

"No, that was the other high school classmate. Just some guy who ran in Portia's circle."

"Just some guy?"

"Tall, dark-haired and trending toward smooth and shallow."

"And born without a social filter, apparently. Who brings up old nicknames like that, anyway?"

"Right?"

"Wait, did you say tall and dark-haired? That's your personal kryptonite. You're not going to sleep with him, are you? Or worse, date him?"

"Probably not," I hedged.

"When I said to scratch an itch, I did not mean with a bottom-feeder." He cleared his throat. "Barnes, you are my best friend in this beer-soaked adventure we call life, and I would happily part with a kidney if yours crapped out, or help you dispose of a body, and I'll even help you move out of that third-floor walk-up someday. But my God, woman, you have the worst taste in men. Bed someone whose bed you're not embarrassed to be rolling out of the next day. More importantly, I don't want you dating the emotional equivalent of Splenda because you think that's all you deserve. You deserve the whole damn world, Barnes."

"So I should find the emotional equivalent of Mexican Coca-Cola? In the vintage glass bottles?"

"The worst, Barnes. You're the worst."

"Fine, I will heed your smug 'I might have found my soul mate, now go find yours' pep talk and lay off undeserving man candy. Now amuse me. What's going on at Valhalla?"

"We finally signed that YA author you adore."

"The one who wrote the gender-flipped Scheherazade retelling?"

"The same," Ian said, the smile evident in his voice.

"Swoon. That's the best news I've heard all morning."

"That's rather sad."

"But I got to start my day with a chocolate croissant from Cordy."

"I hate you," Ian groaned. "My jealousy knows no end. Now, unless you want to rub more culinary triumphs in my face, I do have to leave for the office. My business partner up and left me."

"Hey! I am still responding to clients. You're just the face everyone will see this summer."

"And what a glorious face it is," he preened. "Take care of Momma Barnes. Keep the pup away from the cacao stash. Stop provoking blood feuds with the locals. Write your damn book. Maybe even consider being nice to the good doctor. If not for his sake, then for your own. Carrying this baggage from high school around all summer cannot be good for your inner Bard."

"Just don't kill all my houseplants," I said, blithely ignoring his advice. I ended the call and cranked up some Tom Petty. "He's going to kill all my houseplants," I confided in Puck. My dog craned his neck in my direction, an invitation to scratch behind his ears. "You really do smell nice." My mind flashed to Adam standing in my driveway, my dog gazing adoringly up at him. The image shifted to a younger Adam, his hair sticking out from beneath his battered baseball hat with the split brim. The Adam who'd stumbled upon me mid-obscenity-laden rant when I'd come out from rehearsals to find I'd left the dome light on and my battery had gone the way of Rosencrantz and Guildenstern.

Over a decade ago, beneath a canopy of deepening twilight, he'd driven me home in his blue pickup truck, the two of us chattering on about our favorite classes and the worst movie endings of all time. On and on we'd talked and laughed, falling into a conversational rhythm that had felt like slipping on a much-loved hoodie.

Adam had walked me up the drive and we'd sat on the stairs for a bit watching the fireflies flicker in the tall grass. We had talked for what felt like hours, and when the words ran out, he leaned over and kissed me, soft and sweet and smelling of spearmint.

That version of Adam, I'd thought at the time, might just have been the whole damn world.

The Taming of the Shoe

slipped into The Taming of the Shoe about a minute before our first meeting started, the stiletto-shaped silver bell above the door announcing my arrival. Despite my assertions to Ian earlier in the week that I would consider being more civil to Adam, that didn't mean I wanted to spend a second longer around him than I had to. I figured the less time I spent with Adam, the more civil I could be when I did see him. Take that, logic.

The shop smelled of shoe leather and, if I wasn't mistaken, the heady scent of an Old World vintage—a dollop of floral, a dash of dirt. Tillie spotted me from her perch on the couch and crossed the floor in a swath of peacock silk to hand me one of those comically large wineglasses I'd only ever seen people use as photo booth props. "Thirsty Thursday." She winked.

She'd filled it about a quarter of the way, which meant I should only drink about an eighth of it if I wanted to drive home. Otherwise, I'd have to hoof it. *Well, at least I dressed for a late-night stroll,* I thought as I glanced down at my trainers and leggings.

"I heard about your standoff with Candace. About time someone stood up to that twit," Tillie confided in me as she took me by the elbow and led me over to where Dan and Adam were seated in the patterned chairs and chaises. Tillie insisted these overstuffed behemoths were absolutely necessary if you were ever going to find the right pair of shoes for your feet. I actually found it to be quite the opposite. Once I'd sunk down into one of the enticing chairs, I had little desire to get up and walk around in whatever shoes I'd tried on.

Surveying my limited seating options—join Tillie on the couch, even though she struck me as the kind of woman who liked to sprawl across the furniture, or take the wingback by Adam—I settled on not cramping Tillie's style. With a soft sigh, I folded myself into the wingback, because if nothing else, the high contours of the chair blocked me from having to look directly at him.

"Where's my favorite fur face tonight?" Adam asked brightly. This evening's clothing selection featured a button-down in desert sage that did interesting things to the green in his hazel eyes. He'd rolled his sleeves up to the elbow, and Bard help me, I had no idea why that was such a turn-on. There was something about a man who looked equally ready to dive into yard work or suture a family pet. Also, he smelled nice—a bright citrus with a ginger base.

Studiously not staring at Adam's bare forearms, I managed, "The pup's peccadilloes include a penchant for shoe chewing. Didn't want to ruin Tillie's night."

Our aforementioned hostess nodded approvingly as she laid one of my sister's signature creations down on the table with a flourish. Cordy had even piped the shop's logo—a delicate glass slipper—in silvery icing atop her sinfully delicious chocolate silk pie.

I smiled over the brim of my glass. "Custom job?"

"We keep your sister busy." Tillie preened, clearly pleased that I'd noticed the personal touch. "I like my calorie sinkholes to be pretty."

"Words to live by," Dan agreed as he sipped his wine, his long, elegant fingers wrapped around the glass. Although I would never tell him this, his constantly furrowed brows over his darting hawk eyes and tightly pressed lips reminded me of Vincent Price circa *The*

Raven. Minus the upsetting 'stache. Dan even had that gravel and velvet growl reminiscent of the horror icon. "Miranda, is your father coming as well?"

I shook my head. "He's got class tonight."

"I'll take set notes," Adam offered. "I can catch up with Pete later."

I gave Adam a long, appraising look. Were he and my dad multigenerational besties? When he caught me staring at him, Adam smiled, an easy expression that was as warm and delicious as freshly baked cinnamon buns, and just as bad for me.

Tillie cleared her throat to get the room's attention. "I'm afraid I've got some bad news. Kitty called me last night. Her ninety-three-year-old father broke a hip and she's heading down to Georgia to help him rehab. She'll be there most of the summer. We need to figure out what to do, and fast. Selections are due tomorrow and we're now short a director."

Dan cleared his throat. "I'd like to do the Scottish play. As Shakespeare's grandest tragedy, I think it's only fitting we put it on for our centennial." He looked around expectantly.

I lifted an eyebrow. While it was considered bad luck to speak the name *Macbeth* in theater spaces and all sorts of misfortune and doom were supposed to ensue if you did, we were in a shoe shop. Still, I appreciated Dan's adherence to theater superstitions.

"Good pick," I said, nodding. I knew my mother would have preferred I wrest the tragedy from Dan, because she thought the Bard's tragedies were more high-profile. But truth be told, I preferred the comedies. The women always seemed to fare better in them. Besides, my mother couldn't be everywhere at once and had decided the mainstages subcommittee could be left to its own devices. "I'll take a comedy," I offered.

"Can you two split directing responsibilities on the third?" Tillie asked anxiously. "I'm getting up there, kids. I don't think I have it in me to direct and do costuming."

Dan hummed his disagreement. "I don't think that will work. There's just too much to do in a short span of time. Iz wants auditions and casting next week, with rehearsals in full swing shortly thereafter."

"Agreed," I said. "We need someone who can hit the ground running."

We all looked at Adam.

He snapped up in his chair like a smoke alarm had gone off. "Oh, no, you guys know the drill. No acting, no directing. I'm good with my hands. That's where my theater talents end."

My traitorous id emerged from a cave worthy of Grendel to spin visuals involving Adam's hands. Adam's hands reaching for mine. Adam's hands cupping my chin, tilting my face up. Adam's hands tracing the arc of my collarbone. Adam's hands—

"Candace stopped by the shop this morning and dropped a monster-sized hint to Aaron that she'd be interested in doing the third." Dan rolled his eyes. "Opportunistic harpy."

My id shuddered at the mention of Candace and scuttled back to the safety of the cave. "I don't think that's a great idea," I hedged. "For the same reason Dan and I can't split the third mainstage, Candace can't do it and the dinner theater production." That, and I was pretty sure Candace feasted on the souls of the innocent.

Tillie sighed. "I can ask around, but your mother has already co-opted most of the town into service. Everybody is already on a subcommittee as it is. Besides, if word got back to Candace that we were looking for someone after she offered . . . Well, I've had a good long life, but I worry about the rest of you."

"Could your niece do it?" Adam asked. "She's home for the summer, right?"

Tillie gnawed her lip. "Opal is a freshman in college, hon. That's a lot of responsibility for a kid her age to shoulder."

"Miranda directed a mainstage the summer she graduated from high school," Adam insisted. When I stared at him with a bewildered expression, he shrugged. "I interned a few towns over at the Haas Animal Hospital that summer. How could I pass up *As You Like It*? It's one of my favorites."

Screw it, I'll run home, I decided as I knocked back the rest of my wine and pondered Adam's admission. The thought of him sitting unseen in the audience, watching my directorial debut, both unnerved and pleased me.

"Has Opal taken any theater classes?" Dan asked.

Tillie nodded. "Introduction to the Stage her first semester and Basic Directorial Techniques her second."

I raised an eyebrow. That was more training than I'd had when my mother had thrust me into my first mainstage. "Where is Opal?"

"Mini-golfing with Alice at Peaseblossom's."

"If Opal wants to take on the third play, I'll back her up on auditions, casting—anything personnel related," I said, even as I mentally kicked myself for the offer. I really didn't have time for this.

"I can help her out with any technical aspects, props and lighting, that sort of thing," Adam chimed in. "Tillie, if you can walk her through costumes and makeup, that's another load off her. Dan, you're the marketing whiz. Could you and Aaron assist her on the promotional side?"

Surprised, I gave Adam a grateful smile.

"It could work," Dan agreed in a mollified tone. "If she's up for it."

We all looked at Tillie.

"Worth a text." Tillie shrugged and produced a rhinestone-encrusted phone that proclaimed it was wine o'clock somewhere. That settled it. I wanted to be Tillie when I grew up.

While we waited for Opal's response, Dan talked himself in and out of putting on the Scottish play. Personally, I was over *Macbeth*. It required a delicate hand to avoid veering into scenery-chewing territory. But I'd seen Dan pull off *King Lear*. He could do it, particularly with input from Aaron, who kept their high-end kitchen and cookware shop, Two Gentlemen of Daytona, from descending into tacky Williams Sonoma knockoff territory.

"C'mon, it wouldn't be a centennial if we didn't risk putting on the Bard's cursed masterpiece," I teased. "What could possibly go wrong?"

"What're you thinking on the comedy?" Dan countered, his oh-so-serious eyebrows doing an inquisitive shimmy.

"*Twelfth Night*," I blurted out, without really realizing I'd already committed to it in my head. But it felt right. "Viola's the most resourceful Shakespearean heroine. She'll resonate with a modern audience."

"More so than Beatrice?" Adam asked.

I shrugged. "Viola survived a shipwreck and disguised herself as a man just so she could move about freely in society. Beatrice had it easy by comparison."

"Also, Benedick is kind of an ass," Tillie chimed in.

"Orsino is one of my favorites," Adam added. "Can't go wrong with the duke."

Dan snorted.

"What?" Adam said.

"Orsino is bland."

"Orsino isn't bland," Adam insisted. "He's a flawed character who picks the wrong woman and by some stroke of luck gets a second chance to make it right."

Adam might have been talking to Dan, but his eyes were on me, and I felt hot all over. "Tillie, have you got any more wine?" I croaked.

"Codpieces and corsets, Miranda! I have wine for days." Tillie happily topped off everyone's glasses and passed out pie as I steered the conversation to safer talk of audition times and budgets for costumes, props and sets.

Sometime around nine, the slipper-shaped harbinger signaled the arrival of a tall, willowy figure. The girl shrugged out of her jacket and shook out her dark hair, its geode crystal streaks dancing in the light. "Alice is a cheat," she declared, flinging her jacket behind the register with practiced ease. "She took four mulligans. On the front nine. She knows you don't get mulligans in mini-golf, right?" She flopped down on the couch beside Tillie, eyeing the pie.

"You think that's bad? You should see her at cards," Tillie snorted.

I watched in fascination as Opal devoured the dessert as only wolves and teenagers can. It seemed like not so long ago that Opal had been a shy middle schooler who Tillie had gone to war for when her deadbeat father had decided he wanted his daughter back—an arrangement that was palatable to neither Opal nor Tillie. Unfortunately, the fine folks of the legal system thought that custody of Tillie's niece should go to her father since Tillie engaged in an "alternative lifestyle." Tillie reached out to my sister for legal advice, only to have Portia, fresh out of law school, roll into town for the hearing. The only hearing. After which the thoroughly chastened court had agreed that Opal would be just fine in Tillie's capable hands. Because Portia was the courtroom equivalent of the Mother of Dragons.

Brushing crumbs off a navy TARDIS T-shirt that proclaimed her allegiance to the Thirteenth Doctor, Opal looked each of us up and down in that unnervingly frank way that only teenagers can pull off. "Tillie said you needed some help? You need an usher or ticket taker?"

"Is that what she told you?" I raised an eyebrow.

"She said you guys needed some help." She pushed her long hair off her forehead, an amethyst lock winking in the light and curling around her shoulder. "I'm happy to pitch in. Although you should know, I do not come cheap. I expect minimum wage and unrestricted popcorn privileges."

I glanced over at Tillie, who suddenly seemed fascinated by the peep toe display I'd been so taken with earlier, while Dan pretended to check his fitness tracker. Adam just stared expectantly at me the way Puck did when his food dish was empty. I rolled my eyes at all of them before turning to Opal. "We were thinking something on a slightly grander scale, but I'll throw in popcorn, candy, fountain soda privileges and free tickets for you and your friends."

Opal leaned forward, rubbing her hands together. "Now you're talking."

"How do you feel about directing one of the mainstages? Your choice. We will back you up on production and promotional stuff so you can focus on directing."

"That's kind of a lot." The teenager chewed her lip.

I nodded. "It is." As much as I loathed the thought of working with Candace, that didn't mean I'd throw Opal to the wolves if she really didn't want this. "I'm not going to sugarcoat it. It's stressful and time-consuming, but it's also a total rush, not to mention a great résumé builder. I also promise that I will be your personal Yoda or enforcer, whatever you need."

Opal weighed me with eyes as dark as her hair. Well, some of her hair. I wondered if I was too old to do the geode thing on the tips. Of course, if I was asking myself that question, the answer was probably yes.

Despite writing for the young adult demographic, I found teenagers to be a terrifying mix of unpredictability and sass with a stunning capacity for kindness or cruelty—or both. Which was why I left them to Hathaway Smith. I did not want to be dissected and picked over on Twitter by these insightfully blunt creatures.

"I'll do it," Opal said finally. "As long as you'll help me." She brightened, the expression transforming her face into one of pixie delight. "Can I do a mythology-centric *Midsummer*? Because I always feel like the fairies take a back seat to the humans, and I think there's a lot we could do with Puck, who is basically the Shakespearean equivalent of Loki."

I blinked. "That could work."

"Great, I'll work up some notes tonight and send them over to you."

And just like that, I'd acquired a teenage protégé who was a billion times cooler than I was. That wasn't going to make me feel old or anything.

Hours later, after all the costumes and sets that needed updating had been carefully cataloged into Tillie's rather intimidating spreadsheet, we all staggered out of the shop, full of pie and action items. Waving to Dan as he drove off, I sampled the night air, tangy with salt from the nearby marsh and echoing with the call of the peepers. I loved living in the city, but there was nothing quite like standing under the star-studded sky in the velvet dark of Bard's Rest. *The woods are lovely, dark and deep*, I thought, *but I have a book to write and a deadline to keep,* I finished, riffing on my favorite Robert Frost line.

Clicking my key fob, I started for my car. Nothing. Frowning, I clicked it again. Still nothing.

Head drooping, I pulled on the door handle. Slipping into the driver's seat, I stepped on the brake and uttered a half-assed prayer as I pressed the ignition. My car grumbled anemically before trailing off. Rolling my eyes skyward, I noted that the dome light had been switched to the on position. Of course it had. I thunked my head against the steering wheel. Did AAA service the wilds of Bard's Rest?

Screw it, I fumed. I'd run home and my dad could give me a jump in the morning. While not an ideal situation, at least a run would give me a chance to mull over my next writing move. I just needed to get my reflective vest out of my trunk. In the city, where over half the population texted while driving, any jogger with a functioning brain stem had one, because wearing bright, shiny objects increased your chances of not being nudged by an apologetic Instagrammer in a Hyundai.

"Fleeing the town limits on foot?"

I spun around to find Adam, the blond of his hair sparkling like kindling in the shop light, shrugging into a navy Winters' Tail zip-up.

"It's a nice night for it," I lied as I hastily stashed the vest behind my back.

"How soon the city slicker forgets. It's high mosquito season around here. The minute you start sweating, you're going to be a meal for the masses."

I shrugged. "It's not a big deal." Although to be fair, I couldn't even remember the last time I'd seen a mosquito. As if on cue, something savaged my ankle with a needle-point stinger. I slapped at it as casually as I could and pulled my sock up. "That's why they make anti-itch cream."

"You know they took out the streetlamps on Avon Road, right? When the town declared it a bird sanctuary last year, they removed the lights to encourage breeding. You'd basically be running through prime ax murderer hunting grounds. Or Alfred Hitchcock *Birds* territory. Pick your worst nightmare."

Did riding home in an enclosed space with someone you were actively avoiding but kept popping into your life count as a worst nightmare? Maybe the introvert's version of it.

"Thanks, but I think I'll take my chances," I said, trying to angle my body in front of my car. It didn't work, as Adam easily peered around me.

"Dead battery, huh?" He chuckled. "What have you got against cars, Barnes?"

I groaned. "Left the dome light on. I never learn."

"Amateur hour." He clucked his tongue. "How about a jump?"

"I'd appreciate that."

Adam patted his pockets for his keys. "Crap, my jumper cables are in my Prius. Back in Seattle. I'm driving Pop's truck." He hesitated. "I could give you a lift?"

The hesitancy in his voice made me suspicious. "What's wrong with your dad's truck?"

He jerked his thumb behind him. "See for yourself."

I shuffled forward, pausing beside Adam, and gasped. "Wow." Someone had transformed the truck into a truly tacky moving beige billboard. I'd always admired the clever cat tail logo that swished its way down from the "L" in "Tail" and underscored The Winters' Tail sign in spectacular calico fashion. I just wasn't sure it worked airbrushed in navy on both sides of the truck. Also, the mural of the slightly cross-eyed animals sprouting out of the gas tank seemed a bit much.

I stared up at the night sky, lips pursed, trying not to laugh.

"Bunny 'surprised' Pops with it for their anniversary. I'm not saying there's a direct correlation between that custom paint job and Pop's heart attack, but he did keel over about two weeks after she parked it in the driveway."

"I think I'm about to keel over right now."

"I'd say that's an overreaction, but . . ." He trailed off.

"I think I'll take my chances in the unlit marshlands. I might catch beige madness from that thing."

"Suit yourself. I'll get in my truck and follow you home to make sure you don't get picked off by a backwoods, knife-toting Shakespeare enthusiast."

"You don't have to do that," I protested.

"I do, because if you end up a tragic local headline, I will never forgive myself."

"Tragic local headline?" I raised an eyebrow.

"'Local resident carried off by mosquitos the size of Buicks'?"

"Try again." I folded my arms across my chest.

"'Local resident mauled beyond recognition by fisher cats'?"

I put my hands on my hips. "Fisher cats?"

"Fisher cats are no joke," Adam insisted. "The loss of life and injury to pets each year would surprise you."

"Exactly how many humans sustain life-threatening injuries because of fisher cats?"

From the way he was gnawing his full bottom lip, Adam seemed to be calculating his odds of bullshitting me with made up statistics. "Coyotes. Our coyote population has increased threefold. They have been known to target lone humans."

"Fine." I threw up my hands, trying to stifle a laugh. "You can drive me home. But no more worst-case scenarios involving local wildlife."

"Excellent," he said, playfully bumping his shoulder against mine. "You can ride shotgun."

"Where else would I ride?" I muttered as I followed him to the truck. At least the interior was uninfected by the makeover and relatively devoid of detritus. No food wrappers littered the floor, no unopened mail stashed in the passenger seat, no men's magazines. Although there was a sizable bag of dog and cat treats in the back seat. When he caught me staring at the stash, he looked sheepish. "I don't like being bitten or peed on."

"Words to live by."

"More like a professional hazard." He laughed, the sound of it filling the cab and settling in my chest. "That was really nice, what you did back there for Opal," Adam said.

I shrugged, wedging myself into the corner of the cab, as far away from Adam as I could get. "I know what it's like to be the weird theater kid. It helps to know someone's in your corner. Although it sounds like she already has plenty of good ideas."

"She's a good kid. I'll help her however I can," he said. "As for *Twelfth Night*, the old sets are in rough shape. I don't think they've been updated since you played Viola. That was ages ago."

"Yes, thank you," I said dryly. "Just remember, you're older than I am."

"I'm not old," Adam protested as he drove us out of town and into the darkness, devoid of streetlights. He hadn't been kidding about the bird sanctuary thing. "I'm in my prime."

"We're trilobites compared to Opal. She looks at us the way we used to look at our teachers. We may as well be nursing home escapees."

Adam shuddered. "Okay, we're teenager old, but not *old* old. I'd like to think we've held up better than those sets." He gave me a sidelong glance. "I do have a few preliminary ideas on updating them. Any chance you're free tomorrow night to discuss them? I don't want them to clash with any spin you're thinking of putting on the production."

That definitely wasn't going to work. By some stroke of luck, the doctor's office had called back today with a cancellation for tomorrow morning, and I'd hounded Mom into taking it. I suspected that by tomorrow evening, nobody in the Barnes clan would be feeling very social, except maybe Portia, who was immune to feelings. "I have plans."

"Saturday?"

"Not good either."

"I get it, you've just gotten home. How about next week?"

"I have—" I trailed off. Was there a nice way to say I'd rather be mauled by fisher cats than spend more time with Adam? It was bad enough seeing him in a group setting, but just the two of us for a prolonged period of time? What would I even say to him?

"Oh, come on," he cajoled. "Pencil me in for next Friday. That will give you plenty of time to get your Bard sea legs. Besides, I want to practice on you before I meet with Dan. Pete says his set demands are the stuff of legends. And not the good kind."

"Oh, so I'm your guinea pig?" I asked, frowning at him. "As flattering as that is, I'll probably be doing gopher things for my mom that night."

"On a Friday night?"

"You've met Isabella, yes?"

"This is centennial-related. I'm sure she'll give you a pass. How about next Friday at The Winters' Tail around eight? You can bring Puck. He can meet Lucille. She's been lonely since we flew out here."

"Can't you just email me?" I really didn't want to hear about Adam's girlfriend.

He wrinkled his nose in distaste, and though I was loathe to admit it, it was kind of adorable. "Well, yeah, if we were talking about tax returns. You know the back-and-forth that goes into getting the sets right. Email is not going to get you there. Particularly if you're going to help Opal bring her own play to life. You'll need to get a jump start on yours."

"I don't know," I groaned, but even I could hear the acquiescence in my voice.

"C'mon, Barnes," he said, his smile winsome. "I'll not only feed you and design you gorgeous sets, but I'll stop telling everyone your dog puked all over my good shoes."

"Why would you tell people that?" I stammered.

"Because it's hilarious," he said, his smile trending devilish in the dim light of the truck.

"That's evil," I scoffed, pulling my eyes away from the gravitational pull of his lips curving up like that. "Have you no standards?"

"I don't want to have shabby sets for the centennial. I don't think you do either. It would reflect badly on Pete."

I narrowed my eyes. "Fine."

"Great." He slowed, easing the truck into my driveway. "I'll see you Friday."

"Next Friday," I corrected. The truck shuddered to a stop and I slid out, fumbling for my keys and general sense of equilibrium. "Thanks for the ride."

"Anything to help a car-murdering damsel in distress," he teased. "Give the pup a scratch for me, okay?"

"He is rather attention starved," I deadpanned, but smiled as I shut the truck door.

With a small wave, Adam reversed and rolled out of the driveway. Home. He was going home to his special someone. While I was going upstairs to a four-legged imprudent eater and a new plot line that begged to be explored. Somehow, the universe felt right again.

··········

The Hospital

I awoke, bleary-eyed and still sporting yesterday's clothes. I hadn't just explored that new plot line; I had chased it down and wrestled it into the beginning of a halfway decent middle. I was due a serious raid of my parents' best tea for progress like that. Slipping into jeans, I made for the stairs and paused in the reading nook. Inhaling deeply, I basked in the old-book smell of my childhood hideout from my extrovert sisters and gazed out the window, where—where my car was neatly parked in the driveway.

Frowning, I headed for the kitchen. I found my father sitting at the scarred wooden table where Barnes dinners and game nights had been waged for decades, his head bent over the local paper as he munched on oatmeal and summer berries. Puck lay curled at his feet, eyeing him adoringly. Clearly, Dad had slipped him some sort of predawn deli meat.

"Morning," I said.

"Morning, lambkin," Dad said, glancing up to give me that crinkly-eyed smile of his. "Sleep okay?"

I nodded. Crawling into bed somewhere in the neighborhood of 3:00 a.m. could be considered sleeping okay, right? "Do you know how my car ended up in our driveway?"

"I do," he said, sipping a mug of his Earl Grey. Like father, like daughter. The rest of Clan Barnes was regrettably Team English Breakfast. "Adam texted me this morning to see if I knew where you kept your keys. Something about leaving your dome light on? I told him if he brought me one of those breakfast wraps he makes, I'd ride into town with him, help him jump your car and drive it home."

I stared at my father.

He shrugged, not bothering to look apologetic. "Not that I'm not happy you girls are independent women with brains and spine to spare, but couldn't one of you have done your old man a solid and married Adam? The man grows organic tomatoes and makes his own herb spread."

I pressed my hands over my eyes. "My own father," I muttered. "Willing to parcel me off like chattel for chives and cream cheese."

"It was no trouble," Dad continued cheerfully. "It gave us a chance to talk over sets. Your mother is going to harp on you for revisiting *Twelfth Night*, but I think it's an excellent choice."

I flashed him a grateful smile. "She still in the shower?"

He nodded. "Just finishing up."

"How did she seem?"

"She had her 'Jeanne d'Arc on the eve of battle' face on."

Grinning, I helped myself to a mug of tea. "If she makes a break for it, I do expect your support in the form of that tranq gun. No holding back. You go full-on 'Most Dangerous Game' on her." My stomach rumbled, a stern admonition that it had been a while since the previous night, when I'd downed the smoothie my big sister had poured into a carefully measured travel bottle in the fridge. Once I'd stirred some cocoa powder into the banana kale concoction, it hadn't been half-bad. I knew smoothie theft made me a terrible sister. My only excuse was that I liked to keep Portia guessing.

"You and Adam seem chummy these days," I remarked in what could pass for an offhanded manner. "What with the homemade breakfast sandwiches and all."

"He seems a bit lonely, is all. Coming up from the city and running the practice alone while Walt is recovering from bypass can't be easy."

Oh right, just because my father had birthed an emotional ogre like me didn't make him one.

"He can't be all that lonely," I muttered, thinking of the mysterious Lucille. Okay, the quasi-mysterious Lucille—because honestly, that name didn't evoke intrigue. My money was on Instagram influencer. And blond—she would definitely be a blond.

"He volunteered to build sets with me in the bowels of the theater building in the high heat of summer. Of course he's lonely."

"Who's lonely?" my mother asked as she breezed into the kitchen, her hair expertly pulled into a sleek chignon. I smiled, shaking my head and touching my own haphazard slipknot of a bun. How were we related again?

"Adam Winters," my father supplied cheerfully.

"Well, of course he is," she agreed, clucking her tongue. "The poor thing doesn't know what to do with himself. He practically jumped at the chance to work on sets with your father. I mean, who would do such a thing? It's hotter than the hubs of hell in that workshop."

"When they ask me what I did for love . . ." My father sighed dramatically.

I snickered into the bergamot-scented steam rising from my mug.

"Laugh all you want. I get to pick the music today," Mom said, her tone superior.

I stopped smiling. "It's too early for opera."

"Nonsense," she insisted. "It's never too early for opera. I'm thinking Monteverdi."

I groaned as I bent down and rubbed Puck behind the ears. "Count yourself lucky you get to stay here," I whispered. Puck closed his eyes, leaning into my knuckles. "Be good for Grandpa. Don't roll in dead things."

Puck's eyes hardened in what I can only describe as extreme canine shade.

Straightening, I scooped up the manila folder that contained

Mom's forms and instructions for the procedure. "Can we at least listen to 'Ride of the Valkyries' as we roll into the parking lot? With the windows down? Because I think that would be totally badass."

"Oh, Miranda," my mother sighed. "If you're going to use profanity in this house, I wish you'd choose something of the Bard's. Otherwise, why bother?" She snatched a silk scarf that Dad had brought her from the gardens of Giverny and knotted it around her neck. It was the academic's equivalent of getting armed for battle. "Shall we? I don't want to be late to my own execution."

This time it was my father who snickered.

Outside, Mom plucked an errant crepe myrtle blossom from the birdbath and tilted her face up to greet the morning sun. Rolling her shoulders in a way that was distinctively feline in nature, she slid into the passenger seat beside me, her gardenia-steeped-in-rosemary scent a marked upgrade over the gym sock aroma of the fur face who usually sat shotgun. I plugged in the address for Maine Medical and backed down the driveway as Mom switched the car's Bluetooth connection from mine to hers. Instead of opera, Mick Jagger's ragged plea for shelter filled the car. I heaved a sigh of relief.

"Three daughters and not a Puccini fan among you," she tsked.

We drove in silence down the undercarriage-devouring road as the bright morning rays of the sun skewered the canopy of trees and dappled the wings of the sparrows. Somewhere around these woods lay an abandoned fairy village that Cordy and I had spent countless hours on, lovingly thatching the acorn roofs with pine needles and adorning the walkways with bits of shell and mica. We had labored over it together, year after year, until that summer someone gave Cordy her first cookbook, and then the fairies and I were left behind in favor of spun sugar and candied citrus. Not that I was complaining. I'd rather eat cupcakes than spirits of the air any day. Still, I wondered what had become of it—likely reclaimed by the elements and trampled by the animals.

Mom made a sound too delicate to be considered clearing her throat. Perhaps she sensed I was a million miles away in a realm of thumb-sized cottages and a childhood I could no longer find my way back to. Or maybe it was because I was driving a healthy fifteen miles over the speed limit—a pace that would be considered sedate by Somerville standards, but here would probably get me pulled over. There'd be no living that down, so I eased off the gas.

"Tillie sent over the selections this morning. I see you've settled on *Twelfth Night*," my mother said breezily, one hand waving laconically out the window. "You made such a lovely Viola in high school. But I admit I'm a little surprised you're revisiting familiar territory."

"I've been in over a dozen of the Bard's plays. There's not much at this point that's unfamiliar territory unless I want to venture into the royals or *Coriolanus*."

Mom shuddered delicately. "But why *Twelfth Night*?"

"I've always liked its balance of the whimsical and the practical." I chewed my lip. I didn't want to be psychoanalyzed by someone who made Freud look like a rank amateur, but I pushed aside my reservations and offered, "Viola resonates for me."

"Because she's Shakespeare's greatest secret keeper?" Isabella's smile was disarming, but her tone was sly. Unlike the rest of our family, who found my need for a pen name to be quirky (Cordy) and more trouble than it was worth (Portia), Mom had always understood it. I was her shy middle daughter who only seemed to blossom while onstage—she alone grasped that my creativity flourished when I got to be someone else.

"Because she's a cross-dressing lover of poetry, and if that's not some sort of divine mash-up, I don't know what is," I offered, giving my mother my most guileless smile. I squinted into the sun as the canopy of trees gave way to a startling blue sky smattered with white clouds as airy as Cordy's confections. Mick finished cheerfully kicking everyone off his cloud and then asked us to have a little sympathy for the devil as we headed for the interstate. "Did Tillie mention that Opal is trying her hand at directing *Midsummer*?"

"Ambitious. But a fine play to cut one's teeth on. I hear her mentor is a seasoned theater veteran." She patted my knee again. "I'm proud of you. I know that's a lot for you to take on, what with writing your book and all."

"Subtle. Is that your way of fishing for updates?"

"No, that's my way of telling you I'm proud of you. I know the committee is a lot and you weren't expecting to be adding a mainstage and a mentorship to your plate." She tucked a strand of hair behind her ear. "But now that you mention it, I'd love to hear how it's going."

"Shameless. You're completely shameless," I retorted, but the effect was ruined by the grin tugging up the corners of my mouth.

"You've hit upon something, haven't you?" Mom said, with a knowing smile of her own. "I heard you in the attic the last few nights."

"Being back in Bard's has helped me reconnect with my characters. I've been able to tune out some of the noise that's been making it so difficult to write," I admitted.

"I knew it. I told your father that the creative muse would shake loose once you had a chance to clear your head after this minor setback." Mom preened.

"It was hardly a minor setback," I grumbled. "Everyone hated *Inconstant Moons*."

"There are very few people in life who can say they make a living doing what they love. Would you still consider yourself one of them?" my mother asked, wearing her best Cheshire cat smile, the one she saved for big life talks and epic cribbage wins.

I blew out a breath. Did I still love the agenting? For sure. But the writing? The past days of writing on fire excluded? Sure, but for a while there, the jury had been out. "I really thought I'd written what was best for the series," I admitted in a quiet voice. "With Thad out of the way, the other characters could move forward. But they hated it, Mom. My fan base hated it. It's been so hard to write after that."

"Well, you do write for teenagers. They are prone to hating new things." Mom gave me a fond pat. "Especially change."

"I thought teenagers were supposed to be all 'live your truth' and whatnot," I muttered.

"They are," she said kindly, "but like all of us, they crave the familiar, the routine. It can be difficult—even frightening—to go after something new, something we really want. Particularly when we're not sure how it will pan out."

My thoughts involuntarily flipped to Adam in profile as he drove, the streetlights flickering on his face. The soft curve of his lips, always curling upward, as if he were just a second away from a smile. And the sound of his laugh as it filled up the truck and settled in my chest. "Are we still talking about writing?" I asked, clearing my throat.

"Of course," Mom said mildly. "Now, not that I'm sniffing around for details or anything," she said in a voice that communicated plainly that's exactly what she was doing, "where does young Meg find herself these days?"

"At a crossroads. In her head, I think she knows it's time for her to leave the Guild, that she's the catalyst to unite the Fae and free them from the tyranny of the summer and winter queens. But she's unsure if she's ready to put herself out there to lead the realm in an uprising."

"Well, Meg's been very successful as the spy behind the curtain," Mom said thoughtfully. "But that's what good characters do. They evolve and discover they're capable of so much more than they ever imagined." She reached over, patting my hand. "I'm sure you'll help her see her way through it."

I sighed. "No pressure."

Turning onto the interstate, I steered the conversation back to her. "How're things going with the centennial planning?"

She launched into a dizzying deep dive of budgets and permits, meetings with the zoning board, musical selections and centennial colors, parade schedules, vendor contracts, projected weather forecasts, official merchandizing opportunities, local business tie-ins and her keynote address.

I couldn't help admiring how calm she was, describing her responsibilities and tasks. They sounded like the logistical equivalent of mucking out the Augean stables.

"Did you know it would be so much work when you agreed to do it?"

"Of course," she said airily. "I've been on a committee as far back as I can remember."

"But the head role?"

"Well, I tried to convince your father to cochair with me, but you know how he likes to stay out of the line of fire."

I bit my lip and tried not to laugh. But she was just so dead-on. My father would rather hide out in the sweltering underbelly of the theater shop all summer than wade through the politics of the various committees.

"Why this year?"

"Darling, it's the centennial. Who else was going to do it?"

Who indeed? For who else loved the Bard as much as Isabella Barnes? Who else had lovingly taught his plays and sonnets to novice and master alike over the years? And who else had fundraised with such ferocity for the town and the arts? She was right. Somehow, it felt like a true Shakespearean plot twist that just as my mother was coming into everything she'd ever wanted, potential misfortune and ruin lurked in the wings.

When we reached Maine Medical, I pretended to fumble for the parking ticket at the gate, but really I was reclaiming control of the Bluetooth. With a few finger strokes, I deftly cranked the volume up as the opening strains of "Ride of the Valkyries" filled the parking garage.

"Smart-ass," my mother sniffed. But she was smiling.

"Honestly, Mother. If you're going to use profanity in this car, I wish you'd at least use something of the Bard's. Otherwise, why bother?" I said, mimicking her voice as best I could.

"Canker blossom."

"Much better."

But the moment she stepped out of the car; my mother's smile evaporated. Her lips flattened into a tight line and her hand curled like a talon around her folder. Her navy blouse, loose-fitting per the biopsy instructions, billowed out behind her as she traversed the pavement with steady, resolute steps.

"I could go in with you," I said softly. "In the room, if you want."

Her shoulders stiffened. "Thank you, darling. But I'll be fine."

The thought of her alone and lying on the table, hands above her head, waiting for the needle, brought the first sting of tears to my eyes. I pushed them down hard. Now was not the time. Now was the time to show up for the woman who'd always shown up for me. "I brought my earbuds. The nurse said you could listen to music if you want."

"Thank you, but I'm all right. I'll just compose to-do lists in my head." She sighed. "I had to miss a meeting today with the board of health. Something about the proximity of the petting zoo to the food stands. I just don't have time for this."

I wasn't sure if she meant the petting zoo or the biopsy, but my heart ached at that somber, determined expression on her face. I wasn't as brilliant as Portia. I wasn't warm like Cordy. But damn it, I had one thing going for me—I was occasionally hilarious. So I reached deep into my childhood and pulled out the following gem: "Time to put on your big-girl nether hose and get on with it."

It broke the awful spell. She smiled, ruffling my hair. "Oh, Miranda. You know women didn't wear nether hose."

"I don't care what the Bard said. Pantyhose covers you from toe to waist. Therefore, it covers your nether regions. Hence, nether hose."

"You're absolutely right, darling. Why should men have all the fun?" She squeezed my shoulder. "Come on, let's get this the hell over with," she said, stepping through the automatic doors and into the carefully controlled temperature of the hospital with a devil-may-care ferocity.

Inside, we checked into a bland waiting room full of the requisite outdated magazines. We didn't have to wait very long. When the door opened and a delicate slip of a woman called my mother's name, I bit back another offer to go in with her and instead locked eyes with her. Mom nodded and turned on her heel, head held high.

I waited a few beats until I was certain she wouldn't be coming back out and then found a tiny bathroom that smelled of antiseptic. Leaning against the sink, I let the tears I'd been holding on to earlier come in hiccupping torrents. I wasn't a religious person by any stretch, but I sent up a silent prayer to the universe to watch over the person who'd spent a lifetime watching over me.

Catching sight of my tear-swollen eyes and blotchy cheeks reminded me why I never cried in public if I could help it. My face looked like someone had backed over it with farm equipment. At least I'd been smart enough not to wear eye makeup, because there wasn't a waterproof mascara on earth that would hold up to "I'm with my mom at her biopsy" tears.

After several rounds of splashing water on my face, which only seemed to make the red blotches on my cheeks more prominent, I emerged from the bathroom.

Opening my laptop, I sorted through client emails and looked over our launches for next quarter. When I finished, I scanned my personal email and found one from Opal. Apparently, she'd taken the initiative to post the audition slots for the three mainstages for this coming Wednesday and Thursday. I opened the Excel file and squinted at the casting call spreadsheet posted on the mainstages forum. Every spot for *Twelfth Night* was already filled.

I gulped. Hopefully these people weren't expecting some high level of competency just because my last name was Barnes.

Extracting an actual, honest-to-goodness composition notebook from my bag—something that Ian would have found quaint and Gen Z Opal would have been unfamiliar with—I started in on a to-do list for *Twelfth Night*.

As I wrote, all of the old tricks and tips came back to me. I was nose-deep in a detailed costume list when the door opened. My mom stepped out unaided and, if it wasn't a trick of the light, still perfectly coifed. Hell, she didn't even look rumpled, just a little pale. I looked worse for my hour in the waiting room than she did for hers on the table.

"Well, that was a lot of fuss over nothing," she declared, her expression serene and locked down. Ever the professorial sphinx. "Let's go home, darling. We have a centennial to plan."

"I'll bring the car around."

"Darling, don't be silly. It was a breast, not a leg," she said, rolling her eyes. "It's not like I'm limping."

Behind us, the nurse snickered.

....

The Fire Pit

Despite her stylish exit from Maine Medical, the formidable Isabella Barnes succumbed to whatever meds they'd given her for the procedure and spent the drive home snoozing in the passenger seat surrounded by the sweet strains of her beloved Liszt. I didn't mind Liszt, and some of his waltzes were downright tolerable as a backdrop for composing my writing plans for the afternoon.

As we pulled into the driveway, the sputter of the gravel waking Mom, I glimpsed my father lounging in the garden with a battered copy of *A Moveable Feast* and an expression too sanguine to be anything other than practiced. As Mom stepped out of the car, he reached down behind the chair and lifted a bouquet of wildflowers tied with a sunny yellow ribbon.

Mom heaved a put-upon sigh worthy of a Lillian Hellman play, but she wasn't fooling anyone as she accepted the flowers and a careful hug from him. Seriously, how was I ever supposed to be satisfied with an adult relationship when I had such unrealistic role models?

"The doctor said I'll have the results next week," Mom said as she brushed a spattering of pollen from Dad's shirt. "So we can all be done with this foolishness and get back to what matters." She turned to me. "Speaking of which, don't you have some writing to catch up on? Time to pay the piper, daughter of mine."

"Yeah, yeah," I replied as my furry love bounded from around the side of the house and plowed into me. "I missed you too," I said to Puck. "How about a walk before we're banished to the attic?"

Dad pulled a face. "You make it sound like you're Rochester's mad wife."

"Was she mad, though?" I called as I headed off in search of Puck's leash, snickering as Mom started in on Dad about the male gaze and the lens through which men viewed so-called female hysterics. Poor Dad. He was in for it. At least it would give them something to chew on rather than his inevitable questions about the procedure. Better that he give her a little breathing room. We'd know soon enough what fate had in store.

After a walk in the humid-heavy woods that left Puck panting and me wishing I'd done more than a half-assed job of applying deodorant that morning, I retreated to the attic with a pitcher of fresh squeezed lemonade and snacks for Puck and me.

Picking up a dry erase marker, I stood in front of the ancient whiteboard from my misspent, doodle-prone youth. The board had the same dingy look that white shirts get when you haven't washed them with bleach. But it would do for the back half of the dreaded middle.

As an agent, I'd read hundreds of middles, and I knew better than anyone that this was where it was easy to go astray. This is where a writer had to raise the stakes without going down the rabbit hole of weird subplots. And the best way to get through the middle was to know where you'd come from and where you were going.

I stared hard at the board. I knew where Meg had come from. It had taken a trip to the Meadows to coax her back onto her path, but she was back on it and would pick her friends up along the way. Touching the tip of the marker to the board, I began to diagram the scenes until I could see the narrative thread. With a triumphant cry, I swapped the marker for my laptop.

Maybe it was the octagonal windows that overlooked the weeping willows. Maybe it was the framed photos of my younger self as Juliet and Beatrice. Or maybe it was that the first chapter of *Elf Shot* had been written in this very room. Whatever odd sway this attic held over me, it grabbed tight and shook the words loose.

Hours passed, the summer sun rose and sank over the pond, steeping the sky in orange creamsicle and pink lemonade hues, and still I wrote, lost in the worlds of the Fae. I wrote until Puck woke and demanded to be fed and let out. I filled his bowl and left him in the capable, snack-prone hands of my father before retreating upstairs once more. My only companion now was a dwindling stash of slightly sweaty caramels.

Around ten, intervention finally came in the form of a note under my door in Cordy's familiar scrawl. "You are cordially invited to a meeting of the Barnes progeny at the usual meeting spot. Snacks will be served. BYOS."

I grinned. *BYOS* was Cordy speak for "bring your own stick." I glanced longingly at my screen, where the end of a chapter begged for a few more paragraphs. But the promise of snacks that required sticks called to me like a sticky siren song. "Sorry," I caught myself muttering. "But Cordy uses Ghirardelli. She fights dirty."

Pulling on my trusty Valhalla Lit zip-up, I tiptoed down the stairs, taking great pains to avoid the creaky spots near my parents' bedroom. I grabbed a flashlight, because the last thing I needed was to break a leg picking my way down to the pond. Though it would lend a certain *Rear Window* quality to my already tragic stint in the attic.

Once outside, I rummaged around for a suitable stick. Finding an acceptable Y-shaped specimen, I tugged my socks up over my jeans to keep the ticks at bay and headed down the well-worn path. As I drew near the pond, the weeping willows rustled and dragged their trailing tendrils across my face. Voices floated up from two shadowy figures hunching over a fire and bickering, like something straight out of *Macbeth*.

"Build that fire any higher and it will singe my eyebrows off," Portia warned.

"Right, because looking permanently surprised all the time is a much better alternative to no eyebrows," Cordy giggled.

I smiled in the darkness. The meeting of the Barnes sisters had apparently started without me. I stepped into the clearing, where Cordy had indeed stoked a sizable fire in the stone pit. "Do I need to get the hose?" I asked.

"Apparently, she's expecting the high school volleyball team for a bonfire," Portia sniped, but her cheeks were rosy, lending her face an uncharacteristic warmth. "What if it spreads?"

"We'll run like hell and blame feral teenagers?" I offered.

Portia covered her face with her hands. "You know that arson is illegal, right?"

"No legalese." Cordy wagged her index finger at Portia. "Particularly not when you're drinking from a sparkly flask and have marshmallow on your pants."

Portia hissed and rubbed at a spot on her thigh. She did, however, press the bejeweled flask into my hand. I smirked at the saucy "Pastry Chefs Do It in the Puff" emblazoned in red and unscrewed the top. Sniffing tentatively, I asked, "Special hot chocolate?"

Cordy steepled her fingers. "Extra Godiva liqueur. Just the way you like it, lightweight," she teased. "Where's your stick?"

I brandished my branch. "Gimme."

Cordy forked over a bag of marshmallows, two hunks of Ghirardelli and homemade chocolate-dipped graham crackers.

"Peanut butter?" I asked hopefully.

"As if you have to ask," Cordy tsked as she pressed a tub of freshly ground peanut butter into my hand. "And honey for the health-conscious weirdo."

"Honey on graham crackers is delicious," Portia insisted. "It acts as a glue."

"If you didn't undercook your marshmallows, you wouldn't need them to hold the chocolate in place." Cordy smiled sweetly.

"Not everything benefits from a full flambé," Portia countered.

"Children," I said, skewering two plump marshmallows with my stick, "let's not fight in front of the carbs, okay?" I always split the difference between Portia's painfully pale marshmallows and Cordy's flaming blue ones. Mine were always golden brown and gooey. "Not that I'm complaining, but who called this meeting?"

"I did," Portia said. "Because I'd like a little more information on Mom other than the 'we're home, everything went fine' text from earlier."

Ignoring Portia's piercing gaze, I crouched down and balanced two grahams on one of the flatter rocks that made up the firepit. Smearing a smidge of peanut butter on each piece of chocolate, I pressed them onto the crackers and expertly slid my stick into the fire. "She wouldn't let me go in with her, so it's all secondhand at this point. She walked out of the procedure on her own and slept the entire ride home. That was about it."

"You didn't speak to the doctor?" Portia pressed. "When exactly is she getting the results back?"

The skin of my marshmallows began to crisp to that perfect barley color. Reminding myself that it was difficult for Portia to turn off her lawyerly interrogation skills and that she was as scared as the rest of us, I took a deep breath and said, "I don't have an exact day for you. Mom said sometime next week."

"I don't understand how they can leave us waiting like that. I would be fired if I told a client I'd get them an answer sometime next week," she grumbled. "And I don't save lives for a living."

Cordy and I exchanged a glance.

"Something else on your mind?" I asked tentatively.

Portia shook her head, her hair shining like spools of gold in the firelight and her face locked down like a sphinx. But when she spoke, her voice was uncharacteristically quiet and uncertain. "I'm all out of sorts here." She glanced quickly at Cordy. "No offense. I know this place is home to you."

"None taken," said Cordy

I tamped down a wave of annoyance. I knew that Portia hadn't meant any offense to Cordy. But it didn't weaken my desire to poke her with my marshmallow stick. Cordy had mentioned several times she was saving up to open her own place, and that she was looking around at Portland and Portsmouth as potential locations. No, Portia wasn't hurting Cordy on purpose. She was just so wrapped up in the world of Portia that she seemed to forget the big life decisions of everyone around her.

Pulling the now slightly overdone marshmallows from the flames and sliding them onto the waiting crackers, I considered Portia. She'd ruled this town with a prettily manicured hand, winning accolade after accolade, from homecoming and two-time prom queen to class president, and capping it off with a trip to the podium as valedictorian. What regrets had she left behind here that made her so out of sorts? It wasn't like she'd been the one who'd had a socially scarring experience that resulted in an embarrassing nickname.

"We'll stay on top of Mom until she sorts this thing out. She won't be able to wriggle out of anything while the three of us are hounding her." I took a long pull from the flask and handed it back to Portia. "Drink. Unless you're driving somewhere tonight."

Portia wrinkled her nose. "Miranda, I'm wearing yoga pants. I'm obviously in for the evening."

I rolled my eyes toward the starry sky, spying first Aquila and then Cygnus with its twinkling Northern Cross. I could almost taste the popcorn and feel the scratch of the blanket beneath me on Stargazing Saturdays, when we'd lie out under the stars, my parents taking turns pointing out the constellations and entertaining us with the myths behind them. I wasn't sure where I shook out yet on the whole kids thing, but if I did have them, I wanted both of their grandparents around to teach them about the rowdy heroes and monsters that lit up the night sky.

"In other news," Cordy said brightly. "There's a preliminary test run next Friday night for the dinner theater menu over at Titania's. Invite only. I could use your input on which gelato pairs best with the baked cinnamon apples, and it just so happens there are two seats left at the table."

"Oooh, oooh, pick me," I said, waving my marshmallow stick. Then my face fell. "Damn it, I can't. I'm supposed to go over the set designs with Adam for *Twelfth Night*."

Portia's head swiveled in my direction like a hawk that sensed prey moving in the underbrush. "Adam Winters?"

I took a generous bite of my s'more, the graham giving way to gooey delight. "Yeah."

"I didn't realize you two were working together," she said, her eyebrows doing an impressive job of shimmying up into her hairline.

"Yep. He's doing sets with Dad this year."

"Are you meeting here or at his place?" It wasn't quite an accusation, but it wasn't quite a question either.

"At his place," I said, cramming the rest of the s'more in my piehole.

"And you're okay with that?" Portia asked.

I none too subtly took the flask from her and emptied a good portion of its remaining contents into my mouth. If I was going to be interrogated by Portia, I would do so with liquid courage in my belly. "Yes. Are *you* okay with that?"

"Of course. I'm just asking if it's awkward for you."

"And why would it be awkward for me, Porsche?"

With a sharp intake of breath, Cordy lunged for the flask. "I'm just going to finish—"

"This again?" Portia said, rolling her eyes. "I have apologized for prom night. Profusely."

It was a quasi truth. Portia apologized once for the prom night debacle after much prompting from Cordy. She told me she was sorry that I was so upset by her actions. As if the average person wouldn't be upset to come home to find their prom date sucking face with their sister.

"Look, it's ancient history," I said, reaching for another marshmallow. I skipped the accoutrements this time—I really just wanted to set something on fire. Preferably not a sibling.

"It didn't seem like ancient history," Portia pressed. "I saw the way you two were staring at each other in the driveway the other morning."

"We weren't looking at each other," I corrected her. "He was dropping off Puck, and when you came out, that's when he started staring."

"It's not like that," Portia insisted. "It's just that, well—what happened on prom night was not our collective finest moment. It can be—"

"Awkward?" I suggested, plunging another marshmallow into the flames.

"Yes," Portia sighed. "It can be awkward."

I extracted the marshmallow from the fire and waved it around, making the blue flames dance. "Well, you needn't worry about anything. There's nothing left between Adam and me; we're just working on the same project." I wanted to believe that more than anything, because the thought that I might still be hung up on a guy who broke my heart back in high school with an assist by my big sister—well, that added a Havisham dash of tragic to my already anemic love life that I was wholly unprepared to deal with. I turned my back on Portia, speaking directly to Cordy. "I'll tell Adam I'm busy and we'll have to do it another night."

Cordy shook her dark curls emphatically. "Nope, you two need to work out your unresolved differences." She waggled her eyebrows suggestively. "Over your competing visions for *Twelfth Night*, of course."

I scratched my nose with my middle finger.

Cordy cackled as I glanced back over at Portia, searching that porcelain mask for some sort of reaction. Some sign that she might have something more to say. But no, my sister gazed calmly back at me, serene and untroubled.

"Portia?" Cordy asked. "You in for dinner?"

"I really shouldn't. I have a mountain of work to get through."

As Cordy visibly deflated, I glared at Portia, who stared right back at me, bewildered. But I wasn't letting her off the hook. Finally, she looked back and forth between Cordy and me, realization dawning on her face. "You know what? It can wait," she said. "I'll be there. But I'm not eating sweetbreads again." She crossed her arms over her chest. "I draw the line at glands."

Cordy flashed Portia a grateful look. "I'll make sure Jerome gets the message. Thanks, sis."

I hid my grin in the darkness, because although we Barnes didn't always get it right the first time—particularly Portia, who had apparently been born without discernible empathy—we got there eventually. At least on most things, I thought, watching as Portia continued to stare into the fire, the ghost of a lingering memory flickering in the flames between us.

....

Bard's High

Although the high schoolers had recently abandoned the building to summer vacation, the hallways were buzzing with people young and old, crumpled scripts clutched in their hands. They murmured here, paused there, eyes scanning the lines to find that magic rhythm that transformed the Bard's words into something a modern audience could love.

"Miranda!"

I turned to find Opal, a fierce grin on her face and Hawaiian-print Chucks on her feet. "Look at this turnout! Every audition spot is filled for both nights, and there's even a waitlist. Can you believe it?"

With a wry smile, I thought of all the times I'd paced these corridors, waiting for my own name to be called with white knuckles and sweaty palms. High school productions had been one thing, but none of them came close to that thrill of reading for the summer mainstages. Yeah, I could believe it. "You're in the black box tonight, right?" I asked.

"Yeah." She gnawed her plum-glossed lip. "What do you think?"

"Great space. Don't be afraid to go off script and have a conversation. Sometimes the right person for the role bombs the read-through.

Don't be afraid to ask for something else, their choice or yours." I rummaged in my bag for my extra manila folder of monologues. This was Opal's first time directing, and I'd helpfully prepared—

"That's a fantastic idea," she chirped, whipping out her phone. "I could have them read something off All the World's an App."

I hastily dropped the folder back into the chaotic recesses of my bag. "All the World's an App?" I asked, though I wasn't sure I wanted an explanation. Bard save me from Gen Z and their omnipresent technology.

"Yeah, how do you not have an account? There's an entire section of audition pieces searchable by folio, genre and gender."

Of course there was. "Sounds like you're all set, then," I managed, stifling a shudder at the thought of auditioning with my eyes glued to a phone screen. "Text me if you need anything. Otherwise, good luck."

"That's it?"

I shrugged. "That's all there is to it."

Opal's eyes widened as she clutched her laptop and phone tighter to her chest. "Yeah, I guess it's time to get to it, then." She squared her shoulders beneath her cerulean tee with the silhouette of a wolf on the front, and as she turned, I caught a glimpse of the words "Save Fenris" printed across the back. She had impeccable T-shirt game.

"Hey," I called after her. She spun around, the greens and blues of her hair dancing around her face like the northern lights. "Have fun tonight." Opal studied me for a moment, then flashed that confident grin that only the teenage demographic can muster, before striding down the hallway.

"Bestowing some last-minute advice?" Dan asked gravely, the soft scent of oak moss rolling off him as he stepped up beside me. As usual, he was impeccably dressed, this time in a crisp madras button-down with the sleeves evenly folded back to the elbows and not a hair out of place despite the summer heat.

"Hardly. I'm winging it on a wig and a sonnet and hoping that nobody notices."

Dan eyed my bag, brimming over with audition sheets. "Whatever you say, lovely. You're not fooling anyone." He hummed appreciatively as he took in the crowd of hopefuls. "Definitely some contenders here. I think I see my doomed lead already."

I followed his gaze to where Marty Cabot, chef extraordinaire and owner of The Merchant of Venison, the best farm-to-table restaurant in a fifty-mile radius, stood laughing with Mo Simmons from the First National Bank of Bard. "You can't be serious," I said.

"Can't I?"

Eyeing Marty, he of the fierce beard and twinkling eyes, not to mention Dan's former rival for Aaron's affection, I shook my head. "You cannot cast your husband's ex as Macbeth just so you can kill him onstage."

"Why not?"

"Because you're an adult."

"Miranda, he sits us by the kitchen whenever we dine at his overpriced establishment."

"You mean his James Beard Award–winning restaurant?" I arched an eyebrow.

"He flirts shamelessly with Aaron," Dan muttered.

"Why don't you just tell Aaron you don't want to go there anymore?"

"Because that man's Kona-crusted pork loin makes Aaron's face light up like Le Creuset is on sale." Dan smiled fondly. "I just love it when he smiles like that. Even if he's staring at artery-clogging meat."

I patted Dan's arm reassuringly. "That's why Aaron chose you out of all the eligible bachelors in Daytona. You are a loving, mature partner who can put aside ancient history and even dietary preferences." Dan worshipped at the altar of all things plant-based. He hadn't had so much as a slice of bacon since the Clinton administration.

"Flatterer," Dan scoffed, hiding a pleased smile. "Well, in any event, thanks again for giving me the auditorium. Your young ward had scheduled me in the gym."

"No worries." I shrugged. "We're all in this together. Besides, I think I'm better equipped to deal with the smell of feet than you are."

Dan shuddered. "No audition space should have wrestling mats."

"I don't know. A modern retelling of the Scottish play set in a Planet Fitness could be thought-provoking."

"Heathen," he said with a quirk of his lips. "Any chance you'll change your mind and audition? I think the Barnes sisters as Hecate's handmaidens would be a coup."

"It would be the coup of the century if you could convince Portia to get onstage dressed as a hag," I said mildly. As far as I knew, it was the only argument my mother had ever lost. Portia had never acted in a play, claiming to be above such things. But I had a sneaking suspicion that my perfect older sister suffered from stage fright.

"Oh, come on, the town would love it."

"You're proposing I direct one mainstage, mentor the director of another and act in yours?" I arched a brow. "When do you suggest I sleep during this theatrical hat trick?"

"Your mother used to do it all the time."

"Oh, to be the lowly daughter of the great and powerful Iz," I said, clutching my chest.

Dan made a noise too dignified to be called a laugh.

"All right, I'm off to set up a command center before you talk me into something inadvisable. Good luck on finding your leads." With a meaningful glance over at Marty, I added, "Be the bigger man. For Aaron."

"If you think I'm casting him as Duncan, you're sadly mistaken. That man doesn't get to make eyes at my husband AND get a noble death," Dan tossed over his shoulder as he headed off in the direction the auditorium, a graceful spring in his otherwise dignified step.

My feet easily remembered the way to the gym, although the halls had long since been remodeled. I pushed through the swinging doors, and a squeaky polished floor flanked by plastic bleachers in the school's colors greeted me. Two forlorn basketball hoops faced off on opposite sides of the floor, while a scoreboard, also upgraded since my time here, sat dark. Your standard-issue gym, except for the walls. Admittedly, most schools didn't have scrollwork murals that proclaimed: "Cowards die many times before their deaths; the valiant never taste of death but once," and "To thine own self be true." But as the progeny of artists, we had to have a little flair.

Some thoughtful soul had set up a folding table and chair for me so I didn't have to make camp in the bleachers. I'd hardly finished laying out my schedule, notebooks, snacks and audition sheets when my first appointment, a Bard's High senior named Corey, who worked part-time in the summer at the bookstore, poked her head in. "Are you ready for me, Ms. Barnes?"

"Corey, give me a few years before we start with the honorifics, okay?" I groaned.

"Sorry, Miranda," Corey said, nervously tugging on one of her chestnut curls. "Mom says you're a big-deal literary agent in Boston now. I got rattled."

"I'm in Somerville, not Boston. The big-deal agents are all in Boston. I can't afford their rent."

Corey giggled, her shoulders relaxing a little.

"What are you auditioning with tonight?"

"The 'I left no ring with her' monologue from Act II, Scene II."

"I love that one." I nodded encouragingly. "Go for it. Dazzle me."

And she did. Corey had a liveliness and playfulness to her delivery that I found irresistible. Not quite what I was looking for in my Viola, but definitely a contender for Olivia, who didn't get nearly enough credit as a dynamic character.

"Was that okay?" she asked when she finished, her voice steady, but her left hand still drumming out a frantic staccato against her leg.

"You were great," I assured her. "You're my first audition of the night, so I'm not sure how everything will shake out," I said honestly. "But I'll post the cast list after tomorrow night's auditions."

Behind us, the double doors creaked open. "We're not done here quite yet," I called over my shoulder.

"Oh hey, Dr. Winters," Corey chirped. "Are you auditioning for *Twelfth Night* too?"

My head snapped toward the sound of Adam's laugh, rich and smooth as caramel. "No, I'm just here to sit in on auditions so I can get an idea of how the sets might shape up." He offered me a friendly smile, but there was a mischievous glint in his eyes, as if he were daring me to say otherwise in front of this adorable high school moppet. "How's Meatball?"

"Much better since you gave us that shampoo." Corey beamed at Adam. "She's completely stopped itching."

"Glad to hear it," Adam said. "Call me if anything changes."

"Will do." Corey shrugged into her hoodie. "You need anything else, Miranda?"

"Nah, just keep an eye on your email for the cast list."

When she'd gone, I turned a raised brow on Adam. "Meatball?"

"What's funny is that you would expect Meatball to be some sort of beefy tabby, right? But she's this tiny white-and-gray ball of menace." He shrugged. "I've learned not to judge pet names. Thanks to this town, I currently have a Lady Catbeth, a Clawdius and a Dogberry on my patient list."

"Fair enough," I said, hiding a grin. "What are you really doing here?"

"Just like I said. I'm rotating through auditions tonight, trying to get a feel for the sets."

"How is sitting in on auditions going to help you with sets?" I asked, not bothering to hide the skepticism in my voice.

"It's all part of my process," Adam said, his eyes wide and guileless.

"Have you ever actually designed a set before?" I countered, making a concerted effort not to admire his tan, bare arms peeking out from the sleeves of a T-shirt that complemented his pecs. Damn, was it his work in the shop that made them stand out like that?

"You knocking my creative process, Barnes?"

I opened my mouth, a salty retort on my lips, but just then the doors swung open and a nervous-looking college kid walked in. "Fine," I fumed. "You can sit in the back."

Over the next few hours, I found my Sebastian among the Keene State crew and my Feste from Bard's High. Although it was only the first night of auditions, I identified several other prospects among town notables, including Cat Jackson, the town's new adult shop proprietor, for a sharp-witted Viola; Sheriff Eddie Knight as a delightfully dour Malvolio; and Aaron in the role of Sir Toby Belch. Mild-mannered Aaron was about as far away from the carousing, rowdy nobleman as you could get. But by the Bard, when he channeled his inner boozy man-child, I laughed so hard I worried my jeans might split. The town would be talking about this performance for years. Best of all, Aaron was so lively and engaging during his audition, I almost forgot that there was an interloper with exceptionally defined arm muscles sitting in the bleachers behind me.

With just one audition to go, in walked—no, *walked* was too weak a word—in *swaggered* Byron Greene. "Never fear, your leading man is here."

I cocked my head. "Do you actually use that line on women?"

"Sadly, I've never had the chance to use it before now. But I can tell from your face I should never speak it aloud again." He managed to look chagrined, which I was sure was a new emotion for him. "I'm a little nervous, auditioning in front of the great Miranda Barnes."

"I didn't see you on the audition list," I said, scanning my sheet.

"I'm right there," he said pointing triumphantly. "G. Loat."

"I'm confused, trending toward suspicious."

"G. Loat. Greatest lawyer of all time? It's a riff on the Tom Brady thing."

I blinked. "Get out."

"Aww, c'mon, what's in a name anyway? Am I right?" And when that overplayed pun failed to impress me, Byron ran a self-conscious hand through his dark hair and tried again. "I'm just kidding. I mean, I am the GLOAT of the legal circuit, but I really do want to audition. Please?"

"Really?"

"I'm a lawyer. Acting comes with the territory."

I raised an eyebrow. "What's in it for you?"

"My love and support of this town, of course."

I stared him down, chiseled jaw and all.

"Okay, it's great for business. I always see an uptick after I perform."

"Ah, the universe makes sense again. Who do you want to read for?"

"The duke, of course."

"Of course."

Behind me, Adam snorted. I turned around and gave him a full-on glare. "You mind?"

"Not at all," he said, trying—and failing—to smother a grin. "Please proceed."

The thing was, Byron wasn't half-bad. Orsino called for someone handsome and confident, and Byron was both of these in spades. Even his "music be the feast of love" bit was spot on.

"Have you even read *Twelfth Night*?" Adam groaned. "You're doing it all wrong. You think you're wooing Olivia, but really you're wooing the man who is actually a woman standing in front of you." He leapt up from his seat, and within a matter of seconds, he'd muscled Byron aside. "Allow me."

"Remind me how this informs your process for designing *sets*?" I ground out.

But Adam ignored me, stepping close enough that I could smell wintergreen on his breath. "Once more, Cesario, get thee to yond same sovereign cruelty: tell her, my love, more noble than the world, prizes not quantity of dirty lands; the parts that fortune hath bestow'd upon her." He clasped my hands, and I tried to ignore the tingling warmth that raced up my arms. "Tell her, I hold as giddily as fortune; but 'tis that miracle and queen of gems," Adam pressed, his hazel eyes holding mine. "That nature pranks her in attracts my soul."

My throat had gone so dry that when I swallowed, I swear my vocal cords squeaked from lack of lubrication. But then I reminded myself that I was Miranda H. Barnes. This was my stage. I squared my shoulders and squeezed his hands. "But if she cannot love you, sir?"

Adam's hands slid up my wrists to clasp my upper arms, pulling me even nearer in response to the challenge. "I cannot be so answer'd," he said urgently.

"Sooth, but you must—" I teased.

"Right, because that's how two dudes hang," Byron piped in.

The charged air between us fizzled as Adam dropped my arms and stepped back.

"Seriously, Winters," Byron continued. "Do you have any friends?"

"It's a complicated role," Adam said. "Shakespeare is experimenting with the fluidity of sexual orientation and flirting with the possibility that Orsino might be attracted to a man—"

"The vet doth protest too much." Byron nudged me. "How'd I do, coach?"

"Very well," I assured him, but my eyes were on Adam. What was he playing at? And did he have any idea what Shakespearean theory talk did to me? Bard, I hoped not.

"Just think of how I'll look in my man tights," Byron added, clapping me on the shoulders in full-on bro mode. "Do it, Barnes. If not for yourself, then for all of womankind."

I buried my face in my hands. "If I cast you, will you stop talking?"

"Highly unlikely." Byron grinned. "You want me to read anything else?"

"I've seen enough," I told him. "I'll post the cast lists."

"If anyone needs me," Byron called over his shoulder as he ambled toward the door, "I'll be at the Tavern. Drinking. Talking with other men. While *not* grabbing their appendages."

When Byron's hooting laughter and footsteps trailed off, I whirled on Adam. "What was that?" I demanded. "Do I come bother you while you're in the shop?"

"Well, no, but that's because Pete says whenever you cross the threshold of the workshop, there's bound to be bloodshed. Did you really cut your hand on a measuring tape?"

My nostrils flared as my eyes narrowed.

"Right, not the point." He held up his hands defensively. "I'm sorry—he butchered Orsino. The duke is my favorite. It just hurt the theater lover in me."

"He wasn't that bad," I scoffed. "What is your deal with him?"

"I like the guy, but he's a meathead. You can't make Orsino a meathead."

"Says the former baseball meathead."

"I'm nothing like Byron," Adam said tartly. "For one thing, I haven't slept with half the town. For another, I've actually read Shakespeare."

"Sounds like you really like Byron," I deadpanned.

"You're right, that wasn't fair. He's only slept with a quarter of the women in this town," he said archly. "And I'm sure he's read a sonnet or something. But more likely *Men's Health*."

"Do you have everything you need for your sets?" I asked pointedly.

"Getting there, but I still want your take."

"Is that really necessary?"

"Barnes, this is just the beginning of us working together. How else will I get the backdrop right for your vision? You know what they say . . . sets set the mood."

"Nobody says that," I retorted. I didn't need to spend any extra time with Adam, but I didn't want crappy sets either. "Fine." I acquiesced. "But I can't do Friday. Cordy is running a tasting over at Titania's. Sisterly support and all."

"How about we move our dinner up to tomorrow after the second night of auditions? And now that I know it's Cordy doing the desserts, I'm definitely letting Candace know I'm going to that tasting."

"You know Candace?" I felt a strange twinge in my chest.

"Her dog, Sophie, is a patient," he said casually. "Black lab mix, but more boxy looking than Puck. Maybe you two should get together for a doggy playdate."

"Don't say that," I protested, miming earmuffs. "You're ruining my worldview of Candace as a fire-breathing monster. If she's into rescue dogs, all is lost."

Adam snickered at that. "You know, your place is on my way to Titania's. I could pick you up and save you the trouble of driving yourself, leaving your dome light on and winding up with a dead battery. I'd hate to think of you wandering alone on the dark country roads."

"Let me guess, dark country roads infested with fisher cats?"

"Overrun by fisher cats," he said solemnly. "How did you know?"

"While I appreciate your healthy fear of woodland menaces, I'll drive myself."

He looked momentarily disappointed, but quickly recovered with a grin that was becoming all too familiar. "Do you have any food allergies I should know about?"

"What?" I asked, confused at the abrupt subject change.

"For our dinner tomorrow night. Do you have any food allergies?"

I considered telling him I had an acute reaction to guys who tried my patience, guys who had broken my heart in high school and guys who had a weird fixation on fisher cats, but I settled for shaking my head. "Can I bring anything?"

"How about Puck?"

"That's an odd thing to ask someone to bring to dinner. I'm afraid he doesn't go with much. Hardly pairs with any wine."

Adam laughed, the sound of it rolling over my skin. "You bring the dog. I'll supply the wine and a side of witty banter."

"Well, if it's anything like tonight, we'll be light a course. I'll bring some dessert."

He touched his heart. "You wound me, sweet Cesario."

I held my smirk as he left. But as soon as I heard the doors swing shut and the absence of his steady footsteps, my expression sobered. *Yes,* I thought, *but you wounded me first.*

....

The Black Box

After sitting through the second night of auditions, I beat a hasty retreat to the bathrooms. Even though these too had been updated since my day, students had still scrawled "Andrew is a three-inch fool" and "Evan is a damned, luxurious mountain goat" in black Sharpie, because some things never change. I chuckled softly as my eyes roved over the walls. All bathroom insults should aspire to iambic pentameter.

Looking down, I hastily brushed cheese curl dust off my shirt, because I was not going to Adam's place to dine with him and his girlfriend with cheese residue on my person. I had actually bothered to dress nicely for the occasion, donning a dark-wash pair of jeans and a low-key black eyelet blouse that proclaimed to the world I was an adult, but not trying too hard. Or so said Cordy.

The bathroom door creaked open. "Miranda, you in here?"

"Opal?"

"Need your opinion when you have a sec."

"This is a clear violation of bathroom etiquette. No talking while peeing."

"That only applies when both people are peeing. Meet me in the black box."

Grateful for any excuse to delay heading to Adam's, I spun on my heels and trotted down the stairs to find Opal. Even in high school, I knew how lucky we'd been to have a black box theater—a cozy, square-shaped affair with four black walls and just under a hundred seats flanking the flat floor that drew the audience in close to the actors.

A million years ago or so, when I'd been a junior here, Adam had asked me to prom in the black box. I'd been sporting full medieval garb and an itchy blond wig—a less-than-confident Guenevere in *Camelot*, because yes, we'd occasionally perform things other than Shakespeare. I'd been an absolute wreck, staring at the sets and imagining all of the ways I'd potentially blow the high note in "The Lusty Month of May," when I felt someone slide into the seat beside me.

"You're going to have the whole place eating out of your hand on opening night, Barnes," he'd said.

Barnes, that's right. He'd been the first person to call me Barnes.

I'd jerked at the sound of his voice and spun around to face the senior baseball all-star who had given me a ride home in his pickup the previous week and kissed me on my porch and then vanished. Over the last several days of teenage overanalyzing, I'd settled on the theory that Adam had been drinking hallucinogen-laced hooch and mistaken me for Portia, who he had dated the previous summer—a detail that had made me just uncomfortable enough to work up the nerve to ask Portia what the deal was between them. True to form, Portia had told me no specifics, instead noting with a toss of her blond ponytail that I was "welcome to her sloppy seconds." Real humanitarian, my big sis. Still, she'd given me the green light.

"Correct me if I'm wrong, but that song seems a bit sexed up for high school."

Cheeks flushed, I managed, "I think it's up for interpretation."

"I feel like Lerner and Loewe are using the queen of Camelot to pull one over on us young, impressionable theatergoers."

"You should take that up with the school board. Of course, you'd have to explain to them who Lerner and Loewe are." A question, maybe even a challenge in my voice. If I didn't know better, I would have sworn that in addition to having a healthy bank of SAT words tucked up in that head of his, Adam Winters knew a thing or two about theater.

"Oh, I, uh, I have tickets to opening night," he laughed nervously. "My mom—she makes me go to all of them with her."

"I get pretty good comp tickets if you'd like a pair."

"That's really nice of you, but she got seats up front."

I narrowed my eyes. Tickets went on sale to students first, not to the general public, which meant that to score seats up front, Adam himself would have had to buy tickets. I leaned over close to him. "I call shenanigans."

For a minute he looked like I'd just caught him stealing test answers or something. "Theater reminds me of baseball," he admitted like it was some sort of secret.

"Huh?" I said, cocking my head at him.

"The scenes are like innings, building upon one another until that inevitable final out. The lines and songs have a rhythm and flow to them, just like strikes and balls. And there's this thrill in it where, just like baseball, you only get one shot to get it right. No do-overs, no take-backs. You make contact or you don't."

I'd been performing since I was six and had never heard it framed that way, but listening to Adam, I could see it. I hadn't been to many baseball games, but like the rest of the sophomore class, I'd bought a ticket and donned my Bard's hat to watch Adam and the team take on the Sherburne Wildcats in the division championships last year. Looking back on it, there was a certain undercurrent of excitement that felt like the moment when you stepped onstage, staring into the lights and delivering that first line.

Adam cleared his throat. "And now I feel like an idiot."

I didn't think he sounded like an idiot at all. I liked the way he talked, the way he thought about things and the way he'd sat on my porch, listening to me, taking in my words and mulling them over before responding. For someone who belonged to that upper echelon of popular kids, he was surprisingly thoughtful. "You don't sound like an idiot."

"Well, as long as the queen of Camelot doesn't think I'm an idiot," he said, a nervous laugh bubbling out. "Hey, I know it's over a month away, but I was wondering if maybe you wanted to go to prom with me? As yourself," he added quickly. "I don't have a thing for medieval ladies. Or wigs." He stopped and groaned. "Wow, why am I so bad at this?"

"Yes," I spluttered. "I mean, yes, I'll go to prom with you. Not that you're bad at this. I mean, no offense, but you are pretty bad at this."

We both laughed, but I was suddenly aware of how close he was, and the laughter died off. Around us, the silence grew as the black box shrank to the space of the distance between our lips. I could smell the arctic frost of his sports drink, sweet and cool on his breath.

Never taking his eyes off me, he leaned in slowly. I met him halfway, tilting over as far as the stiff brocade of the dress would let me. Our lips brushed. A soft, searching kiss—

I shuddered, wrenching myself back to the present. I didn't need to keep reliving some stupid high school kiss. Especially not that one. Not when I had to meet with Adam tonight. Adam, who'd obviously left his high school experience in the rearview like a normal person. Adam, who had a girlfriend improbably named Lucille.

My eyes adjusted to the warm glow of the lights along the wall as I traipsed down the narrow aisle to join Opal onstage. "I think I found my Titania," she said glumly, looking up at me from her perch atop a stool. "But it's complicated."

I looked around the theater, completely empty except for the two of us. "Umm, I'm all for postmodern interpretations, but . . ."

"She's in the bathroom." Opal rolled her eyes. "Can you listen to her read?"

"Sure," I said, taking the empty stool opposite her. "How's the rest of the cast looking?"

"Great. All the mortals are cast, I think. Marty Cabot is going to make the best Oberon." She frowned. "Unless you need him for a major role."

"I don't, but you might have to arm-wrestle Dan for him," I informed her. "He wants to kill him onstage. Literally."

"That's just weird." Opal squinched her nose. Laughing, she slid off the stool, stretching her arms over her head. "I'm starving. You want a snack?" She upended her bag over a small table, spilling packages of Swedish Fish, Peanut M&M's and chocolate-covered pretzels, along with a set of car keys and four different kinds of lip balm. She frowned and shook it once more, and as she did, a copy of *Inconstant Moons* slid out.

My eyes widened.

"Yeah," Opal said as she ran a self-conscious hand through her hair. "Sorry, my bag's a mess."

I nodded at the book. My book. "What'd you think of it?"

"Are you one of those adults who closet-read YA?" she asked, the corner of her mouth lifting.

I am one of those adults that closet writes YA, sweet pea, I thought wryly. "Tons of it. Of course, I get paid to do it. Also, my agency represents her."

"You know Hathaway Smith?" On a lesser being, Opal's vocal reaction might have been classified as a squeal. "What's she like?"

I waggled my hand back and forth. "A bit neurotic and insecure, like a lot of creative types." I couldn't resist; I was thoroughly enjoying myself. "But deep down, she's a good egg."

"A good egg? Miranda, she's like the voice of a generation. You have the coolest job ever. You get to work with famous writers and read all day."

"Yes, it's very glamorous," I quipped.

"Can I please have your job when I grow up?" she begged.

I grinned up at her. This fangirl version of Opal was less intimidating than the unflappably cool teen. "How about you start with an internship?"

"Don't even joke. I will camp out at your office."

I could see it—her and Ian squaring off over bagels for geek dominance while debating the latest publishing trends. "I'll want to see a résumé, but consider this an initial impromptu interview. Review that book for me." I knew I was going to wind up with box seats in hell for this, but I was too curious.

Opal's eyebrows knitted together. "So many feels." She picked up my book, running her hands lovingly over the cover. "A lot of readers hate this one because a major character dies." She shrugged. "But I think it's the best one yet. It's authentic. Thad's death was necessary. Meg is now free to fulfill her destiny and unite the realms."

"You think that's what Smith has in store for her?"

"Well, yeah. Meg can't go back to the mortal world now. Whatever is coming in this epic smackdown that Smith has been setting us up for, there's nothing left for Meg but to topple the queens and rule a united realm." Opal chewed her lip. "If she's going to do that, she'll need allies. Personally, I think she should ditch the fae prince and align herself with Dylan."

"The fae stable master?" I arched an eyebrow. "What's wrong with Prince Adrian?"

"Yawn fest." Opal rolled her eyes. "He's perfectly boring. I'm sure he'd be happy to ride Meg's coattails straight to the top. But she deserves better. She doesn't need a man." Her dark eyes glittered with conviction. "She needs an equal."

"Dylan betrayed Meg in the first book," I reminded her.

"Because he didn't have a choice," she insisted. "His only options were to rat out the Guild or risk his entire village being burned to the ground."

"But Meg doesn't know that."

"Not right now she doesn't," Opal agreed. "But the truth will out. Personally, I'd like to think Meg is a bigger person than to let a little betrayal and torture get in the way of the realms' emancipation." She tore open a bag of the Swedish Fish and offered me some. "Besides, if Smith doesn't want Meg to end up with Dylan, how come he keeps popping up?" she asked. "It's like she can't let go of him. When he's on the page, Adrian fades into the background."

She smiled mischievously. "You know what I think it is? Smith wants us to think Adrian is the smart choice. But Smith never does what anyone expects her to do—that's why people love her."

Or burn her to the ground, I thought, mirthlessly. "Okay, let's say I buy that. What would you want to see happen next as a reader?"

"Oh, I know." Opal clasped her hands together in glee. "Adrian is discovered as a traitor to the Guild and Meg has no choice but to off him. The Guild rallies behind her. Enter Dylan."

"Huh." Maybe I should quit the trips to the Meadows and sit at the fount of wisdom of one of my savvier target audience members. "You have a dark streak," I told her.

"Thanks!" She beamed. "So, did I get the job?"

"Send me your résumé and I'll discuss it with my partner."

Just then, the doors swung open, and in strode Jazz Jones, sporting a "Much Ado About Pastry" shirt, complete with powder prints. The light glinted off a tiny rhinestone in her nose as she took her place beneath the spotlight. "Am I interrupting something? Sounds heated in here."

"I'm always heated when discussing literature. It's just that much more fun when you get to do it with a real-life agent," Opal said.

Literature. She'd called my writing *literature*. Squealing would be too much, right? Yes. Yes, it would.

"Oh hey, Miranda. I came in to read for Hippolyta," Jazz offered by way of explanation, "but Opal keeps making me read Titania." She narrowed her eyes. "Over and over again."

"Last time, I promise. I want Miranda to hear what I hear."

Jazz rolled her shoulders like she was preparing for a cage match. Her lovely face transformed to something haughty and regal, a monarch's gleam lurking in her eyes. And from the opening of Titania's "These are the forgeries of jealousy" monologue, I sat rapt, watching her command the stage, that confident honey bourbon voice rising and falling with the meter.

"All hail the fairy queen." I clapped when she'd finished.

Jazz flashed me a grin, the monarch's spell broken as the perky college kid reappeared.

"She's perfect," I whispered to Opal. "What's your question?"

"There's a bit of a conflict." Opal winced.

"This is my first time doing the summer class credit program," Jazz offered, overhearing us. "I wanted to make sure I got in, so I already signed up to do dinner theater."

Dread invaded my belly like a malevolent cold front. "With Candace?" I managed.

She nodded reluctantly. "She's a little territorial about her rehearsal time."

Dogs were territorial. Candace was a Minotaur in heels guarding the entrance to the labyrinth.

"Please don't tell me you're her Juliet?"

"Lady Capulet."

"Ah," was all I could manage. It wasn't that Lady Capulet wasn't a juicy role, but who could pass up the chance to play the fairy queen? Jazz would be a Titania for the ages. The Boston magazines always covered the festival, and Jazz was certainly in the range to merit some ink as a standout performer. But not as Lady Capulet.

My silence must have gone on a beat too long, because Jazz's expression faltered, and she suddenly looked very young under the lights. "I know that's a big ask, but I'm willing to put all the work in and Cordy says I can keep my hours flexible at the pastry shop."

Opal looked at me beseechingly. "Please, Miranda. I need her. No one else is even close. Would you please talk to Candace?"

"Why can't you talk to Candace?"

"Aunt Tillie called Candace a soulless harpy at the last small business owners' meeting. Candace fired back that Tillie was a decade past her relevance date." Opal winced. "I'm afraid that if I tried to talk to her, I'd be another match in that gasoline-soaked feud."

She had a point there.

"There was a loyalty clause in my contract stating that I wouldn't commit to anything that would interfere with rehearsals," Jazz added with a wince.

I closed my eyes to think. On the one hand, I wanted to live out my days in relative peace without having to go toe-to-toe with the likes of fire-breathing Candace. On the other hand, I'd promised to stick by Opal on this mainstage.

I sighed, resigned. "Okay, I'll go talk to Candace. See what I can do."

My protégé and the future queen of the fairies beamed at me.

I tried for a confident smile. It really sucked being an adult sometimes.

"Anything else you two need this evening? Want me to fetch you the golden fleece? Secure the Hope Diamond for Jazz's costume? Procure actual fairies?" I asked.

They laughed, but I saw something intensely unsettling in their eyes: admiration.

"Well, my work here is done," I muttered under my breath. I really had to get going if I was going to be on time for dinner at Adam's. But on the bright side, after what I'd just agreed to do, it no longer felt like the worst thing on my social calendar.

The Winters' Den

You know, there's a good chance he doesn't know we're here yet. We could still peel out of the driveway, make for the town limits and find a drive-through."

Puck rolled his eyes and pawed at the car window.

Lights flickered on, bathing the porch in soft yellow. Mosquitos and moths skittered to life, throwing their tiny bodies against the screen door where Adam's lean figure now stood.

"There would have been hamburgers," I muttered. "You think he will sneak you an all-American, artery-clogging beef patty? Think again."

Puck ignored me, thumping his tail frantically.

"Suit yourself," I sighed, leaning across him and opening the door. I smiled as sixty pounds of determined dog barreled into Adam, nearly knocking him to the ground.

Grabbing the bottle of pinot and neatly tied pastry box I'd sweet-talked Cordy out of, I followed in Puck's wake. It'd already been a full day, and now all that stood in the way of my bed was Adam. I shook my head, my brain scrambled at the thought of Adam and my bed. Or rather, Adam *in* my bed. *Nope*, I told myself sternly, *we're not doing this. We're being polite and productive for the sake of the main-*

stage, but we're not crushing on high school heart crushers with live-in lady friends.

To my relief, Adam didn't open his arms for any kind of weird acquaintance hug, but simply stepped back so I could pass. Still, I was close enough to get a whiff of Italian herbs and garlic—the olfactory mark of someone who'd been cooking pasta. Damn it, why did he have to smell so good? Also, and not that I was complaining (much), but his baby blue Cummings School of Veterinary Medicine tee stretched indecently tight across his chest.

Adam flashed me an easy grin. "Excellent, you brought wine. I hope you don't mind, but I made us pasta."

"I'm pretty sure nobody minds the phrase 'I made us pasta,'" I said dryly.

"For all you know, I could be a terrible cook and you'd have to spend the rest of the night pushing it around your plate to avoid hurting my feelings."

I cocked my head at him. "What makes you think I would avoid hurting your feelings?" As Adam's eyes widened, I smirked and added, "Give it up, Winters. My dad told me you make your own bagel spread."

He groaned. "Yeah, about that, you gotta talk to him for me. He is blowing up my spot all over town. Ms. Saunders came in for a flea preventative for Lily, the world's oldest dachshund—honestly, I think that dog is in her late thirties—and she ended up sweet-talking me out of the last tub of homemade lox."

I offered him the pastry box. "Maybe these will help your lox-lessness? Cordy says you're a sucker for her dark chocolate mousse cups."

Adam cradled the box. "I'm honored and famished. I've been keeping the practice open late, and Mrs. Noodleman just left with Scuppers. Again. That doodle either has a porcupine death wish or a terrible memory. Took me over an hour to pluck all the quills out of his nose. With the added benefit of Mrs. Noodleman trying to set me up with her granddaughter in Iowa."

"I'm guessing Lucille wouldn't appreciate that."

"That's for sure. Lucille doesn't like competition of any kind. But who knows? If the stars align, maybe you'll get to meet the lady of the house tonight."

I nodded, swallowing down the rising sourness in the back of my throat. *That's right, Barnes. Off-limits and out of your league. Always has been. Always will be.*

"I'm dying to hear about auditions, but let me just run upstairs to check on the pasta."

My eyes flicked to the well-worn wooden steps. "You got a kitchen up there?"

"There's a furnished one-bedroom apartment upstairs. I think Bunny always envisioned me living above the practice and taking it over from Dad someday."

"Is that what you want?"

He shuddered. "I'd rather cover myself in honey and roll around in fire ants."

"That's weirdly specific."

"I adore my mother. I just adore her more with state lines between us. Also, her taste in décor is aggressively floral. Silk flower arrangements everywhere and this cross-stitch tissue box cozy in the bathroom. It looks like Audrey II from *Little Shop of Horrors*. I keep waiting for it to try and eat me while I'm in the shower."

"Yikes."

"I know. C'mon, let me get you settled in the office." His smile was wicked. "The old man would have a fit if he knew we were eating in here."

I followed Adam past the pair of exam rooms, where Puck shot nervous glances toward each and whined softly. Adam crouched down to rub my distressed pup behind the ears. "No shots or unfortunately placed thermometers for you, buddy. I promise."

Once Puck's lolling doggy grin returned, Adam straightened and led us through a door that opened into a roomy study. The space was dominated by a gorgeous carved wooden desk and matching round table that had been set with mismatched plates and utensils. The built-in shelves behind the desk were equal parts scholarly texts and well-loved paperbacks. On the far right of the room was a comfy-looking chocolate brown leather couch with a chaise that Puck was eyeing in a decidedly hopeful manner.

"Go for it," Adam told Puck. "I'm sure the old man wouldn't mind if—"

Puck bolted for the couch, clearing the chaise in a single leap, before circling three times and plopping down with a contented sigh.

"Right," Adam said, eyeing me speculatively as if he were wondering what kind of shenanigans I let Puck get away with at home. The answer should have been obvious—all of them. "I'll just pop upstairs." He nodded toward the desk. "I left the sketches out in case you want to get a head start on them. Or you could always rifle through the old man's sci-fi and fantasy collection." He nodded toward the shelves. "I used to sneak the dirty ones out as a kid."

"I suppose that would have been better than any birds and bees talk your mother could have offered," I snickered. Bunny had a brief but memorable stint as the high school health and nutrition teacher. There had been an unfortunate banana and condom demonstration. Adam had been lucky to survive it with his coolness still intact.

He groaned. "Actually, I think I would have preferred one of my mom's half-baked sex ed talks over my old man using a rubber cow's uterus to explain conception."

I blinked. "Wow."

"So you can see why intergalactic alien sex was less traumatic." Turning, he headed for the stairs with a happy whistle.

Settling myself into the buttery soft leather of Dr. Winters' chair, I stared at the stack of sketches before me. Licking my lips nervously, I turned the first few pages, tracing my fingers over the clean lines of what he'd envisioned for Olivia's garden.

I let go of the breath I'd been holding, realizing I'd been afraid I might hate them as an encroachment on my vision for the show. Or maybe it was the thought of hurting Adam's feelings. To my relief, they were so thoughtfully drawn—at once inviting and detailed—to the point that they looked professionally done. I envisioned them springing up around my characters, anchoring them to a time and place that now seemed all the more real.

I flipped through the first act, occasionally humming in appreciation of Adam's attention to detail, until my fingers landed on a sketch of Viola. Though disguised as a man, she sported a riot of red curls spilling from beneath her cap and a familiar stubborn tilt to her chin. My fingers roamed the constellation of all-too-familiar freckles across her nose. He'd somehow made them look fetching instead of being the total nuisance I found them to be on my own face.

Cheeks flaming, I hastily moved onto the next scene when—*click-clop, click-clop*—I jerked my head toward the sound of something moving outside the study.

Puck must have heard it too, because he lifted his head and issued a rumbling warning.

Click-clop, click-clop—the noise sounded again, closer now, although I still couldn't see anything. Puck slid off the couch with a huff and padded over to stand between the door and me.

"Adam?" I called, pitching my voice louder so he could hopefully hear me upstairs. "I think one of your patients might be loose." It wasn't unusual for Dr. Winters to keep a sick pet overnight. But I assumed a free-range one was not the norm.

"Be right there," Adam called down. "Mind taking hold of Puck?"

"On it." I stood up and rested my hand on Puck's head. "Easy, boy." Puck stoically pressed himself against me as a shadow sliced across the doorway. I squinted at the four-legged party crasher, who grunted as it trotted into the light.

"Adam," I yelled again. "There's a freaking pig in here."

Footsteps thundered down the stairs and Adam reappeared, his cheeks flushed and his oven-mitt-clad hands clutching a steaming pot. But instead of shooing said bacon-in-waiting away or showing any sign of surprise, Adam smiled broadly. "I see the lady of the house has decided to grace us with her presence."

I suddenly felt bad about the bacon-in-waiting thing. "You have a pet pig?" I stammered. *Brilliant, Barnes.*

"Lucille is a *rescue* pig," he said, setting down the pot on a trivet. That's right. The man used trivets.

"Yeah, that distinction is not doing much for me in terms of why there's a pig in here."

Adam scratched the little porker behind her ears. "I may have commandeered her from some U-Dub students who were underfeeding her thinking that would keep her pint-sized." He shook his head in disgust. "You wouldn't believe how many breeders don't vet their customers."

I cocked my head, and Puck followed suite. "Can we go back to the part where you pilfered this pig from a couple of undergrads?"

"I like to think of it as the choice between surrendering her to me or an anonymous someone dropping a dime on them to animal control. And by an anonymous someone, I mean also me." Adam's lips thinned. "I don't like to think of any animal suffering, and starving one is particularly abhorrent. Not to mention they were keeping her in a freshman double on campus. That couldn't have been a sanitary arrangement for anybody."

"Is she a healthy weight now?"

Adam tipped his hand back and forth. "She's on the small side at eighty-five pounds. I'd like to see her put on another ten or so." He rubbed her head with his knuckles, and she leaned into it like a cat. "Height-wise, she's perfect. About twenty inches, right where she's supposed to be."

"Is she friendly?" I asked, admiring Lucille's dainty ears. I had to admit, she was pretty adorable, with pearly pink skin and black splotches down her back. Also, she wasn't a Swedish underwear model like I'd originally suspected. So she had that going for her.

Adam tipped his hand back and forth. "She's a little possessive of me, but she hasn't rammed you in the shins yet. So let's go with yes."

"That's not exactly comforting." I shot him an exasperated look. But I sank down to my knees, as both a friendly gesture and a strategic decision to protect my shins, and offered Lucille my palm. Her mud pie eyes flicked from me to Puck. She took a few tentative steps forward, and then another, until her cool snout pressed against my fingers. Then she pushed her head under my hand in the universal animal sign for "Pet me now and a lot, please, thank you."

"Pigs are a lot like dogs. Only smarter," Adam noted.

Puck huffed indignantly.

"Not you, buddy. You're canine Einstein," Adam reassured him. Puck dropped to his back and demanded restitution belly rubs as Lucille watched with interest. "I tried to find her a new home with people who actually understood how to care for her, but as you might imagine, there weren't a whole lot of qualified applicants in downtown Seattle with adequate yard space."

I raised an eyebrow.

"Fine." He threw his hands up. "I didn't try very hard after the first week. She's a very considerate roommate. Nice house manners and never hogs the remote."

Ignoring the spectacularly bad pun, I tickled Lucille's belly, reducing her to throaty grunts of delight. "I can't say I blame you. She's lovely. Is this why you got the place in Queen Anne?"

He ducked his head, grinning. "There's a square footage requirement in Seattle if you want to keep a pig. Plus, she loves to roll in the grass."

"How did you get her here from Seattle? Did you fly with her?"

"Sure did. It's just Lucille and me. It's not like I could find a reliable pet sitter."

So he likely didn't have a live-in girlfriend. It didn't foreclose the possibility he was dating someone though. Also, why did I care? I did not date guys who had burned me in the past. "How does one fly with a pig? Did you buy her a seat on the plane?"

"I bought us a row, actually."

I clapped a hand over my mouth, but the laugh spilled out anyway. "I thought I was an overinvolved pet parent." I rubbed Lucille some more. "I hope he sprang for first class," I whispered. "You're worth it."

"You're not scandalized I live with a pig?" Adam watched me carefully.

"Nah, my old roommate fostered dogs, cats, hamsters, birds, lizards and a chinchilla that liked to hump my laptop mouse. Never a pig though."

The little ham shook herself and made a happy whuffling noise as she headed for Puck. True to form, Puck commenced wiggling at her approach. My dog didn't really care where attention came from, as long as he was front and center. Adam and I laughed as Lucille went snout-to-nose with Puck and let out a squeal as Puck stuck out his tongue and lapped her face.

"Why don't we let them out in the backyard for a bit during dinner? Lucille will ring the bell when she wants to come in."

"You taught your pig to ring a doorbell?"

"No," he said smugly. "But you should've seen your face."

"Ass," I muttered.

"She will kick the door when she wants in." He whistled softly, and both animals followed him out like the pied piper. Well, a pied piper with a really nice ass.

After a pit stop to exam room one to wash my hands, I busied myself opening the wine. Adam soon rejoined me, spooning curly-shaped pasta with a fragrant greenish sauce onto our plates. Cordy the cook would have known what kind it was, but I saw only the promise of carbs.

"What's in the sauce?" I asked.

"Parsley, pine nuts and parmesan."

If it weren't for the whole standing me up at prom and ensuing untrustworthiness, I might have professed my love to the man after the first bite of herby cheesy nutty goodness.

"Tell me all about auditions," he said, tucking into his pasta. "You fill the cast?"

"Yep. Most of them are college and high school students. I did cast the sheriff as Malvolio and Aaron as Sir Toby Belch."

Adam choked on his pasta. "As in Dan's mild-mannered husband, Aaron?"

"Blew me away with his best drunk uncle."

"Now, that is something I can't wait to see. Is Byron your Orsino?" His tone was light, but his eyes fixed on me intently.

"Yes."

"Humph," Adam muttered, stabbing at his pasta more forcefully than necessary.

"What's your deal with him?"

"He's wrong for Orsino."

"He's good-looking, charismatic and confident. He's perfect for Orsino."

"There's more to Orsino than just his looks." Adam's eyes flashed. "The duke has depth. Byron's about as deep as a puddle of contact solution." He put his fork down and looked at me imploringly. "Shakespeare could have made Orsino a fool for not seeing what was right in front of him, but instead, the Bard gives him a second shot to make things right. A character like that deserves to be played by someone whose daily goals include more than just manscaping and flirting with anything with two legs and a pulse." He forced a tempered smile. "But I've never known you to direct anything less than perfection, so I'm sure Byron will be fine as long as he takes your direction. Any other standouts?"

Was that an apology? It kind of felt like an apology. "Do you know Jazz Jones?"

"Yeah, she works with Cordy and sometimes warms up my croissant when your sister isn't looking," he said, with a pointed look.

I blithely ignored this. "Well, Opal really wants her for the lead in *Midsummer*, but she's already committed to dinner theater. That means I have to talk to Candace to see if she'll allow Jazz to split her time."

Adam looked up at me with wide eyes.

"Yeah," I said heavily. "We didn't get off to a great start. I'm just hoping this ends in anything other than a blood feud."

"I'm sure it will be fine. She'll realize you're just trying to create opportunities for Jazz and Opal." He dabbed at his mouth with a napkin. "But if she bests you in a fight to the death, dibs on Puck."

I winced. "Thanks for the vote of confidence."

"I do what I can." Adam took a long pull of his wine. "Other than starting blood feuds, how is it for you being back in Bard's?"

"You mean, besides feeling old as dirt at the high school tonight? Not too bad. I've been able to work remotely while still helping out my parents with the centennial, so it works out. I also love having the bookshop and Cordy's pastries at my fingertips. What about you? Do you miss Seattle? I mean, other than the fact that it rains sideways?"

"East Coast snob," he teased. "You New Englanders don't even have a decent coffee shop out here."

Wistfully, I thought of the alluring siren smell of Diesel that called me home each morning with open, caffeine-laced arms. "Those are fighting words, Winters."

"Bring it on," he said, giving me a quick once-over that made me blush. "I do miss the exemplary coffee and the ability to get takeout after ten. I miss the weekends too. Lucille and I would take the kayak out on Lake Union. We'd paddle over to Ivars—it's this great seafood place where you can tie up right next to the dock—and split a fisherman's platter. Lucille goes wild for scallops. But you know me; I've always loved this place, especially during summer and fall. Seattle doesn't really have seasons like we do."

"How does it work, you being here? Are you working remotely?"

"Not exactly. I'm starting a new job in September, and they gave me the summer off so I could help with Pops. My older brother, Dave—I'm not sure you'd remember him, I think he may have already graduated by the time you were a freshman—he's been coordinating Dad's care back here, so I wanted to give him a break."

While I couldn't put a face with the name, I thought my mother had mentioned Dave. Oh yeah, she totally had. He was the one who looked at butts for a living. "Is he a proctologist?"

"Yes," Adam said, rolling his eyes. "The only real doctor in the family, as Bunny likes to bring up at every major holiday. I was living in Seattle when I got the call that Pops had—had his cardiac event," he managed. "Even on the first flight out, it still took me eight hours to get home. But Dave is in Boston, so he stepped in and took care of everything. Even convinced one of my father's old colleagues to come out of retirement and run the practice here for a bit. But that wasn't going to work long-term. So when I landed the new job, I asked for some time off before starting and they were happy to give it to me. It's a big practice, and because I'm the new guy, I'll be on a large-animal rotation when I get back."

"That sounds great."

"Yeah," he said, digging into his pasta without meeting my eyes. "Before that, I was doing small-animal care at a practice in Fremont. Eventually a spot opened up at Murdoch Veterinarian Services. They're one of the biggest practices in all of Seattle and have an affiliation with SPU, so I might even be able to teach courses someday. Either way, it will be a great way to get a wider breadth of experience."

"Is that what you like best? Small-animal practice?"

"I did some large-animal work when I was in vet school," he admitted. "I prefer to take care of animals that people treat like family members instead of an income stream. But it will be good experience. I'll need that if I ever want to open my own place someday." He sipped his wine and pointed a fork at me. "Your turn. Bunny says you're a big-deal literary agent in Boston. She claims you own an agency."

"Somerville, not Boston. I'm not that kind of fancy."

"Says the woman who owns a literary agency."

"I *co-own* a literary agency," I corrected. "With my partner, Ian."

"The guy who wanted to get the Biscuit Bitch tramp stamp?"

"It wouldn't have been a tramp stamp. Ian's more of a lower-leg-tattoo kind of guy. The man is absurdly proud of his calves."

"Duly noted. So other than being into his own calves, what's your partner like?"

I chewed thoughtfully. "If a book-loving hipster and a sarcastic Wookiee had a love child, Ian would be the result."

"So . . . he has good facial hair, talks trash and reads a lot?"

"*Killer* facial hair."

"How did you guys end up partners?"

"I met Ian forever ago when he—" I couldn't very well tell Adam how I'd met Ian without revealing that I was Hathaway. "He and I met during a young literary professionals' mixer," I said. There, that was vague enough, and they were a real thing. A real thing that the introvert in me rejected like a faulty organ. "We hit it off and found that we shared similar ideas on what an agency should look like. We scraped together the scratch to get it off the ground and we've been working together as co-agents ever since."

"Are you guys *partner* partners?" Adam asked, with a suggestive waggle of his eyebrows.

"Definitely not." I wrinkled my nose. "Ian's like a brother. And not in that 'oh, you should totally be together' rom-com trope. More like an actual blood relative—if I saw him naked, I'd have to double the amount I spend on therapy."

"But you two travel together to conferences and stay in the same rental?"

Funny how that's the detail that stuck out for him in my Seattle conference story. Well, that and the near-miss Biscuit Bitch tattoo. Which was pretty memorable. "Well, yeah. When you're in a strange place, it's not the worst idea to stay with someone who thinks of you as a little sister and has your back. Plus, we like all the same stuff." I pointed to my chest. "Book nerds for life. What about you? You got a *partner* partner in Seattle? Or are you thinking of taking Mrs. Noodleman up on her offer? I'm sure Iowa is lovely this time of year."

"I'm sure Mrs. Noodleman's darling granddaughter, who is ten years my junior, will make some guy her own age incredibly happy. But that's not my scene."

"What is your scene?" I shook my head. "You don't have to answer that."

"I don't mind. Sadly, I don't really have much of a scene these days."

"Fair enough. How did you end up in Seattle?"

Adam sat back in his chair, regarding me. "Sure you want to hear it? It's a tale full of woe."

"But it ends with a pig and weekend kayaking trips for fried food?"

He smiled, but it was a little sad. "I suppose it does." He sipped his wine. "I had an Andrea."

My stomach tightened at the weight he gave that name.

"We started dating our last year at Cummings, and as graduation got closer, she made it clear that she wanted to move back home to Seattle. And me, in my dumbass idealist period, I thought, *Yeah, I think I love this woman.* Moving to Seattle would be an adventure, a leap of faith that I thought would end up as a story we told at our wedding. So after we graduated, I moved out there with her—knowing no one, no family nearby, no connections. We lasted about a month."

"That couldn't have felt good."

"Oh, it gets better. She left me for one of those guys who throw fish down at Pike Place Market. Forearms like a mini-fridge. The worst part though? I ran into them at a farmer's market in Fremont and it turned out this guy made and sold his own artisanal beard tonics. Had his own YouTube following and everything. How's a guy supposed to compete with that?"

I tried. I really did. But a tiny burble of laughter escaped.

"Okay, it's a little funny," Adam admitted. "I mean, it's funny now. But at the time, I was just the most emo guy you could imagine. Moping around Seattle, listening to Bon Iver, hanging out in coffee shops just to hear other people talk. People think of Seattle as this amazing progressive city. And it is. Seattleites are outwardly friendly, happy to tell you about their Peloton and sustainably sourced coffee, but they're also overworked and overcommitted like everybody else, with little time or appetite for widening their social circles.

"Worse, we'd been working at the same pet clinic, this launchpad where all the newly graduated vets worked and waited for their spot at Murdoch or one of the other prestigious places in the city. Except I couldn't stomach seeing her. It was so awkward and I was so miserable that I left before the six-month mark. Wound up at a tiny place in Fremont. It was good experience, but there was no way I was going to get into Murdoch after that."

"But you got there eventually?" I asked.

"Yes, but it was a freak thing. This guy came in one day as I was closing up. He was carrying this stray dog that had just been hit by a car and had driven him to the nearest place he could find. Jack—that's what we named the dog—was in rough shape, but I was able to stabilize him until we could get him transferred to Murdoch. In going back and forth with the team there, I guess I got noticed. Two years later when a spot opened up, they reached out."

"What happened to Jack?"

"He was okay. Better than okay, actually." Adam smiled proudly. "We managed to save his back leg, and the Good Samaritan, this guy named Arnie, adopted him. I still get a holiday card from them every year."

My throat tightened suspiciously. "That's incredible."

"It's the job. I love when we can save them, and even when we can't, I tell myself we gave them their best life as long as we could." He gazed up at me from beneath those light lashes. "But I work crazy hours. Don't have many friends outside of the office, that kind of thing. When I said it was just Lucille and me, I meant it—wow, I sound like a winner. How am I single?"

"You said it," I teased.

"I'm at a point in my career where dating seems kind of overwhelming. Where am I going to find time to meet a woman who doesn't mind sharing domestic space with a pig, or won't chew me out if I have to miss date night because of a work emergency?"

"Because saving the lives of puppies can't wait?"

"That's right," he said solemnly.

"You *are* tragic," I snickered.

"I know, Bunny tells me that all the time. But I take solace in the fact that I save baby animals for a living and I'm an above-average cook. I think that means I can hold out for the right woman this time. At least until I'm thirty-five. If I haven't found my ideal partner by then, I'll revisit my standards."

"I get that," I said. "If someone comes along, great. But otherwise, the agency keeps me busy." And when it wasn't the agency, it was my writing. But I couldn't tell him that. "If it wasn't for Ian, I'd never go out. At home, it's just me and Puck, and it works. I'm so drained after work, I need that time to recharge. But sometimes it can get—" I tried to find a word that didn't make me sound completely pathetic.

"Lonely," Adam supplied quietly, meeting my eyes. "It can be lonely when you want to share some aspect of your day with another person."

Our eyes met.

"Yeah, it can get lonely," I agreed. Of course, in addition to having little time or energy to date, I had the added complication of Hathaway Smith. I'd told exactly zero of my previous partners about it. It was just too messy, too easy for something to get out, and that added another layer of distance between me and whomever I dated. Dating seemed pointless, a future goal I'd get around to eventually. Like making sure I got a will—an omission that still horrified Portia.

He gestured to my empty plate. "Seconds?"

"It was delicious, but I'm so full. Can I help you with the dishes?"

"Nah, I don't want you to see the laundry I left all over the floor upstairs. It's clean, I swear," he insisted. "How about you let the beasties in and get them settled? We can flip through the sketches."

"Works for me," I said.

Outside, Puck and Lucille were snuggled up against each other on the little brick patio, their heads tilted up toward the sky like they were stargazing. As if she could sense she was being watched, Lucille looked over her shoulder at me with a Mona Lisa smile. *Man, pigs really are smarter than dogs.*

I let the pets in and headed for the study. I wanted more wine but I didn't think that would help my equilibrium. It had been a weird night, not at all what I was expecting, I thought as I began to flip through Adam's sketches again. First, Lucille had turned out to be a pig. Second, while I'd expected dinner to be a stilted and awkward affair, it had actually been a pleasant surprise to discover that not only could Adam cook but he could carry the conversational ball. And finally, even though we were coasts apart and we'd chosen vastly different professions, Adam and I struggled with a lot of the same things.

"So, what do you think?" Adam asked from the doorway, holding up the pastry box.

Startling, I snatched my hand back from his drawings. "They're great," I said, nodding my head vigorously. Fumbling for conversation, I added, "They were all snuggled up together when I went to let them in. Makes me feel like a bad dog parent. I think Puck may need a friend."

"Same with Lucille."

"Oh, is there another pig theft in your future?"

"Smart-ass." He smirked, giving the box a little jiggle. "Is it too soon for dessert?"

"Who says that?"

"I was hoping you'd say that," he said, doing what one might call a happy dance—or at least a happy shimmy—as he untied the cord around the pastry box and held up a pair of mousse cups topped with dark chocolate curls. "Initial thoughts on the sets?" he asked, handing over one of the cups and a napkin.

"Stylish and functional without being overly fussy."

Adam ducked his head, his blond hair spilling over his forehead and a hint of color rising in his cheeks. "That's kind of you to say, but I struggled with the last couple of scenes. I feel like the action goes off the rails a bit, so I want to make sure everything feels grounded, at least from a set perspective."

"They're exactly what I would have drawn, only mine would've had stick figures," I assured him. "I had no idea you could draw like that."

"I wasn't just a jock in high school, Barnes. I did take a few art classes." He bit into the decadent mousse, his eyes closing for a moment. "If you weren't here right now, I would be making indecent noises."

"I appreciate your restraint," I said solemnly, taking a bite of my own dessert. "Nobody likes a moaner."

"I'm not sure that's true," he said, his lips curving upward into a knowing smile that was twice as rich as the mousse and ten times more devastating.

I turned my gaze back to the drawings as I internally debated the merits of never speaking again. "I like this one of Olivia's balcony."

"Yeah? Do you think it will work or are you thinking of something more elaborate?" He came around the desk to join me. Side by side, we studied the sketch of the balcony. This close, he smelled of freshly peeled citrus, sharp and sweet, with that enticing spicy note of ginger beneath. "I like that you didn't clutter it up with flowers," I said finally, clearing my throat. "I feel like Olivia is a lot more practical than Juliet. Strictly an English ivy kind of girl." I nodded at the vines he'd drawn.

He frowned down at the drawing and snatched a pencil from the tin. Leaning over, he wrote something in miniscule print beneath one of the hedges. "Sorry, just making a note here."

"Please tell me you wrote 'strictly an English ivy kind of girl,'" I said lightly, but it didn't quite cover the wobble in my tone. Adam's scribbling of that note had brought him even closer. Still, I didn't—couldn't—make myself move away from him. Even though I felt like a damn teenager again. How was it that over a decade had passed between us and I still felt that strange electric hum just under the surface of my skin whenever he was near? Shouldn't I have outgrown that all-consuming adolescent attraction, the one that made you want to kiss someone until you were dizzy and do reckless, sweaty things in the back seat of a car or, say, pressed up against the bookshelves in the fabulously appointed study of a veterinarian?

"Here," he said, pointing to Viola's big reveal in Act V, Scene I, that she was in fact a woman in disguise, and in love with Duke Orsino.

I studiously tried not to look at Viola's face, which shared all the features of my own, but somehow seemed more beautiful when drawn in Adam's careful hand.

"Mmm-hmm," I said.

"Do you think it's too busy?" he asked, oblivious to the heat rising in my cheeks. "There are so many characters coming in and out in this scene—do you think we should put the balcony on hydraulics?" He ran his finger over the character, the motion sending a slight shiver down my back, as if he were touching my skin and not the page. I couldn't seem to stop watching his hands or the way his long fingers moved over the drawings. Had I become a hands girl? Was that a thing? I'd have to ask Ian if that was a thing. But for the life of me, I couldn't remember hands ever being this distracting.

"You were my favorite Viola," he continued, his voice sliding into that faraway quality of someone searching for a memory. "I went to a production in the city a few years back and all I could think was how you played her better."

I flushed with pleasure. "She was my favorite role," I admitted. Truth be told, she'd been the gold standard against which all others were measured. I'd never felt more at home in a character than I had in Viola.

"Because she was a feisty, cross-dressing smart-ass?" Adam ventured.

"Because she was a progressive heroine so far ahead of her time, I'm not even sure Shakespeare realized how subversive she truly was." I licked a whip of mousse off my fingers, a little unnerved to find Adam watching me intently. "You have to admire a woman who finds herself alone in a foreign country and survives by pulling off this masterclass ruse. And just when you think her secret is going to come out, she comes up with a way to keep all the threads from unraveling with nothing but her wits. I respect that."

"Because you're a woman of many secrets, Barnes?" Adam asked, his voice low and teasing, his proximity an unbearable distraction I no longer wanted to ignore.

"You have no idea, Winters." I said, turning and catching his gaze full on, the green and gold flecks of his eyes glittering against the soft brown. Adam was looking right back at me with this odd mixture of longing and fondness, his lips caught between a smile and a question.

It was that look that did it. A look that conveyed desire but no expectation of it. The look that said he wanted it, wanted me, but was a little unsure of himself. That look which was no doubt a mirror of my own.

Arching up on my tiptoes and resting my hands against his chest, I brushed my lips against his, savoring the taste of wine and dark chocolate that lingered there. With a soft sound of surprise, he answered my invitation, deepening the kiss with a gentle sweep of his tongue.

I slid my arms around his neck, pulling him close and drinking in that delicious spicy scent of his. He cupped my face in his hands and proceeded to kiss me the same way he talked—thoughtful and thorough, exploring my mouth with soft, insistent strokes of his tongue.

Pressing me back against the desk, his hands moved from my face, trailing down my arms to rest on either side of my thighs. With one swift movement, he lifted me onto the desk, his hands moving from my waist and back up my arms to trace the curve of my jaw, all the while working me, his mouth on mine.

Then my brain, my traitorous brain, fired off a single, repeating question. *What in the actual fuckity fuck are you doing, Barnes?*

I tried to ignore it, focusing on the sweeping intensity of the kiss. But my inner naysayer had a fine point. This guy had done a number on me in high school. I was what, supposed to pretend it never happened because he made me laugh and his ass looked good in jeans?

The pleasure of the kiss soured, and my eyes snapped open. Pulling away, I firmly pressed my hand against his chest. "I can't."

Adam immediately stepped back. "Too fast?"

I shook my head, sliding off the desk. "This was a mistake."

"What? Why?" Adam searched my face for answers.

"It's just not a good idea," I said, looking around for my bag.

"Why not?" he asked, his expression bewildered. "Barnes, please talk to me."

"Because the last time we started down this road, it didn't end well for me." I cringed at my tone, which was as bitter as the chocolate shavings atop the mousse.

His shoulders slumped. "I thought maybe we were past that."

"It's hard to get past something that we never dealt with in the first place. I keep trying to reconcile the you from high school with the you now. And I'm coming up empty and confused."

"Have you considered the possibility that maybe I've changed since being the idiot teenager you knew in high school? That I regret what happened and I've spent years thinking about how I should have handled it differently?"

No, it actually hadn't occurred to me that he had ever thought of me after that night, but I didn't think pointing that out would be helpful. "I don't know. But what I do know is that I have a lot on my plate right now—work stuff, centennial stuff, family stuff—this isn't a good idea." And with that, I slipped past him, heading toward the door with a somber Puck at my heels.

Scene Fourteen

....

The Garden

The series of sharp knocks on the attic door exploded the dream I'd been having about hazel eyes and set sketches into disintegrating shards of subconsciousness. "Somebody had better be dead," I mumbled, glancing blearily at the clock.

There had been some sort of mix-up at Titania's involving Cornish game hens that required the tasting to be moved to the following Saturday, so I had taken the opportunity to channel all my confusing Adam feelings from that week into an epic writing bender. I now had a decent middle. And an impressive hangover from drinking with Cordy last night.

"Open the door, Miranda," Portia called. "I can hear you moving around in there."

Oh good. Portia had decided to ruin my Sunday sleep-in. "Any chance you've reconsidered your stance on attack dog services?" I whispered to Puck. From his full-body slouch across my ankles, my dog sighed.

"Evil, thy name is Portia," I muttered as I threw back the covers. Stalking to the door, I flung it open to find my big sister in her "weekend casual" outfit of designer jeans, a crisp white blouse and nude kitten heels. Effortlessly put together and so confident in her own skin. I kind of hated her.

"You look awful," Portia said, handing me a glass of some sort of violently magenta sludge. "Here, drink this. It's packed with beets."

I had a general avoidance policy when it came to beets, but I accepted the glass in the hopes of getting Portia out of my room as quickly as possible. I sipped, shuddered and promptly set it down. "Evil, thy name is *beets*."

"Don't be so dramatic. You need to put some clothes on and do something about this."

"This," as far as I could tell from Portia's disapproving hand gestures, was my entire face.

"Is there a reason you're banging on my door this early and forcing me to reconsider my stance on sororicide?"

Portia pointed a perfectly lacquered smoky plum nail toward the window. "She's been deadheading the roses for over an hour."

"So? Mom always gets up early to garden on the weekend."

"She's not wearing any gloves and it looks like she's been crying."

That got my attention. Shuffling over to the window, I could indeed see my mother bent over the roses. With a vicious yank, she tossed aside a drooping head. "That can't be good."

"Do you think she got her results back?"

I winced as Mom decapitated another bloom. "What makes you think that?"

"What else could it be?"

"Any number of things. Maybe Dad is having a torrid affair?"

"With what? A new table saw? The man only has eyes for Mom, farm-to-table food and power tools. In that order," she said dryly.

"It could be centennial stuff," I offered.

"If it were centennial stuff, she'd be ripping off literal heads."

"Fair point," I conceded. "Where's Dad?"

"Left early with Cordy this morning. He wanted to log some inventory. Maybe if you kept normal sleeping hours—"

I held up a hand. "I do not take work-life integration advice from someone who made partner by billing three-thousand-plus hours per year."

She huffed as I continued to watch Mom's jerky movements.

I sighed, the drag of fatigue rounding my shoulders and deadening my legs. All I'd wanted was a nice quiet morning. A walk with my dog. A trip to the Meadows to plot out the next few chapters. A call to Ian to chew over my disastrous dinner with Adam. Or maybe a croissant the size of my head.

Instead, I had twitchy, hair-trigger Portia standing in my bedroom, and potentially an even bigger problem down in the garden.

"Crack of doom," I hissed, perfectly aware it was far too early to be quoting the Bard.

"Stop mumbling and focus," Portia commanded. "Should we tag team? Go down there and demand to know what's bothering her?"

I turned to my big sister. "Is that how you'd handle a client who just got bad news?"

Portia shrugged. "Depends. Am I billing hourly or a flat fee?"

I gaped at her.

"It was a joke, Miranda. A little attorney humor?"

"Nope." I shook my head emphatically. "Definitely too early for that."

Portia rolled her glacial blue eyes. "Nobody gets me."

"The legal mind is a sad and solitary place," I agreed. "I'm thinking we put on gardening clothes and offer to help. If she wants to tell us, she'll tell us."

Portia chewed her lip.

"What? You don't like it?"

"What if the news is bad? What if it's Grandma Bea bad?" Portia asked, her voice fraying along its normally razor-sharp edges.

"Then we'll be there for Mom and help her fight the good fight," I said, trying to keep the creeping incredulity out of my voice. What else did Portia think we would do? Sit around and watch Mom wither away? We were Barnes women, damn it.

My big sister nodded resolutely, but her eyes were wide as dinnerplate dahlias.

"Go put on some gardening clothes," I told her. "Or if you don't have any, whatever passes for leisure wear in the city."

Portia frowned down at her outfit. "This is my leisure wear."

"Damn it, Portia, I know you own three-hundred-dollar yoga pants. Go put them on. And for Bard's sake, lose the heels. I'll meet you outside." With that, I ushered a still-shell-shocked Portia from my room and closed the door decisively behind her.

Puck side-eyed me from the bed.

"I know, I know," I said with a groan. "It's too early for me to adult. I could pull a hammy or something."

My dog blew out an unimpressed breath and rolled over.

"Can we at least agree that Mom's one-woman reign of terror down in the garden takes precedence over your walk? I don't like the way she's eyeing the peonies."

Shrugging into gardening attire of my own—black yoga pants (which did not cost three hundred dollars, thank you very much) and a faded Valhalla Lit tee—I hastily tied back my bedhead curls in a half-assed ponytail and brushed my teeth. I stared at the baleful woman in the mirror, the woman who just wanted to walk her judgmental dog and map out a game plan to write the next few chapters of her book. But noooooo. Instead, our intrepid heroine had to ferret out why her mother was in a snit and taking it out on the shrubbery.

Good talk, I told myself, and headed downstairs with Puck at my heels.

Breakfast might've been nice, but I settled for the warm tickle of the early morning air on my bare arms and the pungent scent of roses. "Morning," I said cheerfully to my mother's back. "Mind if I join you?" I asked as Puck made a beeline for the bushes behind the house.

"Good morning, darling," she replied, without turning around. "Join if you like." Her voice sounded suspiciously waterlogged, like it was choked up with tears or allergies. And my mother didn't have allergies.

"Okay if I use these pruning shears, or do you want me to go Hulk on them like you are?"

My mother sighed. "Really, Miranda."

I smirked as I made a show of carefully snipping deadheads. There was something incredibly satisfying about knowing that you were clearing the way for another glorious bloom. I'd missed this in the city, where I had just enough room for kitchen herbs on the sill, but nothing so glamorous as the dahlias, hibiscus and daisies that reigned supreme in my mother's garden.

Tossing a handful of heavy-headed blooms to the ground, I asked, "How'd you sleep?"

"Same as I always do in my own house," she said, a touch of wryness returning to her tone. "Still burning the midnight oil to finish that draft you promised me?"

"Yeah, yeah," I groused. "Spinning words into gold takes time. How did things go with the zoning committee yesterday?"

Mom's shoulders slumped. "The food booths that require heating sources are too close together to pass, so we'll need to shift around booth assignments."

"That blows. I know how territorial the vendors get over their assigned spaces."

"Territorial doesn't even cover it," she said dryly. "Last year a fistfight broke out between Betty Tilney and Mabel Higgins over who got the spot closest to the gazebo."

"Well, I've always said that kettle corn consumption is a crime of opportunity. Proximity to the raffle in the gazebo is the key to success."

"Mabel had to wear an eye patch for the entire festival."

"That's because Betty squeezes the lemons fresh for her lemonade. Have you seen that woman's biceps? I hope I have guns like that when I'm seventy-two."

"Fistfights between septuagenarians aside," my mother said delicately, "Simon emailed me this morning that the fireworks budget isn't going to cover what we need because there was some sort of water damage in the supplier's warehouse, so everything is more expensive than it should be and it's too late to change vendors."

"Double suck."

"The budget is already stretched so tight this year with the extra mainstage, extra booths, extra tents, extra guest lecturers . . ." She trailed off. "Everybody has an opinion as to how I should be doing this or that differently without offering up any real solutions." She turned around to face me, and finally, I caught sight of her red-rimmed eyes and the beds of purple beneath them. "I'm so damn tired, and I'm all out of fucks to give."

My eyes widened. "That was an excellent use of the f-bomb, Mother."

"I thought you'd enjoy that."

"How can I help?" I asked, relief rolling over me like the nipping morning air. Portia had been wrong. This didn't have anything to do with Mom's results. I crossed to where she stood and gave her a hug. "Give me a list. We'll divide and conquer. Ooh, maybe we can send Portia to kneecap the people who annoy you." I squeezed her even tighter. "You had me so worried. I thought you were out here crying about your biopsy results."

"Oh, that," she said, wiping at her eyes. "Dr. Wu called Friday. Nothing you need to worry about."

"The biopsy came back negative?" I said, hope making my voice leap an octave.

"I didn't say that. I said you didn't need to worry about it."

I pulled back, searching her face. And I knew. I knew it from her grim expression and the way the very marrow in my bones curdled in response. "Do you want me to call Dad and Cordy? Have them head home so we can all talk together?"

She shook her head. "I'll tell them when they get home. It won't change anything."

"Won't change what?" Portia's wavering voice rang out from behind me.

My mother rubbed her chlorophyll-stained fingers together.

"Well, if nothing else, I raised two highly observant women," she said dryly. "What gave me away?"

"Full Hulk on the roses." I nodded to the green streaks on her hands. "I haven't seen you that angry since Portia voted conservative—"

"It was a mock election," Portia interjected.

"Girls." My mother held up her hands. "You're frightening the honeybees."

I glanced at the fuzzy little chubbers lolling all over the nearest azalea like they'd just stumbled out of an all-night pollen-fueled bacchanal. They'd be fine. But beside me, my big sister buzzed with tension. For once, I was doing a better job than the ice queen of holding my shit together. "Maybe you could fill us in on what's going on?"

"It's a tumor." Mom held up a hand as Portia's mouth dropped open. "From the imaging, Dr. Wu thinks the cancer is contained to the mass. There's no evidence that it's crossed any border, but when they do the surgery, they'll remove some surrounding nodes to be sure. I may not even need chemo or radiation."

I tried to follow what she'd said, I really did, but the blood started roaring in my ears after the word *cancer*, and the dew-heavy grass beneath my feet seemed to shift and sway. My mother—the woman who'd taught me passable iambic pentameter before I was old enough for a library card and gotten me through each and every bad review of my books on Amazon—had cancer.

Beside me, Portia's skin had gone a chalky alabaster. "Are you sure?"

"Yes, I'm sure," my mother said gently.

"What about a second opinion?" Portia pressed. "You're going to get one, right?"

"Honey, it's pretty cut and dry. It's going to be fine."

"Then why have you been crying?" Portia asked in a small voice.

"Because the fires I have to put out for the centennial rival those of Beltane."

Portia looked at me, puzzled.

"Gaelic fire festival," I whispered back. "Remember that time Mom taught in Edinburgh for two semesters? She's never gotten it out of her system."

Portia frowned. "So, you've just found out you have cancer, but you're crying because the centennial planning isn't going the way you hoped?"

I cut Portia a scathing look that I hope clearly communicated "Be helpful or get the eff out, sis."

"It sounds like the prognosis is good, right?" I asked, managing not to cringe at the twist of acid in my gut. Thank the Bard I'd skipped breakfast. Yarking in the roses would not improve the situation.

"Dr. Wu said if it had to be bad news, this was the kind of bad news we wanted. I'm going to be fine."

"You can't promise that," Portia insisted, and something in her voice broke, making it wet and wavery. "Don't make a promise you can't keep."

I glanced at my big sister—whose eyes were suspiciously glistening—not entirely sure what to do. Luckily, Mom did. She gathered Portia in her arms and beckoned for me to join her. I clumsily wrapped my arms around them both, grateful for the sense of grounding it afforded my still-shaking limbs.

My mother stroked Portia's golden braid. "You're right. I can't promise that. Any more than I can promise I won't be taken out by Maisy Adams and that death contraption of a trolley she passes off as public transportation. But I like my odds."

I smothered a snicker. Maisy Adams—local tour guide and transportation extraordinaire—had probably gotten her learner's permit right after she helped Moses carry the stone tablets down the mountain. The woman was a nearsighted, blue-haired menace, but no one had the heart to make her hang it up.

"It's not funny," Portia's muffled, teary voice came from behind Mom's other shoulder. "The two of you make light of everything."

"You'd rather I don a black veil and tear my hair out like a Greek chorus on crank?" Mom asked.

My wobbly laugh was louder this time, and if I wasn't mistaken, echoed by at least one other person in this human pretzel knot.

Portia extricated herself and straightened up to her full height. "I expect you to take this seriously. Both of you."

Mom and I shared a long sideways glance. Portia had inherited Mom's smarts and Cordy her wicked sense of rebellion, and there was no denying what I'd acquired from her. The two of us started guffawing.

"Did you just say 'crank'?" I asked.

"I picked it up from my students. Do you like it?" she managed.

"Unbelievable," Portia muttered.

I wiped away the tears at the corners of my eyes. "Thanks, I needed that."

"Me too," Mom agreed, but she still tried for a serious, matriarch-in-charge face. "Portia, my darling. We can't control our fate. But we can control how we choose to face it."

"Middle fingers waving in the air?" Portia said dryly. "I think I'll pass. One of us needs to be an adult." She reached for her phone. "We should get a second opinion. I can get you fast-tracked—"

"I want Dr. Wu to do it," Mom interrupted in a kind but firm tone. "I have a high degree of confidence in her."

Portia looked to me for help. I shrugged, generally a big proponent of letting people make their own choices about their bodies. "When are you going in for the surgery?"

"Soon." Mom's eyes flicked away to a long-abandoned birdhouse, one of those copper-top affairs on a post with wisps of straw peeking out.

"As in, you haven't scheduled it yet?" I asked, suspicion creeping into my voice like the ivy currently choking out the pergola. Yes, I was all for people making their own choices about their bodies, except when it was my own mother and she was being a stubborn dumbass.

As if she could feel the skepticism seeping out of my pores, she waved a dismissive hand in the air. "Dr. Wu can't do it right now, she's booked out. I'm in for October." She tried for nonchalant. With that neatly arranged French twist of hers, she nearly pulled it off.

"Horseshit," I countered. "This is crazy. What if the cancer spreads between now and then?"

"Real life isn't like an episode of *Grey's Anatomy*, Miranda. Not everything happens in the span of twenty-four hours," Mom said dryly. "Dr. Wu is a very talented surgeon, and she's booked up. If she says it can wait, it can wait."

"Is that what she said?" Portia demanded.

Mom said nothing.

"Is this because of the centennial?" I demanded.

No answer.

"Are you at least on a waitlist to get in any sooner, in case there's a cancellation?" Portia piled on.

"Mmm-hmm," Mom said, still staring at the birdhouse. She made a show of checking her watch. "Oh my, I've got to get to that meeting."

"What meeting?" I narrowed my eyes.

"We're voting on the final selections for the grand marshal for the parade," she said archly, daring me to question her.

"We are so not done talking about this." I glanced at Portia for help, but she seemed stuck between cross-armed determination and teetering on the verge of ugly crying.

"I'll look forward to it," my mother said dryly. "You can take a number and get in line with everyone else who has a grievance with me these days." And jutting her chin out, she flounced off, leaving us to stare after her, the pile of severed rose heads at our feet.

"Well, that went well," I breathed to Portia.

"She's dodging us," Portia insisted. "You have to talk to Dad. Convince her she needs to schedule it sooner. I don't believe for a second that Dr. Wu is booked up until the fall."

"Agreed. I'm not an expert, but I'm pretty sure no doctor is like, 'Oh hey, you have cancer, see you in three to four months.' Wait, why can't you talk to Dad?" I hissed.

"Because I'm bad at conversations requiring tact?"

I huffed out a breath. "Fine, bring logic into it."

Portia looked vaguely offended that I didn't try to correct her, but wisely said nothing.

"I am Fortune's bitch," I muttered.

"But you'll talk to Dad, right?"

"Yes, you emotional lightweight."

"Sooner rather than later."

I gave Portia a much-deserved murder glare. "Don't push it."

....

Titania's Bower

I crammed the last of the crumbly coconut macaroon into my pie-hole and wiped my mouth with the back of my hand. Crumpling the paper bag on which Cordy had scrawled "take-no-shit snack for sis" in Sharpie, I tossed it on the floor of my car to deal with later.

I flipped down the visor mirror, inspecting my teeth for remnants and smoothing down my curling hair. I didn't want to roll into Candace's lair looking completely tragic. I honestly didn't want to roll into Candace's lair at all, but I couldn't keep putting this off—Opal and Jazz needed an answer, and Candace had been ducking my calls and emails. Besides, it was this or go talk to Dad about getting Mom to move her surgery date up. Of the two, I'd take the potential for hand-to-hand combat with the Northeast's scariest event planner over the inevitable look on Dad's face when I told him Mom was dragging her feet on the surgery.

Titania's Bower was a mile's drive from the town center, which was probably for the best, given that it was straight out of *Stuffy Southern Architectural Digest* and would have clashed with the sturdy New England sensibility of Bard's charming main street.

Built in the twenties by a tobacco heiress, the mansion was a boxy buxom beauty with huge windows and columns for days. The

Crawford family bought the grand dame sometime in the eighties and had added weeping willow trees and fanciful fountains that featured frolicking sprites and fairy queens. Marla Crawford, the matriarch of the clan, had the idea to convert the seldom-used ballroom into a dining and function space, and Titania's Bower was born.

Over the years, Marla had hired wedding coordinators and event specialists, which helped cement Titania's as the go-to wedding destination in the Northeast. The waitlist, rumored to be three or four years long, had would-be brides signing up before they even had engagement rings on their fingers. But the one thing that had eluded Marla over the years was a top-rated pastry chef. Which was why, each spring when the crocuses were peeking out of the soil, Marla showed up to woo Cordy with promises of 401(k) matching and flexible hours. But my sister, an enigma wrapped in a puffed-pastry shell, had never warmed to the idea of having a boss. At Much Ado About Pastry, even if it was technically owned by our parents, Cordy was mistress of her own menus and frosting budget.

Titania's wouldn't open to the public for another two hours, but the parking lot, nestled in a ring of trees off to the right so as not to wreck the aesthetic, was dotted with cars. The staff and dinner theater actors, I guessed. I'd even spotted what had to be Candace's candy apple red coup, because honestly, nobody else would have the vanity plate "#1 EVNT PLNR."

Out of macaroons and excuses, I headed inside. I asked the hostess, who was studiously wiping down leather-bound menus, where I might find Candace. After giving me an appraising look, she led me down the carpeted stairs and deposited me in front of a pair of doors with a printed sign that read, "REHEARSALS IN PROGRESS—DO NOT EVEN THINK OF DISTURBING UNLESS THERE IS AN ACTUAL FIRE—PER ORDER OF THE DIRECTOR AND HEAD EVENT PLANNER."

"Did you call ahead?" the hostess asked hopefully.

"No. Should I pull the fire alarm to get her attention?"

She winced. "I wouldn't do that."

"Duly noted. I'll just wait here?"

She nodded.

"Thanks." As soon as she was gone, I slipped into the room. Like a damn ninja. Years of acting had taught me how to make a grand entrance, but I'd also had to learn how to move unseen and unheard when waiting in the wings, which made me uniquely qualified for this kind of skullduggery.

Dark, cool and a little musty, the place had all the hallmarks of a storage space—dinged walls and scuffed floors—but someone had taken care to erect a makeshift stage and on it were two bespectacled students making calf eyes at each other.

True to Cordy's previous report, Candace was staging a modern retelling of *Romeo and Juliet* set in some sort of robotics summer camp, if the sets with half-built robots and mess hall vibe were any indication. I wanted to turn my nose up at it, because Shakespeare retellings were not my thing, but the longer I sat stowed away in a corner among empty produce boxes, the more enchanted I became. Juliet in particular stole my attention with an odd mixture of brazen confidence and raw vulnerability that reminded me a little of Opal.

At the front of the modest stage, Candace sat perched on a stool, a curled script in her hands and a rapt expression on her face. I knew that look. Damn it, I knew that look because I wore it every time the lights went down and the curtain went up. Candace was a theater nerd.

I carefully set aside the unsettling realization that Candace and I might have something in common other than two X chromosomes and returned my attention to the stage, where some socially awkward mooning was going on, played to great comedic effect by the two young leads. Who knew that making Juliet an MIT professor's daughter and Romeo a Harvard dean's son would add an extra layer of delicious complication to an already fraught family feud?

The person now standing to my right evidently had. Apparently, I wasn't the only one who'd learned to skulk around, because a thoroughly unamused Candace had gotten the drop on me.

"Miranda, what a surprise," Candace drawled in a tone that

couldn't have communicated more clearly how less than excited she was to see me. She was sporting a dark blazer with—so help me, Bard—pinstripes on the cream cuffs, over black pants and heels with stems as sharp as rapiers. Portia would have sold her soul for a blazer like that. Scratch that; Portia probably had a dozen blazers just like it.

"I love what you've got going on up there. Did you write the adaptation yourself?"

"Yes," she said, her tone suspicious.

"It's seamless. You can hardly tell where his words end and yours begin."

After scrutinizing my face for signs of insincerity—or acne? Who the hell knew what stone-cold killer Candace was thinking?—she muttered, "Give me a second." She clapped her hands and instructed the cast to take a fifteen-minute break. Someone flicked on the lights and the storage space was its sad, sorry self again, the star-crossed lovers just students once more.

"I didn't mean to intrude on your rehearsal. I was going to wait in the back until I could get your attention, and well, I got carried away by the show. So really, it's your fault."

She allowed herself a small smile. It was sharp and hesitant, the way Portia smiled around strangers. As if she didn't trust it or them.

I sighed. "I wish it were just a matter of showing up a day early to the tasting, because that is something I would totally do. But I don't want to bullshit you, and you keep ignoring my emails. I need to talk to you about Jazz Jones."

"My Jazz Jones?" Candace's perfectly plucked blond brows rose in unison.

"Unless there are two Jazz Joneses running around this tiny hamlet, yes."

She crossed her arms over her chest. "I hope you're not going to ask me again if she can quit the dinner theater to take a lead role in the mainstage production of *Midsummer.*"

I cleared my throat. The Wi-Fi in this town might have been total shit but the gossip was lightning fast. "Nothing of the sort. I was wondering if you'd be up for letting Jazz split time between the two. With a little schedule coordination, I'm sure we could make it work—"

"No," she said flatly. "Jazz signed a contract with me."

"She did," I conceded, "but if we figure out a way to make this work, Jazz could get additional credits for her major."

"I don't think so."

"Come on, Candace, this would be a huge opportunity for her," I pleaded.

"You can't run point all over dinner theater because you think it's some low-rent, lesser cousin of the mainstage."

I bit my lip. I mean, she wasn't wrong. Dinner theater had always been something palatable, but forgettable, taking a back seat to the mainstages. She was right—I was being a snob. But I wasn't trying to pluck Jazz because I thought Candace's production was somehow less; it was the role. Lady Capulet was juicy and all, but the opportunity to play Titania, queen of the fairies . . . there was no comparison.

"I don't think what you're doing is low-rent," I said earnestly. "I think it's hilarious and heartfelt. You're not going to have a dry eye in the place on opening night."

"I'm sure," she scoffed.

"No, really. I wouldn't blow smoke like that. Not about theater."

A little laugh squeezed itself through the tight binding of her lips. "Has anyone ever told you what an absolute weirdo you are?"

"I'm a middle child. It goes with the territory."

Clearly, I'd said the wrong thing, because that impassive mask slammed back into place. "Do you think because your last name is Barnes you can cherry-pick someone who's already committed and put them in your own production?"

"It's not for my production. It's for Opal Perkins."

"Then why isn't she here?"

"Because she's a college kid and you have a reputation for being scary as hell?"

She didn't deny it, but looked rather pleased. "So she thought the mature thing to do was to send you over because your mother is the committee head and you think you can force me to give up one of my actresses?"

I groaned. "What in my words or general demeanor suggests that I'm forcing you to do anything? Hell, I'm scared of you too. I sat in the car for ten minutes, pounding macaroons and giving myself a pep talk before coming in here. I just wanted to have a conversation to see if we could make something work for a talented young actress who deserves our time."

Candace blew out a long breath like she was preparing to deal with a recalcitrant toddler. I had that effect on people. "Let me ask you something. If I'd come to you and asked if I could steal one of your actresses for dinner theater, what would you say?"

"Is the role as awesome as Titania?" I asked. "I mean, the answer wouldn't change for me. But I'm curious. Clearly, you've got Juliet all sewn up. Would you be looking for a saucy camp nurse in this scenario? Or a gender flipped Mercutio?"

Candace allowed herself another of those rare, small smiles. "Can't help yourself, can you?"

"Tell me what's better than theater?" I dared her. "Don't say sex. Everybody always says sex as a knee-jerk answer, and there's no way that can be true. Sex doesn't last a fraction as long as a good show."

She smirked. "I was going to say event planning, but a good show still beats out a successful event." She rubbed her temples. "Fine, you can have Jazz. No splitting of time; I'll release her from her dinner theater contract entirely. I don't want to deal with the scheduling headaches."

"Really?" I didn't squeal, but it was a near thing.

Candace lifted an imperious finger. "In exchange for a favor to be named later."

The grin that had been spreading across my face quickly dried up. "Like, your first-born kind of favor, or like, get the word of mouth out about dinner theater kind of favor?"

Candace's smile was thin. "I find children unsettling."

And I found the prospect of owing Candace a favor unsettling.

I gnawed my lip, my mind flashing to Opal and Jazz. It was a no-brainer. Besides, how bad could it be? I thought even as I pushed down a nightmare montage of me having to kneecap someone while Candace looked on approvingly. "Okay, a favor to be named later. But nothing illegal or unseemly."

"Define 'unseemly.'"

I stared at her. "Who's the weirdo now?"

She laughed, and the sound was bright and as unexpected as her smiles had been.

"What made you say yes?" I prodded. "Was it my theater nerd cred?"

"Definitely not," she managed, her laugh growing even louder. "Maybe I appreciate you coming in and asking me like a human instead of demanding things of me."

"You mean like how you rolled up on me and demanded that I not perform anything from the first two folios?" I asked, lips quirking.

Candace actually looked sheepish. "I may have come on a little strong."

"Coffee is strong. You were like a human mace in heels."

She frowned. "Do you have any idea what it's like to be an outsider here? Everybody assumes all your ideas are precious and you couldn't possibly have the love for Shakespeare that the residents of Bard's have. You do all know he was born in England, right?"

I nodded gravely. "I am of a clan that acknowledges the Bard was born on foreign soil."

She made an exasperated noise low in her throat. "It's exhausting not to be taken seriously just because you weren't born here."

"Try being born here."

Candace cocked her head at me.

"After what can only be termed the world's most awkward adolescence, I finally found my place with the theater crew, only to get to high school, when my prom date showed up to my house the night of the dance and ended up taking my hotter older sister instead. Every time I come back here, someone calls me Backup

Barnes. Say what you will, but small towns can be just as psychologically scarring as big-city living."

"That is rough," Candace agreed, making a clucking noise that almost sounded sympathetic. "Was it Portia?"

"You know Portia?"

"Yeah, she negotiated my employment contract with Titania's three years ago. Basically, I can't leave for any reason or I forfeit my bonus and the ability to list this place on my résumé."

I grimaced. "That sounds like Portia. She's, uh, very protective of her clients."

"Yeah, well, I almost didn't take the job because of it. It didn't exactly predispose me to liking your family. And don't get me started on your mother. She who can't be bothered to return a phone call or email. I just wanted to see if I could get some ad space."

"Says the woman who can't be bothered to read my emails or return my calls."

"The difference is, I read your emails. I was just ignoring you."

"Oh, much better," I scoffed. But I couldn't help smiling a little. Was it weird that I kind of liked Candace? "I'll get out of your hair. I know it's annoying to be interrupted during rehearsals."

"I did almost murder you when you came in," Candace admitted.

"I suspected as much," I said with a smile. "I'll catch you at the tasting."

She nodded. "Maybe I'll come up with my favor by then."

Shuddering, I pushed through the doorways and left Candace to her rehearsal. Looking both ways to make sure no one saw me, I took a pen from my back pocket and added "#1" in front of "Event Planner" on Candace's do-not-disturb manifesto. I was a peace-keeping middle child, after all, not a saint.

The Two Noble Pinsmen

'm an albatross," I informed Ian after I'd finished catching him up on the unfolding Shakespearean tragedy that was my current existence. "An emotional albatross."

"You're not that bad," Ian insisted.

"I'm sitting in the car preparing to ambush my dad with the news that I'm like ninety-five percent sure his wife and soul mate of almost forty years is delaying her potentially life-saving surgery in favor of putting on a festival where people don hose and bad British accents."

"Yeah, no. You're an albatross," Ian agreed. "Can we go back to the kissing Adam thing? I'm out of my depth on this thing with your mom."

"No," I groaned. "I'm afraid if I speak his name, it will summon him." I glanced out the window, eyeing the back door of the workshop attached to the basement of the high school. I half hoped my dad would come out so I didn't have to go in to get him. No one wants bad news delivered to them in their sacred space, and that old workshop full of sawdust and sets was my dad's home away from home.

"He's a sexy vet, not a genie."

"He is not a sexy vet," I insisted.

"By your own account, he most definitely is a sexy vet. Why don't you just climb him like Romeo ascending Juliet's balcony and be done with it?"

"First, *you* don't make Shakespeare puns. *I* make Shakespeare puns. Second, I can't just climb Adam and be done with it. There's all this stuff between us. What kind of person would I be if I slept with the guy who broke my heart in high school? It just screams sad."

"Or you could look at it as conquering your old demons and putting the past behind you. Or beneath you. Really, either option works."

"What happened to the 'you deserve the whole damn world, Barnes' speech?" I demanded.

"A fling, Barnes. Just a little something to get the good vet out of your system and give you a boost of confidence. If not for your own sense of self, do it for your book."

"I don't like it. It's too messy."

Just then, the storm-style doors to the bulkhead opened and out walked the mess factor in question. And he was shirtless. "Oh, screw me sideways," I muttered as I slid down in the seat as far as I could go.

"Pardon?"

"Adam's here. Probably taking a break from saving puppies to help my dad out on some sort of shop project. And he's shirtless. He's a vet, for Bard's sake. The man can afford a shirt."

"Cut the guy a break—it's hot here today. Can't be much cooler there."

"Don't you dare take his side." I watched the muscles of Adam's back ripple as he hefted a barrel of wood scraps. Something pooled low and hot in my belly. "Heat is no excuse for showing an excess amount of skin."

"Heat is *always* an excuse for showing an excess amount of skin," Ian retorted.

Of course, it was at the exact moment I was ogling Adam that he looked up and saw me. Feeling the flush of my cheeks, I pointed to the cell and waved him off. "Shit, I gotta go, he's spotted me."

I ended the call amid a hail of laughter from Ian and willed myself to disappear.

"Hey," Adam said, jogging over, his face breaking into a smile. "What are you doing here?"

"I need to see my dad about something."

"I popped over on my lunch break to take care of my mess from yesterday. Have to drive those scraps over to the burn pile or the kids will lift them for bonfires."

"Wouldn't that take care of your problem of having to haul them away?"

"It would, but I'm less likely to set myself on fire than a bunch of kids half-drunk on hooch." He made a weighing motion with his hands. "Responsible adult wins out."

Shirtless responsible adult, I noted, trying to look anywhere except the point where his abs narrowed in that perfect triangle down toward his jeans. I swallowed hard. *Please, Bard,* I thought. *Please don't let my dad come out at this exact moment and see me drooling over his shop buddy.* That would be so hard to come back from.

"How you been?" Adam asked.

"Good, you?" I responded. See, I could be a human.

"I wasn't sure I'd see you before the next meeting."

"And I didn't think I'd see you semi-naked outside the high school, but here we are." Had I just said that out loud?

The corner of Adam's mouth lifted into that half smile, signaling I had in fact just said that out loud. "I can take the hint. I will go and put on a shirt." He wiped his hands on his jeans. "Can we talk about the other night?"

"While you're shirtless?" I shook my head. "No."

"I will put a shirt on, Barnes. Give me a minute."

"I don't have a minute," I explained. "I'm already late as it is. I'm supposed to be over at The Two Noble Pinsmen sweet-talking Ernie into hosting an open bowl night for the centennial. You know how cheap that man is."

Adam winced. "Rumor has it he hasn't thrown out a single bowling shoe since the sixties."

"Right? I have my work cut out for me. Being late is not going to predispose that wannabe Lebowski into hosting a free event."

"I could go with you?" Adam offered. "After I put a shirt on," he added hastily. "My afternoon is pretty light. I don't have a patient until four."

Waffling, I internally debated the merit of bringing a planning committee wingman versus the prospect of having to talk to Adam about our misunderstanding at dinner. My hatred of begging for free stuff won out. "All right, but I need ten minutes alone with my dad first."

"I'll just grab my shirt and meet you out here when you're ready."

I grunted in agreement, and grabbing the pastrami on rye I'd picked up for Dad to soften the blow, I squared my shoulders and marched myself into the workshop. Like any theater kid who'd come through Bard High, I knew my way around it. Still, the scent of fresh sawdust and old soldering pulled me right back to the days where my greatest worries were what part I'd landed and not losing a finger while working on a set.

"Dad?" I called out.

"Back here, lambkin," Dad yelled back. "You just missed Adam."

Yeah, I hadn't exactly missed the shirtless wonder. But no one's father wanted to hear about their daughter ogling some guy. It was unseemly.

"Wow, look at this," I said when I'd found Dad over by the wall of neatly labeled tools. He was bent over, sanding something that looked like a throne.

"Dan thought the other one looked dated."

"Of course he did." I ran my hand over the smooth wood and whistled. "This is gorgeous, Dad. You want a hand?"

"No, thanks," he said, trying—and failing—to hide his alarm. "But I'll take that sandwich if it's for me."

Guiltily, I forked it over.

Dad inhaled. "My favorite." Then he looked at me—really looked at me. "Oh no, what's wrong? You brought me pastrami."

"What did Mom tell you about the biopsy results?"

His eyes softened. "Is that what this is about?" he asked, gesturing to the sandwich. "Honey, I'm okay. Your mom is a strong person, and now that she knows there's something that needs to be taken care of, she's all over it, and we'll be there for her every step of the way."

I lifted an eyebrow. "So you're okay with her waiting until October to have the surgery?"

"October?" He frowned. "Iz said she'd gotten the first available spot that Dr. Wu had. Come to think of it, she never said the date . . ." I could practically see the moment it dawned on him, the sandwich turning to sand in his mouth, his expression souring. "Oh hell."

"I can maybe understand her putting it off until after the centennial," I conceded. "I don't like it, but I get it. But the centennial ends mid-August."

"Our anniversary trip," Dad said, grimacing. "I booked us a week in Scotland in September. I thought she'd need it to recover from the centennial. Maybe that's why she picked October."

"Can you move the trip?"

"Of course we can move it. I always buy trip insurance, and even if not, your mother's health comes first."

"At least somebody thinks it should," I grumbled.

"I'll talk to her tonight," he said, giving my hand a reassuring pat. "After I spend the next few hours berating myself for allowing your mother to slip one by me."

"She is crafty," I conceded. "I just don't get it. I feel like there's this ticking time bomb inside of her, and instead of calling in the bomb squad to deal with it, she's just letting the clock run down," I huffed.

"An apt analogy," he agreed. "I know you're frustrated, but sometimes it's easier for people to focus on festivals and trips instead of, say, their own mortality."

"Oh fine, be all philosophical about it," I muttered.

"You got your mother to the biopsy. Let me take a shot at her."

Relief washed over me, and I leaned into him for a hug. "You're the best."

Dad patted my back reassuringly. "We'll get her there."

"Thanks," I breathed into his shirt. "Thanks, Dad."

As I released him and turned to go, he added, "Oh, and since I'm currently enjoying the favored parent status, I feel it's only right I get to dispense some unsolicited advice."

"Go on," I said with a tiny flourish of my hand. "You've earned it."

"Be nice to him."

"To who?" I asked, confused.

"To Adam."

"Because of the lox thing? Dad, I will ship you freshly made lox from the finest farm share Somerville has to offer."

"Because he's a good partner. I don't want you scaring him off."

"Say the word and I'll happily put on a tool belt and join you in the bowels of the shop."

Dad shuddered, trying to cover it with a cough. "What makes you think I was talking about set building?"

I lifted a shoulder. "Because meddling in the love lives of your daughters for the sake of lox is beneath you."

"You haven't tried the man's lox," Dad called after me. Followed by, "That sounded better in my head."

Still snickering, I emerged from the darkness of the shop and, squinting into the sun, could make out the figure of Adam leaning against the hood of my car. With a shirt on, I noted with a mixture of relief and disappointment. "I'd offer to drive, but you've already expressed your concern over potential exposure to beige madness."

He was right, of course. I drove, and although it was only a ten-minute trip to The Two Noble Pinsmen, I half expected Adam to ambush me the minute we pulled out of the parking lot. But to my immense relief, he opted to describe the progress he and my dad had made on the *Macbeth* sets, noting what a complete pain in the ass Dan had been, changing his mind about a dozen times before settling on his grand vision. Of course, Adam probably hadn't drawn a fetching portrait of Dan in period costume to soften him up like he'd done for me. Or fed him dinner. Bard, why did I have to think about the dinner? And the kissing? I turned my attention back to not driving us into a ditch.

Built in the glory days of candlepin, The Two Noble Pinsmen was a Bard's institution that had stood for over a century. Still a popular high school hangout, the place smelled like lane grease and french fries. I could hear the familiar crack of a ball as it smacked into the pins. What was out of place, but still familiar, was the face behind the beer taps. I lifted my hand to greet a former high school classmate. "Del!"

"Miranda!" the petite, dark-haired spitfire yelled back. "What brings you into this armpit of Americana?"

She hadn't changed a bit. In fact, it was Del and not Cordy who'd first taught me all the words one never used in polite company. "Here to hit your old man up for some free stuff for the centennial."

"Good luck with that," she snorted. "He's tighter than a hermit crab in a too-small shell, and twice as mean."

"I don't even know what that means," Adam stage-whispered beside me.

"And you call yourself a vet," I murmured back to him.

"Dad," Del jerked her shoulder and yelled toward a curtain-covered door behind her. "There are some kids here who want to sell you some Girl Scout cookies."

"Tell them I'm a diabetic," a gruff voice rang out.

"Their parents are with them, they want you to switch political parties."

"Tell them I'm an independent," the voice roared.

I gaped at Del. "What are you doing?" I whispered.

She held up a finger. "Watch this."

Just then, Ernie came barging out from the back. With a balding pate and a paunch he carried with pride, Ernie was sporting a bowling shirt with a feather quill and pins embroidered over the pocket and an expression that could best be described as "don't make trouble in my lanes and I won't feed you a knuckle sandwich." But that hard-boiled expression cracked as his eyes landed on Adam. "Why didn't you say pine tar royalty was here?"

"Because that's a super weird thing to say," Del pointed out. She leaned out over the bar in my direction. "You're welcome for softening him up," she whispered, giving me a hearty slap on the back. To her father, she said, "Some pushy kids were just here trying to sell you something, but Adam and Miranda chased them away."

"Excellent—first round is on me. Why don't you kids have a seat? I got to choke some grease out of the trap, be with you in a bit," he said, lumbering off.

Del rolled her eyes. "One of the pinsetters is acting up again. You know how some families fix everything with duct tape? Well, that's us, but add grease. Head over to a booth and I'll bring you some beer. Been working on something special."

"Cordy said you went to fancy brew school," I teased.

"You'd better believe it. I got a tattoo and everything. The shit I brew is guaranteed to put hair on your chest."

"Unappetizing, but intriguing," Adam piped in.

"Shut up, ball boy," Del tossed back. "Grab a booth. I'll be right over."

We did as instructed, taking a seat in one of the scarred wooden booths, beneath a picture of Ernie bowling, dressed as Shakespeare— or at least what a guy in the seventies thought Shakespeare looked like. There was some unfortunate use of polyester and mustache wax.

Before I could even crack open the slightly sticky menu to avoid looking at Adam, Del brought over a pizza and two beers. "On the house from Dad."

My eyes widened. "It's free?"

She jerked her head toward Adam. "Dad's a real fan of boy wonder here."

Adam preened.

"The beers are from me though. I call this the Prince of Cats."

She set down a pair of pint glasses filled with a rich-looking dark beer. "Peppery with a fuck-all finish," she promised. "Just like a real cat."

I gestured to the spread. "I feel bad enjoying all this since I'm here to piss your dad off by asking for even more free stuff."

"Just give me your honest opinion of the brew and we're square." With a wink, Del sauntered off.

"Someday," I said, pointing at Del's retreating back, "I'm going to be at least half as cool as she is."

"I don't think you're giving yourself enough credit there. You're in icon territory as far as Opal and Jazz are concerned."

"'Icon' is teenage code for 'old,'" I groaned as I extracted a slice. He took his own piece, bobbling the hot pan and accidentally kicking me under the table.

"Sorry," he muttered. "For that, and the other night. Not all of the other night," he added quickly. "Not the kissing. I mean, that was . . . wow. But I'm sorry for thinking we could just ignore what happened between us in the past and skip over it. That was pretty shabby and shortsighted of me. So, I'm sorry."

"Thanks. I appreciate that," I said stiffly, the delicious pizza turning dull and heavy in my mouth. I knew this talk was coming, but it still sucked all the same.

"Would it be okay if we talked about prom?"

I lifted a shoulder. "Yeah, okay."

I didn't tell him that I remembered prom night like it was last night, the memory of it thumping in my heart like a malignant murmur. I could trace it back to the moment when I had just finished unpinning my hair from the Velcro rollers Mom had given me. For once, my hair had looked pretty, falling in still-cooling waves over my shoulders. The phone on my bedside table had rung. It had been Cordy, her voice full of angry tears. By the time I'd called Adam to let him know I was running late, I'd already been halfway to the Grotto, an abandoned park reclaimed by enterprising weeds and pot-smoking teenagers. When I'd returned half an hour later with a fuming, tearstained Cordy, I found Adam on the front porch kissing Portia.

"I don't know what Portia told you." Adam's words sliced through the memory like a knife through hot pizza cheese. "But whatever she said, it was my fault. I got your voice mail saying you would be late, so I was just starting to get ready when Portia called me crying, and at first I thought something had happened to you, so I threw on my tux and I drove right over.

"When I got there, it took me several tries to get her to calm down enough to tell me you were fine but that her prom date had been suspended for cheating, leaving her dateless. Of all the things to cry about," he muttered. "She begged me to take her to prom.

"I told her I couldn't. But she kept crying and all of a sudden she was in my arms, sobbing into my tux, and I felt like the biggest asshole." He scrubbed his hand through his hair. "We had history. It's not an excuse for what I did, but it hurt to see her that way.

"Typical of the dumb male teenager species, I thought I could have it both ways. I thought I could talk to you and we could go somewhere better, like drive to that Pinter play you wanted to see at the Pines that weekend and I could be a good friend and take Portia to that stupid dance and we'd all be fine.

"But then Portia told me she thought she still had feelings for me. That did something to my brain. I started to think about it, her at Harvard and me at Tufts in the fall—it made a certain amount of sense. Geographically speaking."

When I raised an eyebrow, he hurriedly added, "Look, I'm just being honest. Teenage Adam was kind of an idiot."

"As opposed to quasi-adult Adam, who refers to himself in the third person?" I asked.

"Hush, you, you're interrupting my tragic tale of woe." He offered me a half smile.

"Really? Because I thought this was *my* tragic tale of woe. You got to make out with a cheerleader. I was the one left standing on the porch in my prom dress."

"The seafoam green one with the straps," Adam groaned. "How could I forget? I loved the way you looked in that dress. Like a mermaid. In the best sense of the word."

I reached for the pizza pan. "I should go. I'm just gonna take this with me."

"Please," he said, his eyes boring into mine. "If you must go, leave the Prince of Cats."

I kicked him under the table.

"Ow! Okay, as I was standing there, like a jackass, mulling over what to do, Portia was sort of pressed up against me. I tried to be all manly and wipe away her tears and all of a sudden, we were kissing. Then you drove up with Cordy, who was also crying." He paused. "So much crying that night, Barnes."

I didn't offer up that Cordy had been crying because Simone Landry, Cordy's first serious girlfriend, had dumped my sister when she refused to do shrooms with Simone's older cool-girl clique. The Cordy of today would have burned that poser Simone and the Grotto down to the ground with her blowtorch mouth, but the Cordy of yore, while still undeniably cooler than I was, was still finding her high school footing like every other freshman.

"Then I tried to explain the Shakespearean tragedy unfolding in real time on your porch, and Portia—"

I interrupted. "Allow me—this is my favorite part. Portia asked, 'Are you two dating?' And you said, 'No.'"

"I said no," he admitted. "We'd never talked dating . . ." He trailed off, the blush creeping into his cheeks. I wondered if he remembered it like I did, meeting up after school and stealing away to the Meadows, talking for hours about everything and nothing and kissing. Lots of kissing—that all-consuming, the-world-is-on-fire kind of kissing that you only experience when you're a teenager. We'd talked about school and movies and theater, but never us. We'd never talked about what we were to each other. We'd never needed to.

"I really liked you, but you were staying in Bard's to finish high school and I was starting college in the fall. Then there was Portia telling me she wanted to give it another try. I think I knew deep down I didn't want to get back together with her, but things between you and me were so new, and I didn't really know how it would work long-distance."

"So you thought it would be okay to make out with my sister?"

"It wasn't like that," he insisted. "I made a bad decision in the moment. But you—you were like no one else I'd ever met. Still are. I thought I had the girl playbook down pat. I knew what to say. I knew what not to say. But you blew that out of the water. You didn't want to talk about all the things other girls talked about. You didn't ask for anything. You were just happy to be with me, and I never felt like I had to be anything other than me."

"I can see how that must have been so scary for you," I deadpanned.

"Excuse me," he said imperiously, "but do you mind? I'm trying to explain how you intimidated the crap out of me."

"*I* intimidated *you*?" I held up my hands. "Hold on, golden boy. I made *you* nervous?"

"Yes. Yes, you did," he said earnestly. "You made me nervous because you always kept me guessing. Hell, you still keep me guessing. Like when you kissed me at dinner. Didn't see that coming. I would've been less surprised if you'd kicked me in the junk. But laying a kiss like that on me? Not even on my radar of wildest dreams." He managed a shaky half smile. "May I continue? I've spent years rehearsing this in my head and I'm still mucking it up."

"By all means," I said, biting back a smile of my own. Yes, he had been a total shit. Yes, I deserved this long-overdue apology. And yes, he was an adorable groveler.

"I chose what I thought was the safer option—the path I knew with Portia. I am so sorry for being such a coward that night. I stood there like an asshole, watching you turn on your heel and get back in the car. I knew I should run after you, but with Portia hanging on to my arm and Cordy glaring at me like she wanted to rip that arm off and beat me to death with it, I froze.

"I know that it was so much worse for you, but I can confidently say that was one of the worst nights of my life. Even today, if anyone even mentions the word 'prom,' I have this bile-in-the-back-of-my-throat thing and a flashback of clutching your sister's hand, this fake smile plastered on my face, thinking to myself the entire night that I had the wrong girl beside me. Where did you go when you ran off?"

I didn't answer, remembering how I'd driven around aimlessly until I'd come upon the turnoff for Oberon's Woods. I'd gotten out, my prom dress twisted around my legs, looking less like a Disney mermaid and more like an extra in a horror movie, and I wandered until I reached the Meadows. There, I'd sat down in the clearing and cried myself dry, built a fairy ring and imagined myself disappearing into it.

"I tried to find you the next day and every day after that for weeks, but it was like you disappeared off the planet," Adam continued. "I even showed up to your house to talk to you, but damn Cordy and her Spidey-Sense, she came out on the porch to tell me to piss off."

"That doesn't sound a thing like Cordy," I sniffed.

"You're right. She told me to piss off in four different languages. I had no idea she knew Portuguese. Eventually I took your silence as a hint and stopped calling and trying to run into you. I figured I'd screwed everything up and I deserved the brush-off."

"You chose Portia over me. You deserved the brush-off."

He nodded. "I did. I completely screwed up, and I didn't do enough after the fact to try to set it right. Instead, I wallowed in my teenage cesspit of self-pity. I didn't want to be the villain in anyone's story, but most of all yours.

"There were times in college, even in vet school, when I wanted to call you. I'd see a good show and think, 'Barnes would've loved that.' Or, hell, I wanted to ask you to the show in the first place, take you to dinner, tell you everything and ask you if we could start over."

"Why didn't you?" I asked, more curious than angry.

"You ever do that thing where you play out a memory over and over again in your head? You imagine what you'd do differently a hundred different ways. Well, I've done that over and over again with prom night. If I could have just one do-over in my whole life, that would be it. But you can't change the past. I knew I'd blown my chance with you and I'd never put it right. Don't get me wrong, it's not like I never dated again. I dated lots of other women after you. A lot of—" He stopped when he caught sight of my pursed lips. "A few women, here and there," he amended. "But I'd nitpick this one for her taste in books. Or that one for not being funny enough. Or yet another one for talking during the first show I took her to. Who talks during *Miss Saigon*?"

"A complete monster."

"Exactly," he sputtered. "Then I met Andrea, and well, I stopped even trying to date after that. But then here I was, back in Bard's, and you show up in my waiting room, all gorgeous and snarky, with the world's most lovable mutt. I didn't know what to do. I could tell you were still so angry with me, but then there were other times when I felt like you and I were connecting. Then you kissed me." He stared up at me from beneath his lashes. "Why did you kiss me?"

I shrugged. "I liked your set drawings."

Adam's face scrunched up. "I don't know whether to be flattered or put out by that."

"I'd go with flattered. Since I still haven't decided if I'm accepting your apology yet."

"Fair enough." He winced and took a bite of pizza. "I gotta hand it to you, Barnes. I never know what you're gonna say next. Or whether you're ever going to say another word to me again or just stonewall me with those green eyes of yours."

"You deserved the silent treatment you got that first night."

"And the dog vomit on my shoes," he added. "Don't forget that."

"How could I when you keep bringing it up?"

"Sorry about that," he said sheepishly, "and pretty much everything else."

I sipped the Prince of Cats while I contemplated this quasi adult Adam who doted on animals and worked diligently on the sets. This

Adam who had thought of me over the years like I'd thought of him and who wished that things had been different. This Adam who I liked very much.

"We're good," I said finally.

"Yeah?" Adam's mouth tugged up cautiously at the corners.

"Yeah," I echoed. And I knew that I meant it. I didn't want him to be my villain anymore. I enjoyed having him around too much for that. Also, I desperately wanted to ogle him shirtless without feeling conflicted about it.

Before either of us could say another word, Ernie slid into the booth beside Adam, the scent of fresh wax and Pine-Sol wafting off him. "What'd I miss?"

ACT TWO

·········

July

....

The Auditorium

July in Bard's arrived in all its usual face-melting glory. And the heat was only part of it. Chewing on the end of my pen, I watched Byron and Cat circling each other, their body language and lines rich and suggestive as they burned the place to the ground. Seriously, if the subtext got any hotter, I was going for the fire extinguisher.

As accessible as Shakespeare could be, it all hinged on that subtext to translate it into themes that rang true for a modern audience. While *Twelfth Night* lacked those weak-in-the-knees, highly quotable declarations of love found in *Romeo and Juliet*, there was no denying that at its center were two characters exploring a forbidden attraction.

Out of the corner of my eye, I could see movement in the wings, a flash of blond hair, the brim of a faded baseball hat. *Adam*. It might have been my imagination, but it seemed he'd been around here a lot more since his mea culpa over pizza and beer at the Pinsmen the prior week. Also, I couldn't say for sure, but I was pretty convinced he'd grown even more attractive since apologizing. More men should try that. Lifting my hand in a silent greeting, he rewarded me with one of those grins that lit the backstage better than any spotlight could.

Once rehearsals had kicked off in earnest, my evenings had settled into a familiar cadence, beginning here in the high school auditorium—working through scenes with the cast and indulging in Adam sightings—and ending in the attic with finger cramps and hard-won progress on my book.

In another week or two the amphitheater on Will's Island would finally be fully operational for rehearsals. Apparently, there'd been a wood rot issue that not even my father had the expertise to fix, so we were here in the auditorium rehearsing while Tillie worked on costumes and Dad and Adam built the sets. *Adam.* Moving in and out of my field of vision, he had one of those tool belts around his waist. The guy made the male equivalent of a fanny pack look hot. I was doomed.

"Miranda?" Cat's expression was bright and expectant, but also a little sly. Or maybe that was just the natural predisposition of her full lips. She did kind of look like a sexed-up version of Belle.

"Wonderful. You nailed it."

Cat exchanged a knowing glance with her stage partner. "Other than the parts where I dropped my lines twice and Byron stepped in early on his monologue?"

"Well, yeah. The chemistry is there, and that's the most important part."

She didn't say anything, but the way her eyebrows winged up was enough to tell me she didn't believe my bullshit for a minute.

"So you're okay if we knock off fifteen minutes early and head to the Tavern for twenty-five-cent wings?" Byron asked hopefully.

"Or we could pick it up from scene four again?" Cat wrinkled her nose. "I'm not sure how I feel about consuming poultry from a place called the Tavern of Ill Repute."

"You've lived here how long now?" I asked.

"Four months."

"Definitely time to rip the Band-Aid off. Tavern's got the best apps in town. Don't let the dive bar mystique put you off."

"See? I told you it's legit." Byron beamed at Cat. He turned his hopeful expression back on me. "We done here?"

"We'll pick it up from scene four tomorrow night," I agreed. "But we're going thirty minutes later the rest of the week because of the Fourth."

"That's decidedly less fun," Byron groaned.

"Suck it up, Greene," Adam called from stage left. "You want the adoring fans, you put the work in."

"I put the tights on. That's how I get the adoring fans. Go back to your sets, plague sore," Byron tossed over his shoulder.

"Flesh-monger," came Adam's answering retort.

"Scullion," Byron bellowed.

"Fustilarian."

"Three-inch fool!"

"Cream-faced loon!"

And then, in an uncanny display of timing, they both yelled, "Villain, I have done thy mother."

Cat turned to me with a bewildered expression. "Did I just witness a Shakespearean cock fight? I've heard of these."

I nodded. "Not one of the better ones I've seen," I scoffed even as huffs of male indignation rose up around me, "but in these parts they always end in some variation of an insult to one's mother."

Adam stepped out from the shadows, a hammer in one hand and a smirk on his face. "I tailor my game play to my opponent, but I could go all night, Barnes."

"I bet you would go all night with Barnes—" Byron's words cut off abruptly as Cat's foot came down hard on his.

"You guys want to join us for wings?" My leading lady's ensuing smile was determined. Bard bless Cat Jackson and her social-saving graces.

"Thanks, but I'm going to pack up and call it a night." As much as I liked wing night at the Tavern, my book wasn't going to write itself. Besides, I didn't want to be the third wheel to whatever was going down between Cat and Byron. I just hoped it wouldn't flame out before opening night. Their chemistry was pure gold.

"I have some stuff to plow through here," Adam added. He closed his eyes, shaking his head at the layup he'd just handed Byron. But the insult never came, because at that moment, Cat unwound her topknot and commenced shaking out her glossy chestnut hair, and Byron stood watching her, transfixed.

Stifling a snicker, I busied myself with sweeping up my script notes. As Cat and Byron retreated in a hail of bickering over whether the flats or the drums of the wing were more conducive for dipping, I became increasingly aware of Adam and how dark and echoing the auditorium now seemed in the absence of the actors.

"Fustilarian?" I asked, sensing from the citrusy ginger of his scent that he was close enough to hear me. "That was the best you could come up with?"

"I'm out of practice," he conceded, drawing up beside me. "But you have to admit that cream-faced loon was pretty spot on."

"Byron's not so bad," I insisted. "He grows on you."

"So does fungus, but that doesn't mean I'd walk around the gym showers in bare feet."

I stared at him.

"Fine, he's not the worst Orsino I've ever seen," Adam grumbled, his bottom lip dipping into a territory so pouty, I kind of wanted to nibble on it. "But he still bugs me. The way he flirts with"—he stole a sideways glance at me—"everyone," he finished.

"Is it his hair? It is pretty magnificent. I can see how that might be intimidating."

"His hair is most certainly not magnificent," Adam snorted. He ran a self-conscious hand through his own tousled locks. "Wait, do you really think his hair is magnificent?"

"Well, I can't say I necessarily condone the hair gel to follicle ratio, but you can't argue with the results." I waggled a finger at him. "Never figured you for the jealous type, Winters."

"Never figured you to go for the high-maintenance type, Barnes," he shot back, but I noticed he didn't deny that he was jealous. Interesting.

"I don't date enough to have a type, remember? No scene, no type. Just me, the job and the dog."

"Same," he said, bumping his shoulder against mine. "Swapping out the woof for the oink. But if I did have time for a type, it would not include someone with questionable hair gel choices."

"Oh, do tell, Mr. Impossibly High Keratin Standards."

He hoisted himself up on one of the fold-down auditorium seats, settling his arms across his chest in a way that showcased his tan skin. Honor sort of dictated I should do the same, so I perched myself on the seat next to him, praying I wouldn't overshoot it and go ass-over-teakettle into the row behind me.

"Actually, I think it's more of a future state than a type," he began. "Does that count?"

"It sounds very adult. Please continue."

"You know how much I love my job, right? I want that someone who makes me want to tear myself away from work every night just so I can get home to her and our fur babies." Adam gave me a sideways glance from below his thick, sandy lashes, his expression a little uncertain.

"Oh, fur babies are part of the deal?" I teased.

"Fur babies are always part of the deal, Barnes," Adam said, his shoulders relaxing. "I want to have someone to rush home and cook for."

"You're the cook in this scenario?"

"Look at these hands," he said flexing his long fingers out in front of him. "Of course I'm the cook in this scenario. But maybe she bakes. Or she can be the sommelier and music curator of the soundtrack of our life. She'll have a career that she loves like I love mine. We'll spend dinner trading stories about the best parts of our days. Sometimes we'll be on the couch with a bowl of noodles or out to dinner and a show. She'll want to see her favorite Pinter for the third time and I'll agree as long as we can work *Hadestown* into the rotation."

"That is quite the future state," I said, my tone a little wistful.

Because damn if that didn't sound good. And for one brief moment, I let myself be that future state—one hand in Adam's, a Playbill in the other as we waited—grinning like small children—for the stage lights to come up. Adam on the couch in flannel pajama pants, me tucked into his side as we cranked the volume up to cover the snores of fur babies.

"What about you, Barnes?"

I licked my very dry lips. Apparently, all of the moisture had fled, along with my ability to form a coherent thought. I wanted something very similar to what he'd described—the person I could have adventures with, but also the person I could come home to and relax with. The person who wanted to hear about my day—my real day—which would inevitably include coming clean about Hathaway Smith. The part of my life I hadn't been able to trust with anyone I'd been in a past relationship with. My parents, my sisters and Ian—they were bedrock forever relationships. But my romantic relationships had always felt like placeholders, moments in time where I was certain the next page turn was coming.

"I can't just conjure one out of thin air," I protested, although I was generally better on the fly than this. But having Adam this close to me was doing weird things to my brain. My normally dependable neurons were firing off frantic signals that I should scoot closer, brush against him, maybe bump my knee against his and leave it there. "I need to think. Although I will definitely be stealing some of yours."

"Steal all you like." Adam smiled, looking inordinately pleased with himself. And if I wasn't mistaken, he'd just leaned closer to me. Oh yeah, he'd definitely shifted closer. I could feel the heat of his skin through his T-shirt warming the sliver of air between his arm and mine.

"At a minimum," I added, wanting to give him something, "it will include someone who rides the highs and lows of life with me. I'm not talking about the person who nods politely while half listening. I want the guy who crawls into the trenches with me and remembers to bring snacks."

I thought about how much I could have used that guy when fan reactions to *Inconstant Moons* started dropping. Not that Ian hadn't been my stalwart companion, spending hours upon hours that first weekend plying me with tissues and artfully crafted cocktails, but he was also my business partner, and we depended on my income from Elf Shot to bolster Valhalla. There were limits to what I could dump on him.

Just as I'd let myself into Adam's future state, I wrote him into mine. For one brief instant, I saw myself hunched over my phone, mired in bad reviews, and Adam pulling me up from the couch and whispering something hilariously unflattering about the reviewer as he wrapped his arms around me and danced to the soundtrack of our lives. Which trended toward classic rock with some non-pretentious folk.

I smiled at my thought thievery, and evidently encouraged by this, Adam grinned back. "Got it, always bring snacks." He pretended to jot it down, the movement bringing his hand into contact with my arm, and when I didn't move, he left it there. "Store-bought or homemade?"

Before I could answer, the door behind us banged open and light flooded the auditorium. Adam and I sprang away from each other. "Miranda? I need you." Opal called, her voice edged in frustration. "I can't get the blocking right for the mortals fleeing the woods. It looks like a foursome of stoners trying to get off public transportation at the same time."

"Speaking of the trenches," Adam whispered, "I think you're being summoned to them."

I groaned softly. Part of me had really wanted to see where this conversation went. The other part of me wanted my comfy sweats and the refuge of the attic. No part of me wanted to deal with exit cues.

"Don't look at me. I've always hated *Midsummer*," Adam confessed. "Especially Helena."

"Everybody hates Helena," I whispered back, trying to stifle a giggle. To Opal I yelled, "It's all about how you stagger their exits. Be right there."

I turned back to Adam with an apologetic smile. "Duty calls."

"The future state must wait, then." Adam slid gracefully off his seat and gave me a grin that had me doubting my ability to stand without wobbling. "Catch you at the tasting, Barnes?"

Maybe it was the proximity of the words *catch* and *tasting*, but whatever it was, it did nothing for my equilibrium or my exit from the auditorium.

......

The Gardens of Titania

As the rest of Bard's put aside the quills and sonnets in favor of hot dogs and sparklers, I prepared for a different kind of Fourth of July that included fancy hors d'oeuvres and close proximity to my own personal firecracker.

Catch you at the tasting, Barnes. Adam's words shivered through me as I finished zipping up my dress. Did I want Adam to catch me? As much as I wanted to keep the tentative peace that Adam and I had forged, every time I was within ten feet of him, I seemed to want naked and sweaty. It was all very vexing.

"Is that what you're wearing?" Portia asked from the doorway.

"I didn't bring a lot of cocktail options with me," I replied, trying to keep my voice light. For her part, Portia was wearing a flower-print mini with flashes of cream and gold that cinched in at the waist and billowed out just above her knees, pairing perfectly with her nude heels.

"It looks good," she said. "That dress really works with your skin."

I waited for the backhanded compliment to come. Where Portia's dress was interesting angles and colors, mine was flowing sage green silk that whispered against my skin when I walked. But the biting remark never came; instead Portia simply said, "You should leave your hair down."

That was it. No scathing remarks. No commands. Just a recommendation. Maybe Bard's really was softening my sister.

"We should get a move on," she added hastily. "I don't want that harridan in heels harping on us for being late."

Maybe not.

On the drive over, I recapped my chat with Dad earlier that week, since Portia had had to zip back to New York for a few days to close a deal. I'd texted her already to avoid accusations that I was keeping things from her, but I knew she'd want a full download in person anyway.

"Has he had any luck getting her to push it up sooner?"

Fiddling with the playlist and landing on *Postcards of the Hanging*, which seemed fitting for Portia's special style of interrogation, I shrugged. "Not yet. Give him some time."

"He can be really passive."

"He's not passive; he's just not loud and in your face like some people." I tried so hard not to look at Portia when I said this. "Have a little faith in him."

Portia shook her head. "Not good enough." Tapping her chin, she swiveled her neck in that unnerving manner that only big sisters and hawks can manage without serious cervical damage. "What about your book? Is it close enough for Mom to read? Can you pull that lever?"

"It's getting there." I squirmed, not wanting to tell her that I was close but it felt like something was missing. A thread that would tie it all together. "But I still need an ending. She's not going to want to read it until it's done. Even then it needs at least one reread before I can give it to her." I was generally one of those writers who revised as I went, but years of agenting and editing other people's work had left me with the single, iron-clad rule that you should do at least one deep-dive edit before letting someone read it.

Portia blew out a breath. "Well, hurry it up. We'll need to use that if Dad can't talk her into being reasonable." She glanced out the window, the sinking sun catching her hair and setting the gold in it on fire.

"Porsche, you okay?"

"I just don't understand her. If it were me and I knew that I had something like that"—her voice cracked—"like that inside of me, you'd better believe I'd push that team to see me sooner. How can she get up and go about her day knowing there's something inside of her, killing her by inches?"

I wanted to reach out and squeeze her shoulder, but I wasn't sure how she'd take it. "She'll get there," I said with a certainty I so desperately wanted to believe myself.

Portia nodded, but didn't say anything else, riding the rest of the way in silence, making me feel like I'd somehow let her down.

Although Titania's was closed for regular dining on the Fourth of July, the red-carpet treatment had been rolled out for those of us invited to the tasting. The gardens were lit with their signature twinkle lights and lanterns, and the function room used for small weddings—the one that afforded an unhindered view of the lake and the fireworks—was gorgeously laid out. Well, maybe *gorgeous* wasn't the word that most people would use for a camp theme, but somehow Candace had made a classy affair of it. There were birch and pine accents and cloth napkins tied with "merit" badges with our names and skills on it. Mine had the comedy and tragedy masks, while Portia's sported a gavel and the scales of justice. I had to hand it to Candace—she'd struck a clever balance between the fine dining experience one associated with Titania's and that nostalgic sleepaway camp feel.

Our hostess for the evening circulated among the guests she'd no doubt handpicked like a shark on the reef, slowly sizing up the buffet options. The entire centennial planning committee was present—including my parents, who'd driven over from the bookstore—as well as the chamber of commerce heads, the mayor and her wife, several writers and editors from the *Daily Folio* and, if I wasn't mistaken, Elle Folger of *Elle Eats*, the latest darling of the Food Network. But no Adam.

While I was aware that I didn't warrant Candace's attention in this kind of lineup, when our eyes did meet, I pointed to the nearest table setting with its merit badges and flashed a subtle thumbs-up. To my surprise, I was rewarded with a pleased smile before she turned around.

Portia and I made a quick detour to the kitchen to wish Cordy good luck. Sporting a batter-splattered "Don't Go Baking My Heart" T-shirt and barking out commands like a true cake boss, Cordy was fully in her element, and judging from the gleam in her eyes, she was enjoying every moment of it. We got off one quick hug before being ushered out of the kitchen, but I could tell from the size of the cream puff she slipped me that she'd liked the attention.

As Portia made her way over for a chance to meet Elle, who was apparently some sort of vegan maven, I headed toward a corner where Tillie and Alice were talking animatedly with Dan and Aaron. Upon being spotted by my surrogate theater family, I was swept into hugs and kisses and offered bacon-wrapped scallops. Adam or no Adam, the night was shaping up nicely.

When the stream of hor d'oeuvres eventually slowed and Candace rang a triangle—an honest-to-goodness triangle—to get our attention and find our seats, I made my way toward the family-style tables. A voice called my name and I turned to find Jay Park, the senior editor of the *Daily Folio*, smiling broadly at me.

"Jay," I said, taking his proffered hand and shaking it. "Congrats on leveling up to grandfatherhood." According to my mother, Jay had started campaigning to be a grandpa the day the youngest of his three daughters had graduated college. Rumor had it he had stopped just shy of taking out ad space in his own paper to offer lifelong free babysitting to whichever of his daughters had a child first. It was sort of like *King Lear*, but decidedly cuddlier and with baby monitors.

"Twin granddaughters," he crowed, the dimples showing in his decidedly jocund face as he plied me with pictures of adorable, dribbly humans. I made the appropriate cooing noises. Babies would never be as cute as dogs, but that was not something you said to a new grandpa. "You are just the Barnes I've been looking for," he said, breaking out the jazz hands. "'Local girl returns home to rekindle her former theater glory.' I'll run it opening day of the centennial. Above the fold and everything. I'll even send one of our photographers over to get a picture."

I looked around to make sure my parents were nowhere within earshot. Pitching my voice low, I said, "I'll give you fifty bucks if you caption it 'Local woman harangued into service by her well-intentioned but decidedly scary mother.'"

Jay chuckled. "Iz would skin me alive."

"Me too, but it might be worth it," I agreed. "Actually, what about running a piece on Opal's directorial debut, or—" I paused, looking over to where Candace was helping guests find their seats. "How about, 'Dinner theater takes *Romeo and Juliet* retelling to delicious new heights'? I don't think dinner theater's ever landed the coveted Monday spot."

"You've seen it?"

"I've seen enough of it in rehearsals to know that people are going to be talking about this one for years to come. And you'll be the one to have called it."

Jay nodded slowly. "That's a great idea."

I tapped my head. "Every once in a while, I have one." I gave him a wave and made my way to my assigned seat, but instead of the gavel and scales of justice badge I'd expected to find next to my place setting, the badge featured a puppy and a medical bag.

"I hope you don't mind, but Portia wanted to switch so she could sit with some old classmates." Adam was wearing an apologetic smile and a cream-colored linen jacket over a pale blue shirt that looked great with his hair. "Try not to take it too hard. Dave always ditches me at family gatherings because I'm not"—Adam dropped his voice—"a *real* doctor."

"I'm sure legions of grateful pet owners would vehemently disagree," I said, catching that delicious citrusy ginger scent wafting off him, and though I'd put away a respectable amount of appetizers, my mouth began to water.

"Absolutely. Besides, I'd still rather treat pink eye in cocker spaniels than look at butts all day like my brother, the *real* doctor." Adam grinned wickedly.

"Ladies and gentlemen, my dinner companion."

"You're right, my social filter fails me when I'm hungry. That house call took longer than expected. What did I miss?"

"Bacon-wrapped scallops, fancy corn dogs and a whole lot of unidentifiable bits of stuff smeared on toast."

Adam groaned. "You couldn't have let me down easy? I love unidentifiable bits of stuff on toast. Well, that settles it, then. I'm going to hog the bread basket in retaliation." He pulled my chair out for me. "After you."

I settled in beside Adam, removing my merit badge from the napkin and arranging the picnic-theme checkered square in my lap, my knee bumping against his. I swallowed hard as a tingle of heat raced down my bare leg from the contact against the cool crisp fabric of his pants.

"So tell me about this house call that kept you from bits on toast?"

Adam's whole face lit up. "Major is this strapping gray tabby specimen with a penchant for tangling with woodland creatures twice his size. I've had to stitch him up three times this summer. Whatever got him today bit a chunk out of his ear. Took me forever to suture it because he kept batting me with his paw as if to say, 'Hurry it up, human. The backyard isn't going to patrol itself.'"

"Sounds like Major will not be bullied."

"Exactly, although I wish he'd exercise a little more caution. Nothing bleeds like an ear."

I couldn't help but smile at him. He was just so adorable when he was talking about his job.

I was about to ask him to regale me with more tales from the vet files, but our table began to fill up with other guests. We greeted each newcomer and scootched our chairs closer together, making room at the table for a pair of food bloggers and some chamber of commerce members.

Two hours later, I was so full I confessed to Adam that I was contemplating pulling the fire alarm just to get some air. He advised against it, and lucky for him, Candace picked that moment to announce there would be a fifteen-minute break before dessert for people to mingle—or, in my case, to rethink the wisdom of having doubled up on skillet corn bread. I excused myself and made a beeline for the gardens while Adam gallantly offered to go to the bar for us.

Of all of Titania's bountiful charms, it was her gardens that I loved best. Winding and warmly lit with solar lights and flanked by stone fountains featuring the Queen of Fairies herself, her mercurial Oberon and their whole court of winged attendants nestled among fragrant blooms, I could have wandered here for hours and never gotten bored.

Picking my way along one of the stone paths, I came upon the koi pond, the cream-and-orange scales of the fish winking in the moonlight. Settling on a stone bench at the base of a sturdy-looking oak liveried in pale green lichen, I closed my eyes and listened to the water moving over the rocks.

A few minutes later, I heard the scuffle of feet on pea gravel.

"Good seatmates don't let fellow seatmates ponder life by a koi pond without a drink in hand," Adam said, proffering me a flute and sitting down beside me.

I gratefully accepted the bubbles. "Thanks. I don't even know if I can drink this right now. I'm so full."

"Me too, you double-helping corn bread enabler," he teased.

"I regret nothing," I insisted, taking a tiny sip. "Candace sure knows how to put on a show, huh? The food, the camp vibe, her thinly veiled warnings to the press not to discount the dinner theater. I feel like I'm witnessing the dawn of a new, slightly terrifying era."

"Agreed on all accounts. I'm in. As long as there are snacks."

I raised an eyebrow and turned to face him. "Oh, you haven't been back in my good graces long enough to crib my snacks jokes."

Adam drew back with a mock gasp. "But I fetched you bubbly."

"That you did." I tipped the flute to my lips.

He leaned closer, his fingers grazing mine on the bench. "What would one have to do to get back into your good graces?"

Over the rim of the glass, I met his eyes—luminous in the moonlight with swirls of gold and green—like my own personal galaxy. "My good graces?" I echoed, licking the last of the effervescent drops from my lips.

His gaze tracked the progress of my tongue. "Well, yours are the only graces I care about getting in. Your many, many graces, Barnes." His eyes dipped to my lips.

To hell with carefully resurrected relationships, I thought. I wanted naked and sexy. Setting my glass down, I closed the distance and sealed my lips over his. His were hot—a startling contrast to the cool night air—and he tasted like the ginger and lime of the Moscow mule he'd been sipping on at dinner.

His hands went to my face, stroking my jaw as he deepened the kiss. I explored his mouth, kissing him the way I'd wanted to since that night in his office, unhurried and unreserved, achingly thorough. And still he wasn't close enough. My arms encircled his neck, drawing him to me.

His fingers trailed down the side of my face until he'd reached my collarbone. He paused, stroking it with his thumb and making me shiver, before moving down the silk folds of my dress and settling on my thigh, where he could touch the bare skin of my leg through the slit.

"Oh, hey, you two," an amused voice called from somewhere behind Adam. I froze, but Adam, ever the quick thinker, righted himself on the bench, making like he'd just been admiring the koi this whole time.

"Hey, Candace," he said as if I hadn't just laid a honey of a kiss on him. "Is it time to head back in for dessert?"

"Looks like you two already got a head start on it," Candace chirped. "Actually, I was looking for Miranda. My replacement for Lady Capulet has been called away for a family emergency. I'm going to need to call in that favor."

"You owe Candace a favor?" Adam's voice was a speculative whisper.

"Hush, you," I breathed. To Candace, I said, "I'd be delighted to be your Lady Capulet."

"Oh no. Not you. You're all wrong for Lady Capulet."

"Hurtful."

To my right, Adam snickered.

Candace's searchlight gaze flicked his way and the noise died on his lips. To me she said, "It's nothing personal. I was thinking your sister could step in."

"You want Cordy to play Lady Capulet?" I asked, confused. How was that going to work, with Cordy doing desserts?

"Portia."

Beside me, Adam sucked in a sharp breath. He knew as well as I did how Portia felt about the stage. "Acting isn't really Portia's thing," I stammered.

"I'm sure she'll have no trouble picking it up. There's something about her that just screams Lady Capulet."

"Is this payback because of how Portia handled your employment contract with all the delicacy one would expect from an individual born without empathy?"

"Something like that." Candace smirked.

"I'll see what I can do," I said shakily.

Candace nodded curtly. "See that you do." She gazed around. "You know, if I were going to meet up for a rendezvous, I'd have picked the koi pond as well. Can't beat the lighting back here. Just make sure you're back at the table in time for dessert. Wouldn't want people to get the wrong idea." And with that, she spun on her heels to leave Adam and me staring at each other.

"That went well," he said.

"On what planet did that go well?" I hissed, even as we both dissolved into laughter.

"That was worse than being busted by Bunny. I think my nether parts actually crawled up into my lower intestines. I'm not sure they can ever be coaxed out again."

I laughed so hard, I had to balance one hand on Adam's chest to keep from toppling over. Okay, I didn't have to, but I wanted to. It was a very nice, firm chest.

"We should probably head back," I said, wiping at the tears gathering in my eyes.

"Agreed. As soon as my legs work properly." He rose from the bench. "To be continued after the dessert course?" he asked, almost bashful.

I smiled up at him like he'd offered me the moon. I think he wanted naked and sexy too. "Yes, but not here. Somewhere more private. Your place." I stopped, frowning. "Wait, I'm Portia's ride home."

"Don't you have another sister in attendance tonight?"

"Good point. But what will I tell Cordy so she doesn't get suspicious?"

"Tell her I drank too much so you're driving me home."

"Deal."

"Good, I'll spend the rest of the evening thinking of how best to work my way back into your good graces." He stroked one finger down my jawline, and I leaned into it. He grazed a teasing kiss over my lips, pulling away before I could insist on more.

"I think I'd like that." And I think I really would've, but somewhere between the cast-iron skillet s'mores and Adam's fingers beneath the table tracing interesting patterns on my leg, he got a call that Major had opened his stitches. Excusing himself, he promised to text me later, but it did nothing for the heat pooling between my legs.

Despite Cordy's culinary mastery, I barely tasted dessert, the flavor of Adam on my lips drowning out everything else. And after the fireworks in the garden, the planned ones over the lake seemed tame by comparison.

On the drive home, I was restless, only half listening to Portia and completely forgetting to tell her that I'd signed her up to play Lady Capulet. Instead, I rolled down the windows, but not even the cool night air could soothe the electric tingle that Adam had ignited just under my skin but failed to quench.

There was only one thing that would do.

After bidding Portia good night and grabbing snacks for Puck, I closed the attic door and sat down in my chair with a flourish, the laptop springing to life.

I finally knew with absolute certainty what—no, who—had been missing from the action.

Meg strode from the tavern, senses rapier sharp. All night she'd been unable to shake the itch between her shoulder blades that someone had been watching her. Let them come. She'd been spoiling for a fight.

Ducking into an alley, she drew her knife and counted the breaths of the approaching figure. She struck, spinning out of the shadows and swinging her blade up and against the jugular of the soon-to-be-corpse.

"Meg," the figure whispered hoarsely. "Please."

Her eyes went wide at the sound of his voice, but her grip on the knife never wavered. Her memory had been cruel to him, but that didn't mean the years had. He was undimmed, his hair still silvery-blond bright, and the emerald eyes that only the fae possess bored into hers.

"Go ahead and finish it." His strong fingers closed around her wrist, sending a shiver of memories racing through her blood. Dylan, pressing her against an ancient tree, his hands hiking up her skirts. Dylan, his face tender in the morning light beside her. Dylan, silent as the guards dragged her away.

She relaxed her grip, her hand falling to her side. After all that had passed between them, she could no more finish him than take a knife to her own heart. "What do you want, Dylan?"

Tempest Tossed Pizza

Just a few short weeks until the Valkyries ride," Ian singsonged.

"You know it's weird when you refer to yourself as a Valkyrie, right? Mythologically speaking, there were none. Not a single instance of a dude Valkyrie in any of the Eddas." I scanned the parking lot of Tempest Tossed Pizza for any sign of Opal or Jazz.

"A sexist and a spoilsport," Ian observed primly. "Did we have a little bit too much fun last night on the Fourth?"

"Nothing of the sort," I mumbled, exquisitely grateful that Ian couldn't see my cheeks flushing scarlet. I'd definitely had a little bit too much fun last night, but not the kind Ian was alluding to.

"So, did you secure us VIP passes yet?"

"Why, hello to you too. How I've missed you, my cherished business partner, can't wait to see you in two weeks," I grumped. "Thanks for moving up your arrival date a week earlier than expected, by the way."

"Oh come on, Barnes. You're the one who let it slip there was a locals-only party the week prior to the centennial. How could I miss that? Have you gotten me an invite yet?"

"I'm working up the nerve to ask my mother, but she's such a purist about these things. She has this silly idea that a residents only party should be attended by actual residents."

"Did you tell her it's not a party until I roll up in my skinny man jeans?"

"That seems like an odd thing to tell one's mother."

"Miracles, Barnes. Miracles. I expect nothing less. Speaking of miracles," he said slyly, "how's the book coming along? Susannah's called several times. You know she's all sugar and spice. Until she's not. Then it's all, welcome Dunwich, hello Cthulhu."

"I'm nearly there."

"Really, that's fantastic. Can you see the ending yet?"

"Not yet," I admitted, although things were starting to take form. An unescapable battle long in the making. Meg and her allies at the forefront instead of skulking around the edges of the fray all cloak-and-dagger style. There was still the matter of Dylan, however. He was no longer a villain, but I wasn't sure what he was to Meg and what role he would play.

"How was your Fourth? I'm a little hurt you didn't respond to any of my Bill Pullman *Independence Day* memes."

"Hmm?"

"How was the tasting?"

Right, the tasting. My mind unhelpfully flashed to kissing Adam. "It was good," I hedged.

"Oh, come on, Barnes. Out with it."

"Fine, I might have made out with Adam in the gardens and it was so freaking hot until we were busted by Candace. Get this, she wants Portia to play Lady Capulet in the dinner theater. Of course, I completely forgot to tell my sister about this, and she jetted back to New York this morning on some sort of urgent client issue."

Stunned silence ensued. I couldn't call it a first for us, but it was definitely a rarity. "All right," he said finally. "I meant how good were the desserts. But it sounds like you had yourself a double helping of sweets, you backwoods temptress." I could practically hear the smirk in his voice. "Let's review. About a week ago you text me to tell me how you and the good vet settled up on your past. Now we've graduated to woodland shenanigans? Did you learn nothing from the Grimm brothers?"

"You have sex outdoors all the time," I protested. "Forests, national parks, the Arnold Arboretum—hell, I'm willing to bet you've probably had sex in the outdoors camping display at REI. Don't lecture me on open-air extracurriculars."

"Wouldn't dream of it," Ian said mildly. "How was it? I've never been patient enough for the whole slow burn thing."

"Did you miss the part about Candace interrupting us?"

"So, there was a big bad wolf," Ian crowed. "Or should we say, a big bad blond?"

"I hate you."

"You love me," he scoffed. "Didn't seal the deal, then?"

"No," I admitted. "First we got busted by Candace, and then our to-be-continued was thwarted by this cat that ate its stitches and—" I paused. "My life is weird. Anyway, he texted me this morning and invited me over for a late dinner tonight."

"You going?"

I blew out a long breath. "I haven't responded yet."

"It's almost four o'clock."

"Yes, it is."

"What's the problem?"

"It seemed so perfect in the moment, but now that I've had time to think about it . . . I don't think it's a good idea. I'm not great at messy."

"What's messy about it? You enjoy the rest of your summer with a satisfying side of sex. You finish your book. Direct your play. Encourage your mother to make smart choices. Entertain your best friend in style. And come Labor Day, you kiss the sexy vet goodbye and make your triumphant return to Valhalla. What's messy about that?"

"What if I can't just have sex with Adam?"

"I know it's been a while, Barnes. But it's like riding a bike. You'll be fine."

I muttered a string of curses that had Ian doubling over on the other side of the line.

"From everything you've told me, you two have chemistry. What's the problem?" he asked.

I didn't say anything. I was giving him five seconds.

He got it in three. "You like him."

I sighed. "I don't know if I *like* him like him. But I think I like him enough that if I have sex with him and he doesn't feel the same way, I'll be crushed. Also, even if he did feel the same way, and it's more than just sex, we'd still have to end things when the summer is over and we go back to our real lives. So I'd still wind up crushed."

Now it was Ian's turn to let out a long breath. "Yeah, you can't sleep with him."

"I know," I groaned. "I've been going back and forth all day on it. I think I should text him that I can't make it tonight, and when I see him at rehearsal tomorrow, I'll explain we just got back to base and I don't want to endanger our friendship."

"Exactly what every man wants to hear."

"Whose side are you on?"

"Mine. Obviously."

"Thanks, partner."

"Then yours, of course," he amended. "You want me to head up now? I can pack and be there in a few hours. We can binge an entire season of that new series with the dead body on the picturesque island where everyone has lilting accents and wears those ridiculously attractive wool sweaters."

"A tempting offer, but I'm buried here."

"All right, but call me if you change your mind. Otherwise, I'll see you in two weeks."

"Miss you, talk soon." I hit end and banged my head against the seat rest. Swallowing hard, I texted Adam, citing centennial work and assuring myself that it wasn't cowardly to cancel dinner. I applauded my excellent judgment for averting a potential disaster. Who was I kidding? There was no way I could just sleep with Adam. Of course I'd want more. My mind flashed back to my revamp of

Adam's future state, the two of us snuggled up on the couch, pets at our feet. *Let it go,* I told myself as I climbed out of the car and made for the entrance. *Put your game face on and go in there and be a theater Yoda like you promised.*

As I sank into the booth, my eyes roamed the cheerful interior of Tempest Tossed Pizza. With its wall murals of some of the Bard's most famous scenes—Juliet leaning over a balcony while Romeo waited on bended knee with an open pizza box, or Hamlet contemplating a double-stuffed meat lovers instead of poor Yorick—the place was packed with families, happily scarfing down the sunflower-seed-studded crust of the town's tastiest pies.

My phone vibrated on the lacquered countertop. *Time to pay the piper.* I glanced at Adam's text. No problem. Rain check? I ignored it, focusing instead on the homey smells of cheese and tomato sauce.

I didn't have to wait long for a better distraction, as Opal and Jazz were right on time. They piled into the other side of the booth and whipped out their tablets in a disconcertingly synchronized manner. "Let's talk shop," Opal said, gleefully rubbing her hands together.

"Don't worry," Jazz said, taking in my mildly alarmed expression. "I'm here to make sure Opal exercises some restraint." She turned her head, her braids swinging out behind her, to follow a waiter hefting two steaming platters. "And the wings. I was told there'd be wings."

Five birch beers, two baskets of wings, a hummus plate and several hours later, I'd answered all of Opal and Jazz's worst-case-theater-scenario questions, including the transition to Will's Island next week and classic watch-outs for performing in the round.

We were discussing the hazards of bats during nighttime performances when Jazz elbowed Opal. "Isn't that Adam over there? We can ask him what he thinks about that set change with the bower."

My head swiveled in the direction of the takeout counter, where indeed a familiar lanky frame was standing in line. "I don't think—"

"Adam!" Opal sprang up—and before I could get another word out—she was over there, half dragging him back to our table.

"I am Fortune's bitch," I muttered.

"You say something?" Jazz asked, looking up from her tablet.

"Nope." I was just going to have to pretend like I hadn't committed outdoor frottage with Adam while I sat here with a pair of teenagers who were bloodhounds at sniffing that kind of thing out. No pressure.

"You look like you're finishing up here," Adam said, glancing down at the table and then up at me, his expression cautiously hopeful.

"Not at all." Jazz gestured to the tabletop. "We were thinking of getting a pizza."

I stared at the heaping bone graveyard and scraped-clean bowls, my eyes going wide.

"I'm starving," Opal agreed. "I could totally go for pizza. Ever order Caliban's Catch?"

"You can never go wrong with poached lobster and charred octopus," Adam said sagely.

Realizing that him standing there like that was starting to get a tad awkward, I said, "You could join us. If you want."

"Great," he said, quickly settling in beside me as if I might change my mind. Although we weren't touching, I could feel the warmth of his legs near mine. And it made my thighs ache.

After flagging down our waitress and putting in the pizza order, Opal turned her most winsome smile on Adam. "Jazz is trying to talk me out of using an open flame, and Miranda agrees with her. What do you think?"

"I think you should consider the open-air venue and the all-too-real possibility of setting someone on fire," Adam said.

I pressed down on my lips, trying not to smile. "It's a great idea," I told Opal solemnly. "But Adam and I lived through the year that Richard III's cloak ignited because the director demanded there be oil lamps. It left us both a little traumatized."

"The entire second act smelled like burnt hair." Adam grimaced. "People were talking about that one for years. And for all the wrong reasons."

"Hard pass on being a fairy flambé." Jazz patted Opal's shoulder. "I'll just burn bright from the inside out."

"Fine," Opal grumbled, rolling her eyes. "But live plants are still on the table."

"This is your fault, isn't it?" Adam elbowed me. "You told her she could do anything and you'd back her."

"Oh, I'll definitely back you on live plants," I said with a conspiratorial wink.

"You're going to be the best boss ever," Opal said. "Assuming you still want to hire me."

"What's this now?" Adam asked.

"I applied to be an intern at Miranda's agency. Jazz submitted her application to Berklee's summer program, and if we both get in we could be"—Opal's cheeks flushed pink—"roommates," she finished weakly.

"Opal said you represent Hathaway Smith," Jazz said, jumping in to rescue her lady love. "I'm reading *Inconstant Moons* right now. Can you please tell her that I'm obsessed? I don't care what anybody else says, this one is burning shit down," she said with a ferocity that made me want to hug her. Where had these two been when swarms of Amazon reviews had breached the gates and stormed the castle of my self-esteem? I lifted my beer to my lips to hide my smile.

"Also, I think this one has the most Shakespeare references of all her books so far," Jazz continued. "It's too bad Hathaway is all secretive about her identity. She would rock an author event at Bard's Books. She'd fit right in with the other Bardolators."

I choked on my drink, hastily wiping at my mouth. "Went down the wrong pipe," I wheezed.

"Hathaway Smith writes contemporary fantasy for young adults," Opal explained for Adam's benefit. "She writes a series called Elf Shot—it's basically a call to arms for this generation to not settle for the status quo and rise up to change it."

"Oh, I know Hathaway Smith," Adam said breezily. "I have a precocious fifteen-year-old niece." He leaned in close, his tone taking on a conspiratorial edge. "I'm engaged in open warfare with my sister-in-law's brother for the title of fun uncle, so I had to make myself an expert in all subjects that interest teenagers. Reading is no exception. Elf Shot is all Shannon talked about last winter break. Educate yourself or be a social pariah at dinner."

"You should have Bunny stitch that on a sampler," I scoffed, wishing I didn't find his story about his niece so endearing. Instead, I reminded myself that this Adam, this banter, this friendship, was what I could have. Not a messy entanglement and eventual heartbreak.

"What I appreciate most is that Smith doesn't talk down to her audience," he added. "She just tells it how it is and doesn't seem to care if you like her characters or not. Although it's pretty impossible not to like Meg."

"She's everything," Jazz agreed. Maybe I could talk Ian into taking on two interns next summer if things didn't work out for Jazz at Berklee?

"Maybe Miranda could get you an autographed copy or something. Pretty sure you'd secure the title of Funka for that one." Opal winked at Adam.

"Funka?" Adam repeated. A grin stretched across his face, positively transcendent. It did weird things to my stomach. "You're right. Why settle for Fun Uncle when I can be the Funka?"

Jazz and Opal preened.

"I read this post about Hathaway Smith on SpillThatTea. Is it true that not even her editor knows her real identity?" Jazz asked.

"Yeah, what's with the secret identity thing?" Opal added.

"I don't want to speak for Hathaway specifically, but I think it can be a struggle for authors who feel the need to live up to their own hype. Some need that extra distance between them and their readers." I paused, sipping my beer. "There's also the occasional nutter who crosses the line. Some writers want that security of fans not knowing who they are and where they live."

"Sounds complicated," Opal sighed. "But makes sense. There's a lot of crazy on the internet." She squinted at something over my shoulder. "Hey, is that Clinton?" Opal asked, craning her neck. "I want to run some scene notes by them."

"Clinton is playing Lysander," Jazz explained, her eyes fond as she watched Opal rummaging around for her tablet. "Killer baritone."

"Back in five," Opal promised, pulling Jazz up with her.

"Oh, to be in college again," Adam mused, watching them go. "They're good kids."

"They're really good kids," I agreed. Of course, these really good kids had left me sitting next to my personal romantic kryptonite. They were all right kids, I amended to myself.

"I won't try and entice you with dinner since it looks like you put away half the menu, but maybe some wine back at my place?"

I hesitated. Part of me wanted to say yes. But there was a bigger part of me that just didn't want the inevitable hurt that was coming my way if I went down this road. "I'm gonna pass."

He frowned. "Barnes, if I did anything last night—"

"No, I wanted to. But thinking through it today with a clear head, I realize I'm not built for this kind of thing."

"What kind of thing?"

"The just-sex thing," I said. Though even that wasn't entirely true. I was actually not half-bad at the just-sex thing, or the casual dating thing. I'd made a half-assed habit out of dating guys I only half cared about. But there was nothing half-assed about the way I was feeling about Adam. To try and convince myself of anything else would be a lie. "We just got back to being friends. I don't want to screw that up by making it weird."

"Seeing me naked will make it weird?"

My mouth went very, very dry. "Mmm-hmm."

"You want to know what I think?"

I managed the barest of nods.

"I think I look fantastic naked."

"Really?" I stammered. "That's what you got?"

"It needed to be said." He shrugged, not looking remotely sorry about it. "Besides, I'm hardly in a position to argue. I get it," he said, his expression going serious.

"You do?"

"Yeah. You don't want to see where things go because as much as you say we're good, you don't trust me not to hurt you again."

"What?" I sputtered. "That's not it at all. I know how I am, and it's not going to be just sex for me. I like—"

Adam raised his eyebrows, waiting.

"It wouldn't be casual for me," I finished lamely. "And I'm sure you don't want a mess on your hands either."

"Why don't you let me worry about what I want," Adam said, his tone clipped.

"Which is what exactly?"

"Not shutting this down because you've already convinced yourself it can't work."

"But it can't work."

"You don't even know what *it* is," Adam fired back. "You kiss me in the study. Then you tell me it's off because there's all this unresolved baggage between us. So we worked through it and put it behind us, or so I thought. Then you kiss me again at Titania's and now you tell me it's off because there might be a future scenario you don't like. How am I supposed to feel about that? Other than I'm not worth it?" Adam took out his wallet and threw some cash on the table.

"I don't know why you're acting like this. I say I want to protect our friendship and you go off on me."

"I'm not going off on you. I'm frustrated. I respect your choice, but I think you're making it for the wrong reasons. You're assuming I'm going to hurt you. And that hurts." He nodded in the direction of Opal and Jazz. "Would you please tell them something came up at work? I don't want to be rude." He held my gaze for a long moment, as if waiting for me to say something.

But I didn't. I sat there biting back the words that I didn't want him to go. It wasn't him. It was the reality of our circumstances. And maybe my reluctance to feel that kind of hurt again, a hurt I hadn't felt in a relationship since it had been Adam and me on the porch all those years ago.

Adam stood, his shoulders stiff. "Guess I'll see you around, Barnes."

I watched him go, wanting to call him back but knowing it wouldn't do any good. He was right. I didn't want to get hurt. So I was letting him walk.

After limping through the rest of dinner with Opal and Jazz, I drove home, blaring "Just Like a Woman" and singing (off-key) at the top of my lungs. Bob Dylan didn't seem to mind.

"I don't understand men," I harrumphed to Puck as I barricaded the door behind me and retreated to the attic. My dog huffed in solidarity as he settled across my feet.

My thoughts wandered to a desolate plain that overlooked the stronghold of the Winter Queen. I imagined Meg astride her (non-talking) mount, alone and facing down her enemy. No, that wasn't right. I added Meg's friends at the Guild. A small posse of unlikely heroes facing down impossible odds. Much better. Still missing something though.

With a resigned shake of my head, I sighed and wrote Dylan into the scene. I might not be able to have Adam the way I wanted, but that didn't mean Meg couldn't have her happiness. I let my mind go to all the places that Meg and Dylan could go that Adam and I couldn't.

Hours later, my eyes bleary and my fingers cramping, I pushed myself back from my laptop. *The ending.* Bard above, I'd just written the ending. Meg, Dylan, the battle for the realms. The breaking of the fairy ring. Two figures standing over the ruins of it all and holding hands as the world burned.

....

Falstaff's Folly

We will not part from hence—Cesario, come. For so you shall be while you are a man. But when in other habits you are seen, Orsino's mistress, and his fancy's queen."

"No, no, no." I crumpled up the script and tossed it in the grass. "Say it like you mean it. Like you're a duke, for Bard's sake." I glared at Byron and then up at the night sky, praying for patience. It was in short supply apparently, but there were plenty of stars.

Will's Island, a tiny but mighty spit of rock owned by the town, was normally a place of homecoming for me. Especially since I'd literally been born here during a mainstage intermission. But more than that, it was a place of peace, a place where I'd performed, a place where I could comfortably slip on the skin of someone else for a time.

Except right now. Right now I wanted to burn it, amphitheater and all, down to the ground. It had been *a week*. For starters it was fires of the inferno hot, and the mid-July humidity draped over me like the devil's Snuggie. It was also high season for mosquitos, and while the black flies were waning, they still had a foothold out here in the woods. But really, it wasn't the heat, the humidity or the flesh-eating bugs fanning the flames of my bad mood.

Onstage, Byron's mouth worked like a hooked fish. Beside him, Corey fidgeted in her farthingale, looking for all the world like a forlorn teenager and nothing like my wily Olivia. After a few moments, Cat, dressed in a man's doublet and still managing to rock it, strode out onto the stage, her boots echoing in the night air, and murmured a quiet word to Byron. But he shook his head vehemently, the stark white ruff around his neck accentuating the movement.

"This has to stop," he told her. Then he whirled on me, his cape swirling in an angry tempest of blue. "What is going on with you, Miranda? You've been a total shit to us all week."

Corey sucked in a breath and nervously pulled at her wig. "Now you've done it."

"It had to be done," Byron insisted.

"What my less-than-eloquent and emotional inferior is driving at—" Cat offered.

"Hey!" Byron yelled.

Cat blithely ignored him. "Is that you seem a little tense."

"You're endangering your reputation as the non-firebreathing Barnes sister," Byron sniped.

I shot him an exasperated look.

"Well, you are," he mumbled. "We're all volunteers here, Miranda. Doing our best. Sweating our asses off, I might add."

Sighing, I raked my hands through my sweaty hair. "You're right. I'm sorry. I'm stressed out that we only have two weeks left of rehearsal and so much left to do."

"Sure it doesn't have something to do with the lack of a certain vet with an aversion to shirts hanging around our rehearsals?" Byron asked.

I reached for my water bottle, chugging it so Byron couldn't see that he'd hit the mark. I hadn't heard from or seen Adam in over a week. Not that I'd expected to, since I'd been the one to send him packing. But that hadn't stopped me from looking over my shoulder at rehearsals in the hopes of seeing a flash of that familiar blond hair. I knew he was angry with me, but I had thought we'd slip back into our familiar rhythm of friendship, just with less sexual tension. Apparently, I had misjudged the situation.

"Miranda?" Byron pulled me back to earth. Gloomy, Adam-less earth. "If you want," he said gently, "I can take my shirt off right now and walk around giving unsolicited advice."

"This is why I do the talking," Cat muttered.

"All right, all right," I conceded, throwing up my hands. "Yes, I've been a shit. No, it has nothing to do with a lack of shirtless men and everything to do with work and the centennial kicking off in two weeks. That being said, I promise to check my stress at the dock and not let it pollute the rehearsal space from now on."

"See that it doesn't," Byron sniffed. "It's bad enough you eat cheese curls on the boat. You're getting cheese dust everywhere. The only thing orange on boats should be the life preservers."

"Don't push it," I growled, but I was smiling despite myself. It was Byron's boat, after all. Yet another unwritten rule of the centennial was to always make sure you cast someone who had a boat. I inclined my head to Byron. "Duke, from the top, if you please."

Byron bowed low and started his monologue. I knew I needed to get my head in the game. *Twelfth Night* was coming together beautifully, but that didn't mean I could let up. Between looking in on *Midsummer* and helping Mom with her centennial to-do list during the day and rehearsals and working through client emails and edits to my book at night, I had a full plate. So why did the days feel so long and pointless?

After line notes, I pulled Byron aside and apologized again. I received a noogie for my trouble, which just went to show you I really didn't understand guys at all.

I piled onto the *G.L.O.A.T.*—yes, that was actually its name— along with the rest of the cast and watched as Byron did a quick head count to make sure we had everyone. Amidst the opening strains of "Don't Stop Believin'," we set off on the twelve-minute boat ride back to the town landing.

Despite my apology, the cast was still cutting me a wide berth, so I was stretched out comfortably in the stern, counting stars, when my phone buzzed.

I knew better than to hope at this point that it would be Adam, but I still scrambled to see who it was.

Need you, Ian's text read. No emoji, no meme.

On a boat. Call you when I get to the landing? I replied.

To my surprise, he sent me a local address. Long story, will explain when you get here.

Upon reaching the docks, I said good night to the cast, making sure I thanked them for their hard work. Then I plugged the address Ian had given me into my phone and headed out.

When I arrived a few minutes later, I stared up at the handsome Tudor, admiring the white paint gleaming beneath its dark wood lattice and smirking at the hand-carved sign above the door that proclaimed the place "Falstaff's Folly" in a font that would have made Chaucer drool. Leave it to Ian to find the bawdiest vacation rental in town.

I made my way up the steps, ignoring the chubby little satyr leering at me, and grasped the brass knocker. Before I could let it fall, the door swung open and there stood Ian, his hair disheveled and his Fitz and the Tantrums T-shirt sporting visible stains. "Mathilde left me for an investment banker."

"Lady scoundrel!" I flung my arms around him, hugging him hard. "Oh wow, I can actually smell the bourbon oozing out of your pores." I inhaled deeply, catching the whiff of slightly sour garlic. "Parmesan truffle fries?"

"You hardly smell like roses yourself," he grumped into my hair. "I've been kicked to the curb in favor of a prepubescent numbers pirate. What's your excuse?"

"Rehearsals on a bug-infested island. I call it 'Eau de Heat and Deet.' You like it?"

"You stink, but I'll take what I can get."

I stepped in and stared around the lavishly furnished living room, dominated by a stone fireplace, an emerald couch and a painting of the Bard in a rather jaunty-looking doublet. On the coffee table was a grease-stained takeout bag, a half-eaten box of Mass Hole Donuts and a nearly empty bottle of bourbon. "Wow."

"I'll be all right. I am like the golden chanterelle of men," he assured me.

"You make people ill if eaten raw?"

"I am available for the shortest of seasons and gone before you can blink," he snorted. But he was smiling and joking. A smiling and joking Ian was an Ian who was going to be okay.

"I hope you don't mind, but I moved up my rental date because I really need a change of scenery. I had no in-person meetings scheduled, but if I need to, I can always head back."

"Happy to have you here." I squeezed his arm. "I'm so sorry."

"Well, as your precious Bard would say, it is better to have loved and lost than never to have loved at all."

"That was Tennyson."

"Damn it. Still holds true though," he muttered, flopping down on the couch. "How are you?"

"Oh, this week has been a delight. We've finally started rehearsing out on the island, so I've added a daily boat ride to my evening commute. And my mother is still refusing to move up her surgery date."

"Double suck. How are things with Adam?"

I plopped down beside Ian and helped myself to a donut hole. "I told him I valued our friendship too much to risk it and he called me out for being unwilling to give things a try. He's ghosted me all week and skipped the committee check-in on Wednesday." It felt good to tell Ian all that, but something in my chest still hurt all the same. "But in the win column, I've channeled all of my anger and annoyance into writing."

"I've funneled mine into expensive booze and truffle fries. So you're way ahead of me there. Is the manuscript close?"

I hesitated. As I'd worked my way through the draft, revising and polishing it until it resembled something people would actually pay money to read, I'd realized that I hadn't just written the ending of this book. I'd found the ending for the series, which was super inconvenient, given I still had one more book to write per my contract. I planned to spend the next few days thinking through whether I could extend Meg's story in a believable and satisfying way. But I wasn't hopeful.

Normally, I'd have bounced this kind of thing off Ian, but he just looked so sad, and I'd already saddled him with running the agency all summer. I didn't want to add one more stone to his pockets. "It's getting there, don't you worry," I assured him. I'd figure something out.

Resting my head on his shoulder, I sighed heavily. "Right now I want to focus on you. I'm sorry about Mathilde. Anyone who would choose an i-banker over you is obviously an idiot. You deserve the whole damn world too, you know."

"I know." He leaned his head on top of mine. "We're a couple of sad sacks, huh?"

"Not entirely." I held up a finger, rummaging around in my bag and extracting a cream envelope sealed with gleaming red wax. I handed it to him with a flourish.

"Is that what I think it is?" Ian slid his fingers under the seal, red shavings falling to the floor. His eyes greedily scanned the invite. "Attire: Pixies or Petticoats. Hobgoblins or Homburgs?" He raised an eyebrow. "Barnes, are we going to a sex party?"

"Yes, with my parents," I deadpanned. "The locals-only party is a costumed bacchanal in the woods, the likes of which would make Caligula blush like a schoolgirl."

"I knew it," Ian said triumphantly. "It's always the quiet ones."

"Or, you know, *Midsummer* is one of the mainstages this year. We're doing fairy folk and Victorians as a nod to Opal's restaging."

"Don't ruin all my fun," he said, although he'd brightened considerably since I'd arrived.

"Wouldn't dream of it. Now, where's my bourbon? I was promised bourbon." I cracked my knuckles. "We've both had the shit kicked out of us this week from a relationship perspective. Should we institute Break-Up Protocols?"

Ian's eyes lit up. "Don't tease me, Barnes."

"Go get them. I know you brought them." Ian was the only person I knew who owned *Ghostbusters*, its sadly inferior, but still highly watchable sequel and *The Real Ghostbusters* on DVD.

"Bill Murray at his finest," he said gleefully, springing up from the couch. "Be a dear and find the remote if you can."

I glanced up at the painting of the Bard over the fireplace. "Like you could have handled that better."

Two Gentlemen of Daytona

I rapped on the glass panes of the bright blueberry-colored door, jiggling the "Kitchen is closed, bon viveurs" sign.

"You're late," Dan chided without any real heat as I stepped past him into the warm glow of Two Gentlemen of Daytona. Despite being allergic to all things culinary, I'd always loved Dan and Aaron's place with its gleaming cookware and spotless demo kitchen where Aaron taught classes on everything from cracking eggs to mastering savory soufflés. If I ever decided to assume the mantle of adulthood, I was going to let that man teach me how to make an omelet.

I held up a manila envelope. "It was worth it to wait the extra thirty minutes for these."

"Tickets?" he asked hopefully.

"Tickets," I sighed contentedly. "Wait until you see how the colors came out on yours. I thought that palette would be too dark with the font, but you nailed it."

"Ye of little faith." Dan held out an imperious hand, but even his dignified manners bowed to the childlike excitement of fresh tickets. "They're gorgeous," he breathed as he riffled through them.

"That reminds me, don't forget to buy your tickets to the dinner theater."

"Must we?" Dan sniffed.

"I still have room at my table if you and Aaron want to join." Actually, I probably had at least three extra seats now that I wouldn't be asking Adam to go with me, a thought that hurt me all the more because I know he would have loved Candace's twist on the tragic tale. "But don't wait. Once word gets out, they're gonna go like tiny hats at a steampunk convention."

"They're called fascinators," he informed me dryly, handing over a glass of iced tea with berries and mint. "You really think dinner theater will finally notch a tally in the win column?"

"I do," I assured him, snatching back the tickets and heading for Tillie before he could grill me further. As I deftly maneuvered around the glass jars of whisks, apple corers and handheld cheese graters, Adam looked up from behind a display of Le Creuset baking dishes. We locked eyes, Adam looking away first. Great, this wasn't going to be awkward at all.

"Where's Opal?" I asked Tillie, handing over the tickets with a flourish. "I have to turn these lovelies over to the box office tomorrow morning; this is our only opportunity to ogle them with the reverence they deserve."

"Still on the island," Tillie said fondly. "Your love for the theater is contagious."

"Sorry?" I offered with a not-sorry grin.

"Nonsense." Tillie waggled her fingers and took a long sip from her glass. "There are much worse diseases you can give someone." She winked. From somewhere behind her, I heard Adam choke on his drink. When he'd recovered, I offered him a hesitant smile and a chance to steer the conversation away from communicable diseases. "How are the sets coming along?" I asked politely, my eyes straying to where he'd left the top two buttons of the blue check Oxford undone. Not that I was staring or anything.

"If it weren't for Pete, we'd all be naked and afraid in the corner.

But somehow, he keeps whittling down the punch list. Of course, if someone would stop changing his mind on the layout for a certain Scottish castle—"

Dan threw up his hands. "Excuse me if I'm looking for tartan perfection. The dragon on that coat of arms was cross-eyed."

"It was no such thing," Adam said mildly.

I snickered into my glass and sank into the nearest chair, content to dip my toes in the conversational tide pool as my fellow committee members traded good-natured barbs and thinly veiled threats. It took the pressure off me to carry on as if nothing had happened between Adam and me. Mostly, I just felt relieved that he hadn't ducked the meeting because of me.

Today had been full of running last-minute plans over to the permit office, tracking down a notary public for some zoning documents, dropping the final parade route maps off at the sheriff's office, grabbing a quick lunch with Ian to make sure he'd eaten something that qualified as a nutrient, catching up on client emails and powering through three hours' worth of rehearsals. Even though I wanted nothing more than to curl up in sweats with an old A. S. Byatt paperback and not talk to another soul for the rest of the day, I was happy I'd showed up. Particularly if Aaron kept refreshing the charcuterie plate.

When the conversation moved on from the remaining action items to lighting schemes and filters, I beat a hasty retreat to the restroom. I marveled at the selection of hand soaps lined up on the marble counter—Tuscan Brunch, Moonrise over Aspen, Crepes by the Seine—all of which were for sale in the shop. I snapped a picture of the crepes-themed one and texted it to Ian, asking if I should buy some for the office. He responded that bathrooms should not smell like somebody shat in a creperie. Which settled it. I'd be buying a half dozen.

When I emerged, I paused by the window, an impressive array of novelty timers catching my eye. As I debated between the chef-hat-wearing raptor or the glow-in-the-dark TARDIS for Cordy's Christmas stocking, the shop lights lit on two figures leaning against the hood of a magnificently beat-up sedan. Opal and Jazz were kissing the way only new couples do—fingers wound in each other's hair and bodies pressed tight—as if nothing else in the world mattered. I envied the simplicity and surety of the kiss.

"Aww, young love," I breathed to the empty back room. Or so I thought.

"Where?" Adam asked from behind my shoulder.

"For the love of Bard!" I jumped, nearly knocking over the timers. "What are you doing back here?"

He held up a roll of paper towels. "Tillie makes Dan nervous. He sent me for reserves." Adam cocked his head at me, that half smile cautiously tugging up the corners of his mouth. "What are *you* doing back here? You wouldn't be avoiding a titillating discussion of bump cues, would you?"

"I was coming out of the restroom when I saw our fledgling director and her lead actress," I whispered, as he stepped to the window for a closer look. "Don't make a thing of it."

"You mean, like you're making a thing of it right now?" he asked innocently.

"I'm not making a thing of it," I insisted, but otherwise let it go. I was relieved that he was speaking to me again. "They're cute. Young love and all."

"Oh, I don't know that young love is all it's cracked up to be. It's all fast and hurried. There's something to be said for the slow burn," he said, his mouth curling around each word as he drew back from the window. "The buildup and the waiting."

I cleared my throat. "We should get back," I mumbled. "Dan is not going to be pleased that—" My phone buzzed and I stared down at the unfamiliar number with a Maine area code. "Excuse me," I said to Adam and accepted the call. He gave me a little nod and turned to go.

"Hello?" I asked in a tone as cold as an ice pick that I reserved for denizens of the seventh circle of hell and telemarketers.

"May I please speak with Miranda Barnes?"

"This is she," I replied.

"Hello, Miranda. This is Dr. Caroline Wu. I'm your mother's oncologist."

The ice instantly melted into watery, knee-buckling fear. "Yes?"

Adam's retreating form halted in the darkness.

"I'm sorry to disturb you, but I just received a call from Sherburne General. Your mother collapsed at a dinner this evening and has been admitted. I've been unable to reach her husband, Peter Barnes, and you're listed as one of her emergency contacts."

"Is my mom okay?"

"The attending on duty said it seems to be exhaustion, possibly dehydration. They're running some tests. They'll keep her overnight out of an abundance of caution regardless."

"Is this because of her cancer?"

There was a long pause. "Your mother needs to focus on her health, Ms. Barnes. I have recommended several times that she needs to prioritize it."

"You mean like moving up her surgery from October?" I said, with just a hint of bitterness.

There was a long pause on the line. "While I always respect the wishes of my patients, I have made it abundantly clear to your mother that I can take her as early as she wants. She just has to want to." After another span of silence, she added, "Perhaps this episode will help clarify things for her."

I winced. With everything that had been going on with centennial prep and my book, I'd let this one get away from me. I should have stayed on top of Dad to continue working on Mom to get her to move up her date. And now this had happened. "Crack of doom," I muttered.

"Pardon?"

"I said, thank you for the call, Dr. Wu," I managed. "I'll head over to Sherburne right now." I hung up and fumbled blindly for my bag, spilling a third of its contents on the floor. "Damn it," I breathed, dropping to my knees to retrieve my things.

The scent of fresh citrus filled my nose as Adam crouched down beside me and joined in the search and recovery. "You okay?"

"Yeah, thanks," I said, accepting a notebook and a small vial of essential oil that, miraculously, hadn't shattered. I so didn't want to be the reason that Dan complained his shop smelled like an aggressive bouquet of geraniums. "I need to go."

"Are you all right to drive?"

"I'm fine. I barely touched my drink."

"That's not what I meant," Adam said, keeping his voice low and quiet. "You look as if you've just seen Hamlet's ghost."

"My mom is at the ER over in Sherburne. She collapsed. She has cancer."

"I know," he said softly. "Pete told me."

"Oh."

"I didn't want to pry," he said quickly. "I figured if it was something you'd want to talk about, you'd tell me. Or not. That would have been fine too." He cleared his throat. "Can I give you a ride? Or keep you company?"

"You don't have to do that."

"I want to."

I opened my mouth, a multitude of explanations for why I didn't need a ride crowding the tip of my tongue. Besides, how was I going to ugly cry and use my sleeve as a tissue if he was in the car with me? But my objections fizzled as I gazed up into the calm harbor of his eyes. "Thanks," I heard myself say. "I'd really appreciate it." I offered him a shaky smile. "Let me just call my dad first."

"Good plan. We could swing by and pick him up on the way."

"I don't know where the card game is this week," I said as I dialed. "Do you?"

Adam frowned. "I wish I could call my old man. If he weren't in Florida, he'd be there."

After being shunted to voice mail, I sent a quick follow-up text. "He didn't pick up, but I'll keep calling and texting. I know they take breaks."

"Old-guy bladders," Adam said gravely. "I'll tell Dan you left something at the landing and need to get it before rehearsals tomorrow."

I nodded, grateful I wouldn't have to face anyone else while my joints were all Silly Putty. Willing myself to move, I opened the back door and stepped out into the cool night air, the sound of crickets gently pressing down on my jumping pulse. Of course, in my general panic, I'd forgotten about our *Midsummer* lovers in the parking lot.

"Miranda," Opal squeaked as she and Jazz hastily broke apart. "We were—"

"The tickets are in if you want to see them," I said quickly. The two undergrads squealed and streamed past me.

In the quiet of the truck, I called my sisters. Away at an overnight conference in Portland, Cordy was nonetheless calm and measured as she told me she'd be home as soon as she could. By stark contrast, Portia melted down in the middle of some exclusive New York restaurant, despite my assertions that I had it under control. She sort of dropped the phone or hung up on me, I wasn't sure, but I thought she said she was on her way as well. I thunked my head against the headrest. Everything about this situation sucked, and it was getting worse by the minute.

A few moments later, Adam climbed into the driver's seat, handing me a travel mug and a shortbread cookie wrapped in a cocktail napkin. "To settle your stomach. Because if you hurl in here, I'll never be able to take a woman out in this again."

"You take women out in this?" I managed a weak smile.

"Just the ones willing to overlook this vehicular eyesore and like me anyway."

I nibbled on the shortbread. "That must be quite a short list."

"It's actually a Post-it note with one name on it." He reached out and tentatively patted my shoulder. "Keep eating. You're looking less like a puke liability by the second."

"Nice."

It was about forty minutes to the hospital in Sherburne over suspect country roads with stingy lighting. I weathered the bumps and dips, running through every worst-case scenario in my mind. The doctors had been wrong; the tumor had metastasized to my mother's brain; her body was shutting down. The tumor had spread to her bones. Her lymph nodes.

My descent into darkness was interrupted by Dad's call. While I was initially grateful for the distraction of bringing him up to speed, I struggled to hold it together as my throat tightened with the tears I was trying to hold back. When we hung up, I stared out the window into the inky black, taking deep, gulping breaths to steady myself.

"Barnes?" Adam's voice was hesitant, cutting through the darkness that was swallowing me by inches.

"Yeah?" I croaked.

"Could I ask you something?"

"Depends on what it is," I said, bracing myself.

He took a deep breath. "It's just that I've always wondered—if you could go anywhere in the world to see a show, where would it be?"

"What?"

"Humor me. This is important stuff."

"The Minack in Cornwall," I said, without hesitation.

"Solid pick. What would you see?"

I imagined that legendary open-air theater of stone overlooking the sea. Only the Bard would do. "*The Tempest*."

He raised an eyebrow, the shadows of the road flickering across his face. "Self-serving."

"I know, I know. But all that water and rock. Imagine Prospero's 'indulge me, forgive me, and set me free' monologue. What about you?"

"You're going to laugh."

"I won't," I insisted.

"*Little Shop of Horrors* at the Sydney Opera House."

"I lied," I snorted. "That's ridiculous."

"No, it isn't," he insisted. "I've given this a lot of thought. Think of the acoustics in that place during 'Mean Green Mother from Outer Space.' In an Australian accent. Now, that would be a religious experience."

"There's something very wrong with you."

"That's what my mother keeps telling me."

I glanced over to find him watching me out of the corner of his eye. I offered him a shaky smile.

He returned it, his steadier than mine. Turning his gaze back to the road, he found my hand and gave it a squeeze. I squeezed back, grateful for the warmth of it. Grateful for the conversational distraction. Grateful for him. Right up until he started whistling the opening strains of *Little Shop of Horrors*.

When we finally reached Sherburne, Adam let me out at the entrance and went to park. Walking in, I lost what little equilibrium I'd gained. For a moment, I just stood there, suspended in the night air, my feet unwilling to cross over into the artificial chill of the hospital.

Inside was worse. Once I'd proved who I was to the triage nurses, they plied me with stacks of forms and questions about previous medical conditions and insurance plans that I wouldn't have been able to answer about myself, never mind my mother.

Finally, just when I thought I couldn't fill out another damn yellow, pink or white form in triplicate, they took me to her. Instead of the rush of reassurance I expected to feel, that water-in-the-knees sensation returned—in triplicate—and would have leveled me if I hadn't grabbed the doorframe. Mom was sleeping, but she didn't look peaceful. She looked less, somehow, her face drawn and her body small and curled under the scratchy blue hospital blanket. How in the hell had I missed this? So consumed by my own petty problems, I hadn't seen what was right in front of me.

I plopped down beside Mom in a plastic chair devoid of comfort and back support and texted my sisters. Then, with nothing left to do but wait, my body broke into heaving waves of silent, shaking sobs. That's how Adam found me, crying without sound and no dry end in sight.

He gathered me into his arms, his T-shirt taking the brunt of my tears. "You're an ugly crier, Barnes," he murmured, stroking my hair.

"Ass," I hiccup-sobbed, and pulled him closer. Even if he was a bit of an ass, even if I'd more or less metaphorically sent him packing, even if I had no idea what I wanted from him, other than the fact I *wanted* him, I couldn't think of a single person whose arms I'd rather have wrapped around me at that moment.

The Waiting Room

Hours later when I awoke at ungodly o'clock, that shivery, bleary spot between 3:15 and 4:45, Adam was gone, but I was not alone. "Porsche?" I asked in a voice roughened by sleeping open-mouthed in the overly assertive air-conditioning of the hospital waiting room.

My big sister sat ramrod straight, a pale vision in pressed trousers and a suit jacket. Or maybe she was a hallucination, because who the hell wore a suit jacket in New England in July? "Dad is with her," she said quietly, "but he doesn't know much. What happened tonight?"

I wiped what I hoped was an inconspicuous amount of drool from the corner of my mouth. "She was out cold when I got here. Nurse said it was exhaustion and dehydration."

"Did she seem tired this week? Was she doing too much? How could you—"

I held up a hand, using my sleep-roughened crypt keeper voice to full advantage. "Stop."

"Miranda—"

"Listen. Just listen for once in your inquisitorial existence."

Portia fell silent. Hell, I fell silent too, because I'd never spoken to her that way. But I was all out of tears and fucks to give.

"I love Mom more than anything, but I'm not her keeper. She's an adult. So, before you ask me any questions starting with 'How could you,' I want you to ask yourself what an actual human being with feelings would do in this situation. And then do that."

The air that whistled out between Portia's blazing white teeth sounded suspiciously like a hiss. "Basic common sense would dictate you'd—"

"I'm going to stop you right there," I gritted out. "I've been here helping Mom out as much as she'll let me while you've been back in New York. If her health was of such concern to you, you should have been here."

"Right," she sneered. "Because all of us have flexible jobs like you do."

"My job isn't that flexible," I shot back. "I've been making this work because it's important."

"Are you saying I don't think Mom's health is important?"

"I'm saying I'm not your assistant. You can't *direct* me to take care of things you're too busy to do—or, frankly, that you don't have the stomach for." The last part dropped like an anchor, dragging the temperature of the room down with it.

Portia narrowed her eyes. "What the hell is that supposed to mean?"

I met her impassive bird-of-prey stare with my own level gaze, the one I hoped would soothe the ice maiden before me and not, say, incite a knock-down, drag-out brawl. "This is something we've all got to face as a family."

Portia clasped her hands so taut in her lap I thought I could hear the tendons squeak. I waited for the excuse, some big deal or acquisition. But she looked away, her eyes moving over the outdated magazines and faded silk floral arrangements. "I'm not good at death," she said finally. "I'm afraid that's what's at the end of this for her. That she'll wind up like Grandma Bea."

I nodded, holding my breath lest I scare her off with the obvious remark that death was eventually coming for us all. But I knew what she meant.

"I'm not strong like you or Cordy. I always seem to be the one that needs comforting, even if I barely knew the person who died. I'm a liability at a time when no one needs one."

"You're not a liability."

"I am when it comes to Mom," she insisted. "I can barely breathe around her. One minute I want to hug her and the next I want to shake some sense into her."

"I think that's a pretty normal reaction when it comes to our mother," I said dryly.

"I don't think it's good for me to be around when I'm off-kilter. My head keeps telling me I need to leave her alone, to give her some space."

"What's your gut telling you?"

Portia wrinkled her nose. "You know I don't think like that."

"I know. That's why I'm asking."

Her fingers worked furiously in her lap, as if she were trying to shred something. "That I need to be here, even if I make it worse."

I nodded, managing a half smile. "That's what my gut says too. That's why I'm here. So why don't you stay here with me and Cordy, and we'll get through this together."

"Easier said than done." She let out a laugh, but it was a dry one. "Do you ever—" She shook her head. "Never mind. It's stupid."

"Say it. I'm so sleep deprived, there's only a fifty percent chance I'll remember it later."

Portia snorted delicately, running her calculating gaze over me like I was one of her deal sheets. "It's not just this situation with Mom. I always feel a little off-kilter when I'm home."

I sat up a little straighter. "Say more on that."

Her eyes narrowed, but when she saw the sincerity in my own, she continued. "I'm still me, accomplished and successful, of course."

"Of course." I swear I kept the eye roll out of my voice.

"But when I'm back in Bard's I feel like an earlier version of me. A version that's not as, let's say, seasoned and mature as me right now."

"You mean, you feel like the high school version of yourself?"

She nodded. "Yes."

"Me too," I admitted. "I think it's something about going home again. I mean, there's the whole 'Mom does my laundry and cuts the crusts off my sandwich' regression that everyone always jokes about. But I think it's more than that."

"Say more on that," Portia said hesitantly, trying on my words for size.

"Like you, I too am a badass," I said solemnly. "I own my own agency. Most of the time I love what I do for a living. How many people can say that?" I pushed the hair out of my face. "And most of the time, I feel okay in my own skin. Not like an Amazonian queen like you or anything, but I've found my people, my place. Except when I'm back here. Don't get me wrong. I love Bard's. But when I'm here, I feel like that insecure drama club wallflower that I was in high school. It's like muscle memory takes over. I feel less confident in myself. Even though all those things I have are still waiting for me at home. So yeah, I hear you when you say you feel like an earlier version of yourself."

Portia blew out a long breath. "I feel like that high school prom queen and class president who needed to win at any cost. Whatever the cost," she said with a sideways glance at me. "I know you probably don't believe this. But I've changed."

Schooling my face into my best locked-down expression, I made a noise that could be considered agreement.

It didn't fool Portia. "Fine, I'm still as cutthroat as they come," she admitted. "But I'm more ethical about it. There are lines I don't cross."

I tried to stop the dizzying montage of Portia garroting a mansplaining colleague with his own tie, rolling his body into a garbage bag (double bagging it, of course) and tossing it into some undefined body of water. I really did.

"I see a therapist," she admitted. "Dad knows about it, but nobody else. At first, it was just someone to talk to about work stress. Setting some boundaries at the office so I don't burn out by forty. But lately, we've moved on to heavier things, like why I feel the need to do the things I do. Or not do. Like not apologizing for what I did to you in high school."

"Porsche, it's been a long night, you don't have to—"

"I want to. I'm tired of carrying it around with me. I knew you liked Adam. But I convinced myself that it wasn't serious and that I needed him more in that moment than you did."

"Did you even want him back?" I asked, trying not to make it an accusation, but the air needed clearing. "Or did you just tell him that so he'd go to prom with you?"

"I thought I wanted him back. Not because you were dating him and I was jealous or anything, but Adam and I made sense. So what if he didn't exactly light my fire? We made a certain amount of sense. That's what I told myself when I put my own needs, my own drive to win prom queen and finally wipe that smirk off Kendall O'Day's face for swiping junior prom queen out from under me—" Seeing my expression, she amended, "Not the point. The point is, you're my sister and I should never have done what I did. I'm sorry, Miranda."

I sank back, staring up at the infernal vents that kept pumping chilled air into the room. I glanced over at Portia, whose eyes had taken on a distinctive watery cast. Yes, she had been a selfish, self-absorbed teenager obsessed with winning—even about something as dumb as prom queen. If I was being entirely honest, she was a bit of a self-absorbed adult too, still obsessed with success. But she was trying. She was trying to share her stuff and be a human. I could at least try and be a human too. "You're my sister. Even if you're a complete pain in my ass, I still love you."

"I love you too," she sniffled. "I'm sorry I ruined things between you and Adam."

"You didn't ruin things . . . permanently." I leaned over, gingerly patting her knee.

"That's a relief. I like Adam. Not like that, of course. If I'm being honest, it's still a little awkward even now when I see him. When I think of how I behaved that night and what I cost the two of you . . ." She trailed off before setting her jaw and continuing. "I'm not great at apologizing, but I promise I'm working on getting my shit together." This time it was Portia who leaned over, squeezed my hand.

I squeezed hers right back, delighted at her rare usage of profanity. "We're all working on getting our shit together," I assured her. "Some of us are just getting there faster than the rest," I said with a deliberate toss of my hair.

Her eyes widened. "Are you—are you making a joke at my expense right now?"

"Porsche, have you ever known me not to make a joke in tense, stressful or otherwise uncomfortable situations?"

"Good point," she said, dabbing at her eyes. She rummaged around in a bag that cost more than most authors' advances and offered me a granola bar. "Here, I almost forgot. Adam mentioned you'd only eaten a cookie on your way over here. That was hours ago. I thought you might be hungry."

As if on cue, my stomach bellowed like a primordial nightmare rising out of the depths. "Thanks," I said, gratefully accepting the bar. Even if it advertised itself as vegan protein. "You saw Adam?"

"He was sitting here, watching over you. But he told me that I was supposed to tell you he was catching up on emails. I sent him home, told him I would give you a lift. He agreed, but only after I told him where the spare key was so he could check in on Puck."

"Oh." I tried to hide my smile as she raked me with her "I know all, I'm Portia" gaze.

"You two a thing?"

"No," I said hurriedly, swallowing down a lump of sticky granola and cashew. At least I hoped it was cashew.

"But you like him?"

"It's complicated." Taking a page from Portia's playbook, I studied the outdated magazines with an intensity reserved for my favorite clients' manuscripts.

"Complicated because relationships are generally complicated or complicated because you two have unfortunate history that I played a part in?"

"Complicated for other reasons."

"Because you like him and he likes you and you live on opposite sides of the country?"

"Something exactly like that."

"It's too bad we live in a time and place where there's no technology that would make long-distance relationships possible," she deadpanned.

"Long-distance relationships never work out."

"They work out just fine as long as you structure them right and the expectations of both parties are clear going in."

"Are we talking about long-distance relationships or mergers? I lost the thread there."

"Depends on what you mean by merger?" Portia gave me a knowing smile.

"Ew, no lawyer humor." I sat forward. "Are you saying what I think you're saying?"

"That I've been in a long-distance relationship for almost two years now? Yes."

"Umm, what?"

"I met David at an M&A event a while back; we were both speaking on panels. One thing led to another, we went back to his suite and the rest is history."

"You've been dating a guy for two years and haven't told any of us?"

"I didn't say I was dating him. We have a long-distance relationship. Once a quarter, we meet up at my condo or his town house in Chicago for a weekend of fun."

"You meet up with a guy for sex marathons?" I croaked.

"Oh, Miranda. Don't be so crass. We occasionally surface to dine. There are some wonderful restaurants in Chicago."

"Ew, ew, ew." I mimed earmuffs. "I am not emotionally prepared to hear this right now."

Portia smirked. "What I'm saying is, you can define a relationship however you want, but whatever you call it, it's whether or not it works for you. David and I have impossible schedules and no time for the work and effort that come with more traditional relationships."

"Ladies and gentlemen, Portia Barnes. Stone-cold sex panther."

"Charming." Portia's tone was as withering as her expression. "Perhaps instead of looking for every reason why things can't work with Adam, you could look for a way to make it work. You might surprise yourself and find that something outside of the regular metes and bounds of a cookie-cutter relationship suits your needs."

I was suddenly hit by a dizzying montage of sex marathon weekends with a naked and heavy-lidded Adam. Swallowing hard, I managed, "Maybe."

"Well, if you have any questions about the finer points of sex marathon weekends, you let me know," she said, patting my hand. "Or in general if there's anything I can do for you. I've been a bit difficult about Mom lately."

"I'm so glad you said that. Because I do have a few ideas."

"Yes?" Her tone was suspicious and somehow businesslike again.

"You can start with no longer force-feeding me beet smoothies. Actually, all smoothies. No more offering me fruit mush of any kind."

Her lips twisted into a vulpine smile. "That's reasonable."

"And," I said, subtly edging away from her, "I may have told Candace Thornton you'd play Lady Capulet in dinner theater."

Portia nearly toppled out of her chair as she squawked, "You did what?"

The Back Porch
of The Winters' Tail

H ere goes nothing," I muttered to my furry wingman. Puck thumped his tail happily. Maybe he'd misinterpreted my words for "I will gladly share this pepperoni and cheese masterpiece with you." Cheeky mutt. I rang the doorbell and waited, my fingers drumming an erratic staccato against my jeans.

It was worth standing in the needle sting of the mosquito haze to see Adam's face stretch into a broad grin. "I didn't order a pizza."

"What about a mutt with suspect manners and home brew? Well, not my home brew," I amended. "Del's home brew."

Adam swung the door open wide. "You brought beer? You may enter."

"You have low standards."

"I'm just relieved you're not some late-breaking skunk emergency."

"Just what every girl wants to hear," I said, handing over the pizza.

"Yeah, yeah. Come inside before you let all the winged malaria in. Lucille and I were debating where to get takeout tonight. She was campaigning hard-core for Thai, but this is so much better." At the sound of Lucille's name, Puck's ears pricked up hopefully. Keeping the box level, Adam crouched and rubbed Puck's head. "She's out back, buddy. Follow your nose." He rose to stare at me, his hair falling over his forehead and his expression speculative. "I'm not complaining, Barnes, but to what do I owe the pleasure this evening?"

I held up the six-pack. "This is how I say thank you for driving my blubbering existence over to Sherburne the other night."

"I like where your head's at." Adam chuckled, his eyes roving past the beer and over my faded *Into the Woods* cast T-shirt, coming to a full stop on my face. "But you didn't need to do this. It was no trouble. I'd have done it just for the pleasure of your blubbering company."

"Ass," I muttered, smiling. "Maybe I wanted an excuse to see you," I said, my words bolder than I felt.

"I'm in. I just bought these new citronella buckets from Stan," Adam offered. "He claims they will put out such a stink that the bloodsuckers will scorn the property for years to come. We could crack open that home brew and eat dinner on the porch."

"Dinner al fresco sounds great," I said, following Adam through the darkened office, the files neat and orderly and the faintest whiff of antiseptic lingering in the air. "But you should know, if Stan's claim has any merit, all bets are off. I will fight you tooth and nail for his stash. It's everyone for themselves when it comes to rock-solid bug protection. And I should warn you, I'm a shameless hair puller."

"Never figured you for a hair puller, Barnes." He shook his head in mock disapproval and held the back screen door open for me. "Would have thought your mama raised you better than that. How's she doing, by the way?"

"Subtle."

"Had to be said," he said with a crooked smile.

"Released this morning. Pretty wiped out. We all were."

"You get a chance to talk to her?"

"Bits and pieces. Mostly I just repeated 'I love you' and 'Please don't ever do that to us again.'"

"I sense a 'but.'"

"But there's still so much to talk about. She can't keep running on fumes. She needs to take it down a notch and focus on her health, which means," I said with a sigh, "that she'll need to rely on us. Which is not one of her strong suits."

Adam studied the shiny silver metal bug pots. "So you're going to wait a day or two and then drop the hammer on her?"

"That's the plan."

"You all right with that plan?"

"Yeah, I'm the one who suggested it. I thought a unified Barnes daughters front would be a bit much tonight."

"Makes sense. I assume your sis is currently stuffing the patient full of pastry?"

"Actually, Cordy had a date tonight with some hotshot sous-chef she met at a conference. I left Mom in the tender care of Portia."

"I'm a little afraid for your mother." Adam winced.

I snorted. "I think it will be good for both of them."

"Definitely," he agreed. "Or you'll return home to an active crime scene. One or the other."

"I'm willing to take that chance." I shrugged. "This may sound selfish, but when Portia volunteered to hang with Mom tonight, I jumped at the opportunity to get out of the house."

"It's not selfish to let someone else have a go at it. You've been shouldering a lot of this."

"Still feels selfish."

"As someone dealing with a stubborn, aging parent from the other side of the country, feeling selfish goes with the territory. As does that crippling feeling of inadequacy."

"Yeah?"

"Oh yeah." He nodded, and his eyes found mine. "It's hard to watch them get old. My dad's been this larger-than-life figure my entire life, and he's slowing down. By inches—but slowing down all the same. And someday, he's not going to be here, and I don't want that day to come any sooner than it has to."

"Exactly," I said, nodding emphatically. "My mom is the glue that holds us together. It's why this cancer thing is such a slap in the face. If it were me, I'd do anything to make sure I got as much time as I could."

"Aging parents are kind of like teenagers. You want them to act like adults, but instead you have to stand by and watch them make their own idiot choices."

"Maybe it's payback for having to raise us as teenagers."

"I was a model teenager," Adam insisted.

"The same model teenager who turned the visitor's dugout into a petting zoo?"

"You knew about that?" He looked momentarily stricken. "Okay then, enough about my sordid youth, let's crack this pie open." He nodded to a hanging wooden swing bedecked with—what else—floral cushions. On the wooden chest serving as a table, I caught sight of this month's copy of *Dogster*.

I raised an eyebrow.

"I like to keep up on my patients," he insisted.

I stared at him. Hard.

"Okay fine, I have dog envy."

"I knew it! I knew you were a doggler."

"A doggler?"

"A person who ogles dogs. You know that person who walks down the sidewalk and doesn't notice an attractive member of their preferred sex, just their adorable Australian shepherd mix pup? Then stares with utter admiration and longing to pet the little floof? You're a doggler."

"I'm not sure what to say to that," Adam said with a slightly bewildered expression.

"You already have a porcine member of your fam; why not add a canine component?"

"That's the thing. Lucille's a little picky with the company she keeps."

"She gets on fine with Puck," I said as I settled on the surprisingly comfortable swing.

"Yes, but he's the exception," Adam sighed, neatly folding his long frame in beside me. "Just this morning Lucille terrorized Sandy Ellington's puggle. Chased the thing around the waiting room until it nearly passed out."

"To be fair, puggles are kind of unsettling mouth breathers."

"No argument there. But it's not like she has a stellar track record. She tried to orchestrate the downfall of Remy, my neighbor's spaniel." When he saw my expression, he hastily added, "She pushed him down a flight of stairs with her snout. We've been disinvited from all future BBQs at Mike's place. And that's a real shame because he has one of those high-end smokers."

I winced. "What about cats? Cats don't take crap from anybody. Would Lucille like a feline companion?"

"Decidedly not. There was an incident with a couple of cats that were boarding here last month. Let's just say I don't think Mr. Courtney will be bringing Pooka, Millie, Biscuit and Blue back here anytime soon."

I winced. "Well, Puck loves Lucille. We just have to find you a Puck."

Adam's eyes sparked with playfulness, his mouth forming a question.

"Don't ask to co-op my dog," I warned him. "I've cut men for less."

"Not quite what I had in mind." He smirked. "Forgot napkins. Be right back. There's a lighter by the foot of that ottoman. Want to get those candles going?"

"On it," I called as I crossed the creaky floorboards. There was something so satisfying about the hiss of a fresh wick and that first flicker of inky gray bug smoke. More importantly, it gave me something to do with my hands as my thoughts tumbled around like a persistent permanent-press cycle, tossing and spinning the words I wanted to say to Adam into a jumble. It wasn't like I'd spent the drive over mentally rehearsing what I planned to say or anything. *Why is it so hard to tell him what I want?*

"Let's have a look at that brew," Adam said, sinking back down beside me and laying out plates, napkins and cheese.

I handed over the plain cardboard six-pack and the earnest brown bottles with nothing on them but chalk scrawl.

"Shandy?" Adam asked, eyebrow winging up. "What are we? Peasants?"

"Del made this special for me," I retorted, snatching the brew away. "If you don't want this delicious blood orange concoction, you can go drink whatever swill your dad keeps in his fridge. He's a Bud heavy kind of guy, right?"

"Please forgive my beer snobbery," Adam said quickly. He loaded up two plates and handed one to me. Taking a long sip of the beer and savoring it, he let out an appreciative sigh. "I think I'm ruined for all other shandy. And potentially all other women, Barnes. Hot pizza, cold beer, fascinating company and an adorable mutt? A guy could get used to this."

"I hate to keep harping on this, but again, low standards." I swore, the warmth creeping across my cheeks had nothing to do with the muggy night air.

I took a hearty pull off Del's beer. *Now or never, Barnes.* "I like you."

"I like you too," he said, smiling back at me.

A nervous laugh bubbled out of me. "I know I've been really hot and cold, and I know it's been confusing for you. It's confusing for me too. I just didn't want to get hurt. Not because I think you'd do it on purpose. It's just the situation itself. That being said, I think you're right. Shutting down whatever this is without giving it a shot because I'm scared was the wrong decision."

"I appreciate that more than you know." He touched my arm. "I'm really sorry I went dark on you for a week. I was confused and hurt. But that's not an excuse. I should have handled that better."

"Apology accepted, that's two from you in one summer," I teased.

"Well, don't expect any more. I plan on being perfect from here on out."

"I'll hold you to that." My fingers drummed restlessly across my jeans. "If you're up for it, I'd like to enjoy the time we do have together. Here in Bard's. No labels, no expectations, no promises."

"No games, no agendas, no secrets," Adam agreed, his hand closing over my fingers, quieting them and somehow electrifying them at the same time. "Just you and me. Putting everything out there. Being open and honest with each other. If something is bugging you, you tell me. If we're moving too fast, you say something. I'll promise to do the same."

"Absolutely. We'll enjoy the time we do have together."

"You know, you don't have to make it sound like a meteor is going to hit the earth tomorrow," he said, arching a brow. "We're both around here until Labor Day, right? We'll just take it one day at a time. Starting now. Fresh start."

I shook my head, a smile curving my lips. "Our origin story is a little warty, but the best ones always are. I'd like to think we're adult enough that we can acknowledge our tragic backstory but still move forward."

Adam leaned closer. "Does moving forward involve kissing you again? Because I would like that very much," he said, his eyes on my lips.

"I definitely think that's in the cards."

His hand traced patterns over the knee of my jeans. "You're right, fresh starts are juvenile. How about a reboot, then? I hear reboots are adult."

My heart resumed its quickened thumping, but this time it was for an entirely different, more pleasant reason. I leaned forward, my mouth within brushing distance. "Why not? It's all the rage," I teased against his lips. "It's like producers can't come up with an original idea without plundering the treasure chest of our misspent youth."

His hands trailed up my arms, cupping my face. "Keep talking nerdy to me, Barnes. See where it gets you," he murmured, his voice going all husky.

I ran my hand over his soft T-shirt, the muscles beneath taut and warm. "I'd very much like to see where it gets me," I whispered, tracing the line of his jaw and savoring the scratch of stubble across my fingertips. "But I should warn you," I purred as I abandoned his face in favor of burying my hands in his sandy locks, "I'm a hair puller."

....

The Stronghold of Isabella Barnes

I shoved the last of the Pop-Tart into my mouth, savoring the perfect ratio of candy-coated frosting and fudge. Behind me, Portia made an audible noise of distress. I whirled on her. "You do you. I'll do me. No more beets—you promised."

Portia nodded solemnly. Then, because she was Portia, perfection incarnate, she pointed at the corner of her mouth and then to mine. "You've got something . . ."

Rolling my eyes, I was saved the need to return fire as Cordy barreled into the kitchen. Her raven hair, wet and shining, was piled haphazardly atop her head and there was a "let's do this" gleam in her eyes that, frankly, scared me.

"Do you really think it's a good idea to confront Mom about personal accountability when you've got one of those?" Portia asked, gesturing to Cordy's neck.

I followed the direction of Portia's finger, and—"Is that a hickey?"

Cordy's hand flew to her collarbone. "Damn it," she sighed. "Be right back."

Portia and I waited until she cleared the kitchen to start laughing.

"Don't suppose you've got a matching one from Adam?" Portia teased.

"No, I do not. Hickeys are for sex-crazed teenagers. And Cordy. Apparently."

We dissolved into giggles again, only marginally pulling it together when Cordy reappeared with a higher-necked T-shirt and a glare. "You two finished?"

"It's a sad state of affairs when Cordy is the voice of reason," I drawled. Portia made a valiant attempt to stifle her laughter, but biting down on one's lip can only get you so far.

"I liked it better when you two were polite but distant toward each other," Cordy huffed. "I thought we were ganging up on Mom today." With more flounce than flourish, she went over to the oven and withdrew a tray of pastries that perfumed the air with a mouth-watering blend of orange blossom and vanilla.

"We are," Portia said smoothly. "But you sidetracked the proceedings when you came downstairs with a hickey the size of a PopSocket." She leaned forward, her hair falling in a golden curtain over her pale lilac silk blouse. "Did it hurt?"

I stepped between them, holding my hands up like a TV hostage negotiator. "Would you two give it a rest? Dad's ploy to keep Mom in the garden isn't going to hold forever. You can only ask someone the answers to the *Times* crossword puzzle so many times before they fake a gastrointestinal emergency. Save your verbal cage-fighting skills for Mom."

"I told you she got some last night." Cordy winked at Portia. "She's so sassy."

I stared at my sisters with a bewildered expression. "Wha—what are you talking about? I didn't 'get any.'" Truth be told, I actually hadn't. Adam and I had gone as far as two reasonably responsible people could go without having contraception in the house. An oversight that Adam had apologized profusely for until we'd both dissolved into laughter at the fact that we used to carry such things around in our wallets and now we carried punch cards for our favorite coffee joints instead. Not quite the ending to the evening I'd been envisioning—but in some ways the night had been just right. Besides, it was going to be worth it to watch Adam's eyelids flap like window shades again the next time he saw me naked.

"Well, not a hickey," Portia said, rolling her eyes at Cordy. "But you got a little something something. The contentment is radiating off you."

"Agreed," chimed in Cordy. "It's got you all take-charge and salty. I like it."

"Yeah, I'm super content you two are acting like asshats right now," I grumped. "Can we stick to our original plan of a unified front? Caring and concerned, but firm."

"She and Adam made up," Cordy confided to Portia. "And made out. A lot."

I groaned, covering my face with my hands. "Remind me why you're my favorite sister?"

Portia huffed. "That's unfair. I should be back in the running. I'm doing dinner theater for you."

"You're doing dinner theater to settle your blood feud with Candace," I corrected. "Consider it penance for the number you did on her employment contract."

"Portia's doing dinner theater?" Cordy gleefully rubbed her hands together. "It's not even my birthday."

"Miranda's right," Portia said quickly, the apples of her cheeks pinking up. "We don't want to waste this opportunity."

"Oh, we are so talking about this later," Cordy crowed. "It's been years since you—"

"Cord," I said, pushing a two-tone note of warning and pleading into my voice.

"Right, Operation: Make Mom Act Like a Grown-Ass Woman is a go," said Cordy, expertly balancing her plate of bribes.

"Stick to the plan," I begged as I grabbed the recyclable tote with its weighty contents and hefted it on my shoulder. "Portia, no making Mom cry."

"Fine," Portia muttered. "Tie my hands."

Without any additional sisterly bickering, we slipped single file out the back door and into the garden, the scent of honeysuckle carried on the breeze. A goldfinch lifted its head, dandelion yellow wings flashing in the sun, decided we meant no harm and went back to drinking from the stone birdbath. Basking in front of a backdrop of righteously red phlox sat the queen of the garden in a wide-brimmed sun hat. Her summer king sat beside her, doing a number on the spine of his crossword puzzles book.

At our approach, Isabella Barnes lifted a brow, her makeup light but in place. Gone was the pale, rumpled woman I'd seen curled up in the hospital bed. This woman had gone to the trouble of using brow filler. "Is this an ambush?" she asked, her voice mild.

"Think of it as an intervention," Cordy said, and held out a plate. "With scones."

Mom reluctantly accepted one, and without looking at Dad, she said, "I suppose you were the honeypot tasked with luring me out here?"

"You've always been a sucker for a pretty face, darling," Dad murmured. "I'm just lucky it's mine that does the trick." He reached over and took her hand. "Hear us out, Iz."

I looked over at Portia, whose delicate hands were balled into fists at her sides. I slid forward and brushed my hand against hers, just the barest hint of contact, to remind her I was there. Portia's fingers unfurled as she drew a deep breath and faced our mother square on. "We love you so much. But we were frightened by what happened the other night."

Mom started to protest, but Portia, her mouth as thin and sharp as a scythe, shook her head and said, "Please let me finish. We know this diagnosis hasn't been easy for you. We know it's scary, and we're all scared too, but"—Portia's measured voice wavered—"we love you and we want you to be around for years to come."

"I plan to be around for many years to come," Mom said dryly, eyeing the lot of us like we were an active wasp's nest and she was uncertain from whence the next sting would come.

"But that might not happen if you don't face this head-on," Cordy chimed in.

"What do you mean, if I don't face this head-on?" Isabella demanded, her voice cool as the iced tea in her glass. "I got dehydrated. I fainted. End of story."

I cleared my throat. "Mom, this isn't really about the other night. It's about taking care of yourself and putting your health first. It's not just us who have noticed either. Dr. Wu mentioned she recommended pushing up your surgery."

She waved her hand dismissively. "I want to make sure that your father and I could still go away to Scotland for our anniversary in September."

"Oh, Iz," Dad began. "We talked about this."

"Don't you, 'oh, Iz' me, Peter Barnes. I don't want your pity," my mother sniffed, casting an imperious glance in our direction, "and I certainly don't need any running commentary on how I choose to address my illness."

"That's the problem, Mom," I sputtered. "You're not addressing it. You're ducking it."

For a moment, her eyes blazed with defiance, and in them I saw Portia's resolve, Cordy's confidence, and my own pigheaded stubbornness. But rather than cower before this maternal glare, I leaned directly into its path, daring her to say otherwise. Beside me, I felt Cordy and Portia standing strong. "Am I one of those mothers that pries into any of your affairs? Do I dictate how to live your lives?"

I opened my mouth but Portia jumped back into the fray. "Let's not wander from the point," she said briskly. "This is about you and your life right now."

"Don't you take that tone with me, Portia Livingston Barnes."

My eyes widened. Wow, Mom was going right for the throat with Portia's full name. Poor Porsche. As the eldest, she'd been tapped to carry on Mom's maiden name. I'd gotten a much better shake on the middle name front.

"Well, what tone should I take with someone who's insisting on—"

"Porsche," I said softly, shaking my head. I turned to my mother. "Mom, we love you. We're not trying to meddle. But we're all scared shitless right now."

Mom sank back into her wicker throne. "Cancer took my mother. Stole everything I loved about her and whittled her down to a husk. I won't let cancer do that to me. I won't let you girls see me like that. Planning the centennial, going away for my anniversary, having you girls home for Thanksgiving and Christmas—I'm not willing to let cancer take those from me. If this is my last year on this earth, I'll go out my way."

"Mom," Cordy said softly, "you don't have to go out like Grandma Bea. They caught her cancer too late."

"You have a good prognosis," I added, gently. "But you can't let this cancer sit inside of you, expecting it to stay dormant until you call it up to do your bidding. It's not one of your centennial committee minions."

Portia and Cordy stared at me. I shrugged. Mom's mouth quirked into an almost smile. We spoke the same language. "It's time for you to go boss your cancer around too."

"We're not asking for huge concessions here," Portia said, firmly steering the conversation back on track. "Just call Dr. Wu and get your surgery scheduled sooner. I'm sure Dad can move the anniversary trip, right?"

Dad nodded. "Of course we can."

"We will be right by your side, Mom," Cordy added. "You're going to have the whole Barnes clan in your cheering section as you kick cancer to the curb."

"I don't need you making a fuss over me," Mom said.

"Well, too bad," Portia said. "We're family and this is how we roll." She looked over at me and I nodded approvingly.

Mom stared out over her hydrangeas, their purply blue blossoms heavy, but not quite bowing the bushes with their weight. She studied her snapdragons, their petals soft and pink and begging to be touched. Finally, her gaze landed back on us, the children she'd tended and watered and nurtured all these years. "I'm afraid," she said in a small voice. "I'm afraid that once I go down this road, I can't turn back. Today it's surgery, but what if it's chemo and radiation tomorrow? I don't want some half life." She wiped at her eyes where tears had caught like dew on a spider's web. "I certainly don't want to walk down Main Street and watch everyone pitying me," she added fiercely.

"I'm pretty sure no one would dare pity you," Cordy interjected. "Not to your face anyway. You're too scary for that."

I bit my lip and pretended to admire the patina forming on the sundial.

"We're getting ahead of ourselves," Dad said, drawing an arm around Mom. "One step at a time, my darling."

"But there's so much more I want to do with my life, Peter. I'm not ready for this. It couldn't have come at a worse time."

"I don't think it ever comes at a good time," he said, pulling her close. "You're still going to do all of the things you want to do with your life. You just have to cross this one off the list first."

"How about I sweeten the pot?" I reached into the tote and withdrew a three-ring binder that contained a copy of my manuscript. I'd finally gotten it to a place where it was readable by another human, and I'd spent the wee hours of the morn printing it out on our ancient printer and three-hole punching it.

Mom's eyes, which still had a watery cast to them, sparkled with delight. "I don't believe that's sweetening the pot so much as making good on what you owe." Still, she held out her hands for it.

"You know, I could play hardball with this," I said, holding it just out of her reach. "Pull a queen of air and darkness like Portia—"

"Hey!" Portia cried.

"I also believe that Portia would advise me that I'm well within my rights to hold on to this until you actually have the surgery, but"—I handed it to my mother—"I know you'll move it up the first chance you get."

"Darling," my mother sniffed with the regal air of a queen, "you're a rank amateur when it comes to guilting family." Still, she hugged the binder to her chest. "Very well. I will move it up. After the centennial," my mother said firmly.

"Right after the centennial," we echoed in agreement.

"Which you will let us help with," I added.

"Pains in the ass. The whole lot of you," my mother declared. She turned to Dad. "How did we raise such headstrong, stubborn girls?"

"We had great role models," Portia, Cordy and I chorused, in perfect unison.

My parents shared a commiserating but somehow fond glance.

"Well, go and fetch my tablet," the queen of the summer garden commanded. "There's no time like the present to get started on my centennial punch list."

And, once more in perfect unison, we groaned.

ACT THREE

....

August

Scene Twenty-Five

Will's Island

With just forty-eight hours to go until the kickoff of the centennial, Bard's thrummed with an energy that imbued its residents with the ability to walk faster, talk faster and crank like an overcaffeinated writer on deadline. Windows and lampposts that were bare at breakfast were adorned with event posters and banners by lunchtime. Smiling sprites and pixies appeared in the freshly weeded flower beds for the children's fairy walk. Tents billowed in the summer wind and rows upon rows of booths stood at attention. And in anticipation of the onslaught of Bardolators, some of the townsfolk had already busted out their best corsets, farthingales, doublets, hose and British accents.

Seeing the town blossom like this made all the work worth it. There hadn't been one night this week that I'd crawled into bed before midnight. Wresting control of the final punch list from my mother had been like trying to take Puck's favorite tug toy away—I nearly lost an arm and my dignity. But with Cordy and Portia at my side, we'd persevered.

When not begrudgingly rehearsing for dinner theater, Portia employed her uncanny knack for plowing through administrative red tape and razing obstacles to the ground like a conquering queen.

I'd like to believe that whole story about her making Ethyl Roberts, a long-time zoning clerk, ugly cry was an exaggeration. Just like I liked to pretend that every time I used a dangling modifier, a word fairy didn't die, she was just sleeping.

By stark comparison, Cordy employed a much softer touch, coaxing and calming the booth exhibitors and festival vendors into compliance. I suspected pastry was involved and fervently hoped Cordy hadn't slipped half the town a mood-altering substance in her special triple chocolate bribery brownies.

But finally, Saturday had arrived. Other than the final few dress rehearsals, I was officially done with my centennial duties for the week and could focus on . . . other things. With that firmly in mind, I slipped into the cool darkness of the high school's basement, a sprinkle of golden sawdust floating in the air and the rhythmic bang of a hammer greeting me. Holding a pastry bag in one hand and coffee strong enough to burn a hole in a worktable in the other, I admired the solitary figure's back, the way his muscles strained beneath his T-shirt as he hammered away, giving him the appearance of a modern-day Thor.

As if he could sense the steam rising off my thoughts, Adam turned.

"Brought you something sweet," I said, waving the bag.

"You sure did," he murmured, his eyes taking in my faded *Once Upon a Mattress* raglan with a hunger that had nothing to do with pastries.

He crossed the distance, sliding his arms around my waist. Pulling me close, he grazed my lower lip before surging forward to claim my mouth. I groaned softly as my hips ground against his. His hand slid over my thighs. "Have I ever told you how much I adore your legs, Barnes? I just want to wrap them around me," he said, backing me up against a sawhorse. "I suppose I could take those bags from you, but the thought of you having no free hands, entirely at my mercy—"

The back door banged open, a familiar whistle hitting me like a December squall—

"Hey, Adam, I found those—" My dad stopped, nearly dropping his recyclable tote. "Screws," he finished weakly, taking in my red face and Adam's proximity to all of my . . . parts. "I'll just go . . . put them . . . somewhere . . . back there." Without meeting my eyes, he stumbled toward the prop room. When he'd cleared the threshold, disappearing behind a giant cauldron, I whacked Adam's shoulders.

"You didn't think to mention my dad was here?" I hissed.

"I didn't think he'd be back from the hardware store so soon, and you were wearing that T-shirt—I completely lost control of my ability to make responsible adult choices." He gazed up at me through golden lashes. "You do things to me, woman. I almost ran a table saw through my hand this morning thinking about you."

"You think about me with my dad working ten feet away from you?" I wrinkled my nose.

Adam's smile was rueful, but not altogether repentant. "Can't stop thinking about you. Besides, it's not like he knows what I'm thinking."

"He does now, grabby hands," I groused. "Here," I said, handing him the bag of sandwiches and travel cup. "I got two. Maybe you could give one to my father as a 'sorry I singed your eyes with a sight that can never be unseen' gesture."

"You're just going to leave me here? With him?" Adam said, his eyes going wide.

"Yup," I said, not even feigning remorse. "I'm off to the final costume check with Tillie to ensure that Byron hasn't talked her into a last-minute codpiece."

"Well, there goes my appetite." Adam frowned. "Guess Pete can have his pick of these. See you at the landing tonight at seven thirty?" Adam asked, brightening. "I'm excited to finally meet the infamous Ian."

I hadn't exactly been hiding Ian from Adam, but my partner had promptly buried himself in work as he pushed through the last vestiges of his breakup with Mathilde, and I wanted to respect his process. Also, he'd sort of been slacking on basic personal hygiene. While I could easily overlook that, I didn't want that to be Adam's first impression of my best friend. "Careful what you wish for," I teased and pulled him in for one last searing kiss.

"THAT'S WHAT YOU'RE wearing?" I eyed Ian's moss green pants and leather thong sandals. "Were there no shirts left in town?" I asked, keeping my voice loud enough to be heard over the partygoers at the dock.

"Why would I cover this up?" he asked, running his hands over his bare chest. "You think I work out for my health or something?" Ian cocked his head, his crown of gilded antlers catching the light.

"What are you supposed to be?"

"I'll have you know I'm a cervitaur—half deer, half man. Try and keep up, Barnes." He cocked his head at me. "What are you?" he asked, gesturing to my silvery ballet dress with whimsically cut tulle petals for the skirt. He fingered the translucent arm pieces that swathed my arms in trailing leaves, delicate as spider silk, and then pointed to the circlet of silver for my hair that held even my wild crimson waves at bay.

I spun around so he could see the gossamer wings. "Fairy of the wood," I said, turning back around and frowning down at my feet. I loved everything about the costume Tillie had made special for me except these sandals. They were an affront to footwear, looking like they'd been woven together from wisps of silky fabric and prayer. I'd certainly kill myself on the tree roots before the night was over, but at least I would die looking ethereally lovely.

"Adam is going to keel over when he sees you," Ian assured me. "I can still give him the surrogate big brother work over though, right?" Ian asked.

"Putting aside the fact that nobody takes you seriously with that facial turf? He knows Portia. In terms of older sibs, it doesn't get more terrifying than that."

"Fair point," Ian conceded. "But can I at least be a little standoffish? I'm not sure I can help myself from emitting that 'you'll never be good enough for her' vibe. It's coded into my BFF DNA." He grinned at me. "Remind me of the protocol for this party?"

"First, don't drink the homemade hooch. I know it's pink and bubbly and smells like flowers, but that stuff will leave you with a face-melting hangover for days. Stick to something where you can identify the ingredients."

"Where's the fun in that?" Ian demanded.

"Second, if for some reason we get separated, the last ferry leaves at midnight, not five past midnight. If you don't make it on, you can either swim home or sleep in the costume cabin and call a friend to bail you out in the morning."

"Why would we get separated?" Ian waggled his eyebrows.

"Because you're a shameless skirt chaser, the alcohol will be flowing and everyone's in costume," I said, ticking each reason off on my fingers.

"Fair enough. Don't drink the hooch or miss the boat home."

"Words to live by," a familiar voice said. I turned around to find Adam. Now, I'd never been one for Victorian romances, never swooned over puffed white shirts or the pants that I maintained were the early cousins of hipster skinny jeans. Top hats didn't thrill me, and I was bored by purely-for-show canes. But Bard help me, Adam looked like Sherlock Holmes—not the Cumberbatch version, but the grittier Robert Downey Jr. boxer version, right down to the deep burgundy vest and the shirt open at the neck beneath a swinging black overcoat.

"That's a very fetching costume, Barnes," Adam managed, taking in my barely there costume.

"You call her Barnes too?" Ian demanded.

"Since high school." Adam winked. He stared expectantly at me. Right, I was supposed to be doing introductions, not standing here ogling Adam in period costume.

"Adam, this underdressed peacock is my best friend and business partner, Ian."

"Ah, the vet," Ian said, extending a hand. "Of the dubious back-story."

"I am Jackass, MD," Adam admitted, taking Ian's hand with a grin. "At least according to Miranda's phone. Even though I technically am a DVM, not an MD—oww!"

Removing my elbow from his ribs, I asked, "Is that really the way you want to play this?"

"Don't take it personally. If it's any consolation, I'm Agent Immature," Ian sniffed. "You make one off-color joke at a launch event and—"

"'One off-color joke,' are you serious right now?" I glared at Ian and then shifted it over to Adam. "And you. We agreed we weren't going to tell people about that."

"I agreed to no such thing." Adam winked conspiratorially at Ian. Without looking at me, he took hold of my hand, his thumb absently running circles over my palm.

"I heard you have a boat," Ian said. "How come we're not on it?"

"It's my father's boat," Adam clarified. "I don't drive it that often and dockside parking will be at a premium, so Miranda graciously agreed we should take the ferry over."

"For the safety of everyone," I said solemnly as the crowd began to shift as we started the boarding process.

If I'd ever worried about what it would be like when my best friend met the guy who made my heart race, I needn't have bothered. On the short ferry ride over, I barely got a word in as Ian and Adam discussed everything from the restrictive nature of Elizabethan-era socks to obscure Kolsch beers. For my part, I sat between them, enjoying their banter and allowing myself to wonder if this wouldn't make for a great future state, to be sandwiched between one's two favorite guys. I pictured us in downtown Boston, the three of us in a back corner of some Ian-selected wine establishment, talking until last call. But I shut it down as quickly as it started. How would that work with Adam in Seattle and me here? I needed to focus on what I had with Adam right now and not on anything else. Great strategy, Barnes.

As the island came into view, I elbowed Ian. "Heavy on the merriment, light on the debauchery. There will be kids at this thing."

Ian ignored me, leaping to his feet and leaning over the side of the boat, his face lit up like a little kid's. "Is this where the mainstages will be?"

I nodded as I joined him. "The amphitheater is closed off tonight for the party. But you'll see it next week." While the centennial kicked off in two days on the first Monday in August, the mainstages ran from Thursday through Saturday of both weeks, meaning I'd have a bit of time early in the week to enjoy the centennial activities.

"Did any of your"—Ian waggled his eyebrows and mouthed the word "book" so that only I could see it—"take place here?"

I shook my head. "No, but at some point, I'll show you the Meadows."

"I'd like that."

I glanced sideways at my partner. I still hadn't worked up the nerve to tell him that after much consideration, editing and handwringing, I'd finished Elf Shot. There wasn't going to be another book, and that was a problem contractually and financially. Whether it was the fear of thinking I'd disappoint him or the fear that he'd try and talk me into another book, I wasn't quite sure. All I knew is, my insides churned every time I thought about telling him. But for now, that was a future Miranda problem.

We gamely followed the train of partygoers up the winding path through the twinkle-lit woods to the clearing atop the island, where a floating dance floor waited. Each corner of the square was flanked by a towering column of birch, wound tight with lights. Strings dotted with star-shaped lanterns connected the columns and crossed the center in X patterns, giving the impression of an open-air lightbox.

Winding paths of pillar candles lit the way from the dance floor to Cordy's dessert offerings and the aforementioned hooch, served in a giant copper cauldron. I pointed to it wordlessly, looked over at Ian and shook my head. Then I jerked my head toward the bar, where the high school drama coach, dressed like a monk, was serving up beer and wine in exchange for donations for the fall musical.

I didn't recognize the all-female band dressed as pixies, but I could appreciate the "Ordinary World" cover they were picking their way through as couples of all ages danced beneath the star-speckled night sky in bare feet and boots. Off in the distance, a group of teen fairies had built a bonfire and were lighting off paper lanterns, their wavering husks weaving toward the clouds.

"Wow." Ian whistled softly beside me. "It's an orgy of lights."

"Light on debauch," I reminded him as we headed toward the dessert table, where a mortal-eating ice queen in icicle-pick heels stood laughing with a sugar plum fairy whose rainbow wings were made out of real lollipops. I knew, because I'd licked one this morning.

I waved to Portia and Cordy, who beamed back, waving in that synchronized sisterly way. "You guys hungry?" I asked my male companions. "I'm pretty sure the Northeast is about to plunge into a months-long sugar shortage, but it was worth it. The Oberon opera cakes are life changers."

"Don't have to ask me twice," Ian said, rubbing his hands together. "Cordy, my culinary love, I've missed you," he called out, and she ran over to him for a bear hug.

Best friend entertained, I turned to Adam. "Food or booze?"

He shook his head, the light illuminating the barley and honey tones in his hair. "Dance with me, Barnes?" Adam held out a hand and led me onto the dance floor just as the band struck up a Crowded House cover. His arms encircled my waist, sliding over the gauzy fabric. I shivered, enjoying the heat of his hands.

I pressed in closer, drinking in the clean smell of his skin as it mingled with the smoke of the bonfire and the tang of the grass. "I could do this all night," I said, then added as an afterthought, "as long as you don't step on my feet. I will cry if you step on my feet."

"Wouldn't dream of it," he murmured, bending his head to brush a kiss across my lips.

I surveyed the other couples on the dance floor, waving at Dan and Aaron, the former dressed like a proper Victorian and the latter in forest green wings and laurel crown, and Sheriff Eddie Knight, my pitch-perfect Malvolio, and his wife, Camilla, both looking like they'd stepped out of a Victorian daguerreotype.

We swayed as the band moved from Crowded House to Lorde, Adam taking the up-tempo opportunity to twirl me. I laughed, my hair and wings swinging out behind me, my dress swirling around my knees. He pulled me in, brushing a sweet sweep of his lips across mine, just right for a dance floor packed with friends and family. "I love the way you smile when you think no one is watching, Barnes."

"How could I not? It's the Saturday night before the centennial, my punch list is done, I've got an amazing cast ready to put on a flawless *Twelfth Night*, my best friend is here and I'm dancing with a devastatingly handsome Victorian gentleman."

"You think so?" he said, half purring, half growling into my ear.

"Definitely the first part. Verdict is still out on the gentleman aspect," I teased, pulling him down so I could reciprocate the whisper. "But I'm not sure I want you to be a gentleman anyway." I ran my hands over the fabric of his vest.

"As my fairy queen wishes," Adam replied, one hand meandering down from my hip to my—

"Well, if it isn't my favorite rump-fed runion and my decidedly less cranky directorial muse," Byron crowed from beside us. He'd gone full fae, rivaling Ian for the amount of visible pectoral expanse and donning what equated to leather hot pants and a pair of black wire wings. If the *300* franchise devolved into a fairy spin-off, this would be its aesthetic.

Cat, absolutely killing it in an indigo steampunk dress, complete with a monocle and black lace gloves, rolled her eyes. "And if we would like our director to remain cheerful, maybe we could give her some space."

"Yes," Adam agreed, "like the opposite end of the dance floor, the bottom of the lake or even another zip code. But only you, Byron. The lady can stay."

"Come on, Winters, I'm happy for you two. This 'will they or won't they' side drama was fun to bet on and all, but—"

"You bet on us?" I interjected.

"Beside the point," Byron said smoothly. "All I'm saying is, try not to blow it."

"Right back at you, you stewed prune." Adam smirked. He inclined his head to Cat. "Just remember, you're too good for him."

"Always," she assured him with a tinkling laugh as she led a still-protesting Byron to a corner of the dance floor.

"This is what you get for casting him as a duke. It's gone to his head," Adam grumbled, but he was smiling.

We laughed and danced together until the band announced they were taking a short break. Thoroughly parched, we headed toward the bar, where we saw Ian attempting to charm Candace.

"Oh man, your partner is barking up the wrong tree," Adam whispered, his lips tickling my ears. "Do we tell him?"

"Absolutely not. I want to see how this plays out."

"Heartless, Barnes. At least let me go wingman. I like Ian."

"And I like Candace," I protested. "But I appreciate your budding solidarity. Go for it," I told him, trying to ignore the swell of affection I felt for Adam in that moment. "Grab me some bubbles while you're at it, please?"

While Adam played wingman, I basked in the smell of pine and the sounds of joy. Though I was not normally one for parties, I felt at ease here, or at least the most at ease I was ever going to feel while dressed as a half-naked fairy queen.

I caught up with my parents and sisters, and then with Tillie, Alice, Opal and Jazz, who'd gone in together on a seasonal fairy theme. I didn't want to play favorites, but Jazz's autumn fairy with her blazing crimson wings and golden skirts were winning the night. I even managed to slip down to the costume cabin where the props were kept and do a final spot-check on everything. Because I was nerdy like that.

By the time I'd run down to the cabin and back, it was fully dark outside and the band had returned, stirring up the crowd with a revved-up version of "Hungry Like the Wolf." I found Adam over with Emmeline McGandry, Portia's zoning board nemesis and one of Adam's patients. Well, her trio of cats, Lucy, Ethel and Hazel, were his patients. I joined in their shared laughter as Adam put his arm around my waist and Emmeline described her one and only disastrous attempt at trying to walk her feline pack on leashes. There had been a revolt of sorts involving claws.

"I'll be marveling about the logistics of that one for a while," I whispered to Adam after Emmeline had headed for the bar.

"Me too," he whispered back, kissing my temple. "Cats were not made for leashes."

"Truer words have seldom been spoken. Seen Ian?"

"He's around."

"Around?" I echoed.

"He struck out admirably with Candace, and last I saw, he was talking Del's ear off about craft beers."

"For the best," I said.

"For the best," Adam agreed.

"We should remind him about the last ferry. I'm about ready to call it a night. Can we take the next ferry out? My feet are barking in these sandals and I—damn it."

"What's wrong?" Adam asked, frowning.

"I left my phone and keys at the costume cabin when I snuck down for a final prop check," I groaned.

"Why don't I run down for you?" Adam offered. "You can have some more time with Ian, say your goodbyes to everyone. Besides, if I keep staring at you in that costume—well, it's kind of like staring at the sun. I'll go blind and senseless."

I leaned forward, kissing him soundly. "That's very sweet of you to offer. How about I go with you? You'll never find my stuff. I tossed it . . . somewhere."

"All right, we'll be back before anyone knows we're gone. The quickest of detours." He turned on his phone flashlight and we picked our way back down the hill, Adam regaling me with his favorite parts of Ian's crash and burn with Candace. Slipping into the cabin, I shucked out of the feet-eating footwear, savoring the bare floor beneath me. "I'll take the back room, you take the front," I told him.

After a few minutes, Adam called out, "Found them. I just had to think, where would I stash my stuff if I was a brilliant but short-on-time director? The answer is the scarves bin, in case you're wondering."

Standing in the warm light of the cabin with Adam, his hair gleaming like late summer honey and his eyes so perfectly earnest, all of my resolve to go back up that hill crumbled. Instead, a slow, steady need kindled low in my stomach. Wordlessly, I crossed the floor and locked the door, the click loud and deliberate.

"Barnes?"

Padding softly across the floor, I rose up on my toes to kiss him. Just a quick sweep of my mouth over his. "A slightly longer detour, I think," I said, this time pressing my lips to his and savoring the sweetness of punch I found there. With my tongue, I traced the map of his mouth, grazing my teeth over his bottom lip and nipping lightly. Then I stepped back to admire my handiwork.

Adam stared at me, face half-lit and half-shadowed in the moonlight, his lips slightly parted, with an expression that was equal parts dumbstruck and delight.

"Scratch that," I said, offering him a saucy grin as I moved in close again, running my hands up his chest. "A much longer detour," I whispered against his mouth. His lips curved into a smile and parted. His tongue found mine as he pulled me to him, his hands running up and down the length of my bare arms in time to the rhythm of his kiss. A rhythm, I might add, that was downright devastating and dizzying all at once.

Coming up for air, I trailed my fingertips over the heavy brocade of his crimson vest. "This is very much in my way," I admonished him in mock disapproval. With quick fingers, I proceeded to relieve him of his coat, vest, undershirt—by the Bard—how many layers of clothes was this man wearing?

With a soft laugh at my exasperated expression, Adam turned my face up to his, sealing his mouth over mine and deepening the kiss again, this time moving those hands up the length of my back, over my shoulder blades, back down to the curve of my hips. With one deft motion, he hoisted me onto the dressing table, one hand steadying me and the other slipping beneath the silky fabric of my dress to stroke my breast.

I leaned against the mirror, arching my back, and as Adam tugged at my dress, what little remained of the structural integrity of the fairy garb gave way. Cool air claimed my bare skin, sparking a shiver up my spine as Adam's mouth trailed hot, teasing kisses down my throat and lower, over my collarbone. I bit down on my lip, trying not to giggle, until he reached my breasts, flicking his tongue over my nipples. I gave up, letting out a gasp as I pulled him to me, my hands winding in his hair as his talented mouth worked each breast in a delicious teasing motion that had me twisting beneath his touch.

"Pants, pants, pants," I muttered, fumbling with his not-quite-true-to-period trousers. "Did people just not have sex in the Victorian era?" I fumed. With a triumphant cry, I managed to undo whatever overly complicated buttons were holding them in place and—wow. It had been a while and—just wow. I grinned up at Adam with a positively filthy expression.

He buried his head back between my breasts, murmuring, "That's one of the things I love most about you, Barnes. I never know what you'll say next." He resumed that maddening game with my nipples, flicking his tongue over one, nipping at the other. A game that had me squirming beneath him, but a game that two could play.

With a wicked grin, I slid one hand between us, my hand finding him. Gently, I encircled him with my fingers and stroked up and down until I was no longer the only one breathing hard on that dressing table.

"You're just full of surprises, Barnes," Adam said.

"Condoms," I panted. "We're going to need condoms."

"You mean you don't have any in that armada of a bag?" he asked, and I swear he was smirking against my cleavage.

"No, that's my theater bag. Why would I have condoms in my theater bag?" My eyes widened in horror as I thunked my head back against the mirror. "Wait, do we not have condoms? Again?"

Adam lifted his head, his expression unreadable. "Well, I didn't want to be one of those guys who always has a condom at the ready, but after last time—"

I slapped his shoulder. "Do you have one or not?"

His smile was downright smug. "I have one."

"Excellent," I sighed in utter relief, sliding a hand down him.

He groaned, pulling away. "Hold that thought. A wild woman ripped the pants from my body. They're around here somewhere."

I muttered about a dozen of those words that nice people don't say as Adam searched for his pants. And I was never so relieved as when his hand shot up in the air, a silver packet between his fingers.

He rose slowly, running his hands up the inside of my legs as I stretched them wide to make way for him. When he was fully standing there between my thighs, he leaned in to kiss me. My hands encircling his neck, I wrapped my legs around him, hooking my ankles, and pulled him against me.

He inhaled sharply, stroking my cheek, then trailing his hands down the curve of my breast and settling between my thighs. With long, capable fingers he slipped inside of me, working me slowly at first and then picking up speed. Moving deeper, he put a finger right on that tiny pulsing spot and bright splashes of color exploded across my field of vision. My back arched and my mouth came down hard on his, gasping in surprise.

"Stay with me, Barnes," Adam murmured, drawing back to watch my face. His motions quickened until I was rocking my hips against him, my back pressed up against the cool glass of the mirror.

"My turn," I breathed and reached for him again, stroking, teasing my fingers up and down the length of him. He groaned, leaning into my touch and giving himself over to it. I flashed him a wicked grin and wrapped my hand around him, sliding up and down in smooth strokes, eventually yielding to harder, more urgent motions.

When I was sure he was approaching that point of no return, I twined my free hand in his sweaty hair, pulling his mouth to mine. "Now," I whispered. "I want you now."

Adam pressed his forehead against mine. "Are you sure?"

I tightened the circle of my legs around his back. "Yes, yes, yes."

With a grin, Adam tore open the foil packet and readied himself while I traced ragged circles over his back. Shifting his weight forward, he gently guided my hips over him, settling into me. I sighed happily and wasting no time, the two of us quickly found our groove—a steady, driving rhythm that brought my entire body to electrifying, jolting awareness.

I closed my eyes, sinking into that delicious, building feeling of oneness. Adam's hands were beneath me, curved around my ass and tightening as we moved together, while mine spanned the smooth cords of his back muscles, rising up and down in time with the roll of my hips.

We rode together, the pace quickening and the urgency growing with each of Adam's thrusts until that white hot tremor sparked within me and caught fire. Frantic, I snapped my hips against him, he answered, driving deeper and faster. My eyes flew open and I let out a sharp, shuddering gasp. Adam's gaze was locked on my face, his hazel eyes wide. Looking at me like I was the whole damn world.

I cried out and came. I came so hard my left foot cramped, but I didn't care, I just pulled him into me as I came, shouting what I'm sure was brilliant literary nonsense. Adam gripped me tightly, both of us cresting and falling over the edge.

We sort of slid off the dressing room table after that and onto the floor in a sweaty, satisfied tangle of limbs.

In the ensuing silence, I thought for one terrible moment it might be awkward between us. But Adam chased it away, pulling me close against him and pressing soft kisses against my collarbone. He sighed happily, the breath tickling the hollow of my throat. "I think you broke me, Barnes."

"Well, you definitely broke my costume," I snickered. "As open-minded as everyone is around here, I don't think going back to the party nude is an option."

"Worth it," he grunted. "When I regain control of my legs, we'll go find you something else to wear. It was very convenient of you to take advantage of me in the costume and props cabin."

"All part of my plan," I said, leaning my head on his chest.

"Well, I'm all yours. Do with me as you will."

"Oh, I plan to," I grinned at him wickedly, and pulled his mouth down to mine again.

Scene Twenty-Six

....

The Shanna-Banana

I awoke staring into the face of an ass head, its marbled eyes reflecting a miniature naked version of me, complete with unmistakable sex hair. Yelping, I shot up, inadvertently smacking into the warm body that lay beside me. Adam let out an indignant cry and startled awake.

"What the—" But he stopped as his gaze settled on the furry head of Bottom. He burst into rolling peals of laughter, laughing even harder as I pointed first to the bed and then the curved canopy of greenery and flowers that arced above us.

"We had sex in a bower," I managed, wiping at my eyes.

"With an ass head in attendance." Adam ran a hand through his matted blond hair. He had good sex hair too, I noted with satisfaction. "How did we not notice that last night?"

"It was dark, and we were in the middle of a sex marathon?" I offered. I patted his bare arm, admiring how the sun filtering in from the tiny window—I stopped. *Sun.* "Craptarts."

"What?"

I glanced at my watch. "It's seven thirty. In the morning."

Adam squeezed his eyes shut and commenced braying like—

well, an ass. "I guess we missed the last ferry out," he said between his sad attempts to catch his breath.

"It's not funny," I insisted.

"Yes, it is. We have sex amnesia. Passed out after several incredible rounds and woke in a strange place missing time." He stretched and yawned. "I haven't felt this good since I was an undergrad."

"Doesn't change the fact we're going to need a lift off this island."

Adam reached for me. "We'll call in the cavalry. Eventually."

"WE SHOULD HAVE swum," I whispered to Adam as his family boat sidled up against the docks and a cry of hoots rose up from within. Candace was at the helm, her blond hair tucked under a navy Titania's Bower hat. Of course Candace could drive a boat. She probably knew all sorts of other useful life skills, like how to administer first aid and operate a crockpot. Clearly, Candace was a good person to have on hand for emergencies. Besides, she had contented herself with just a small smirk as she took in Adam's rumpled costume and me in the shreds of my fairy costume with Adam's dress coat over it.

Ian, on the other hand, couldn't have communicated his shit-eating grin any louder. "Thank you for texting me in your hour of need," he crowed as he jumped onto the dock.

"You and I have different ideas of the cavalry," Adam muttered.

"I knew he'd be highly motivated to find someone who'd drive your boat this early," I murmured. I squinted at the side of the boat. "The *Shanna-Banana*?"

"That's what my dad calls Shannon, my niece, his granddaughter. It started when she was little and sort of stuck."

"I'm sure teenage Shannon loves that," I muttered.

"The scorn factor is high," Adam admitted.

"And you guys told *me* not to miss the last ferry out," Ian tsked.

Candace swept past Ian with a magnificent eye roll. "Miranda, Cordy made you a special hangover tea—she said you'd know what that meant." She pressed a travel mug into my hands. "Adam, I'm supposed to tell you that the foil-wrapped croissants are heated. Does that mean something to you?"

Adam's face split into a broad smile as he took the bakery bag and his matching travel mug. "Sisterly approval. All right! This day just keeps getting better."

"Wait a second." I leaned over and sniffed Candace.

She drew back. "May I help you?"

"*You*," I said, pointing at her, "smell like *him*." I pointed at Ian.

"Of course she smells like me," Ian started. "We've been on this boat together—"

"He spent the night at my place," Candace interjected breezily.

"Plot twist," Adam called between mouthfuls of hot pastry.

"You dog," I chided Candace.

"He was just so cute," she said, batting her lashes. "He followed me home. Can I keep him?"

We both burst into decidedly unladylike guffaws.

"I think I've been used for my body," Ian said in wonderment. He turned to Adam. "I love this place!"

"Want a croissant?" Adam offered, holding one up. "Cordy packed me an extra."

"Best. Morning. Ever." Ian hooted as he made his way down to the bow of the boat.

"Nice work," I said to Candace.

"You too," she said evenly, laughing as she put the boat in reverse.

As we headed to the mainland, the sun shining on the water and Joni Mitchell warbling on the tinny radio, I stood on the starboard side, humming along and occasionally blushing at the memories of last night. Unlike Adam, I claimed no sex amnesia. While I couldn't remember the exact moment we passed out on a prop bed, setting in motion events that would enable Ian to taunt me for years to come, I could remember the way Adam's hands had mapped my body. The way he looked at me, hungry and wanting every inch of me. The way he'd held me, like I was precious and special and worth holding on to.

"A farthing for your thoughts?" Adam had maneuvered his way over to me, negotiating the gentle rocking of the boat.

"Cheapskate."

"Sovereign?"

"Now you're talking," I smiled as his arm slid around my waist, his hand resting on the curve of my hip. Something stirred in my stomach, and I had to remind my brain that we'd just had a full helping of early-morning athletic sex. "Last night was incredible, but all of this—"

"Oh no, you're not going weird on me, Barnes. Are you?"

I wasn't sure what he meant by "weird." I was generally weird to begin with. So I stuck with, "No. I just meant, having your best friend and former nemesis pick you up after a night of wild sex is a lot."

"Oh, that. Yeah, Ian's never going to let you live that down. But hey, Candace is being pretty cool about it." He kissed the top of my nose. "Can I cook you dinner tonight?"

My heart did this strange flip-flop thing. Yes, there had been some part of me that had feared it would be awkward the morning after. But he wanted to cook me dinner. "I'd like that."

"How about seven and you bring the pup? I'll make you a home-cooked meal before we eat funnel cake and fair food for the next two weeks."

"Is eating funnel cake and fair food for two weeks a problem for you?"

"Nope," he said planting another kiss on me. "I just want an excuse to see you tonight."

"It's just—" I looked back and Candace and Ian. "Word is going to get out."

"Ian, are you going to tell half the town about this?" Adam called.

Ian shrugged. "Most of the people I know in town are on this boat, so probably not."

"Candace, how about you?" Adam asked.

"I didn't tell anyone about your little tryst in the woods—why would I start now? Although I would be particularly tight-lipped if someone could cover the last hour of my ticket shift this afternoon? I've got an early evening wedding and the groom is a bit of a head case."

"I'm on it," I said.

Adam grimaced. "I would join you, but I have to drive over to Dale this afternoon and pick up an order of medical supplies. We're almost out of syringes. But it could keep a day or two."

"No way. Ian, want to sell tickets with me?"

"Will there be snacks?"

"Of course," I snorted.

"Then count me in," he said.

"What is it with you and snacks?" Adam teased.

"Happy snack, happy life."

"I'm pretty sure that's not the expression."

I shrugged. "And yet, it's so on point, it's hard to argue with it."

The *Shanna-Banana* shifted beneath us as it dipped against the wake of an oncoming boat. Adam instinctively pulled me closer, steadying me against him. I gazed up at him and found him staring back at me, neither of us saying anything, just pressing against each other and grinning like loons.

LATER THAT AFTERNOON, Ian and I sat in the middle of Main Street with our best customer service smiles on. Although the centennial officially started tomorrow, there were plenty of Bardolators out and in full costume, strolling up and down the street, peering into shop windows and posing for selfies.

Although Bard's had started offering event tickets online years ago, we still sold a fair amount in person each year. It probably helped that Ian and I were seated in a booth made to look like a puppet show stage and were decked out in period garb I'd snagged from Tillie. Mine was more serving wench than fine lady and Ian's was more pirate than nobleman, but it worked.

"So," Ian said, neatening up the piles of tickets. "How was it?"

"We're in the middle of Main Street. I am not talking about last night with you. I'm a lady."

"A lady who had sex in a costume barn and had to be rescued in the *Shanna-Banana*?"

"It was a cabin, not a barn." Dropping my voice, I added. "Okay, fine, the sex was amazing."

"And?"

"And I am not going into details."

"That's not what I meant," Ian prodded. "I mean, are you freaking out?"

"Not presently, no. I mean, I'd prefer the whole town not find out. But yeah, I'm otherwise fine. I know things between us can't last, but I'm prepared for that."

"Why are we assuming things can't last? Now that I've seen you two together, I'm getting a vibe that you're more to each other than just a roll in the costume barn. Definitely for you and I'm pretty sure for him as well."

"Oh, in the eighteen hours that you've known him?" I teased.

"Guys can sense when other guys are into their best friends."

"Oh, is that like the average guy's version of Spidey-Sense?" I snorted.

"There is nothing average about this guy," Ian protested, running his hands over his chest. "Just ask Candace."

I cleared my throat and pointed to the cute couple in matching dresses approaching our booth who had clearly heard him. "I got this one," I told him. "Because you're gross."

The couple asked for the Shakespearean combo, which included tickets to all three mainstages. But when I gently suggested they might also want to check out *Romeo and Juliet* at the dinner theater, they readily agreed and upgraded to the Queen Elizabeth package, which included all shows and a free drink and appetizer at Titania's.

"I'm proud of you, Barnes," Ian murmured after the pair had happily departed with their tickets. "That was quite the upsell."

"The dinner theater is that good," I promised. "Wait until you see it tomorrow night."

"Can we go back to the Adam thing?"

"Do we have to?"

"You like him."

"I do." I patted his hand. "That's why I slept with him."

"You more than like him."

"So what if I do?" I said, my voice a little hopeless. "It's not like it's going to work outside of Bard's. I knew that going in. I'm just going to enjoy the time I do have with him."

Ian's mouth curled into a speculative smile. "We do live in a hybrid age, Barnes."

"Your point?"

"My point is long-distance relationships aren't what they used to be. Nor are traditional working environments. Look at you—you've worked this whole summer remotely. With my help, of course. I think you should at least consider the possibility that whatever this thing is with Adam, it might not have to have a Labor Day expiration date. That's all."

"Are you trying to get rid of me, partner?"

"Of course not. But I would never stand in the way of your happiness. Valhalla isn't the office, it's us. You and me, Barnes. So it doesn't matter where we are, geographically speaking. You could spend time with Adam in Seattle for weeks or even months at a time, explore a relationship, see how it feels and what it's like to live in a city that just named a hockey team after a sea monster."

"You make a valid point. I would look pretty hot in a Kraken jersey." I rearranged the ticket stacks and card reader, trying to school my face into a calm mask. So I hadn't been the only one who was starting to think that me working remotely without sinking the agency was a possibility. "But I would miss you," I insisted.

"What's not to miss?"

"I'm serious."

"I am too. But think of all the fun filters I could use on Zoom, and I'd come visit and make you two do all the cringe-worthy tourist things and demand we eat at Biscuit Bitch at least once a day. So how about you stop using the geographic divide as the insurmountable obstacle?" He turned his bright smile on the approaching gentleman in the crimson jerkin. "I got this one," he whispered.

While Ian upsold the nattily attired Bardolator, I let out the breath I hadn't known I'd been holding. It wasn't like I needed my partner's permission to work remotely, but it was a relief to hear he was so on board with it if I wanted to. The question was, did I want to?

We fielded several rounds of ticket sales, Ian turning up the charm and selling an impressive amount of Queen Elizabeths. When the line dwindled down to nothing, he turned to me with that familiar "I'm going to annoy you, but I'm going to ask anyway" Ian face.

"I don't want to talk about Adam anymore," I said, holding up a preemptive warning hand. "Move on to another topic."

Ian's smile was wicked. "Excellent transition, Barnes. I couldn't have put it better myself. Let's talk about your book. When can I read a draft?"

My face fell. My best friend had just offered me a remote partnership and a potential path forward, if I wanted it, with Adam in Seattle. And I hadn't had the decency to talk to him about something that would affect our partnership. I was a most notable coward.

"Ian, I need to tell you something."

His playful expression gave way to his intent listening face. "Of course. What's going on? Did your mother hate it? Do you need a pep talk?"

"No, my mother loved the book."

"So what's the problem?"

"I finished it."

"That's great—"

"I finished the series, Ian. I don't think I can drag it out over another book."

"Oh." He exhaled loudly. "Okay."

"Okay? We're counting on that income and—"

"How long have you been sweating telling me this?" Ian asked, his eyes narrowing.

"I dunno, a few weeks? I've been racking my brain to see if I can stretch it out over two books without a bunch of filler, but I just can't, Ian."

"Why didn't you tell me instead of tying yourself up in knots like this?" He frowned, a real honest-to-goodness look of disappointment on his face. "We're partners. We don't keep stuff like this from each other."

"I've had a lot going on," I offered lamely.

Ian fixed me with a level gaze. "I'm not angry about the book. It's no different than what we'd say to any of our writers. If you're finished, you're finished. We'll figure it out. But the fact that you didn't say anything, that you kept this from me—that hurts."

"I know. I'm sorry." I grimaced. "I already felt like I was sticking you for the summer by leaving. Then Mathilde ended things and I didn't want to pile on."

"Right, but I bounced back pretty quickly from that. What's the excuse for the rest of the time? When I was literally less than a mile away from you."

"Cowardice?"

Ian was quiet for a long moment. "Barnes, I love you. You know that, right?"

I nodded meekly, waiting for the *but* I knew was coming.

"But sometimes, it feels like you were raised by wolves. And I've met your parents. Stubborn, but definitely not *Canis lupus*. I also get that you're a middle child and want to keep everyone happy. But you can't pretend you don't have needs too. The thing is, you gotta let people in. The right people. Not the asshats. You have to learn to trust the people you pick to be close to you and be up front about your needs, otherwise you're not really in a ship together, whether that ship is a relationship, a friendship or a partnership."

"Wow, how long have you been waiting to use that one?"

"Since I realized what a wall-building, withholding pseudo-adult you can be sometimes."

"Ouch."

"I'd like to think I've done better than most people at chipping away at that facade of yours. But I'm not going to hurt you. Nor am I going to drop you like panties at a Jonas Brothers concert just because you're a human. Did you cut me loose when I was going on a one-man tear through Somerville after Natalie broke up with me?"

"I forgot the summer of your man capris." I shuddered. "Thanks for reminding me."

"Or what about the time Frankie was in that biking accident? Who slept on my couch for a week, ran our then-fledgling office and still went with me to Mass General every day?"

"Even with a fractured pelvis, your sister still held it together better than you did."

Ian waved me off with his hand. "The point is, I let you see me all man-crying and vulnerable because I never worry about whether you'd leave me at the first sign of me being a human. Being a human is totally allowed and expected with your closest friends."

"But I do share with you," I insisted. "You're the first person I called when I found out about Mom's diagnosis. I tell you lots of things."

"Just not the stuff you think is too hard for me to handle," he observed mildly. "But when it comes to stuff you want, stuff you need, you have a tendency to go sideways. Whole person, Barnes. You love the whole person. Bumps and uglies and everything."

"I'm sorry," I said. "Can you forgive me? For this level of ugly bumps?"

"Don't be ridiculous," Ian huffed, waving a hand at me. "We are not tragic YA characters who are going to spend the next sixty pages of our lives moping around and listening to what passes as emo these days. Of course I forgive you." He frowned. "Talk to me. You have that constipated look."

"That's my thinking face," I shot back. "Of course you're right—not about my face—but the trust thing. You've never let me down, Ian. You've more than earned it."

"And you will send me the manuscript. Tonight, wench."

"And I will send you the manuscript tonight, pirate," I grumbled.

"Excellent." He wiggled his fingers. "I'll have a look, and then we'll figure out how to frame this to Susannah. Together."

"Together," I echoed.

"How about a *Die Hard* marathon at the Folly tonight?"

I winced. "Dinner with Adam."

"Oh, that's way better," Ian agreed.

"I could see if—"

Ian laid his hand over mine. "No, we can do a *Die Hard* marathon anytime. Do dinner with Adam."

He didn't say it—didn't have to say it—but the implication was there. The centennial kicked off tomorrow: two weeks of fun and frivolity, a few days of cleanup and then a little time off before Labor Day. If I didn't do something about it, I'd have only about thirty days to enjoy time with Adam, and the thought struck me like a slap of cold winter's wind to the face.

"Oooh, here's an idea." Ian clapped his hands together. "You could wear your wench costume to dinner."

"Remind me why we're friends?"

"*Best* friends," he amended. "How about this instead—" And all of the humor drained out of his face. "How about you tell him how you're really feeling and what you want."

I opened my mouth to protest, but shut it, because he was right.

"And that's why we're best friends, Barnes." Ian smirked.

What's in a Main Street

Arm in arm, Adam and I walked down Main Street. Overhead, the summer night breeze jostled the old-fashioned light bulbs hanging over the street in a twinkling canopy of lights. The scents of baked apples and meat pies wafted up from the food booths in delicious greeting. Everywhere you looked, people were decked out in dresses and doublets, ruffs and collars, laughing and talking animatedly as they moved among the tents, bursting with glittering jewelry, hand-bound notebooks and feather-plumed pens.

"You look positively fetching in that dress, Barnes."

"This old thing?" I teased, smoothing down the midnight blue silk of my dress. I'd opted for an Elizabethan corset, a style that was less rigid than the classic Tudor but still emphasized my waist. I'd debated the farthingale to keep my skirts in the classic bell shape for the evening, but ultimately skipped it given that we'd be sitting most of the night. "You clean up nice too."

"I wore my nice period costume pants tonight. The ones that haven't been peed on."

I raised an eyebrow.

"By a patient," he hastily added before pulling me in for one of those searing kisses of his. "You have this glow about you to-night."

"Maybe it has something to do with the excellent dinner you fed me last night and the after-dinner activities," I teased, lightly nipping at his bottom lip.

"Oh, did you enjoy the dessert, then?" he asked, his fingers wandering down the length of the corset.

"Dessert that lasts all night is the best kind of dessert. Breakfast was lovely too."

"Waking up next to you without an ass head present is always lovely," he added.

I flushed with pleasure at the memory of waking cocooned in Adam's arms, the morning light streaming in and my bare back pressed up against his smooth chest. The way he'd smiled at me through morning mussed hair, trailing kisses along my collarbone. My hands twisting in the sheets as he'd rolled on top of me.

He swooped in for another kiss, a long, slow kiss that stole my breath and ability to form coherent sentences. "People are going to see us," I managed.

"Let them. Unless you'd prefer not to be seen kissing me."

I thought about it for a grand total of three seconds. Deciding I didn't care in the slightest who saw, I kissed him back for all I was worth.

When we finally broke apart, Adam slipped his hand into mine and we continued down the stalls. I'd never been much for hand-holding; I found it annoying when you had an itch or your hand got sweaty. But with Adam it was different. It was connection. A tether to my own personal source of happiness.

As we walked, stopping at tables piled with plumes, vials of perfumes and perhaps my favorite—scores of the Bard's works in leather-bound, paperback and even miniature form—I wondered if Adam and I could always be this happy. Were we the stuff that long-term relationships were made of, or were we destined to burn out? And did I want to find out? Or did I want to take what fate had offered us: a graceful exit at the end of the summer?

Stealing a sidelong glance at Adam, his hair golden in the sinking summer sun and a soft smile on his face as he took in everything the centennial had to offer, the fear of heartache and mess seemed small in comparison to the gift of getting to be with Adam.

"You know, markets and mainstages were always my favorite part of all this when I was a kid," Adam said, pulling me back to the present.

"And now that you've seen behind the curtain?"

"I enjoyed my stint on the centennial committee. There is a certain kind of Zen one enjoys when building sets. But I think," he murmured, drawing me beside the falconers and austringers tent for another kiss, "I think it's the company of the beautiful and accomplished Miranda Barnes. I feel like centennial royalty right now. A guy could get used to this."

Our eyes locked, and in that brief moment, every single sound and smell of the night market dropped away. I wanted to tell him that maybe while it wouldn't always be costumes and codpieces, there could still be an us after Bard's. It would no doubt be full of mess and miscues while we figured it out, but I did think we could figure it out.

"Well met," a voice rang out, shattering the moment to glittering pieces. In front of an impressive wig display stood Ian, decked out in a gold and crimson ensemble, complete with fiery red cloak.

I sighed. Ian always had impeccable timing. I'm sure he was due an off moment now and then. But I still sort of wanted to murder him. Instead, I said, "Well met, bestie. Glad to see you decided to tone it down tonight."

"I tone down for no one, Barnes." He tapped his decidedly off-period watch. "Let's away, friends. Our Uber is nigh and I want to make sure we get a good seat."

"You know we have assigned seats, right? It's dinner theater," I told him, but I let him usher us down the winding path of booths toward a waiting car. Pardon, a "Ye Olde Uber," per the calligraphic sign stuck in the back window. Everyone was getting into the centennial spirit, it seemed.

———

Inside Titania's, the menfolk went off in search of the bar, while I stood taking in the birch trees and Camp Verona flags that flanked the transformed banquet room. It even smelled piney—none of that artificial air freshener crap, but honest-to-goodness sunbaked tree sap.

"You like?" Candace asked from behind me, trying to keep her tone casual.

"I love it. You really did think of everything," I laughed. "Although I'm not sure I want to know where you got that stuffed racoon, do I?"

She frowned. "No, you do not." She ran a hand over her immaculate French braid, as if searching for wispies. The gesture reminded me so much of Portia, and yet—for all the polished and diamond-sharp qualities that she and my big sister shared—Candace couldn't hide her nerves. Or the fact that at her core she was a big nougat of theater nerd, just like me.

"Thanks again for helping to rustle up a sell-out crowd tonight," she added, her tone almost shy.

"A lot of that credit goes to Ian. Man's got a knack for salesmanship. I just put the word of mouth out and brought Dan. Because his mouth alone should have tickets sold out in the next twenty-four hours for the entire run."

"Clever."

"You should see me when I put my agenting hat on. I can be downright devious."

"I'm having trouble with the whole Miranda as a literary mercenary thing," Candace drawled. "But if we're sold out for the duration, I'll reconsider my opinion on who the scariest Barnes sister is."

"That's all I ask." I grinned.

She jerked her head toward the "Nature Hut," where Ian and Adam were chatting in line waiting for drinks. "Think you two will continue on after all this?"

"I hope so. Despite all my best efforts to make a mess of it, I like where we've come out. Now I guess we discover what happens next."

"Nobody says you have to get it right the first time. The important thing is that you get there eventually."

"Wise words from a wise woman." I waggled my eyebrows at her. "You know, if you ever want to make an honest man of Ian, I'm here for it."

"I'm not sure I've met a woman alive who would be up to that task," she chuckled. "Unlike you and your adorable pet doctor, I think that Ian and I are like comets streaking across the sky—destined to flame out. But what a ride." She looked down at her phone. "It's getting to be that time; I should go rally the cast."

"Good luck out there," I told her.

Candace leaned over and hugged me, so briefly that at first I thought maybe she'd lost her balance. But women like Candace didn't lose their balance. They were born with their own gravitational pull. Smiling tentatively, she smoothed out wrinkles in her camp uniform that weren't there and strode off. No sooner had she disappeared behind the curtains than the room begin to fill out.

When the lights went down, I sat rapt, basking in the rhythm and flow of the math nerds turned star-crossed lovers. I had to smother down a delighted laugh as Portia took the stage, clad in a bespoke power suit. Apparently, she and Candace had decided she should play Lady Capulet as an overly involved, high-powered working mother from Cambridge.

Intermission came too soon, but it provided me a chance to finally introduce Opal properly to Ian as our potential summer intern. Unsurprisingly, Ian took to her immediately, weaving her a picture of the publishing and agenting scene that had the two of them excitedly drawing up plans for next summer.

I found Adam over at the s'mores table and soon we were sticks deep in milk chocolate and marshmallows and chatting excitedly about what we'd loved in the first half, when a still-costumed Portia slipped from behind the curtain, crooking her finger at me. Then she surreptitiously pointed at Ian.

"I'm being summoned," I whispered to Adam.

"I'll snag us some extra chocolate," he promised.

"You are so the man for me," I exclaimed, kissing him before heading over to where Portia stood cutting an intimidating figure in her power suit, which probably had been pulled out of her own closet and not the costume one. "You were fantastic out there," I said, hugging her.

"You made me actually feel a little sorry for CEO Capulet," Ian added. "Well done."

Portia preened. "Thank you, but I didn't call you both over to fawn over my star-making performance. I had a look at Miranda's contract today like you asked and, well—I couldn't wait. There's wording that clearly supports the substitution of an alternative project in the event that the series is concluded early, in Miranda's sole discretion, of course. Not only that, but you can do it without any kind of penalty or blowback. Well, at least legally anyway. Relationship-wise, you may have some groveling to do."

"Thank you!" I squeezed her hand. "I always feel better when you look at my contracts."

"Of course you do," she said with a toss of her hair. "Writing is your thing. Contracting is mine."

"And being charming is mine. Let me take a run at Susannah," Ian insisted. "I'm hard to resist."

"That remains to be seen," Portia scoffed.

"Hey, I'm charming. Jackass, MD over there digs me."

"Adam likes everyone." Portia's lips quirked. "Some more than others, I think," she said with a look that couldn't have been more pointed.

"That's what I said," Ian agreed. The two of them regarded me with matching expressions of interest.

"Stay out of it," I admonished both of them. "I will sort this out."

I was saved by the lights overhead flickering on and off, an indication we should head back to our seats.

"Well, don't wait too long," Portia cautioned. "Our doubts are traitors and make us lose the good we oft might win by fearing to attempt."

My mouth dropped open. "Portia, did you just quote the Bard?"

"When in Bard's," she smirked, sauntering off toward the curtain.

"You heard her, time to get a move on, Barnes," Ian teased. "Time waits for no one." He grinned at me. "That's Chaucer."

The Amphitheater

I held up my hands for silence as the cast closed in around me in a tight knot, the nerves and opening-night excitement wafting off them. "Now," I began, "take a deep breath, find your rhythm, your voice. Pluck the magic out of the air. Pick up that golden thread and hold it fast. Leave everything on the stage tonight and each night. Because there are no second chances. This is it. Your one shot at immortality on this island. That's all you get."

"Did she just go full Baldwin on us? What's next, Cadillac or steak knives?" Byron whispered to Cat. "Hey, Barnes, I wouldn't take up a second career as a motivational speaker."

While some of the cast laughed nervously, I pretended to be exasperated. Byron could be such a patsy sometimes. But a very effective tool. I leaned forward, pitching my voice low like I was repeating a secret. "Okay, how about this? You're the best damn cast I've ever worked with. You've already performed the greatest miracle of them all: You've resurrected the dead. You've breathed new life into these long-dormant lords and ladies, fools and villains. It's time to let them loose." I looked around at them. "So what the hell are you waiting for? Go get your costumes on, powder your faces and blacken your eyes. It's time to set the Bard free."

The cast whooped and scattered, and for a brief moment, I felt a pang of longing to go with them, to lose myself in the excitement. Maybe I would try out for some local theater when this was all over. Particularly if that sandy-haired man dressed in stagehand black would come see me. As if he could sense me, Adam looked up from his last-minute prepping and hit me with a smolder that would have melted the panties right off a lesser woman.

Watching him, his head down and the light catching his hair and the soft, determined expression of his face, made my heart stutter. It was time to tell him, I thought. Tonight. No more beating around the bush. I had to put it out there and go for what I wanted. And what I wanted was Adam.

Giving him one last look, I slipped out stage left and down the wooden stairs, taking in the boisterous mix of locals and Bardolators decked out in period costumes, masks and feathered hats as far as the eye could see. The smell of popcorn mingled with bug spray as the audience pored over their programs and took selfies of themselves in the open-air theater beneath a rising full moon in the purpling sky.

I made my way down the aisles of pine benches, a line of soft white lanterns above my head to light my way. Beyond that glow, the trees and bushes had been adorned with twinkling fairy lights and brightly burning lanterns, giving the island's woods an otherworldly charm.

A hand reached out and grabbed my elbow. I yelped in surprise to find Portia smirking up at me from her seat. "I believe the time-honored expression is break a leg?" Beside her sat Candace, Cordy and Ian. There were two empty seats next to them draped with my father's tweed jacket, which he insisted made him look professorial. On the other side sat Tillie, Alice, Opal, Jazz and Dan, all grinning at me like I'd hung this particularly gorgeous sturgeon moon. And it hit me—even as they were snapping pictures of me in my little black director's dress—I'd never filled a row before. Not like this.

Before I could burst into a full-on ugly cry, Portia was on her feet, hugging me with a ferocity that both threatened to knock me over and somehow steadied me at the same time. "You're going to be great tonight," she whispered.

I squeezed her back, sniffling a little. "Thanks, sis. But just so you know, I'm not crying. I got dust in my eye."

"Of course."

"Where are Mom and Dad?" I asked, dabbing at the dust-related tears.

"Last I checked, Mom was overseeing the punch preparation. I think Dad was heading backstage to see if your man needed anything."

"He's not my—" I stopped. "Thanks, Porsche."

"Back at you. By the way, your ragtag band of reprobates," she said, jerking her head down the aisle, "cleaned out the florist for you and the cast. I don't think there's a stem left in town. But I did manage to talk Ian out of bringing one of those tacky condom bouquets from Cat's shop. You're welcome."

"You're a good person," I said solemnly, and leaning over her to wave to the rest of my friends and family, I called out, "I'll see you all after the show." A chorus of "Knock 'em dead" sprang up in my wake. I waved once more and wove my way up the center aisle.

True to Portia's word, I found Mom over by the concessions. Dressed in a lavender sheath dress and swathed in a cream and gold accented cashmere shawl that seemed to float around her, she was leaning far too close to an enormous punch bowl. I gently tugged her back from the edge of dress-staining oblivion. "Hey, I thought you were done haranguing all of our wonderful volunteers for the evening?" From behind my mother, Edina Rodgers and Priscilla Gordon tried and failed to cover their snickers.

"What are you doing out here?" she exclaimed. "Shouldn't you be backstage?"

"Nah, the cast is in costume and makeup. They won't need me for a bit," I said with a glance back over the rippling crowd. "Up for a quick walk? To settle my pre-curtain jitters?" I asked, all doe-eyed and guileless. I was fine. But I wanted to maneuver Mom into her seat. After two nights of the mainstage, she needed to be off her feet.

"Perfect," my mother said, clasping her hands together. "That will give me a chance to do a final walk-through."

Edina, who had been busy ladling punch into plastic crystal knockoff cups, flashed me a grateful look. And as soon as my mother's back was turned, she hurriedly beckoned Pris to dump another bottle of champagne into the bowl.

"I'm sure everything is perfect, Mom. Cordy, Portia and I triple-checked everything. You know, so you could enjoy yourself? Maybe not decimate next year's volunteer pool?"

She shot me a sheepish look and pulled her shawl tighter around her shoulders. Grinning, I followed her past the concession stands and the Bard's Rest branded souvenir tables where people could purchase a dizzying array of period gloves and masks as well as glow sticks and other light-ups for the younger set. I would feel bad about this shameless commercialization of the Bard except that the profit would go back to the town for the schools, community programs and tire-eating potholes.

Mom slipped between the stand selling crimson seat cushions with the Bard's face on them and, my personal favorite, the candy apple table where Earl Winston had been leveling up on his use of caramel and candy on honeycrisps for years. Waving at him and mouthing "I'll be back," I followed Mom, picking my way carefully down the brush and roots to the water's edge.

"It's magic," Mom said after a few beats of silence. "You can always feel it. The way it courses through the crowds at the mainstages. Nothing feels quite like it." She smiled, her face half-hidden in the shadow of an elm. "This might be the best year yet."

"Because you roped all of your children into a form of indentured servitude?" I teased.

Her mouth curved up at the corners. "Well, I won't pretend I didn't enjoy watching your sister's version of playing nice."

"I'm sure Emmeline McGandry was just kidding about Portia never being welcome in the town hall again."

"Emmy is a softie. She'll come around in a decade or so," Mom assured me, her eyes tracking the bobbing progress of the boats still making their way toward the dock. "I remember the night when you stepped onto that stage as Viola. It was just like tonight, clear and crisp."

"Oh, come on, you can't remember all of my performances." I nudged her.

"I remember your last performance on this island like it was yesterday," she insisted, reaching out to stroke my hair. "Conceal me what I am and be my aid. For such disguise as haply shall become the form of my intent."

"Not bad," I conceded. "One of Viola's best lines, to be sure."

"Portia the lawyer. Cordelia the chef. And my Miranda the . . ." She paused, crooking an eyebrow. "Actress? Agent? Writer? What guise tonight, darling?"

"Head gopher to Isabella Barnes," I said solemnly. "Pretty sure that's the one that will get me a bunch of free drinks around town. Everybody feels bad for me."

"Smart-ass," she snorted. But she took my hand, hers surprisingly cool. For a few beats we stood there, side by side, listening to the lake lap the stones. I saw myself, a ganglier version in braids and braces standing next to my beautiful mother—less lined and less gray, but no less determined or beautiful.

"Did you talk to Ian yet?"

"Yeah, you were right." I grimaced. "While not happy that I kept it from him, he told me we'd figure something out with the publisher. He's heading out tomorrow. He's got a couple of meetings back in Boston he wants to get in, and he thinks calling Susannah from his office will give him some sort of power boost."

"Did you point out that he's not Sauron and Valhalla is not Mordor?"

"No, dang it. But I should have. Next time."

She arched a perfectly penciled brow and squeezed my hand. "You've accomplished what every writer of a series aspires to. Left nothing on the table. What you've crafted is an ending that is so earned, so deserved that even your fickle fans won't be able to do anything but love it. It's the best thing you've ever written."

"Thanks, Mom." I rested my head against hers and tried not to get dust in my eyes again. I wanted to savor this moment, store it away for later when someday it would inevitably be just me standing at the water's edge alone. And damn it, that memory would not include blubbering.

"You know, I was thinking tonight that I've had over fifty years of mainstages on this island—forty with your father, and about thirty with you girls. Whatever way my fate twists, I am the luckiest woman here tonight."

The chill that prickled down my spine had nothing to do with the nip in the night air. "Mom?" I asked, my voice threaded with uncertainty.

"Oh, I'm not trying to be maudlin, my darling. It's just—I want that for you. Whatever *that* is for you, I want you to be comfortable in your own skin, to look back and think you were the luckiest. That whoever stood by your side, whoever held you in their arms, or who you held in yours, made you feel like the luckiest."

I raised an eyebrow. "Are you meddling in my love life? Mother, this is an unexpected turn of events."

"Yes," she said dryly, "and if you're not married off post-haste, I'll take to my bed like Mrs. Bennet."

"Now, that I'd like to see," I scoffed. "You're really not bred for the consumptive lifestyle, considering you can't sit still for more than a minute at a time."

She sighed heavily. "Sometimes, I regret having raised such stubborn, willful daughters."

"No, you don't," I said, elbowing her gently.

"No, I don't," she agreed. "Not for one minute."

I pressed my forehead to hers.

"You want to know a secret?" I whispered. "I've got you and Dad, Portia and Cordy, that whole band of lunatics in the third row and maybe someone waiting backstage. Throw in my dog, and I think that makes me the luckiest too."

———

"CUTTING IT CLOSE, Barnes," Adam called out softly as I slipped behind the curtain, the heavy velvet rolling over my bare wrist and muffling the sounds outside.

"Please," I said, pointing to the shadows where a costumed duke and his lords had their heads together. "They don't need me."

"But I do," he said, sidling close behind me. "I'll take every minute you're willing to give me." His finger lazily traced the path from my elbow to my shoulder, making me shiver.

"That's convenient," I murmured. "Because I plan on monopolizing all of your time tonight after celebratory drinks." I spun around to face him, my arms going round his neck. "Shall I describe my plans to you in great detail?"

"In great detail, please."

From behind me, the sound of someone loudly clearing his throat had Adam and me springing apart like guilty teenagers.

"Ah, Adam. I see you've got your hands full," my father said cheerfully. Clearly, he'd gotten his sea legs back beneath him and was prepared to have a little fun at Adam's expense.

"Sets look great," I told him, leaning in for a bear hug.

"Only the best for you, sweetheart. Although I'll say that this one over here"—he jerked a thumb toward Adam, but there was a fond smile tugging at the corners of his mouth—"made sure everything was perfect. He was here by six this morning, making sure everything was right for you."

"I thought we agreed we wouldn't tell her that," Adam mumbled.

I smirked. Though I'd woken to an empty bed this morning, Adam had left a note that he'd had a few things to take care of at the office. And tea—the man had left me a mug of tea. It was even better now knowing that he'd come here to the island to make last-minute tweaks for me.

"Any man pact we had went out the window when you took up with my daughter," Dad said dryly.

"At least I know where she gets her delicate wit from," Adam grumbled.

"You obviously haven't spent enough time around Isabella," Dad scoffed. "Did you remember to add that extra piece of tape to the floor trap? Byron keeps missing his mark."

Adam sighed. "If only the man's ego were less than twice the regular size. He might be able to see his feet."

"Don't be petty," I teased him.

"Yes," Dad agreed. "Jealousy is an ugly emotion, Adam."

"I'm not—" Adam threw up his hands. "Only the best for Lord Byron."

"Technically, I'm a duke," I heard a familiar, cocksure voice ring out in the wings.

I snickered as Adam rolled his eyes and retreated backstage. When he was out of earshot, I turned to my father. "Be nice to him. I like this one."

"I can tell. But what kind of father would I be if I didn't give him a hard time?"

"A progressive one?"

"Where's the fun in that?" He patted my hand. "How's your mother holding up?"

"I caught her micromanaging the punch preparation. I rectified the situation though. The punch should be twice as boozy as usual."

"That's my girl." My father winked, then glanced at his watch. "Your mother will be onstage any minute to introduce the play. I should probably find some of that punch."

"Make it a double for her," I said. "You guys are in third row center," I told him and gave him one more squeeze. As he turned to go, I called out softly, "Dad?"

"Yes, hon?"

"Thank you."

"The sets were no trouble. Adam did the heavy lifting."

"I'm not talking about the sets. Just thank you. For everything."

He smiled as he disappeared behind the curtain, softly humming, as he always did when he was happy. I really was the luckiest.

Outside, the din of the crowd died away as stagehands lit the torches and the master of ceremonies took the stage. In a voice that had dominated lecture halls for decades, my mother introduced *Twelfth Night*, touching on the themes of gender and identity. I risked a peek, peeling open a small fissure in the curtain. Just as I'd suspected, the crowd was putty in her hands, hanging on her every word, drinking from the generous fount of her Shakespearean wisdom—and some liberally mixed punch.

As she bowed, the curtain rose, and the lights flared. Byron tromped across the stage and bellowed, "If music be the food of love, play on. Give me excess of it."

The audience never stood a chance.

As it turned out, Adam and I didn't either. Only leaving my side for set changes, he stood with me in the wings, breath and hands held. We laughed softly as Cat wooed and wowed, a coy and yet strangely vulnerable Viola. We brayed along with the audience, hands over our mouths, as Aaron ruled the roost as the riotous Toby Belch, playing for laughs as Cat and Byron played for hearts.

If the first act bubbled like freshly popped champagne, then the second and third were tantalizing appetizers working up to the hearty entrée of act IV and the bittersweet chocolate of the final act. I couldn't even remember intermission, only that I was mobbed by the cast, and that Adam . . . Adam was by my side for all of it, savoring this Shakespearean feast with me.

When that curtain fell after the final line and the audience erupted into thunderous applause and wolf whistles—which originated in row three with Ian or Dan or maybe both—I grasped Adam's hand tightly. "They did it." I grinned like an idiot. "Look at them," I cried, pointing to the beaming and sweaty cast lining up for the curtain call.

"You did it," he said, drawing his arms around my waist. He nudged me forward as Cat and Byron appeared to drag me out onstage for a director's bow. I in turn gestured to my cast, Adam and the rest of the crew, even tipping my head to my father in the third row. And for one golden moment, everything was perfect.

....

The Fairy Ring

The sun shone through the floral-patterned curtains—orchids maybe. I rolled over to find an empty bed, but I could hear Adam moving around in his apartment kitchen, humming along with the building hiss of the teakettle.

"Hungry? I could make you an omelet," he said, returning and handing me a mug of Earl Grey. "Do you have anything on the agenda today?"

"Nope." Last night, the curtain had fallen on the final night of the centennial. Cleanup would start tomorrow, but today, the town took a collective breath.

"Any chance you'd like to spend the day with me? Lucille is an excellent hiking buddy. We could pick up Puck and go to Oberon's Woods. Pack brunch?"

"That sounds delightful." I couldn't imagine a better offer than a day with just Adam, me and the pets. The last two weeks had been a whirlwind ride of mainstages and madrigals, fair food and far-thingales, and Adam had been with me every step of the way, but there had been so much going on. I'd wanted to talk to him about life beyond Bard's but couldn't seem to find the right moment. I wanted to do it right, when it was quiet and I could lay out my thoughts about splitting time between Somerville and Seattle in a way that made sense. That, and I was a huge honking coward.

"There's just one thing I need to do first," I said, crooking my finger at him.

He climbed onto the bed and made his way slowly up my body, leaving a trail of devastating kisses on my bare skin until he reached my mouth. "You need something, Barnes?" he teased.

"Just all of you," I replied before pulling him down on top of me.

An hour later, fully satisfied and freshly showered, we drove to Oberon's Woods with Puck and Lucille. The weather was warm but there was a slight breeze and plenty of shade as we picked our way over rocks and along little brooks. Adam and I chatted about the mainstages mostly—how good the cast was, how on point the sets were and how relieved we were that I'd talked Byron out of a codpiece.

When we eventually reached Mustardseed's Meadows, I touched Adam's elbow to stop.

"Here?" he asked.

"Perfect place to lay down a blanket."

"I know what I'd like to lay down on a blanket right now," he teased as we made our way across the meadow, unrolling our blanket and unpacking our picnic provisions. Puck and Lucille, excited to be off leash finally, broke for the clover in a madcap chase as Adam and I proceeded to gorge ourselves on croissants and mimosas.

"All right, confession time," I admitted. "I have an ulterior motive for suggesting this place. To the Meadows, I mean. As opposed to other picturesque spots of Oberon's Woods."

"Ominous," Adam hummed. "I like it."

"Nothing of the sort. I wanted to show you my favorite spot in all of Bard's. This is it."

"Not Will's Island?" he asked.

"Don't get me wrong. I loved performing on the island all those years, and *Twelfth Night* will go down as one of my favorites there, but . . ." I hesitated. "This is where I lost and found myself again." I stared at Adam, his eyes warm and open, his expression soft. "Come on," I said, sitting up and brushing crumbs from my jeans. "I want to show you something." I rose and offered him my hand.

His face lit with curiosity, he took my hand and pulled himself up. His hand in mine, he followed me across the meadow until we reached the place where the grass had grown over, but if you looked hard enough you could still see the stones.

"There," I said, pointing to them.

Adam stared thoughtfully at the ground for a bit. "Huh, there's a rock circle." He turned to me, a question in his eyes. "What am I looking at?"

"You asked me where I went on prom night," I said, my tone a little uncertain. "I drove to Oberon's Woods."

"In your prom dress? Oh, Barnes." Adam shook his head ruefully. "How are you not a horror movie cautionary tale?"

"Ass." I shoved him playfully. "To be fair, I wasn't exactly in my right mind. You see, I'd just come from my front porch where a scene out of a horror movie starring my boyfriend and my sister was playing out." I smirked up at him. "Anyway, I eventually made my way to the Meadows and had a good cry. As I sat here, I started to think about what it would be like to disappear."

Adam frowned. "I thought this was going to be a fun story."

"It is. Stay with me," I assured him. "I envisioned this girl, someone stronger and braver than me, but who also wanted to disappear. This girl, she heads into the woods after a blowout with her friends to clear her head, and instead she stumbles into a fairy ring. A fairy ring that drops her into the fae realm in the middle of a war between the summer and winter queens."

"That's funny, that sounds just like—" Adam's eyes widened. "Hathaway," he breathed. "Miranda *Hathaway* Barnes."

"Aww, you remembered my middle name," I said, nudging him.

"How did I not—Barnes, you're famous."

"I'm book famous." I shrugged. "I think that ranks somewhere below 'this one time I went viral on the internet' famous. Doesn't count for much, and even less so for me because of the pen name."

Adam looked at the ring and back at me. "You're telling me you came out here the night of prom, sat down in this meadow, built this circle of stones and wrote *Elf Shot*?"

"Yeah, that's not quite how it happened. I didn't flee my own porch with a laptop in hand. I sat here and sketched Meg and some basic story threads out in my head. From there I shut myself up in the attic for the weekend and stitched together an outline for the first book. Took me a year or so to get it all down on paper and then another to edit it. But yeah, Elf Shot was born right where you're standing."

"First, I just want you to know that I am trying so hard not to fanguy all over you right now. Second, I have a million questions. But mostly, I just want to tell you how incredibly hot it is that you're her. Or she's you. Whatever, you know what I mean. Damn, Barnes, you write a good bloody battle scene."

I tried not to preen.

His eyes went comically wide. "I've always told Shannon that I felt like I knew Meg, and in her infinite teenage wisdom, my darling niece would roll her eyes and tell me that was the point of a main character. But I mean, I like *know* know Meg."

"Oh, I'm not Meg. She started out as a mostly stable, occasionally volatile mix of Portia and Cordy, but over the books she's grown into her own character. I wish I were more like Meg. Meg just puts it all out there and damn the consequences."

"I don't know about that, Barnes. Meg always keeps you guessing as to her next move—is she going to stab that fae warrior in the gut or what—and there's that signature snark of hers."

"Okay, I'll grant you that her sharp tongue is mine," I conceded. I leaned into him, resting my head on his shoulder. "I'm not good at this. I've never told anyone I'm . . ." I faltered on the words. Were we dating? That somehow felt both presumptuous and inadequate all at once. ". . . involved with that I'm Hathaway Smith."

"But you told me," he said, his voice bordering on what sounded suspiciously like wonder.

"When I created Hathaway, I did it to keep a boundary between me and my fans. They have a lot of opinions. A *lot* of opinions. It's just easier for them to direct that at someone else. Someone else who can take it." I smiled self-deprecatingly. "But like Meg, Hathaway sort of took on a life of her own, and she became a barrier when I wanted to get close to someone. I used to think, 'Well, I won't tell this guy about her, he's just a fling,' or 'This is nice, but it's run its course, so I won't be telling him about her.'"

"So what you're saying is, I'm not a fling?" he teased, but there was something behind it.

"Oh, come on. You know I like you," I said. "I trust you. With all of me."

His arm tightened around my waist. "That is very good to know, Barnes. Who else knows about Hathaway?"

"You, sir, are now a member of a very small, very elite circle that includes my parents, my sisters, Ian and my publisher. Oh, and Puck, of course. He's my furry sounding board."

"Of course."

"Is this why you came home to Bard's this summer?" He chewed his lip. "Not to put too fine a point on it, but my niece has mentioned a hundred or so times that the next Elf Shot is overdue."

"Yes, thank you for that," I said dryly. "I've been struggling since *Inconstant Moons*. The fan reaction was . . ." I trailed off.

"Unfair and unkind?" he offered.

"Something like that," I agreed. "There's just something about this place that shakes the words loose. So yeah, I came home to write, but got a lot more than I bargained for—Mom's diagnosis, the mainstages, forging scary alliances with event planners, patching up my relationship with Portia and . . . others."

"Oh, so now I'm an other?"

"You're so much more than an other," I said, squeezing his arm. "I'm not good at defining things."

"Says the woman who redefined the fairy genre," he quipped. "Sorry, I haven't quite gotten my head around the fact that you're Hathaway Smith. 'Honored' isn't the right word. Neither is 'grateful.' Touched? I'm touched you told me?" He shook his head. "No, I love. I love that you told me."

There was something in that word, the way it skittered over my skin when he said it.

"Well, I love that I told you."

We stared at each other for a long while, the breeze lifting my hair and blowing his across his eyes. Behind me, I could hear two four-leggers joyfully rampaging through the brush, but I dared not turn my head, lest this moment snap.

"What happens next?" Adam cleared his throat. "With the book, I mean."

"O-oh," I stammered because I thought he'd been asking about us. "It goes through a heavy-duty editing process. When I get back to Somerville, Ian and I will hole up in the office for a while. There are whiteboards and sticky note insults involved. At the end of it, I emerge with a draft that's ready for Susannah, my editor out of New York, to work her magic."

"Sounds like you've got everything you need back at home base."

"Oh, I think I could write anywhere," I said quickly, hoping the meaning would land. "If this summer has taught me anything, it's that I can be flexible." I thought that might brighten his expression, but though he stood beside me, the look in his eyes told me he was somewhere else. "Adam?"

"Still processing," he said, forcing a smile.

"The Hathaway thing?"

"Yeah. Not so much that you have a pen name. That makes sense. It's more that you have this other side of you, this whole different world you operate in."

"Is that weird for you?" I asked.

"No," Adam insisted. "It's just that I didn't realize how complicated your life is. This bestselling writer with all these deadlines and expectations in addition to your day-to-day as an agent. Then there's your mom's cancer diagnosis you're working through. How do you do it all, Barnes?"

"I have a killer support system, and like you, I love what I do, so it feels less like work and more like just my life."

"So many balls in the air though," he said thoughtfully.

"Does it change things for you?" I asked, not sure I wanted the answer.

"Not the way I feel about you." He leaned over, kissing me lightly on the lips. "I'm glad you told me."

"Me too," I said, staring down at our entwined fingers as we stood before the fairy circle. But I wasn't sure either of us meant it.

....

The Tavern of Ill Repute

On a normal night, the Tavern of Ill Repute was a boisterous locals' bar with deep, dark wood and portraits of the Bard's most infamous villains, from the legendary Lady Macbeth to the silver-tongued Iago, gracing the scarred walls. It was the kind of establishment where sometimes you went home with a hangover or missing an article of clothing, but you never questioned it and always thought it was worth it in the morning. Now as all three casts converged in the back room, there arose such a cacophony that I'm sure it was breaking several of Bard's noise ordinances, which might have been a problem if the sheriff and fire chief weren't already in attendance.

Traditionally held the Friday after the festival shut down on Sunday, the cast party was in full swing. Castmates were sharing stories and appetizers, snapping selfies and signing one another's cast T-shirts and indulging in some much-deserved revelry after the long and hectic week of packing away the props and storing the sets for the season.

As I moved among the actors and crew, congratulating each one of them and blubbering a bit over Opal and Jazz as I hugged them,

I was reminded of how much I'd missed the camaraderie of a good run—that bittersweet mix of relief and sadness that it was over—and the promise of the next one. But somehow tonight seemed more bittersweet than years past, the evening seeming to speed by around me, leaving me behind.

The likely source of my funk stood on the other side of the room chatting with Cat and Byron as if nothing was wrong. And on the surface, it all seemed fine. Adam and I had spent the last few days working to close down the mainstages, but it all somehow felt different. As if Hathaway had driven a wedge between us despite all of Adam's protestations to the contrary. A wedge the size of the bottomless chasm that separated the summer and winter fae courts and ever widening by the second.

But when I'd asked him what was wrong, he'd claimed he was tired from centennial cleanup and changed the subject. Labor Day was seventeen days away (but who was counting), and every day that passed it felt more and more like ours was becoming a tale told by an idiot (me), full of sound and fury (okay, maybe not so much that part, but hey, we all took liberal license with the Bard from time to time) and signifying nothing.

We were running out of evenings, so I resolved, as I slid into his truck at the end of the party, that it was tonight or never.

"Good party," Adam said, backing out of the parking lot.

"Yeah. Good party," I said, staring out the window.

"Barnes, you okay?"

"Yeah," I breathed. "Wait, no. No, I'm not." I turned to him. "What is happening with us? I feel like since I told you about Hathaway everything feels different. And not in a good way."

There was a long pause before he responded, and when he did, his voice was soft and deliberate. "It's not the Hathaway thing, Barnes. I have just been giving this thing between us a lot of thought. And every way I turn it, I don't see it working out."

His words, though carefully chosen, still landed like a slap, rocking me backward.

"What do you mean?"

"I don't see how this works beyond Bard's. We both have these incredibly full lives and people who depend on us."

"I hear you," I said, taking a steadying breath. "I agree that in terms of our careers they're pretty full, but I thought you wanted more than that. *I* want more than that. I want someone to come home to. Not just someone—*you*. I think there's a way to make this work. I don't need to be at Valhalla on a daily basis to do my job, Adam. I could spend time out in Seattle with you. Find a rental, fly home when I'm needed. It would afford us time to figure out if we work outside of Bard's."

"I would never ask you to do that," he said quickly. "I know what Valhalla means to you."

"You're not asking me," I pointed out. "I offered. And I wouldn't have offered it if I didn't think it would work."

"That's a lot of pressure to put on a relationship," he countered glumly.

"I'm not asking you for a guarantee. I'm trying to give us a chance to see where it goes."

"I don't want to be that selfish person who makes someone uproot their whole life," he protested.

"This is different than what went down between you and Andrea," I said softly. "I'm walking into this with eyes wide open, Adam. I know the risks."

"But what about what you'd be giving up?" he said, his voice shredding. "I see you with Ian, the friendship and partnership you two share. How could I take you away from that? From Valhalla? Your writing? You said Ian's a big part of your editing process. You need him. And your whole family is back this way too. What about your mom? I felt so helpless letting my brother take the brunt of my father's care. How could I ask you to take care of her from afar?"

"Because it wouldn't necessarily be a permanent move. At some point we'd decide one way or another where we live. Maybe we split the difference and move to the middle of the country? I hear Kansas lays claim to the biggest ball of twine and was the birthplace of Pizza Hut."

Adam didn't laugh. "I've worked really hard to get where I am. I almost lost my shot before and I'm not going to go off track again. I won't ask you to do the same."

"Why aren't you hearing me?" I asked. "I wouldn't be going off track by being in Seattle."

"You have clients and a business to run. Are you just going to leave all that to Ian?"

"That's not what's going to happen," I said. My tone was a little frostier than I intended, but I didn't like the implication that I hadn't thought this through. "Like I said, it would be a temporary thing while we figure out what we want."

"I don't think I can do temporary. The more time I spend with you the more convinced I am that I . . . that I care about you very much and I don't want to get hurt again like that, or worse, hurt you when temporary no longer works."

"Hang on," I said, straightening up in my seat. "Aren't you the one who accused me of shutting things down without giving them a chance? That's exactly what you're doing here."

"It's different now," he insisted, turning onto the dirt road.

"Why, because you're the one having reservations?"

"Because I think I love you," he bit out. "But I also love what I do. I don't want to stall out again. I don't want to have to start over somewhere new. And I don't want to have to choose between loving you and loving what I do," he finished, his voice breaking and his knuckles white on the wheel.

"Are you listening to yourself right now?" I sputtered. "You're walking away because you love me?"

"That's exactly it."

"I get it," I said tartly. "Do you have any idea how unnerving it was when you asked me to put aside our past for the chance of something better? All that insecurity and years of feeling I wasn't good enough—I put all of that aside for a chance with you. Even though I knew it might blow up in my face and I'd be hurt again. But I did it. I did it for a chance to be with you. Hell, I took an even bigger risk and told you about Hathaway because I didn't want that as a wall between us, something standing in the way of us moving forward. Because I trust you and I want to be with you."

"This isn't like one of your books, Miranda. It doesn't all come out right in the end because you will it so," he said, though there was no derision in his voice, only weary defeat. "I just want to get out while we can still get out clean. Without dragging this out and hurting each other until we both reach the same conclusion, that there isn't a way for this to work."

"That's officially the most asinine thing I've heard come out of your mouth all summer," I fumed. "News flash, you don't want to hurt me? It's a little late for that. But hey, if you want to be a coward, if you want to shut this down without giving it a chance, then by all means."

He pulled into my driveway and not a moment too soon. I swung open the door and beat a hasty retreat to the porch. In the glare of the headlights, I was grateful he couldn't see the tears streaming down my face as he pulled away. "Nothing good has ever happened to me on this porch," I muttered to no one just before the dam broke and I ugly cried all over the creaky steps.

Mustardseed's Meadows

All hail the fairy queen," I said bitterly, raising my mimosa-filled tumbler to the empty meadow. With the other hand, I reached for the slice of Cordy's mousse cake I'd liberated from the fridge and crammed a large bite into my mouth. No fork, no napkin, no manners required for this pity party.

How in the actual hell had this blown up in my face so spectacularly? It physically hurt to hit replay on the events of last night, and yet I kept doing it over and over.

I should call Ian, I thought numbly. Tell him I wouldn't be working remote from Seattle after all. Or sending him single-origin coffee and fresh Dungeness crab. But the thought of calling him and explaining how I'd crashed and burned just made it that more real. So I ate more cake. I would give myself this day, this cake-and-crying fest in the Meadows. I had cried Adam out of my system once. I could do it again. And then I would pick myself up like the grown-ass woman I was and pull my shit together.

My grand plans were interrupted by the crunch of underbrush and feminine voices.

"Please tell me Portia didn't chip me in my sleep?" I muttered under my breath. "Or put one of those find-a-wayward-person apps on my phone?"

"Please tell me she isn't eating cake with her hands," my older sister whispered.

The answering snicker was definitely Cordy's.

"How did you find me?" I asked.

"I might have seen you crying on the porch and Adam's truck pulling out of the driveway in a hurry," Portia admitted.

"And you didn't come check on me last night?" I demanded.

"I needed reinforcements. I am wholly underqualified to deal with"—she made a vague gesture toward the general area of my face—"this."

Cordy plopped down on one side of me, flask in hand, and Portia settled herself neatly down on the other side, expertly balancing a pastry box. "And I'm the reinforcements, obviously. To answer your question, this was the natural place to check when you weren't at the house." Nudging me, she asked, "You want to talk about it, mopey?"

"Adam and I ended things." I reached for the flask. "No, that's not right. Adam ended things."

"Why?" Portia asked.

"He moved to Seattle for a girl after vet school and it didn't work out. I thought he might feel differently about things with me. About us maybe trying something a little more flexible, like me splitting time between Seattle and Somerville while we figured things out. I was wrong."

"Ouch," Cordy breathed.

"Oh, I'm not finished. When he said he didn't want to hurt me I told him he was a coward."

"So it went well, then?" my little sister said, squeezing my shoulder.

I groaned. "I should never speak. I should just keep my mouth shut and write books. Nothing good ever comes from me speaking."

"I actually think you're quite funny," Portia said. She slid her dove gray nail through the tape of the bakery box. "Here, you get first pick."

I reached for a petit four and popped it into my mouth. "Thank you."

Cordy handed me the flask. "Drink up. I'll drive your car back."

That made me start crying all over again. "You two are the best," I sniffled. "He told me he loved me. I don't understand how you tell someone you love them in one breath and in the next you say you're giving them up."

"Oh wow," Cordy breathed. "Did you say it back?"

"What? No. He positioned it as 'I love you, which is why I can't be with you, because I'll hurt you.' It didn't feel right."

"Do you love him?" Portia asked, her voice as gentle as I'd ever heard it.

"Yeah, I think so," I admitted as a flood of memories of the summer smacked into me: Adam tending to Puck, me tracing my fingers over his carefully drawn set sketches, the relief I'd felt making up with Adam in the Pinsmen over pizza, making out in the gardens of Titania's, Adam holding me in the ER of Sherburne, undressing Adam in the costume cabin, sex in a bower and sex just about everywhere else and, finally, the way he'd looked at me on the opening night of the mainstages—like I was the whole world.

"So what's your plan?" Portia pressed, her tone still careful, but more urgent.

"Sit here and drink until the booze and cake run out."

Portia snorted delicately. "I meant about Adam."

"What do you mean what's my plan? It's over. He doesn't want me. Or doesn't want to hurt me." I wiped at my eyes. "Whatever. The end result is the same."

"So you're going to leave it at that?" Portia probed.

"I think the message was pretty clear, Porsche."

"But you didn't tell him you love him," she insisted.

"Whose side are you on?" I said, frowning at her.

"I'm on the side of reason," Portia retorted.

"I think what she's trying to say is maybe last night didn't go the way you wanted it to," Cordy interjected, "but maybe there's still more to be said. Sometimes people react in the moment and it's not necessarily the right reaction and when they've had some time to think about it, they wish they could have responded differently."

"Maybe Adam was asking you to give him some reassurance?" Portia added. "Validation that you love him too."

Cordy and I both turned to stare at her.

"What? I listen," Portia huffed. "I'm just saying, it sounds like you didn't get to tell Adam you love him and maybe he needed to hear it because he's unsure of himself because he got burned in the past. Maybe he needs to know that you have skin in the game too."

"I offered to work from Seattle while we figured things out. I feel like that's putting a fair amount of skin in the game."

"Regardless of what happened with him and Andrea though, it was shitty, the way he reacted," Cordy added. "You have every right to be upset right now. And eating cake with your fingers."

"Right?" Still, I considered what they'd said, turning their words over in my mind. "Maybe I should tell him I love him. That way I've put everything on the table, and if he still doesn't want something with me, then at least I've put it all out there."

"I think that's wise," said Portia.

"We'll always back you," Cordy added.

"Because we love you," they both chorused.

The Driveway of The Winters' Tail

The squeeze in my chest relaxed as I pulled into the driveway and saw the beige monstrosity parked in front of The Winters' Tail. I'd never been so relieved to see those cross-eyed animals rising out of the gas tank. Flinging the door open, I nearly face-planted on the gravel. *Easy, Barnes. Turn the car off. Take a breath.*

Before I could even make it to the porch, the screen door swung open. Steadying myself, I pared down all of the thoughts jumbling around to just two things I was certain of and opened my mouth to speak the words: *I more than like you, you ass. I love you. We'll make it work.*

"Oh, what a surprise! Hello, Miranda."

It's a good thing I took that breath. Because the sight of Bunny, Adam's mother, was so incongruous, it stole my breath away. It'd been a while since I'd seen Bunny, but she still had that look of someone who's decided that the FDA wasn't credible when it came to sunscreen. She reminded me of those mango chews that Portia snacked on—orange and leathery and completely dehydrated.

"Hey, Mrs. Winters," I squeaked. "Back from Florida?" I asked as my eyes scanned the slice of waiting room behind her for signs of Adam.

"Walt and I just got back last night," she said, beaming. "Loved the sun, hated the bugs."

"I bet the palmetto roaches are enough to make you rethink peep toes." Bard, I should never speak out loud.

Uncertain of what to do with that, Bunny tittered anemically. "Are you here to see Walt?" It was her turn to peer past me, looking around to see if there was a sick or injured pet in my vehicle. Without turning around, I knew Puck would have on his best "come hither and let me out of this car" good-boy expression. "Walt, I think you have a patient," she called over her shoulder.

"Oh, Puck's fine, thanks. I'm actually here to see Adam," I stammered, just as Dr. Walter Winters took up his post by his wife. Unlike Bunny, this man had clearly heeded the call of sunscreen and proper nutrition and exercise. If I ever wanted the genetic blueprint for what Adam would look like in his AARP years, this silver-haired fox with the same hazel eyes and winking smile as his son was it. "Nice to see you, Dr. Winters. I was checking to see if Adam was around? Some centennial business I need to wrap up," I added hastily, ever mindful of Bunny's bloodhound's nose for gossip.

"You just missed him." Walt frowned. "He left for the airport this morning."

"Adam flew back to Seattle?"

"I think he was a little burned out from the centennial. He said he was looking forward to getting back to his routine," Walt offered. "Wanted to take some time to himself before he started his new job. Did he mention he was starting a new job? He's joining a large practice," he added, unable to keep the paternal pride out of his voice.

"Yes, he seemed very excited about it. You two must be so proud," I said numbly while my mind flashed to Adam stepping off a plane, not a hair out of place, Lucille in a bespoke pink pet vest and leash beside him. Adam, walking through the airport terminal, relieved and delighted to be somewhere less messy, less complicated and completely Miranda-less.

"He didn't leave without tying up something, did he? That's not like him," Bunny commented, but her eyes, pool blue, had taken on a shrewd cast.

"Nothing like that. I just had a question for him. Not a big deal at all. I'll email him," I replied as smoothly as I could. I didn't have it in me to dodge and weave with Bunny right now. My body felt like someone had stolen every oxygen molecule out of it, and my bones were bending in on themselves. "Well, so very nice to have run into you both." Thank you, manners. Thank you for not completely deserting me in my hour of need.

Walt wished me luck, but I could still feel Bunny's appraising gaze on me as I retreated down the porch steps.

Gone. Adam had gone back to Seattle. He'd left without so much as a goodbye. Without so much as a text. I wasn't even a loose end that warranted tying up. I'd come to tell Adam that I loved him. And he'd slipped out stage right.

"Right," I wheezed as I pulled away, watching Adam's parents waving at me from the porch. The squeeze in my chest returned with reinforcements, its clutch iron and cold. Puck whined softly beside me, reshuffling his bulk so his head rested on my leg. I stroked the soft fur behind his ears.

And as my treacherous mind whirled through the best and worst of Will's breakup lines, it stopped on *Twelfth Night*. Maybe Adam had left to spare me the real hurt after all—leaving abruptly as he did—so he didn't have to tell me that, even without the distance, it would never have worked out in the long run. I supposed I should have been grateful for this last kindness.

"Give me now leave to leave thee," I murmured, quoting Adam's beloved Orsino.

ACT FOUR

....

September

Scene Thirty-Three

....

Clan Barnes Headquarters

Cordy dropped down so that she was eye level with the gold leaf precariously perched upon the shiny chocolate dome. "Too much?"

"You put gold leaf on a truffle. You sped past *too much* hours ago and blew it an air kiss." Portia patted Cordy's shoulder.

"Says the woman who brought three-hundred-dollar champagne. Is it aged in gold-leaf bottles? Where does one even find champagne that costs three hundred dollars?" Cordy demanded.

"The Village." Portia shrugged, smiling. There was a playfulness to her tone that hadn't been there the last time we'd all been in Bard's together.

My throat involuntarily tightened at the thought that an entire month had gone by since I'd stood in the driveway of The Winters' Tail, heart in hand. "I brought these," I said, forcing cheerfulness. I held up several bound copies of my final manuscript.

"Did you bring enough for all of us?" Portia asked.

"That depends—how many bottles of stupid-expensive champagne did you bring?" I teased. Glancing at my watch, I went over and straightened the dish towels that Mom kept hanging by the oven. I wanted everything to be just as she'd left it. Even if the three of us had spent last night decimating the liquor stash. That was in the study anyway—it didn't count.

Even so, all would be forgiven, because today was a new day, a slightly cloudy but not overly cold fall day when Mom would walk through that door after what turned out to be a four-day stay at Maine Medical. In typical Mom fashion, she'd written off her post-surgery complications as nothing. But Dad had told us that she'd had a rough time of it with the drain, prompting Dr. Wu to insist Mom stay a few more days to heal. I didn't know her personally or anything, but I kind of wanted to kiss Dr. Wu on the mouth.

"Can you grab that box of strawberries?" Portia called over to me. "I'm famished."

"Oh, honey." Cordy clucked her tongue. "Just no." She plucked a truffle from the bottom layer and handed it to Portia.

"Can I have the strawberries too?" Portia asked hopefully. "It will be like a chocolate-dipped strawberry." Before Cordy could shake her head, she added, "Word on the street is—and by the street, I mean Candace—Titania's is moving up their annual play to make you their head pastry chef by the holidays. I hear they're throwing in a car allowance to sweeten the package. But I think you should hold out for that and a black box discretionary fund."

"Happy to hear them out like I do every year." Cordy shrugged.

"Could be a great opportunity to get your name out there . . ." Portia trailed off mid-sentence. "But it's not what you want, is it?"

"I'm not sure what I want, but I feel like I'm getting closer to figuring out what that is," Cordy admitted, rearranging the truffles into a more stable formation. "I love working with Mom and Dad, but I think I might be ready to go out on my own." She bit her lip. "It feels weird to even say it. Please don't mention it in front of them. I want things to settle down around here first. Then I'll start announcing big life changes."

Portia reached over the counter and patted Cordy's hand. "I'll be your first customer."

"I'll fight you for that privilege," I called, pulling out the carton of strawberries and—because I found the thought of naked straw-berries upsetting—grabbing a can of whipped cream.

Cordy snatched one of the manuscripts, turning it over in her hands. "I still think you should have called it *A Lusty Winter*."

"Cord, I love *As You Like It* almost as much as you do," I assured her. "But my readers are teenagers. *A Lusty Winter* just wasn't gonna fly with that demographic, or their parents."

"Ian agreed with me," Cordy retorted.

"Yes, but I'm ninety-nine percent sure that Ian named our liter-ary agency after an airbrushed reimagining of 'Ride of the Valkyries' he saw on the side of a van. Nipples and breastplates were involved. His vote doesn't count."

"He did get you out of that last Elf Shot book with minimal bloodshed," Portia pointed out. "His vote should count twice. But never tell him I said that." She tapped her chin thoughtfully. "Al-though I do suppose there are quite a few dead bodies piled up in the Hall of Winter at the end. So maybe 'lusty' doesn't work for other reasons."

I turned to Portia. "You read the first draft?" I asked, utterly touched.

"Of course. It's not like I sleep anyway. Might as well read some-thing good. I'm just excited this version won't have any typos in it."

"Keep it up and you'll be getting an 'I Heart My Big Sister' mug for Christmas," Cordy said, elbowing Portia. "She's looking at you with those big baby deer eyes."

"I do not have big baby deer eyes," I insisted.

"Who else has read it besides us?" Portia asked.

"Apart from fam? Ian, and the usual suspects at the publishers. Oh, and Opal and Jazz. Figured I owed them an advance reading since I data-mined them."

"How did they take the big reveal?" Cordy asked.

"Other than making me autograph a bunch of stuff and agree to do one virtual book club for them and all their friends as penance for my ruse, they seemed pretty stoked."

"Did you send it to Adam?" Portia asked, her voice light as the whipped cream.

I gave her a half-hearted smile. "Yeah, that would have been a little weird. Haven't heard from him since he took off for Seattle without a word." *Twenty-three days ago,* I added silently. But who was counting?

In some ways, it really was like high school all over again. One moment he'd been there in my life, and the next he wasn't. For every time I thought about him, every time I thought he might laugh at this or that with me, every time I longed to be wrapped around him—I couldn't bring myself to pick up my phone and text him. He'd made his choice loud and clear.

"I'm okay," I repeated. It was almost true. As the days wore on, things had returned to the way they'd been before my summer in Bard's. It was me and Puck in the city again. Early-morning walks and takeout on the couch. Drinks with Ian. Weekly Barnes Face-Time calls that Portia now attended regularly, even though she still griped about the loss of a billable hour. Publishing contracts and book launches. Calls to clients and publishers. Only now there was an emptiness that hadn't been there before.

"Yeah, you're selling it," Cordy snorted.

"Fine, it's like I'm walking around without a vital organ. Nothing seems to work or feel right these days," I admitted. "I still can't get over that I showed up at his parents' place to tell him I loved him and we'd figure out a way to make it work."

"Which would count for a whole lot if he knew you'd shown up," Portia retorted.

"I'm not the one who fled to Seattle."

"I'm just saying, if I'm ever unfortunate enough to fall in love," Portia said with a sniff, "I wouldn't relinquish that without a fight."

"Hard to fight for something when the other person is a no-show," I muttered.

"Ease up," Cordy said, a warning in her voice. "If Miranda says she's done, she's done."

Had I said I was done though? Why was that thought so dismaying?

I climbed onto a stool by the counter and reached for a truffle. Cordy swatted my hand away and deftly extracted one for me. "Now, can I please get a subject change that doesn't involve my tragic love life?" I looked at Portia. "Throw me a lifeline. How's New York?"

Portia examined her peony pink nails. "The same. My clients insist the world will burn to the ground if I don't get to this deal today. As soon as I put out one fire, another one springs up in its place. But"—she hesitated, looking unsure of herself—"I signed up for this yoga retreat with Candace in upstate New York in December. We have to sign some sort of waiver because they collect our phones at the beginning of it. No internet access for forty-eight hours."

"That sounds amazing," I said. "Think you can stick to it?"

"Knowing that Candace will be there to rip my arms off and beat me senseless with them if I try to sneak something in, I'm highly motivated not to game the system," Portia said dryly.

"That would certainly put a damper on your sun salutations," Cordy agreed.

I reached for the strawberries and smiled at my big sister. I was proud of her. She deserved some downtime. More importantly, even if they'd started off as mortal enemies, she deserved a high-octane friend like Candace who could talk her into an all-weekend yoga retreat.

I tried to keep my mind on the conversation, but I found it hard not to think of Adam now that I was back in Bard's. Sure, the last time I'd been here I'd made that grand gesture of driving over to his place. But maybe my sisters were right—it's not like he necessarily knew that. On the other hand, the silence over these last three weeks and change had been pretty deafening. That being said, I wondered if I still had a card left to play, and if I did, would I be willing to play it?

Paws thundered down the stairs. "They must be coming down the road."

Portia went to the window. "Puck can hear their car even though we can't see it yet?"

"Puck can hear the delivery guy when he's in the condo next door. Never underestimate the auditory prowess of a dog when food is involved. You know how Dad spoils him."

"Yeah." Cordy rolled her eyes. "It's Dad who's spoiling him."

"Ah, I see them now. Good boy!" Portia said, leaning over and giving Puck a scratch behind the ears. It wasn't much in terms of the normal rubdowns Puck was accustomed to, but he took it for the gift it was intended to be and leaned into it.

Cordy and I busied ourselves neatening the counter and arranging the champagne flutes, while Portia waited by the door. We watched as Dad got out of the car, came around to the passenger side and opened the door for Mom. We chuckled as she stepped out, rolling her eyes at the gesture, but allowing Dad to take her arm anyway.

"Welcome home," we chorused as she stepped through the door. She looked around at the kitchen, exasperation and fondness warring across her pale but smiling face. "That's funny, I don't remember ordering a side of smart-asses."

"But it comes with booze and truffles," I said, and we swarmed our matriarch, mindful of her bandages, hugging her as tightly as we dared. Mom was home—not entirely out of the woods, but on the right woodland path—and that was enough.

Scene Thirty-Four

···········

SpillThatTea.com

Posted by @HathawaySmithRevealed
12:00 AM, September 30, 2021

As the Bard once wrote, 'tis now the very witching time of night.

And what better time to come clean?

I began writing the Elf Shot series in high school and finished the first novel in my parents' attic. Back then I was so sure of myself. But after the release of *Inconstant Moons*, I lost my way in a tide of self-doubt. All these years, I had prided myself on creating Hathaway Smith as a buffer between me and your expectations for Elf Shot. As if deep down I knew that if I let you all in, I'd let you all down. But even Hathaway wasn't enough to get me through this. Going home this summer, I found my voice again. It turned out that to write the book you all deserved, I had to go back to where it all began.

Sometimes when you return to the past, you find things you missed. This summer, I found something that I'd thought had been lost to me for good. But much like writing this book—I discovered that when I was able to put aside my fear in favor of seeing where this path took me—it was mine again to win or lose.

In doing so, I realized I didn't need Hathaway anymore. Not only did I no longer need her, I realized she had to go. For far too long I'd hidden behind her. I'd gotten so good at hiding, in fact, that I'd forgotten how to fight for what I wanted.

She goes and I stay. And I'm here to tell you like it is:

The Winter's Flaw, due out early next year, is mine. I'm here to claim it. Warts and all.

It will be the final book in the Elf Shot series.

I know that many of you may have strong feelings that there will not be a fifth book. But the truth is, Meg's story is finished, and to drag it out over two books would be a disservice to her and to all of you. This is the best ending I can give Meg. And you.

Sometimes in life we have to pull back the curtain and put away the mask. We must embrace our own truths, face down our past hurts and own our insecurities and break down the walls that prevent us from going after the things we want most in life. In other words, sometimes you just have to put it all out there and hope your intended audience hears you.

To steal one last line from the Bard . . .

The wheel is come full circle: I am here.

Sincerely, Miranda Hathaway Barnes

Epilogue

....

All the Best Shakespearean Plays Have Them

Draining the last of my tea, I powered down my computer. Slipping into my Valhalla zip-up, I patted my pockets to make sure I had my keys. It was go time. Since I'd come out as Hathaway, I'd learned that my readers didn't seem to mind my general social awkwardness. In fact, they seemed to find me rather charming. So I kept getting invited to book signings, and to my surprise, I found myself—okay, I was still nervous—but I found I didn't completely hate them. Best of all, this one was early enough and close enough that I could still make it home at a decent hour to consume an entire ribs platter from Redbones and watch Netflix with Puck until we passed out. Not a bad little Friday night.

As I slung my bag over my shoulder, Ian swung into my office. "Sure you don't want me to come? We could hit up that microbrew tasting over by MIT afterward."

Like the best of literary wingmen, Ian had gone with me to a couple of my first forays into the public spotlight as the woman behind Hathaway Smith. But with each passing one, I found I didn't need him there. "Nah, I'm not sure my liver can take another night of debauchery."

"You loved that Lambrusco tasting at Spoke last night. Don't even pretend otherwise."

I had, but I didn't want the hangover that would inevitably ensue from back-to-back benders with Ian. I needed to be in fighting form for Sunday rehearsals. Now that I'd finished Elf Shot, I'd had more time on my hands to revive my acting career, and by some miracle, I'd landed a role in a Pinter play over at the Lyric.

"Are you sure? It's right by the Asgard, which is steeped in runes. I'm just saying."

Ian was campaigning hard for a Norse YA with a slacker Valkyrie for a protagonist. I needed to get that man a girlfriend. Or a hobby that didn't put both of our livers at risk. "I'd be a total lightweight tonight. Besides, I don't want to be rushing out of the book signing. Bad form to jilt your local neighborhood bookseller and all."

"Look at you owning your authorhood," Ian cooed. "Text me if you change your mind and I might let you play wingman. Otherwise I'll see you Monday. Kisses to the intern."

I waggled my fingers. "Have a cold—no, have a snobbishly room temperature one for me."

"Beer should not be so cold as to mask its impurities," Ian yelled as he closed the door.

Behind me, the soft scrape of branches and the October wind against my office window reminded me that the season of pumpkin beer and Halloween movie marathons was upon us. With a small smile, I headed for the door. Gazing around the quiet office, surveying the shelves upon shelves of our clients' books, I spared a glance at the small, empty office in the corner, still a storage space—at least until Opal joined us next summer. It was way too early to start cleaning it out for her, but it was a nice reminder that summer would come again.

The walk to Porter Square Books was lovely and crisp, with just the right amount of briskness in the air to rev me up. I reviewed the backup list of questions given to me by Tish, the senior bookstore manager, just in case it took some time for the audience to warm up. In my experience, the teens who read Elf Shot rarely needed any kind of social lubricant. They came armed with questions and theories they'd already vetted on Reddit. But it never hurt to be prepared.

Still, all the preparation in the world couldn't quiet the jolt of nerves that trilled through me as I turned the corner and saw the line. Wound around the corner and spilling into the parking lot were bundled-up teens and college kids, many clutching *Inconstant Moons*, now in paperback, its blue cover with a blood-tipped crescent moon winking in the streetlights. I didn't need the hastily scrawled message on the outside chalkboard to tell me the event was sold out, nor did I really need to see that giant author photo. Why had I thought adding a little mystery to my smile was a good idea?

Rapping lightly on the side door, I waited until Tish, their candy-red cat-eye glasses perched atop their corkscrew curls, admitted me into the warmth of the store. A frequent patron of the bookstore since long before they'd ever sold mine, I barely recognized the place tonight. The neatly labeled shelves had been pushed to the outer edges, the bistro tables and the chairs in the café put away to make room for the sea of gray folding chairs that were a prerequisite at any author reading.

"Whoa," I said softly, but evidently not softly enough, as Tish chuckled beside me.

"We're not just oversold, we're at 'straining max fire code numbers, try to cram in one more body and the fire department will shut us down' capacity," Tish said gleefully as they pointed to the unsigned books just waiting to be purchased.

"That is a crapload of books," I observed.

"We've got more in the back," they assured me.

I nodded, dumbstruck. Luckily, Tish, with their confident smile and practiced ease, made it clear I was in good hands. *Take a breath, Barnes. You've got this.* And after a few breaths, I realized I did. Hate it or love it, Elf Shot was done. In a few months' time, *The Winter's Flaw*, my final book, would be out in the world and in the hands of these readers. And finally, Hathaway Smith could be laid to rest.

A little red-cheeked and windblown, the crowd shed their outerwear with abandon, some bellying up to the coffee bar while others jockeyed for seats. I watched them with fascination—this pack of readers—a population that I'd once held at a distance for fear of upsetting them, though now I just delighted in their energy, their love of books and, if the line at the counter was any indication, massive quantities of doctored caffeine.

When Tish finally called for attention, they settled the whole lot of them down with a mere flick of their hands. Without further introduction, as we'd discussed, I stepped forward to the battle-scarred podium. "My name is Miranda. Some of you may know me as Hathaway Smith. But you can call me Barnes." The place erupted in thunderous applause peppered with some rather encouraging hooting.

When they'd quieted, I added, "I guess you could say I'm doing the rounds for *Inconstant Moons* a little late." This elicited some good-natured snickers. "But I know why you're really here." I could feel the shift in electricity, a rising buzz that wound its way through each of them, tugging them forward in their seats.

I licked my finger and opened my advance reading copy of *The Winter's Flaw*.

"Meg stared down the snowy abyss, a jagged slash that left mountainous pockets of scar tissue on the otherwise unmarred landscape of the winter queen's realm . . ."

I didn't stumble once during that first chapter, the words as familiar to me as the lines on my palms. Readings were often a blur to me, a passing smear of breaths and pauses. Here too soon and gone too fast. But tonight, the words wove their way through me like a golden, pulsing thread, tethering me to this world as I guided the audience through Meg's.

"Thank you, Miranda," Tish gushed when I'd set my copy down. "That was a wonderful teaser of things to come." They turned to the crowd and asked brightly, "Are there any questions?"

Hands shot up like midsummer weeds, tenacious and plentiful. The questions ranged from softballs like "Where do you get the inspiration for Meg?" (Answer? My sisters, but please don't tell them. It will go to their heads.) to groaners like "Did you really need to kill Thad?" (Answer? Yes, I really did. Thad was a weasel.) mixed in with those long ramblers that were really more commentary than questions, like, "Wouldn't you say that when Meg spares the winter queen, what she's really doing is paving the way for a unified realm, and isn't that a social commentary on the fractured state of our current legislative branch . . ." (Answer? Sure.) And of course, "What are you writing next?" (Answer? Hell if I know. Ian had done a masterful job negotiating me out of the last Elf Shot book, but in the process, he'd promised my publisher I'd give them a new standalone book by summer. Good times.)

Question after question, I answered each the best I could—even when someone asked me if Meg went into battle commando. (Answer? Honestly, I've never considered that. But since she shares many a common characteristic with the berserkers of old, the possibility has to be considered.)

"Well, as much as we'd like to keep going all night," Tish said smoothly as my own voice began to give out, "I'm sure there are a lot of you who would like *Inconstant Moons*, newly out in paperback and fifteen percent off in the shop today, signed. You'll also receive ten percent off if you preorder *The Winter's Flaw* with us tonight. How about just one more question? Yes, you. You in the back."

The scrape of a chair being pushed back. Then a throat clearing.

Tish nodded encouragingly as a rush of hot and cold sensation surged down my spine. I lifted my eyes to the speaker with a mixture of hope and dread, knowing who I would see staring back at me.

"Can you give us a hint as to what might happen to Meg and Dylan in *The Winter's Flaw*?" Adam and I locked eyes in the crowded room where the windows had steamed up from the warm bodies inside and the cold beyond. All of my stage bravado as Miranda the author slipped away until I was just Miranda, one big, exposed nerve in the face of the man who'd made off with—and broken—my heart twice.

I cleared my own throat—once, twice—until I found the words.

"My agent would murder me if I gave away the ending." We weakly smiled at each other. "But what I will say is despite their somewhat ill-fated beginning and after all of the intrigue, espionage and a fae war that threatened to rip the literal fabric of their universe apart, one might conclude that maybe they have earned the possibility of an ending standing beside each other. If they can claim it," I added. "Sometimes people have the most brilliant ways of sabotaging themselves and losing the things that would make them most happy."

It was as if I'd set the audience on fire, fanning the flames of excited whispers and side discussions and, if I wasn't mistaken, a rather smarmy "I told you so."

"So you're saying Meg could forgive Dylan for everything, just like that?" Adam asked.

"Yes, because in this theoretical ending that I'm not revealing, Meg knew Dylan was worth it. Or maybe it was because half the realm had been slaughtered and he was the last functioning immortal left standing," I quipped. "Guess you'll have to read and find out."

The room collectively snickered.

"This will come as a surprise to absolutely no one," I said, offering the audience a self-deprecating smile, "but I think the Bard said it best. The course of true love never did run smooth." There went the appreciative crowd again. But I could only see the man whose face mirrored my own tension and want. "That answer your question?"

"Nearly. Just one more, if you're willing."

Tish put a hand on my shoulder. "In the interest of time—"

"It's okay," I said, my eyes locked on Adam. "He can ask it."

"You recently came out as Hathaway Smith to your readers. In that post, you end with a line from Shakespeare. I believe it was 'the wheel is come full circle: I am here.' What did it mean?"

"What did you think it meant?" I shot back, a second too late before realizing that we were still in a crowded room of strangers. I tried again. "This year I lost—and found—my way back to writing. To do that I had to let go of the things holding me back. If I've learned anything from this experience, it's to never leave unsaid who you are and what you want. So when I wrote I was here, I meant I was here and open and ready for wherever the future may lead."

The room may as well have been empty; my words were only for Adam. I knew it. And I was certain he knew it.

"Thanks to everybody for their thought-provoking questions." Tish clapped their hands and shattered the moment. "Let's have a round of applause for Miranda."

After an embarrassing amount of time spent standing and wondering what the hell to do with my own hands while people clapped for me, I was ushered to a table where I signed book after book, wrote silly dedications and drew fairies in the margins. I even wrote a "most likely to do battle without undergarments" dedication for the teen who'd so boldly inquired about the state of Meg's underwear preferences.

Like the fans who stood in line, I waited anxiously. Any minute I knew Adam would step up to the table, book in hand, explanation on his lips. But as the line dwindled, so did my hopes. Adam was nowhere to be found.

Maybe he was just here to get a book signed for his niece and had backed out because the line was too long and—I cut myself off before I could finish the thought.

When the very last book had been signed and my left hand ached with cramps, Tish walked me to the door, thanking me profusely for staying late and hinting how they'd love to add another signing. In a daze, I readily agreed, all the while still looking around for Adam.

Outside, the first snowflakes of the season were falling, their lacy skeletons illuminated in the streetlights. Another reason October was my favorite—you got the fiery beauty of the falling leaves and the occasional snow flurry—nothing that would stick—but a crystalline promise of things to come.

Under the streetlights, Adam was perched on a bench, a pastry box in one hand and a book in the other. "Someone taught me I should always bring snacks to an apology," he said.

"Wise words." It had been almost six weeks since I'd last seen his face up close like this, but I remembered each curve, each dimple like it was an hour ago. And it hurt.

"You were wonderful tonight," he said.

"Home field advantage has its perks." I squinted at his advanced reader's copy of *The Winter's Flaw*. I wondered if it had been Ian, Cordy or Porsche who had slipped it to him. "You already knew the ending and asked about it anyway?"

"I wanted to hear your take on it."

"I wrote it. That's pretty much my take on it," I said dryly. We stared at each other, Adam looking away first.

"I can't imagine what it must be like to say goodbye to a world you created and the characters that live in it," Adam said. "Your ending was perfect."

Better than our ending, I thought ruefully. Still, I was determined not to make this weird. "High praise from the reigning Funka. Would you like me to sign that for your niece?"

He shook his head, clutching the book. "I couldn't give this one up. That last line . . ." A snowflake flamed out of the sky and lit on his lip. It was gone in an instant. "Did you mean what you said back there?"

"About half the realm being slaughtered and Dylan being left standing as one of the only functioning immortals? Yeah, I did."

"Your post. About you coming full circle. You being here. Did you mean it?" he asked, a catch in his voice and his eyes holding mine.

I didn't answer him. "What are you doing here, Adam?"

"I live here."

"What?"

He pointed in the direction of Arlington. "I live over there in an overpriced but sure to rise in value single-family fixer-upper. It has a private yard for Lucille and everything."

"What happened to Seattle?"

"After I left Bard's, I drank a lot of craft beer, grew an embarrassing beard and started that new job. I was miserable. Lucille is a great listener, but she can be really judgmental for a pig. She definitely took your side in all of this, which was surprisingly hurtful." He offered a small smile. "I tried to resign myself to the fact that I'd lost you twice because I can't seem to get out of my own way. But I couldn't stop thinking about you. Then somebody with a New York address mailed me an advance copy of your book."

Of course it had been Portia.

"I tried not to read too much into that last chapter. I told myself that Meg and Dylan winding up together at the end, standing over that fairy ring, was a happy accident."

"I don't write happy accidents," I deadpanned.

"About a week later after I'd finished your book, I got an exclamation-filled text from my niece. Apparently, her favorite author had come out to the world. I read your post over and over again. I started to think that maybe if you could put yourself out there like that, maybe I could too. Maybe I could start living my own truth."

"Your truth was leaving your new job and buying an overpriced fixer-upper?"

"It's going to go up in value, we both know that." He smirked. "I thought more along the lines of facing up to the fact that my new job wasn't what I wanted. I don't want to treat livestock. I want patients that people treat like family members."

"They don't have those kind of jobs in Seattle?"

"Not going to make it easy for me, huh?"

I stared at him impassively.

"I didn't want to be in Seattle anymore. I moved out there for the wrong reasons, but couldn't admit to myself I'd made a mistake. But after this summer, I decided it wasn't worth perpetuating that mistake anymore. Not given what it cost me." He smiled sheepishly. "I started looking for a new job, emailing my old Tufts connections. Found a small practice over in Arlington, flew back and forth several times to interview and every time I was here, I looked at places. Once I accepted the offer, I bought one of them. Packed up my life in Seattle, which, sadly, didn't take very long, and here I am."

"That's a lot of change."

"It is. But my new partners, Mira and Beth, are phenomenal, and I couldn't be happier that we all share the same philosophy when it comes to our patients. Bunny is a little disappointed I won't be doing the large, prestigious practice thing, but she still gets to tell her canasta club that I'm a partner. She just leaves out the part that it's a three-partner practice."

I giggled. "I'm sorry. I can just picture Bunny's face."

"I know. Worth it for that alone." He grinned, but it was short-lived. "Even after I landed here, I didn't want to show up on your doorstep asking for another shot and putting the same kind of pressure on you that I put on my past relationship." He looked down at the book in his hands. "But this book. That post." He glanced up at me. "I thought—no, I hoped—that 'I'm here' might be for me. Because the truth is, Barnes, I've come here tonight for you. Tonight and always, if you'll have me."

Weeks, I'd been waiting weeks to hear these words, and yet my feet didn't move, remaining rooted to the sidewalk as if the cold in the concrete had seeped into them and hardened me where I stood.

"I was so convinced that I couldn't be happy if my career wasn't exactly what I planned. But even when I thought I'd finally gotten everything I wanted, it didn't make me happy. My life had become so much more than just work. And when you were gone, my life shrank again. There were no more hilarious rehearsal stories shared over dinner. No more watching you duke it out with the town's scariest event planner. And I didn't wake up next to a single ass head. Not even once. I've missed so much about you." He paused. "But most of all, I missed the sound of your snicker, lovely and derisive all at once."

"Ass," I said, trying not to laugh.

"Always," he agreed. "For weeks I've been envisioning grand gesture scenarios designed to win you back that I'm sure Ian will tell you about later in graphic detail. But showing up here tonight was the only one that felt right. That way you could gracefully extricate yourself if you didn't want to see me." He gestured around. "See? Exits on all sides."

"You've been talking to Ian?" I huffed. "Bearded traitor."

"Who do you think suggested skipping all the grand gesture scenarios?"

"Well, he wasn't wrong." I harrumphed. "I'm not much for improbable rom-com endings."

"Yet here we are, standing in the streetlights, outside your book signing, in the snow."

"It's a flurry. Besides, that kid over there is spray-painting the side of the T. He's misspelling the word 'majestic.' I think we're okay." I pushed a crimson strand of hair away that had escaped the hat Cordy had knitted for me. "You really hurt me when you left. You gave up on us. I know you thought you were sparing us a bigger hurt down the road, but you shouldn't have been the one to make that decision for the both of us. You bolted when things got hard." I crossed my arms over my chest. "I know it's not a particularly glamorous description of this ride we call life, but I want someone in it with me for the long haul—the ups and downs, goods and bads and all the weird in between. I'm here for all of that. Are you?"

"I'm sorry it took me so long to get here. Because this is exactly where I want to be. With you. In the weird." Adam stood, making a show of brushing a modest amount of tiny flakes from his jacket. "I didn't come here tonight to demand anything from you. I just wanted to let you know . . . that I'm here for all of it too. If you decide you want me."

I chewed my lip. There were a million self-preservation-based reasons to send him from this place, never to darken my doorway again. And there was just one really good reason not to. I stared at him. Hard. Then I grabbed his arm. "You're such an ass."

"I really am." He grinned. "But that doesn't stop me from wishing for the tempest who blew back into Bard's and seized a main-stage and my heart with both hands. The woman who kisses me like the world is on fire. Literary agent and co-owner of Valhalla Lit.

Lover of snark, bearded traitors and rescue dogs. My Viola, my Hathaway, you secret-weaving enigma of fae worlds. I want you, Miranda Hathaway Barnes, in all your forms. And all your parts. I love you."

"I guess that maybe I love you too." I pointed to my heart and smirked. "Apparently, I've been walking around with this Jackass, MD–sized hole right here."

Adam surged forward, cupped my face with his hands and kissed me until my knees buckled. "I had this whole groveling thing planned out, and if that failed, I was going to come back with Lucille and beg some more," he gasped, when he came up for air. "You think puppy dog faces are emotionally manipulative? You should see the full-on pig pout."

"Less talking, more kissing," I grumbled as I pulled him back down.

"Get a room!" I heard a voice call.

I jerked away from Adam, my eyes landing on that kid with the spray can. "Get a dictionary, you jack monkey. It's a 'j,' not a 'g,'" I yelled, pointing at the brick. I turned back to Adam. "Where were we?"

"I was just going to remark upon your gentle disposition and tender wit."

I snorted. "No, you weren't."

"No, I wasn't." He pulled me close again, wrapping his arms around my waist. "I was going to say that Shakespeare really did say it best." He pressed his forehead to mine. "I would not wish any companion in the world but you."

"Oh, for Bard's sake, that's not fair," I drew back and brushed my lips over his, grazing the bottom one lightly with my teeth. "You know I'm a sucker for a Shakespearean ending."

Acknowledgments

After a decade of near misses in the publishing industry, I thought I'd give it one more go with something completely different. Enter Maggie Cooper, lover of words and champion of would-be dreams. Nothing makes me happier than partnering with a fellow Bostonian. Maggie, you are so kind, supportive and funny and somehow manage to be one of the scariest negotiators I've ever known.

To Kate Seaver, thank you for taking a chance on me and being legitimately disappointed there's no real-life Bard's Rest. I cannot believe how much you've transformed this story. Thank you for your patience and dedication.

To Jessica Plummer and Chelsea Pascoe, the creative duo at Penguin, for taking pity on a tragic social media case like myself, and Mary Geren, for staying on top of everything and always being so nice about it.

To Flor Fuertes, thank you for bringing Miranda and Adam to vivid life. Your art thrills me.

To Nikki Terry at Orange Custard, who translated all of my gibberish requests into an actual author website.

To Sarah of Sarah Jordan Photography, who talked me onto a literal ledge for that picture.

To the talented Leigh Stanfield. I don't even know where to start, but I don't think it's an overstatement to say that I've learned more about writing from you than any course I've ever taken. Thank you for reading all of my stuff and letting me read yours. I can't wait to hold your books in my hands.

To Christy, who reads all my stuff and roots for me anyway. Thank you for being there for me every step of the way. You are the best kind of listener and an even better friend.

To my Pitch Wars 2017 class and my Pitch Wars mentor, Emma Wicker, the only person to ever claim she wanted to lick something I wrote. That book never hit, but you taught me a valuable lesson about revision, perseverance and the importance of funny comments in the margins.

To Amanda, Anna, Katelyn, Melissa, and Michelle. I stole everything I love about Miranda and her crew from all of you. Sorry not sorry. You're the greatest group of friends anyone could dream up.

To Big and Brougham, my menfolk and the inspiration for my favorite character in this one. Someday I'm going to write down all of our past youthful transgressions in scary detail and the world is going to weep. And snicker.

To Julie, who helped get my mind and body in a place to write this book.

To Peter, Carota and Huff. It's easy to write male characters when you have buds with hearts of gold and questionable senses of humor.

To Amy, Amena, Barb, Goose, Conboy and Sean. Because work would have sucked without you. And you just can't write a funny book when work sucks.

To my furry sounding boards, Moneypenny and Fiona. It actually doesn't count as talking to yourself if your dogs are with you. And to Susan, Mindy and Molly, who brought Fiona home to us.

And now to bring it all home (because home is where the fam is):

To my parents, thank you for keeping straight faces when I brought home my first work about my general disdain for my little brother in the second grade (and thank you for keeping it in the attic in its original binding all these years). You raised me steeped in books. It was the best way to grow up. All your support, all those trips to libraries and bookstores, all your advice to stick with writing—it paid off. I've seen my lifelong dream come to life on these pages. Couldn't have done it without you.

To my brother, the subject of that aforementioned masterpiece. John, you're such a good brother, a good person and a Funka for the ages.

And finally, to Gorbey. When married, working full-time and parenting at warp speed, there is little time to write. Thank you for helping me carve out that time. There's no one I'd rather be in the trenches with. Bring snacks.

For the
LOVE
of the
BARD

....

JESSICA MARTIN

Discussion Questions

1. If you could live in Bard's Rest, would you, and if yes, what would be the name of your Shakespearean-themed store-front? Note: This author's vote is for Much Ado About Dumplings, which a friend came up with *after* I'd already written and deeply committed to Much Ado About Pastry.

2. The Barnes sisters are a talented bunch. Would you most like to have Miranda as your literary agent, Portia as your attorney, or Cordy as your personal chef?

3. Early on, Miranda struggles with writer's block. What do you think ultimately helps her push through it? What serves you best when you're trying to solve a conundrum?

4. Clan Barnes is a close-knit crew. What do you think of the way they interact with one another and weather family crises? Ready to sign up to be an honorary Barnes?

5. Miranda and Adam have to overcome their past to move forward. Miranda struggles to trust Adam as a result of what happened on prom night, while Adam wrestles with his guilt. If you were in Miranda's shoes, could you move forward and forgive Adam? If you were Adam, would you be able to forgive yourself and move on?

6. If you could write the next chapter in Miranda's life, would she still be a writer? A literary agent? Both? Neither? If you are choosing to have her continue on as a writer, what's her next project?

7. Puck is a pivotal character in that he advances the plot and contributes to Miranda's emotional well-being. Would you like to pet him a little or a whole lot? (Hint: This would be a perfect moment during book club to steer the conversation to pets.)

8. Miranda and Adam each derive deep satisfaction from their careers. When the future of their romantic relationship clashes with their careers, they must make difficult decisions. Did you agree with their choices? Did they feel authentic to you?

9. Unsurprisingly, Miranda drops a lot of Shakespearean quotes over the course of the novel. What's your favorite Shakespearean quote or insult? Yes, you can use Google. This author loves muttering "crack of doom" under her breath when something goes awry.

Author photo by Sarah Jordan McCaffery

Jessica Martin is a lawyer by trade, a writer by choice and a complete smart-ass by all accounts. Based in the suburban wilds of Boston, Jess shares her life with a finance geek, a small sass-based human and a pair of dogs named after Bond characters.

CONNECT ONLINE

JessicaMartinBooks.com
SeeJessWriteStuff
OhForTheLoveOfBard

Ready to find
your next great read?

Let us help.

Visit prh.com/nextread

Penguin
Random
House